Thomas Woodbine Hinchliff

South American Sketches

Or, A Visit To Rio Janeiro, The Organ Mountains, La Plata, and The Parana

SALZWASSER VERLAG

Thomas Woodbine Hinchliff

South American Sketches

Or, A Visit To Rio Janeiro, The Organ Mountains, La Plata, and The Parana

Reprint of the original, first published in 1863.

1st Edition 2022 | ISBN: 978-3-37500-503-0

Verlag (Publisher): Salzwasser Verlag GmbH, Zeilweg 44, 60439 Frankfurt, Deutschland
Vertretungsberechtigt (Authorized to represent): E. Roepke, Zeilweg 44, 60439 Frankfurt, Deutschland
Druck (Print): Books on Demand GmbH, In de Tarpen 42, 22848 Norderstedt, Deutschland

SOUTH AMERICAN SKETCHES;

OR

A VISIT TO RIO JANEIRO,
THE ORGAN MOUNTAINS, LA PLATA,
AND THE PARANÀ.

BY

THOMAS WOODBINE HINCHLIFF, M.A., F.R.G.S.

LONDON

1863.

T. Picken, lith. Day & Son, Lith^rs to the Queen.

FALLS OF ITAMARITY.

PREFACE.

IN visiting South America I had the satisfaction of fulfilling a long-cherished desire. As a school-boy I had wandered in imagination among the forests of Brazil; my fancy had been fired by Sir Francis Head's description of the Pampas; and I had latterly conceived an eager wish to compare the Andes with the Alps. I started from England with the intention of seeing these three regions in the course of a year's absence; and though I was unfortunately compelled by circumstances to abandon the third division of my plan, yet I derived so much pleasure from all the novel scenes of Brazil and the Republics of the River Plate, that I am anxious to call the attention of others to these comparatively unfrequented countries.

My visit to Brazil was short, but it enabled me to

wander among the exquisite scenery of the Organ Mountains, the beauty of which can hardly be surpassed in any country of the world; to make many delightful expeditions from the neighbourhood of Rio Janeiro; and to see some of the results of modern skill and energy, in a journey to Juiz da Fora, in the province of Minas Geraes. Roads and railroads in many directions, are affording immense assistance to the material progress of Brazil, and the experiment of a Constitutional Empire in the Western Hemisphere has met with a success which must be highly interesting to a traveller. The grandeur of the forests, the infinite variety of ferns and flowers and fruits, the beauty of the birds and insects, and the sublimity of the scenery, all exceeded my highest expectations: and I wish to point out for the benefit of other wanderers, that the limits of a Long Vacation are sufficient to admit of their spending five weeks in the cool season among the splendours of Brazil.

I passed several months in Buenos Ayres and the neighbourhood, where the kindness of friends and relations introduced me to all that was most agreeable and interesting both in town and country life. The society of Buenos Ayres is remarkably hospitable and pleasant, the climate is generally delightful, and it would be difficult to find anything more healthy and invigorating than the free and independent life of the estancias, or country estates.

Availing myself of a good offer, I made an expedition up the river Uruguay to the neighbourhood of Paysandù, about three hundred miles from Buenos Ayres, where I had a very favourable opportunity of enjoying plenty of sport on the estancia of a friend, and of thoroughly examining that district of the Banda Oriental.

Later in the year I ascended the river Paranà to Rosario, Santa Fé, and the town of Paranà, which was then the capital of the Argentine Confederation. After an agreeable visit for a week at the latter place, I started with a friend to cross the rarely-visited province of Entre Rios, and a journey which was both amusing and exciting brought us to Nogoyà and the neighbourhood of Gualeguay. Here we spent a fortnight at the estancia of another friend, riding to all parts of the surrounding country and familiarising ourselves with the life and pursuits of the estancieros, among whom we found many of our own countrymen. Ultimately we left the province at Gualeguay, and had an interesting voyage down the river in a small schooner which in due time, but not without difficulty, brought us into the neighbourhood of Buenos Ayres.

Much as I regretted the necessary abandonment of my intended journey across the Cordillera, I was partially repaid by witnessing the excitement of the civil war which caused it. The armies and navies of a South American republic, though capable of doing much mischief among themselves, cannot fail to be amusing to European travellers. I trust and believe, however, that the Argentine people are beginning to see the folly of their frequent wars and discords, and are preparing themselves for such a career of steady progress and prosperity as would naturally be expected in so fine a country. I hope that the railroads and important undertakings upon which they are now engaged for opening communications and developing the resources of their vast country, will turn their natural talents and energies into sober and useful channels.

Foreigners have been making great progress on both sides of the river, and those Englishmen who go out to engage in the profitable pursuits of sheep-farming in that part of the world will generally find fellow-countrymen within reach. Bad government and turbulent partisans have been the only serious drawbacks to the prosperity of the country, and there is at present every symptom of the evil times having come to their end. Even in the midst of their internal discords, the various governments have been sufficiently wise in their generation to recognise the importance of conciliating foreigners and encouraging the immigration of Europeans: every man who embarks his capital and labour upon the estancias of the River Plate is not only benefiting himself, but contributing his quota to the prosperity of a country which must soon become great and important among the nations of the earth.

The railway which is about to be made from Rosario to Cordova, with its ultimate ramifications through the provinces of La Plata, cannot fail to open up very great sources of wealth in what may even still be considered as almost a new world. Cotton and corn, wine, fruits, and tobacco, will be brought within the reach of a short and easy transit to Europe. The healthy climate and the vigorous life of the country will be strong inducements for all who try it to persevere in their efforts: and with the increased conveniences which every year is producing, I cannot help feeling sure that La Plata is destined to be great.

I have endeavoured to give a short but faithful account of all I saw and heard, in the hope of inducing others to go and judge for themselves. The journals which I kept and the letters which I sent to England have afforded the materials of this volume; and I have adhered to the plan of describing my journey and various expeditions in order as they occurred. This has involved the necessity of retracing my steps for my second visit to Brazil; but, considering the various effects of different seasons upon the climate and vegetation of the countries described, I thought that this was the best system to adopt.

The illustrations, with the exception of that which is taken from an interesting photograph of the ruins of Mendoza after the earthquake, are from rough sketches taken by myself upon the spot, and completed by the kindness of my friends. The map is upon too small a scale compared with the immensity of the country to enter upon much detail, but it is sufficient to give a general notion of the mighty basin of La Plata with the adjoining territories.

In conclusion, I wish to express my thanks to the

many hospitable friends who rendered my visit to South America one of unmixed pleasure and satisfaction; and if any of them derive the least amusement from the perusal of these pages, I shall feel very greatly pleased at having been able to give so slight a proof of my grateful remembrance.

T. W. HINCHLIFF.

LONDON:
May 27, 1863.

CONTENTS.

CHAPTER VI.—*continued.*

CHAPTER VII.

AN ESTANCIA IN THE BANDA ORIENTAL.

CHAPTER VIII.

LIFE IN THE BANDA ORIENTAL.

CHAPTER IX.

GAUCHOS AND WAR.

CHAPTER X.

RETURN TO BRAZIL.

CHAPTER XI.

SCENERY OF THE ORGAN MOUNTAINS.

CHAPTER XII.

VISIT TO THERESOPOLIS.

CHAPTER XIII.

EXPEDITION TO JUIZ DA FORA.

CHAPTER XIV.

LA PLATA AND PARANÀ.

CHAPTER XV.

PARANÀ AND SANTA FÉ.

CHAPTER XVI.

TRAVELLING IN ENTRE RIOS.

CHAPTER XVII.

LIFE AT LAS CABEZAS.

CHAPTER XVIII.

VOYAGE DOWN THE RIVER FROM GUALEGUAY.

LIST OF

ILLUSTRATIONS.

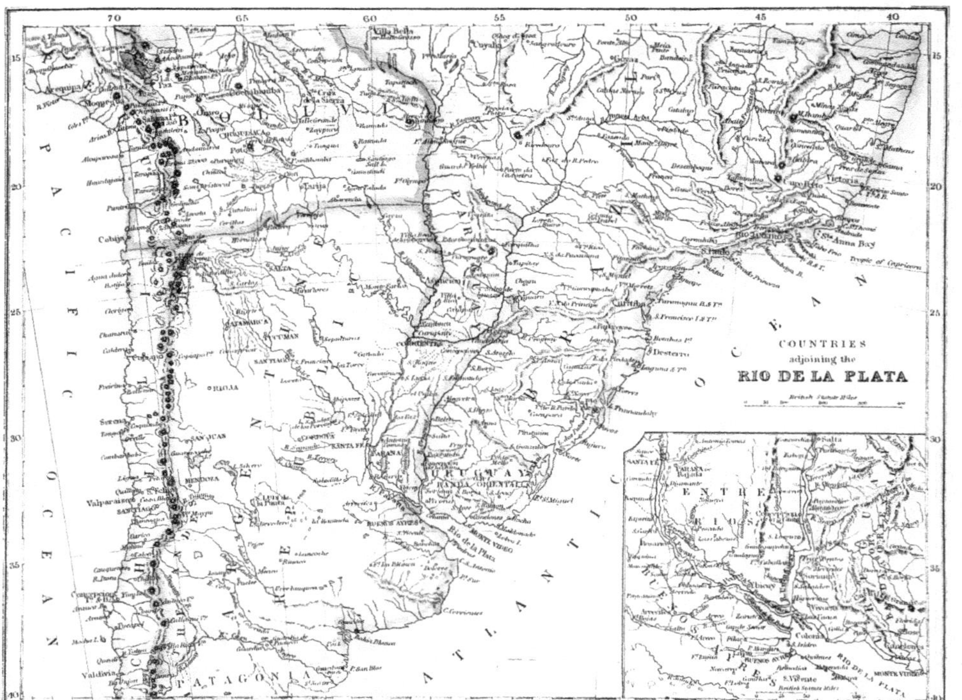
COUNTRIES
adjoining the
RIO DE LA PLATA
BOLIVIA
URUGUAY
BANDA ORIENTAL
PATAGONIA
PACIFIC OCEAN
ATLANTIC OCEAN
ENTRE RIOS
BUENOS AYRES
MONTE VIDEO
Rio de la Plata

SOUTH AMERICAN SKETCHES.

CHAPTER I.

VOYAGE TO RIO JANEIRO.

START FROM SOUTHAMPTON — LISBON — FELLOW-PASSENGERS — MADEIRA — DIVERS — A JUMP FOR IT — TENERIFFE — FLYING-FISH — ST. VINCENT — DRYNESS OF THE ISLAND — WHALES — FERNANDO NORONHA — PERNAMBUCO — A GALA DAY — PINEAPPLES — JANGADAS — BAHIA — ORANGES — CADEIRAS — EARTHQUAKE OF MENDOZA — FATE OF M. BRAVART — CAPE FRIO — RIO JANEIRO — BEAUTY OF THE HARBOUR — NOISY NEGROES COALING THE SHIP.

EARLY in the afternoon of April the 9th, 1861, I sailed from Southampton in the Royal Mail Company's steamer Magdalena, with a light north-easterly breeze to help us on our way towards the sunny South.

A kind friend had accompanied me to the ship, and introduced me to Captain Woolward; and, surrounded by the comforts and luxuries of such a noble vessel, I soon found that there was nothing further to be desired. Many have recorded their impressions on leaving England for distant countries; for my own part, I may fairly say, that next to the natural regret caused by parting with my friends, the predominant feeling was intense satisfaction at having got rid of all the trouble and worry of preparing for a long absence; and I even derived a grim pleasure from reflecting that it was then quite useless to remember anything that had been forgotten.

The cliffs of Old England were soon out of sight as we rushed through the dancing waves with 800 horse-power; the sun set with a clear sky, and when the first stars showed themselves, 'Great Orion' was exactly over the bowsprit. Having a fancy of my own for considering this a very favourable augury, I turned into bed with the full conviction that we should have a prosperous voyage. We ran through the Bay of Biscay with scarcely a ripple on the sea; saw a glorious sunrise behind the Spanish hills on the 12th; and about six o'clock in the morning of the 13th we were steaming up the Tagus into Lisbon. Four days had made a great change in the temperature: here the hills were covered with the verdure of full spring, and the heat during the middle of the day was too great for walking with any pleasure. I went on shore after breakfast with a fellow-passenger, and by keeping to the shady side of the streets, we managed to explore a good deal of the city; but about two o'clock we were very glad to get some shelter in a cool room of the Braganza Hotel. Two hours later the coaling was over; and, with some addition to our passengers, and a famous supply of vegetables and eggs, for which Lisbon is justly celebrated, we left the beautiful Tagus behind, and said farewell to Europe for the present.

I was not long in finding some agreeable companions among the passengers; several of them were young South Americans, who, after a few years of study and travelling in Europe, were now returning home in great spirits. The most remarkable looking man, however, was a many-scarred Garibaldian colonel, who had been a friend and companion of the chieftain from his early adventures at Montevideo to the events of 1860. With a tall commanding figure, of immense power, long iron-grey hair, and the eye of an eagle, he looked a true leader of men. He was one of the many discontented after the affairs in Sicily and Naples, and falling into disfavour with Victor Emmanuel and Cavour, he had made up his mind to try his fortunes once more in the New World, where he had formerly been engaged in all kinds of operations, from fighting in the Banta Oriental to surveying the Patagonian frontier of the Argentine Confederation. There was also a pleasant Belgian count, who, not liking the political prospects of Europe in general, and of his own country in particular, had determined to settle with his family on an *estancia* which he owned on the banks of the Uruguay.

The usual course of the mail steamers, after leaving Lisbon, is to run direct for St. Vincent, in the Cape

Verde Islands; but, owing to a lucky chance, we were this time destined to have a peep at Madeira. The Empress of Austria was wintering in that lovely island, and the Magdalena was ordered to call there with a young officer of the Austrian Court bearing despatches, and charged with certain boxes which we shrewdly conjectured to contain the latest productions of Parisian taste for the Imperial lady. So when I came on deck early in the morning of the 16th, we were lying off Funchal, near enough to distinguish everything on land, in the light of a perfectly beautiful spring sunrise. The Captain had promised us a few hours on shore, but it was found that there were no moorings for us, and he was obliged to stay no longer than was necessary to land the Austrian. It was tantalising enough to see the beautiful hills and snow-white villas, all surrounded with exquisite vegetation, without being able to set foot among them; but we were compelled to confine our amusements to trading with the natives, who came off in a shoal of boats as soon as they ascertained that we were not from Brazil with the assumed proportion of yellow fever patients.

'Branches they bore of that enchanted stem,' the banana, with heaps of oranges, vegetables, fish, and flowers; mats, baskets, and Canary birds; feather-flowers and shawls, sticks and inlaid boxes. Crowding round the ship's side and climbing the gangway, chattering and screaming in broken English and Portuguese, they opened the market in a very animated style; while another boat, containing a couple of divers, afforded infinite amusement to those who were not engaged in commerce. These fellows, wearing nothing but a light pair of drawers, dived with astonishing accuracy for sixpences and shillings, thrown into the sea at a considerable distance from their boat. The water being as clear as crystal, we could watch their bodies glancing like fish far below the surface; and, as they never missed their aim, and many of us gave them all the remains of our English silver, they must have realised a small fortune. The first bell was rung to clear the ship of the speculators who had boarded us, and half an hour later they had a second warning. The ship then began to move, and we thought the fun was all over. But presently we saw that the whole fleet of boats was racing after us with all their might, as if they were trying to keep up with the winner at a regatta; the men were all screaming in Portuguese and broken English, and we could make out, 'Hi! you stop, Captain!' 'Oh, Lor! stop; you got man!' &c. &c.

'What's all this about?' said the Captain.

A quartermaster reported that one of the dealers, in his anxiety to make another sovereign, had not left the ship.

'Very well, then; tell him he must jump overboard, if he does not want to go to St. Vincent.'

In vain he pleaded that he could not swim, as it was

certain to be a falsehood; the ship was going faster and faster, the huge paddles thrashing the sea into waves; so he plucked up his courage, and gallantly plunged head-foremost over the side. After a few moments' disappearance, he came to the top like a duck, and was just beginning to show his talents as a swimmer, when the nearest pursuers caught him by the collar, and dragged him into their boat — a dripping victim to the love of lucre!

Next morning we passed Teneriffe, though at a long distance. The neighbourhood of the island was indicated by large masses of cloud, which would have hidden the Peak, even if we had been much nearer than we were; and in passing, we received the first drops of rain since leaving England. But all was soon bright as we went southwards — gentle breezes and clear skies put everybody in high spirits; and the purple-crested 'Portuguese men-of-war,' floating tranquilly on the dark blue sea, seemed to enjoy it all as much as anyone. Multitudes of flying-fish, frightened by the steamer, flew right and left in coveys, offering us many opportunities of seeing that they have a true flight, although it is limited by the rapid drying of their fins. I frequently saw them fly nearly a hundred yards, without touching the water; and the quick glitter made by the motion of their broad filmy fins had a very pretty effect in the sunshine. Now and then they raised themselves enough to come on board our tall ship; and I observed that the large fins, which act as wings when wet and pliable, stiffened very quickly on exposure to the air. Meanwhile, the heat increased daily; and though it was not too severe to prevent some of us from indulging in leap-frog and various athletic exercises under the awning as we crossed the tropic, we were quite satisfied with more gentle movements when we reached St. Vincent, in the Cape Verde Islands, on the morning of the 21st.

The island of St. Vincent would apparently be useless to the world, if it did not contain a harbour which is very convenient as a coaling station for steamers. At a distance, the height of its hills and their fantastic forms give it a very picturesque appearance; but on coming nearer, there is nothing to see but a burnt-up wilderness of barren mountains. The inhabitants are contained in a small dirty village, close to the shelving beach of the bay; but in the greater part of the island great bluff rocks descend precipitously to the sea. The most remarkable of the mountains is called 'Washington's Nose,' its outline being a close imitation of that patriot's profile. Foreign consuls live in a few little villas stuck down upon the barren rocks; but it is difficult enough to imagine how they can exist in a place where there can be no amusement or occupation, except what may be derived from the arrival of ships. I was told that sometimes it does not rain at St. Vincent for two or three years together, and such fruits and provisions as are consumed are all brought from St. Antonio or other islands.

The bay is overlooked by a scrap of a fort, which serves to maintain the dignity of the Portuguese, though it is scarcely larger than the flag on the top of it. The authorities must have a dismal life, with no satisfaction but that of making other people uncomfortable by putting them in quarantine on every possible pretext.

Between the islands of St. Vincent and St. Antonio is a very remarkable spot, called Bird Island. It is almost exactly like the upper part of the famous Swiss Matterhorn, rising straight out of the sea, and entirely composed of formidable rocks; even the snow patches of the mountain are partly imitated by the guano of innumerable sea-birds, which sit lazily on the rocks, digesting their dinner and contemplating the scenery.

As soon as the ship anchored, the coal-barges began to come alongside, towed by a little steamer of about forty tons, which had come out from England under canvass. In this excessively dry climate, the black dust was intolerable; and I was glad enough to go on shore, though I was told that there was nothing to be seen, and that nothing grew on the island. This, however, like most of such statements, proved to be not altogether true. There were certainly no public buildings or picture galleries in the miserable little village, but it was very amusing to see the natives, of various races, from tawny to genuine wool, coming to look at the new arrivals, and tempt them to purchase work and feather-flowers. A small but animated negro ball was going on in one house; and while the mammas were dancing, their little darkies enjoyed themselves in the sand outside. There is something very attractive in the young of most animals. Puppies and kittens are delightful; but there is nothing so charming in its way as a batch of little bright-eyed niggers playing, stark naked, on a sand-heap. Passing through the village, we followed the line of the beach for more than half an hour, and then turned inland, to ascend one of the nearest hills. Walking was disagreeable, for the sand was deep, and burning hot to the feet; and when we got to the hill, we found it was covered with disintegrated rubbish. However, we succeeded in getting a fine view of the harbour, and then turned our attention to the only green spot which we could see on the island. This proved to be an extensive thicket of tamarisk, growing in deep sand, and consisting of very handsome bushes. There was scarcely any other plant or flower to be found. I only met with a single specimen of a tall and handsome *Orobanche* with large yellow flowers, a very pretty borage, a few grasses, a *Frankenia*, and two or three other plants, sadly scorched by the blazing sun. After about three hours' walk in the hottest part of the day, we were glad to get back to the town, and take shelter in a queer little store called the Café Bilhar, where we refreshed ourselves with a bottle of good Yankee cider, and waited till it was time to go on board. The billiard-table was unluckily *hors de combat*; if it had been blessed with cushions, we might have tried a game, in spite of the filthiness of the cloth.

About four o'clock we sailed, passing very near some whales, which had been lucky enough to escape the crew of a large vessel just starting homewards with a full cargò of oil. In the course of the next two days we passed the track of the outward-bound India and China ships, and it wàs indeed a goodly sight to see those 'tall argosies,' with every sail set to catch the gentle breeze. On the 26th we crossed the Line, but there were no ceremonies to celebrate the event. In these degenerate days, when so many ancient faiths are rudely shaken, the God of the Sea has come in for a share of neglect; and the Royal Mail Company, after voting Neptune a nuisance, has abolished him entirely. For a day or two, between losing the north-east, and meeting the south-east trade-winds, the heat was very sultry and oppressive; the motion of the steamer always made a little air on deck, but it was easy to imagine the sufferings of those who are becalmed on the Line in a sailing vessel.

On the 27th we passed the extraordinary island of Fernando Noronha, used as a penal settlement by the Portuguese, and said to have so dreadful a reputation that ships hardly like going to leeward of it. It consists of a series of sharp hills, the most remarkable of which rises perpendicularly like a monstrous lighthouse, and was distinctly seen from the deck at a distance of forty-five miles.

Early in the morning of the 29th I first saw South America, the ship having anchored off Pernambuco. The mail steamers lie about a mile outside the Recife, a coral reef, which extends, with few interruptions, like a regular sea-wall, for nearly 400 miles along the coast of Brazil. At Pernambuco it is parallel to the beach, and nearly a quarter of a mile distant from it: the fresh sea-breeze sets inland, and the first thing that strikes a stranger is the splendid effect of the waves breaking on the reef, and rushing upwards in pillars and towers of spray. Opposite the northern end of the city a wide opening admits of the entrance of vessels into a natural dock formed between the main land and the Recife; but the roughness of the sea, combined with the exorbitant charges of the boatmen, prevents most passengers from landing unless they are obliged to do so. A friend kindly came off to see me; and after luncheon, accompanied by the Captain, I went ashore in his boat. This little craft was extremely light, and after the pattern of a whale-boat, stem and stern alike; the crew consisted of four magnificent negroes, each a Hercules in build, and the *patron* or master, who had got preternaturally fat from constantly sitting still and steering, guided the frail vessel with marvellous skill among waves, which, whenever we were in the hollows, completely hid us from everything but their towering green crests.

The first thing I observed in Pernambuco was the narrowness and dirt of its streets; and it is wonderful that, with the sea close at hand, some good system of drainage has not been adopted. I should have been very sorry to show my respect for the New World by kissing the earth of Pernambuco. The city is essentially a place of business, but by no means interesting to a spectator, and I should think that no one would settle there willingly. It is not, however, generally unhealthy; and, though nearly level with the sea, it is preserved from excessive heat by the constant sea-breeze, which usually keeps the thermometer at about eighty-five degrees. The rain-fall is heavy, and amounted to about 130 inches last year.

It happened to be a gala day in honour of the election of a president or governor, and my friend took me to a large square in the further part of the place to see what was going on. His Excellency was showing himself at a balcony, and a large ecclesiastic, in purple garments, was apparently performing some kind of benediction; after which the band struck up, and the soldiers drawn up round the square fired running salutes of musketry in very fair style, to the intense disgust and astonishment of numbers of mules laden with oranges, bananas, and other delicacies, which suffered considerably from the violent kicking. The pineapples from the neighbourhood of Pernambuco are probably the finest in the world, and are by no means to be confounded with the little yellow knobs furnished to the London market from the West Indies. Their flavour is perfect, and their size and generally handsome appearance make them the finest fruit that can be imagined. They are frequently fourteen or fifteen pounds in weight, and a resident in Paraiba told me he had seen them as large as twenty-two pounds. We had no time to spare, having to return to the ship in the teeth of a fresh breeze, which raised sea enough to be exciting in our little boat, particularly as we knew that in the event of an upset we might speedily become dinner for sharks. Our stout *patron* steered us admirably, however, and I got on board just in time to see one of these monsters of the deep hauled on deck by the sailors who had caught him. In spite of sharks, the Pernambuco fishermen carry on their trade in most extraordinary little vessels, called *jangadas*, or catamarans; these consist of four logs of cork palm, thicker at one end than at the other, and pinned together into a wedge-shaped raft, having a single plank for keel, and just large enough to hold three or four men standing, or squatting on little stools. A rough mast carries a three-cornered sail, and with no protection from the water, which flows over the craft at its own sweet will, they sail about at a very tolerable speed. They seldom meet with accidents, and fill the markets of Pernambuco with some of the ugliest fish in the world.* Dr. Kidder, who once made a voyage in one of them, reported that they were breezy, watery, and safe.

Four o'clock comes; the anchor is up, and we are off again, running down the coast with glorious skies and gently rippled seas, bound for Bahia, where we arrive early on the morning of May the 1st. Lovely is the view which meets us as we jump on deck. Soft showers have been falling in the night, and now the glorious sun makes the whole air redolent with life and growth as it comes perfumed from the luxurious shore. Streets and villas rise one above another on the steep and lofty banks where the city is built, and every scrap of ground not built upon is covered with brilliant green masses of palms, bananas, and the numberless productions of a tropical climate; while far away to the south stretches the beautiful bay for thirty miles, surrounded by undulating hills, hazy in the blue distance.

I went ashore at once with the mail-boat, and walked to the Consulate through the fruit-market. This trade is principally carried on by negro women, many of whom are fine specimens of humanity, though generally tending to obesity; like most of their race, they delight in gaudy dresses, and I think Mr. Lance would say it is a very picturesque sight to see a group of them in blue, red, or orange muslin gowns, with large white turbans and earrings, chattering round a stall covered with oranges, bananas, mangoes, pumpkins, melons, and huge bunches of the gorgeous flowers of Brazil. This, too, is the head-quarters of the little marmoset monkeys, small enough to curl themselves into a champagne glass, and proving an irresistible temptation to paterfamilias, whose children stuff them with fruits for the rest of the voyage. Whole boat-loads of the famous navel-oranges are waiting on the shore, and the negro in charge only grins as your boat glides past him, and you pick out a fine specimen for immediate consumption, giving him a familiar nod by way of payment. These oranges are very large, full of juice, with thin skins, and not a pip to bless themselves with. Scores of sedan chairs, called *cadeiras*, with negro bearers, are ready to carry you up the hill; but the Englishman gallantly takes the steep zigzags on foot, and soon arrives on the high plateáu, where there is almost always a balmy breeze to refresh him after the close heat of the town.

On returning to the ship, I found that it was entirely in the possession of a legion of devils in the shape of negro coalheavers. The sacks are brought in huge lighters to both sides of the vessel, and two gangs of darkies get them on board by walking aft with ropes, on the same principle as the man-of-war fashion of hanging a man. If they would do their spiriting gently, we might swallow our coal-dust with a better temper; but they insist on stamping the deck as hard as their naked feet can do it, to the accompaniment of a dismal howling chant, which irritates quiet people to the last degree. All things, however, have their end; and about four o'clock we sailed for Rio Janeiro, armed with a stock of southern papers, which had been left by the homeward mail.

We found plenty of bad news from the Rio de la Plata, or the River, as it is generally called. Civil war between Buenos Ayres and the Federal Government was imminent; and the city of Mendoza, at the foot of the Andes, had been destroyed by an earthquake on the 20th of March. I fancy this event caused very little sensation in England. People who overflow with charity when half a dozen men are killed by a Lancashire boiler, look with the most perfect *sang froid* on the destruction of whole thousands at the other side of the world. The facts, however, of this disaster were sufficiently appalling. Mendoza was one of the principal cities in the Argentine Republic, with a population estimated at nearly 20,000. Situated at the foot of the Andes, it was described as the garden of the country, and was the charming resting-place of travellers between the burning plains and the freezing passes of the Chilian Cordillera. In two minutes all was destroyed. The city was literally reduced to a heap of ruins; about 15,000 people perished; and the few survivors could not easily distinguish the streets in which they had lived. Walls and fences were destroyed, and wild cattle and horses trampled the gardens and vineyards

CATHEDRAL OF MENDOZA AFTER THE EARTHQUAKE.

to destruction, whilst other districts were ruined by torrents of mud. The villainy of man added to the horrors of the scene. Miscreants, who survived the earthquake, or came in from the neighbourhood, drove hard bargains with miserable wretches who were entombed by fallen stones and brickwork, and screamed in vain for help, if they could not promise a sufficient reward. The smell of the ruined city, with its slain thousands, is said to have been utterly intolerable.

The accompanying illustration of the remains of the cathedral is copied from a curious photograph which I obtained in Buenos Ayres, and gives a better idea of the destroying force of an earthquake than any with which I am acquainted. Singularly enough, M. Bravart, a French *savant* of some eminence, who had foretold the destruction of the city by an earthquake, was himself among the victims. He was known to have made very valuable collections during a long residence in South America, and, on behalf of Professor Owen, I afterwards made inquiries about them at Paranà, through the English and French ministers, but I found that a claim had already been set up by some of his relations in France, with a view to their being probably forwarded to Paris.

The principal watchmaker in Buenos Ayres, which is about 800 miles distant from the scene of this awful calamity, told me a curious fact in connection with it.

One day he observed with astonishment that his clocks suddenly differed twelve seconds from his chronometers; and when the news arrived, about a fortnight later, he found that the pendulums of the former had been arrested at the moment of the destruction of Mendoza.

On the morning of May the 4th, we rounded the grim and lofty rocks of Cape Frio, where we fell in with rough water for the first time since leaving England. At the back of this dangerous headland H.M.S Thetis was lost some years ago; and the risk of approaching it was formerly increased by the fact of the lighthouse being at the height of about 800 feet above the sea, so that it was very frequently hidden in clouds; but a new light much lower down has been completed within the last year. Early in the afternoon, we saw high rocky islands ahead, and a few hours later we had the satisfaction of finding ourselves in the splendid bay of Rio Janeiro.

Who shall worthily describe the beauties of that which is perhaps the most beautiful place in the world? The European traveller who visits Rio for the first time, if he has any appreciation of natural beauty, cannot fail to be entranced with the scenery that awaits him; and, whatever fate may attend him in Utopia or Sirenia, he may be pretty sure that he will never see anything more lovely in this lower world. As the noble vessel dances over the blue waves to the shining islands in the distance, the excitement continually increases. Telescopes are produced; the palms are seen waving over the sea-borne rocks; and that — yes, that — is the renowned Sugarloaf. We slide between a twin pair of granite islands rising abruptly from the sea, covered with palms and cactus and innumerable green shrubs stretching down towards the water, and presently we see the narrow entrance to the harbour. A mighty rolling swell sets inland, and already we can see the long masses of white surf chasing one another up the rocks, against which the waves chafe in perpetual wrath. The fort of Santa Cruz, trumpery enough, perhaps, in these days of Monitors and Armstrongs, but imposing in appearance, guards the right hand of the entrance; and on the left the perpendicular precipices of the Sugar-loaf mountain, though unarmed with man's artillery, look down awfully on the intruder.

Man, however, makes his voice heard, through the medium of a speaking-trumpet, as we run through the huge swell close under the walls of the fort; a rough brazen blast is supposed to ask the name of the ship, and our captain answers in an equally unintelligible way across the roaring surf which thrashes the walls of the parapet. A few more plunges, and we are in the smooth water of the harbour. Close round the shoulder of the Sugarloaf is the shining bay of Botafogo, the banks of which are covered with white villas, glittering in the sun like diamonds among the emerald-green vegetation; and that long building like a palace is the Lunatic Hospital. A little further on the same side is the Gloria Hill, studded with gardens and houses, and crowned by a conspicuous church. Then comes the city itself, covering not only the water-side, but numbers of low hills immediately behind, above which a range of luxuriant mountains culminates in the sharp needle-like point of the Corcovado, 2,100 feet above the level of the sea. The harbour, though only entered by the narrow gateway between the fort and the Sugarloaf, is about twenty-one miles in length, and eighteen in width at its upper end; it is, in fact, a lovely lake, studded with exquisite islands, and surrounded by forest-clad hills; high above which, at a distance of thirty or forty miles from the city, rise the fantastic peaks and pillars of the Organ Mountains, soaring faintly through the haze to a height of 7,000 or 8,000 feet. As we passed the man-of-war anchorage, and saw the ships of all nations clustering near the busy city, and basking on the bright water, the whole scene was bathed in the golden glory of approaching sunset; long streamers of light gleaming through the gaps of the mountains swept across the bay, illuminating here and there some tall mast or palm-crowned island, and the boyish dreams of Fairyland were realised.

Off the Gloria Hill we were boarded by a swarm of officials, custom-house officers, &c., who took every precaution against possible smuggling. I fancy the Brazilians must exceed all other nations in their wish to swell the amount of apparent revenue, for they seem to think it worth while to impose duties on articles for Government works. They entered into a contract with English people for an iron lighthouse, to be placed on the dangerous Abrolhos; and the ship which brought it out last year, instead of stopping at the Abrolhos, so that the erection might be at once proceeded with, was compelled to go all the way to Rio, discharge her cargo and reload, after paying duty on Government property! Of course the delay and expense were considerable, and apparently for no better object than that of transferring money from one pocket to the other. So at least I was informed.

The mail steamers moor about a mile from the city, alongside an island which is used as a coal depôt, and which has in that capacity realised a large fortune for the proprietor. Early next morning I was aroused by the diabolical noises of a large gang of negroes employed to coal the ship. On they came in slow procession, bearing the coals in flat baskets on their woolly heads, howling a dismal chant and grinning when they saw how disgusted we were with their performances. A proportion of them were armed with a detestable instrument of tin, in shape and size very much like the rose of a watering-pot, and containing a few pebbles, which they rattled incessantly as they stamped along the deck; having listened to this devil's music for an hour or two, I can fully understand the strong objection of a dog to having a kettle full of gravel tied to his tail. The noise and the dust were distracting; so after breakfast two or three of us jumped into a boat rowed by four darkies, and landed at one of the quays of the city.

Some of the Africans at Bahia and Rio were beyond all comparison the finest men that I have ever seen. The most powerful tribe are bronze-coloured rather than black, and their splendid developement of muscle fully comes up to the ideal of ancient sculpture.

CHAPTER II.

ARRIVAL AT BUENOS AYRES.

THE MARKET AT RIO—FEATHER FLOWERS—HOTELS—CARRIAGES—GARDENS—AQUEDUCT—BUSINESS ACTIVITY—PURIFICATION OF RIO—YELLOW FEVER—THE CONSUL'S HOUSE—A CRUISE IN THE HARBOUR—THE SUGARLOAF MOUNTAIN—BOTAFOGO BAY—FEAT OF A MIDSHIPMAN—TRANSFER TO THE MERSEY—A HEAVY SWELL—CAPE PIGEONS AND ALBATROSSES—STORY OF ALPACAS AND LLAMAS—LOBOS ISLAND—MONTEVIDEO—QUARANTINE—THE PAMPERO—THE PARAGUAY, PARANÀ, AND URUGUAY—SHALLOWNESS OF THE RIO DE LA PLATA—LAND AT BUENOS AYRES.

WALKING up the stone steps among a crowd of porters and boatmen of every colour, from jet black to dirty yellow, we found ourselves at once in the open market-place, surrounded by all that mixture of dirt and luxuriance which is eminently characteristic of a city in hot latitudes. Dinah dressed in the most 'gorgeous array,' sat on a basket surrounded by heaps of grapes, bananas, melons, mangoes, and alligator pears; and dirty Sambo chattered by her side, holding half-a-dozen scraggy fowls by their legs with their heads draggled in the mud, and apparently negotiating a barter for his live stock. Close by were mounds of delicious oranges, and stalls covered with strange fishes, reminding me of some which figure in Raphael's picture of the Miraculous Draught. Huge prawns abounded, and, with all due deference to the Isle of Wight, I believe I may say that the Rio prawns are considered the finest in the world; when curried they make one of the standing dishes of the country. Greatly amused, we passed through the busy throng, and reached the Rua Direita, which is the finest street in the place, and turning to the left found our way up a hill with some barracks on the top, whence we had a general view of the harbour and a great part of the city. As we were in the beginning of the cool season, the weather, though of course hot, was by no means oppressively so; and we fully enjoyed a ramble about the streets and squares for a few hours. The buildings are by no means handsome, and most of the streets are excessively narrow. Shopkeepers in the best quarters pay enormous rents, but get very little frontage to display their goods, which are generally sold at exorbitant prices. The famous feather-flowers of Brazil are among the greatest attractions to foreigners; but I would advise no one to buy them at Rio Janeiro, as they are both better and cheaper at Bahia. Hotels are very few and bad, but outrageously expensive, and I should imagine that a first-rate establishment of this kind, conducted on proper principles, would be a good speculation at Rio. A friend of mine was charged £13 sterling for eight days' stay at one of them; and at another they asked ten *milreis*, or a guinea, for a bottle of champagne; such charges as these, combined with small and dirty quarters, show that there must be room for improvement. The most convenient vehicles are neat cabriolets, but there are plenty of omnibuses, which are always drawn by four mules. Some of the Brazilian grandees have exceedingly amusing turn-outs. My gravity was sorely tried by seeing a good-looking carriage, with the regulation allowance of four mules, leisurely crossing a square. A negro coachman and footman sat in front arrayed in a red, green, and blue livery, which would astonish even a Belgravian flunkey, and looking as proud as two peacocks; while four other negroes in the same uniform, and ambling on mules, brought up the rear. The narrowness and crowded state of the streets make it rather difficult for a foot passenger to keep to the pavement; but he is constantly rewarded in his walks by finding himself emerging upon some pretty spot, where palms, and bananas, and gorgeous flowers overhang his path by way of prelude to the beautiful suburbs, where the earth appears to revel in the luxuriance of her own productions.

The opera house is very fine, and some of the more distinguished European performers are, when possible, secured. The public garden makes a pleasant retreat; but the botanical garden, a few miles out of the city, with its wonderful avenue of monstrous palms, deserves its world-wide reputation. The most striking piece of architecture is a very fine aqueduct, which was built to supply the inhabitants with clear fresh water from the hills. The effect of its lofty arches rising through the green clumps of palms and other fruit trees in the suburbs is very striking. The most fashionable side of Rio is the southern division, where the Gloria Hill and the neighbourhood of Botafogo bay are occupied by many delightful residences.

In the city itself the spirit of business engrosses all attention, and every street is full of activity. The Exchange is crowded during business hours, and loungers seem out of their element. Everybody looks as if his whole existence depended upon some transaction in sugar, coffee, or tobacco. Immense numbers of negroes crowd continually up and down the streets with heavy bags and bales, keeping always on the move like strings of ants, laughing, joking, and singing as they trot along with their burdens. Rio is unfortunately by no means clean, but the City Improvements Company, with the support of the Government of Brazil, has undertaken to purify it completely, and there is no reason why they should not succeed.

Before the sudden arrival of yellow fever, about a dozen years ago, the delights of this neighbourhood must have been almost without a drawback; but that horrible scourge has given many a severe blow to society, though, at the worst, it was not nearly so destructive as in many cities of the United States. Fortunately, it has been much less violent in the last few years, and very possibly it may depart as it came; but in the hot months of January, February, and March, the risk is considered serious. The Austrian consul at Montevideo told me that in a long residence at Rio during the worst yellow fever seasons, he had carefully kept statistics on the subject, and had come to the conclusion that the mortality was in proportion to the badness of living among different sections of the community. Thus, he said the Italian residents lived most poorly, and suffered most; next to them he classed the Germans, and then the French, as both cleaner and better fed; lastly, he said the English suffered least of all, because they lived well and drank good brandy and water.

I fortunately had a letter of introduction to Mr. Westwood, the English consul, who kindly asked Captain Woolward and myself to dine with him in the evening. We returned to the ship, and about sunset, on as lovely a day as was ever seen, we were rowed through the shipping towards the consul's house on the Gloria Hill. In about half an hour we landed on some rocks, among which a gentle swell was swaying languidly, and ascended, by a sloping path overhung with the shady foliage of trees on each side, and ornamented with lovely creepers and orchids, till we passed into the garden and reached the house, which, with open doors and windows, was cooling itself after the heat of the day.

I had the pleasure of finding that Sir Stephen Lushington, the English Admiral on the station, was one of our party, and he was good enough to offer me the hospitalities of his flag-ship, the Leopard, for the remaining two days of my stay at Rio; so after a very delightful evening we broke up with an understanding that I should visit the Leopard about noon next day. An old negro, with a lantern, lighted us under the balmy trees to our boat, which was waiting among the cool rocks, and in about half an hour we reached the Magdalena again, after having an excellent opportunity of seeing from the water the singular effect of the city illuminated by countless gas-lights. The long line of beach is for several miles brilliant with them, for they are placed nearer together than in England, and the many suburbs which crown different hills with their various lights make a charming scene in the darkness.

About one o'clock next day I was rowed to the Leopard, and found the Admiral ready for a start. His barge was alongside, rigged with two tall white lattern sails, and manned by a dozen splendid blue-jackets: the sweet sea-breeze was just beginning to ripple the water, and my heart bounded with delight as we flew towards the eastern side of the harbour. There is no greater admirer of Rio Janeiro than Sir Stephen himself, and I was fortunate indeed in having such an able *cicerone*. Never shall I forget the enjoyment of that day and the next; it was the very perfection of 'lotus-eating.' For hours we glided over sunny bays, and between lustrous islands covered with masses of palms, cactus, ferns, and aloes, mixed with mangoes and other trees of intensely green foliage and impenetrable shade, many of them trailing into the water, which reflected every leaf and flower on its surface. Then we recrossed the harbour for a cruise in the lovely scenes of Botafogo Bay, out of which rises, to the height of 1,200 feet, the astonishing cone of the Sugarloaf Mountain. Here we landed for a while on an island, the Admiral wishing to take me to the top of a small hill to enjoy one of his favourite views. As we returned, the sun was fast sinking, and a golden glow stealing over palm and cactus, and all the wonders of that glorious vegetation, and warming the fantastic shapes of the Organ mountains in the distance, produced a kind of sleepy enchantment which seemed to deprecate the interruption of human speech. The sailors themselves seemed to feel the spell, as we made the most of the dying breeze, which soon failed us entirely. 'Stand by the sails,' said the Admiral, and in a few moments everything was stowed away with man-of-war precision. 'Out oars,' and away flew the boat with the united strength of twelve true sons of Neptune, away and away over the shining water to dinner on board the flag-ship. All honour, by the bye, to the midshipman of the day, who was one of the very, very select few who have reached the granite crown of the Sugarloaf—an enterprise which ought at once to admit him to the fellowship of the Alpine Club; for the rock is nearly as steep as rock can be, and far too profusely ornamented with prickly cactus instead of beds of snow.

Those of us who were bound for the Rio de la Plata, or River Plate, as it is generally called, were transferred to the branch steamer Mersey; and on the 8th of May we steamed out of the harbour of Rio Janeiro. I left the place with sincere regret, for little did I then imagine that circumstances would induce me to return there in the autumn for a visit of some length. Inside the fort the water was smooth as a mill-pond, but, as we exchanged challenges with the officials, we dipped and plunged into the swell which sets in from the Atlantic. This is sometimes tremendously heavy in bad weather; and I heard that an island not far from the entrance, which is used as a prison, was once so covered with the sea for several days together, that some of the prisoners were drowned in their subterranean dungeons, while their keepers were scarcely able to save themselves from starvation during the impossibility of procuring any assistance from the city.

On sped the gallant Mersey, and tender stomachs suffered all those agonies which, if previous experience had not assured me of my own invulnerability, might have checked my ardour in seeking pastime on the bosom of the ocean. My old friend the Colonel pointed out to me a Brazilian priest, and, with true Garibaldian instinct, remarked that we should have very bad weather. The sailors fully concurred in this opinion, and I fancy that plenty of hands would have scarcely objected to pitch Jonah overboard if they had not been appeased by witnessing the sufferings of Jonah himself. He counted his beads patiently, but all was of no avail; he bowed his yellow head over the ship's side as he acknowledged the supremacy of the pagan Neptune. The strange forms of the Rio mountains faded in the distance as we sank and rose over the swell which told of past gales to the southward.

On the following day the weather was still fine, and I was greatly interested in watching the whale-birds, albatrosses, and Cape pigeons flying in the wake of the ship. In these latitudes I have gone on deck before dawn and seen with the first ray of light the sea-birds in full activity. Who shall say whence they come, or whither they go? I have watched them for hours together in their weird flight. No motion of the long wing is perceptible; they cross at right angles the water foaming beneath the strokes of the paddles, and with a wild swoop turn and turn again, now and then dipping to pick up some scrap thrown overboard; but the long outstretched wing never seems to move as they pursue their course all day long in utter silence. No wonder that the seaman fancies he recognises the ghosts of departed brethren; and no one who has read the wondrous verses of Coleridge can help realising to himself the feelings of 'The Ancient Mariner.'

One day, when the rough weather prevented most of the passengers from enjoying themselves on deck, I took the opportunity to make the acquaintance of an elderly man, whose dry weather-beaten complexion looked like that of a genuine traveller. I found that he was intimately acquainted with Peru and Bolivia, as well as the Argentine Confederation, and had spent many years of his life in those countries. He was an agent for buying South American wool, and especially that of the alpacas and vicuñas of the Cordillera. Amongst other things he told me that he was well acquainted with Mr. Ledger, and gave me an extraordinary account of the manner in which that enterprising man succeeded in introducing the alpaca into Australia.*

According to my informant, Mr. Ledger, after a residence of several years in Peru and Bolivia, was seized with an idea of supplying Australia with a stock of alpacas. With this view he made a preliminary journey across the Pacific to ascertain if proper pasture could be found for them, and having, with the aid of

* The substance of this story was contained in a letter which I addressed to the *Times*, nearly twelve months ago, and I see it is also alluded to in the *Quarterly Review* for January last. The figures given in the two accouuts do not exactly agree, though there is no discrepancy in the main.

an Indian satisfied himself on this head, he returned to Bolivia. The next difficulty was to leave the country safely with the llamas and alpacas which he purchased. The Government, actuated by the old spirit of exclusiveness, had absolutely forbidden the exportation of these animals, wishing to retain the monopoly of the trade in their wool. Finding that it was impossible to ship them from their own country, he determined on making an immense circuit which would lead him with his flock to the coast of Chili. He started from the neighbourhood of La Paz, near Lake Titicaca, and began one of the most arduous journeys ever undertaken, under difficulties which, according to my informant, no other man could have mastered.

The animals march very slowly, and great care was necessary to provide for their proper rest and food. In addition to the constant fear of being stopped, he was obliged to make anxious search for proper halting-places, and to provide for their security at night. He had to pioneer his way by unfrequented routes in an almost unknown country, and to submit to delays at every addition to his flock on the march; taking care, above all things, never to move them forward by any route till he ascertained that they would find the ichù, a pasture which is indispensable to them. His intimate acquaintance with the language and customs of the Indians enabled him to utilise them to the utmost, and saved him from many a difficulty; while his firm will and good constitution enabled him to defy the severe trials and transitions of the climate of the Andes.

At last he approached the point at which he intended to cross the Argentine frontier, near Jujuy, and here he heard that he would certainly be stopped by the authorities, who were looking out for him. Leaving his flock in a place of seclusion and security, he went forward alone, and boldly took the initiative with the guard. Assuming the character and appearance of a jovial traveller, he brewed punch, and plied them with such potent doses that they sank into a torpid sleep. Then he returned to his treasures, and quietly crossed with them over the frontier into safe ground. He arrived at Jujuy and Salta, in the Argentine territory, thence, by winding and excessively difficult marches, he contrived to pass safely over the dangers of the Chilian Andes, and ultimately arrived at Caldera, the port of Copiapo. There, after obtaining a supply of food for them, he took them on board ship, and in November 1858 landed at Sydney with a mixed flock of 276, consisting of llamas and alpacas, with their cross breeds, and a few vicuñas.* This journey was a marvellous triumph of patience and perseverance, occupying altogether, as I was told, a period of nearly four years. The result was eminently satisfactory. These immensely valuable animals are now thriving in Australia, and

* A quotation from a Sydney paper is my authority for the exact number, which my informant was not sure of.

increasing so rapidly that they are already talked of as a very important element in the future wealth of our colonies.

In the course of a year I four times made the stormy passage of about 1,200 miles between Rio Janeiro and Buenos Ayres; but in spite of priests, prophecies, and prognostications, this first was the quietest of them all. The voyage, including nearly a day's stay at Montevideo, occupies a week; and on every occasion the wind has in that period gone exactly twice round the compass, generally blowing hard from every quarter in turn, forming in this respect a most singular contrast with the voyage from Southampton to Rio, during the greater part of which the steady trade-winds may be depended upon, and bad weather is quite the exception to the general rule. The hurricane wind of the coast is called in Spanish El Pampero, which, rushing from the lofty slopes of the Cordillera of the Andes, races over a thousand miles of Pampas, in which there is scarcely a mound to break the effects of its ferocity. It may be compared with the Euroclydon of the ancients, only, as everything in the southern hemisphere is turned topsy-turvy, instead of coming from the east, it is a furious and cold south-wester.

On the evening of the 13th, the returning greenness of the sea was enough to assure even a novice that we were approaching land; and the ship's course was altered to the westward as we drew towards the Rio de la Plata.

A ticklish point to be passed is Lobos Island, or the Island of Seals, a few miles off Maldonado. I was informed that there used to be a lighthouse on this island; but according to South American tactics, the proprietor of the fishery, asserting that the light was prejudicial to his interests by frightening away the seals, contrived to procure its removal to the mainland. The result of this is that navigators to the River Plate, knowing they must leave this dangerous island on the right hand, are compelled to watch carefully, and see when the lighthouse at Maldonado dips behind the island; and the island being so low that the occultation only lasts for a few seconds, even if the ship is in her proper course, the observation requires some nicety. If she is to the northward of her course, and passes between the island and the mainland of Maldonado, the result will be her sacrifice, for the sake of this seal-catching monopolist. Several of us, besides the officers, were on the *qui vive* with night-glasses; the occultation was observed, and next morning at an early hour, when I went on deck, I found that we were anchored at Montevideo.

The first matter of general interest was the question of whether we should be put in quarantine. The worst part of the yellow fever season was over when we left Rio, and, in fact, there had hardly been a case; but we knew we should be looked upon with suspicion, and the health officers avail themselves of every excuse for applying this system of torture. If a man has died of apoplexy or been washed overboard in a gale, or done anything else whereby it appears that there is one soul less than there ought to be, quarantine is immediately enforced. We had had no fever or other calamities, but, to our great disgust, we were compelled to hoist the yellow token of impurity. The reason of this was, I believe, that the French packet at the beginning of the month had landed a man who died next day of fever—a circumstance which had frightened the authorities horribly, and made them very indignant. Such regulations appear very stupid; but, after all, there is some reason for the burnt child to dread the fire. Montevideo suffered terribly a few years ago from an incursion of Brazilian fever. For my own part, I did not care much about it, as I knew I should visit the city before long; but the passengers whose voyage ended here were furious at being shipped off in a huge barge to expiate their supposed uncleanness on an odious place called Rat Island. Another victim was an officer of the Yankee frigate who came alongside us to ask for letters. He imprudently put his foot upon the ladder, and, though he did not attempt to come on board, he was immediately seized by the myrmidons of the Board of Health, and compelled to spend the rest of the day with us, in spite of his earnest remonstrances.

Montevideo is so named from a hill about 490 feet high on the western side of the harbour, which, though insignificant in itself, is remarkable enough from its isolated situation in a flat country. It is difficult to imagine how it got there, but, at all events, it is extremely useful as the site of the lighthouse. The city looks very picturesque from the sea, white and shining in the purest atmosphere that can be imagined. The greater part of it stands upon and covers a long tongue of land, and it is thus incapable of expansion, except in one direction; property is, therefore, extremely valuable, and immense rents are paid for houses in the best situations. The custom-house and public buildings near the water are extremely handsome, and the domes and towers of the churches are seen to peculiar advantage from the fact of the city consisting principally, like all those in Spanish America, of one-storied houses with flat roofs, or *azoteas*. Many of them, however, are furnished with *miradors*, or raised look-out towers, where people can enjoy a fresh breeze and a fine view. The harbour was full of shipping, and a little to seaward were some fine men-of-war of various nations. The Yankees were represented by a huge frigate, the 'Congress;' and as she rode there in all her beauty, no one thought that a few months later she would be demolished by the fratricidal 'Merrimac.' After looking about us all day without being permitted to land, we were not sorry to move up towards Buenos Ayres in the evening. The pilot came on board, and we were fairly in the Rio de la Plata. There was nothing to see but an expanse of yellow water, and

I turned into bed rather earlier than usual; but about the middle of the night I was roused by the roaring of a Pampero, which had come upon us at last in earnest. The noise was inconceivable, and though we were far up the river, the ship was knocked about more than in the whole way from Rio. She quivered from stem to stern, and no one was sorry when the storm moderated, a little before daylight. The Pampero corresponds in nature to the well-known north-easter of the British Isles; and if any one can imagine the effect of such a blast upon the human frame after being for three weeks in a vapour-bath, he will have some notion of our feelings on this occasion. To complete our misery, when we arrived at the outer roads of Buenos Ayres, we were put in quarantine again for twenty-four hours, during the whole of which the Pampero whizzed through our very bones, and many of the passengers suffered considerably.

Unmixed evil is fortunately as rare as unmixed good; while we are 'cribbed, cabined, and confined' by the bitterness of the Pampero and the cruelty of the health officers, it is a capital opportunity to take out the map and contemplate this mighty river. Those who wish to study it thoroughly in all its ramifications should consult the valuable works of Sir Woodbine Parish and Lieutenant Page:* I only propose at present giving a general

* 'Buenos Ayres and the Provinces of La Plata,' by Sir W. Parish, K.C.H. 'La Plata, the Argentine Confederation, and Paraguay,' by Lieutenant Page, U.S.N.

reader some idea of what he might perhaps not at once realise to himself in a hasty consultation of the atlas. Here we are then, anchored in the outer roads of Buenos Ayres, with about three fathoms water, and about four miles from land. The city is partially obscured by the clouds of dust which are being blown off shore by the Pampero, and the land on the opposite side of the river is entirely invisible, because, though somewhat hilly, it is about thirty-five miles distant: the land on that side is seen but rarely from Buenos Ayres, and when seen it is a certain indication of coming rain. Judged by its name alone, the Rio de la Plata, or Silver River, this wonderful mass of water would be considered an impostor, for its colour is yellow; there is no silver anywhere near it, and even a silver currency has vanished to make way for dirty bits of paper. Nevertheless, the river is a grand reality. From Montevideo to Point Piedras, on the southern side, where the water is generally fresh, it is nearly sixty miles wide; and after navigating upwards for 120 miles we find that at Buenos Ayres it has only dwindled to rather more than half that width. The two main rivers which compose this stream are the Uruguay and the Paranà; the former, rising in Brazil, divides the southern portion of that empire and the Republic of the Banda Oriental from the Argentine provinces of Corrientes and Entre Rios, and is about 900 miles in length: the Paranà is again subdivided into the Paraguay and Paranà, which meet at Corrientes, and thenceforth unite in the common name. The highest waters of the Paraguay are about the latitude of 13° south, above Cuyaba, in the Brazilian province of Matto Grosso; while the Paranà comes from latitude 16° south, in the province of Goyas. The importance of the whole river may be seen in the fact that the Paraguay is now navigated by a steamer without difficulty as far as Cuyaba, about 2,000 miles from Buenos Ayres, in the heart of one of the most valuable and productive districts in the whole world, which only requires steam communication to develope its immense resources. Steamers have long been running up the river as far as Asunçion in Paraguay, which is 800 miles from Buenos Ayres, and while I was in the country the first steamer penetrated to Cuyaba, Lieutenant Page having previously ascended in the 'Waterwitch' as far as Albuquerque and Corumba. All these huge rivers are fed by many powerful branches, and united form the estuary called the Rio de la Plata. The width of this vast expanse I have already alluded to: it is a great pity that the depth is not more in proportion. There is good reason to believe that the water was formerly much deeper, but large vessels are now always obliged to lie in the outer roads about four miles from the city, and those that draw more than sixteen feet are frequently obliged to remain at nearly double that distance. The outer are separated from the inner roads by a dangerous bank, and all vessels except quite small craft must make a long circuit to enter them. The Rio de la Plata is a grand sight with all its fine array of shipping, but if it were half as wide and twice as deep as it is at present, it would be ten times more useful. I shall have more to say about these rivers in due course, but as the quarantine officers have now released us, we will go on shore in a whale-boat.

On the 16th the wind was still blowing hard from the south-west, and dead against us; but as soon as we were signalled to lower the hateful yellow flag, some boats came off from shore. I and some half dozen other passengers jumped into one of them, and good as the boat was, we had hard work to beat to windward in very rough water; but soon after noon we landed at the end of a long and excellent pier. The shallowness of the water used to prevent boats from getting to the shore, and the old-fashioned way was to finish the last few hundred yards in high-wheeled carts: the pier, however, almost always prevents the necessity of this very disagreeable and risky proceeding, which is only resorted to when the water is exceptionally low.

CHAPTER III.

LIFE AT BUENOS AYRES.

CIVILITY OF CUSTOM-HOUSE OFFICERS—STREETS OF BUENOS AYRES—THE PLAZA DE LA VICTORIA—THE FOREIGNERS' CLUB—SUGARPLUMS AND MATÈ—THE BOLSA—DOWNWARD PROGRESS OF THE PAPER DOLLAR—RELIGIOUS LIBERTY—THE RECOLETA—'ASSASSINATED BY HIS FRIENDS'—A BUENOS AYREAN QUINTA—THE OMBŨ TREE—PAMPEROS AND DUST-STORMS—CRICKETERS ABROAD—A DEAD HORSE—FIRST VIEW OF FLAMINGOES.

I HAD the pleasure of being met by my cousin, Mr. Parish, the English Consul, with whom I walked along the pier, preceded by my goods on the heads of a couple of active darkies. At the shore end is a neat building, like a summer-house, where passengers' luggage is examined by the custom-house officers, and I at once conceived a pleasing impression of the place from the great civility with which this operation was performed; certainly I have seldom been so well treated in Europe: and I may truly say that this favourable impression was daily confirmed more and more during a residence of several months. The general brightness and cleanliness of the city are very striking, especially to those who have last come from the tropical dirt of

Brazil. The lofty domes and white towers of the churches and Cabildo stand out in clear relief against the pure blue sky, and the marvellous freshness of the air has a most exhilarating effect on the system. The main part of the city stands upon the same level as the wide-expanding Pampas, about fifty feet above the river, and as every street towards the river ends in a steep incline, each shower washes the place thoroughly, and carries off all impurities into the capacious bosom of the La Plata. Two sets of streets at right angles to each other, and 150 yards apart, divide Buenos Ayres into a system of equal squares exactly like a chess-board. The official plan of the city gives thirty-one streets running east and west, and twenty-nine running north and south; many of these are incompletely built over towards their extremities, but the principal streets are thus about two and a half miles in length. The *quadras* or squares are of course not hollow squares, but blocks of houses facing outwards to the streets. All the older houses and great part of the newest consist of only one floor, and are arranged in two or three courtyards or *patios*, into which the various rooms open. Many, however, are now built upon the more familiar plan of *altos* or upper floors, with lofty front and elaborate decorations.

One remarkable feature in the country is, that on the Buenos Ayrean or right bank of the river there is not a particle of rock for hundreds of miles, nothing but alluvial soil; you may look upon the surface for many days' journey, or you may dig to the depth of many feet, but you will never find a stone as big as a marble to throw at the head of any of the troublesome and savage dogs that fly at you; whilst on the Montevidean side of the river you find abundance of gneiss and granite without the slightest difficulty. The whole country from the eastern slopes of the Andes to the banks of the Uruguay appears to be an immense alluvial deposit, brought down by innumerable rivers, and covering the bed of an ancient sea, whose former presence may be inferred from the numerous beds of marine shells, and probably also from the saltness which still characterises a large proportion of the inland streams. In the island of Martin Garcia, opposite the point where the Paranà pours its waters into the Rio de la Plata by the Guazu channel, is quarried the granite with which the streets of Buenos Ayres are paved and the best houses are built, though plastered brick is the most usual material for the latter. This island is very near the Montevidean, or Banda Oriental, side of the river; and as all vessels, except small craft, are compelled by the shallowness of the water to keep close to it on their passage up or down the Paranà, it is carefully fortified, and looked upon by the Buenos Ayrean Government as a Western Gibraltar.

The stone is brought over in a rough state, and great pains are taken in paving the streets with blocks, which contain on an average about a cubic foot; but the surface, though very hard, is extremely irregular, and causes desperate wear and tear to the fashionable carriages, to say nothing of the terrible jolting which afflicts the nerves and muscles of their occupants. In all probability a few years more will induce the authorities, who have always an eye for improvements, to remedy this inconvenience by employing their convict labourers in squaring the stones. Numbers of paviours are employed already; they work in gangs, but instead of each man hammering in a stone at a time, four of them work together with a four-handled rammer. The foot pavements are too narrow, and often raised one or two feet above the carriage-way, involving the necessity of two or three steps.

Buenos Ayres has increased so very greatly since it threw off the yoke of Old Spain, and it is becoming so fertile and profitable a field for European emigration, that it deserves more notice than has been given to it by Europeans in general. Scarcely anything is known of the country in ordinary society; the commercial intelligence comes in from time to time stating the price of hides, wool, tallow, and ounces; but few are aware of what an extensive field the Argentine republic opens for future developement. To get a notion in the first place of what the city itself is, a stranger must throw aside many previous prejudices, and place himself, to begin with, either in reality or imagination, in the middle of the Plazà de la Victoria. This is a fine square in the centre of the frontage towards the river. On the west side are the Cabildo, or town hall, with a lofty tower and fine English clock, on the right and left of which are the courts of law and the Policia; on the north side is the cathedral, a very fine building, approached from the square by a handsome flight of steps, close to which is the bishop's palace. At the north-west corner is the Colon theatre, only second to the finest in Europe, and in every way far superior to those of the second order. The east side, parallel to the river, consists of a long arcade, filled with shops, in the middle of which is an entrance to the large square and parade-ground of the Spaniards, close to the ancient fort, which is now replaced by a fine custom-house; and the south side is lined with shops and handsome buildings. The square itself is large and planted with rows of Paradise trees, among which on holidays the people assemble in great numbers to see displays of fireworks and other amusements; in the middle of it is a very fine obelisk surrounded by iron railings, and crowned with a figure of Liberty to celebrate the deliverance of the Argentine republic from the government of Spain.

There are no small cabs to be hired in the city, but in this square and at various stables there are always better carriages for hire with two horses than I have seen in any city of Europe. A ride to any part of the city costs twenty-five paper dollars, or rather more than four shillings; but considering the different value of money and the excellence of the article, this can hardly be called excessive. Not far from the Cathedral, in the Calle St. Martin, is the Strangers' Club, to the privileges of which any foreigner can be introduced by a member; and so great is the hospitality of the residents, that few respectable visitors to Buenos Ayres are left for many hours without a ticket of admission, which admits them gratis to all the privileges of the club for three months; after which they can either become members on payment of the entrance fee, or if their stay is to be limited, they can still enjoy the luxury on payment of a small monthly subscription.

Here, besides the journals of the country, are to be found all the best English, French, German, and Italian papers brought out by the European mails; and it is his own fault if every Buenos Ayrean resident is not as well up in 'Punch,' 'Charivari,' and the 'Times,' as if he were in London or Paris, only five weeks after their publication. A handsome billiard-room is in the club, and refreshments of all kinds are supplied at the cost, of course, of those who desire them.

The native productions, with the exception of articles of food, are extremely limited; but hundreds of shops kept by English, French, Germans, Italians and Spaniards, supply all the necessaries and most of the luxuries of European life. The Italians are especially great in *confiterias*, or pastry-cook's shops, the taste for what schoolboys call lollypops being excessive among all ages and classes of the community; the inordinate consumption of these produces disease of the teeth—a too common detraction from the general loveliness of the ladies. If you leave your box at the opera between the acts you would probably bring back a packet of *dulces* for the ladies, and many a pair of white kid gloves has been spoiled by their sticky propensities.

In addition to the shops there are several excellent markets, where not only meat and bread, but quantities of beautiful living birds, skins, feathers, and all kinds of country curiosities, are to be found: the famous *yerba*, or Paraguay tea, made from the leaves of a species of ilex in that luxuriant climate, is sold in vast quantities, to make the favourite drink of the country; and another staple commodity is a small gourd, with the stem for a handle, which forms the teapot, or *matè*, from which it is imbibed, like a sherry-cobbler, the *bombilla*, or silver tube, being put into the *matè* before the hot water is applied. This is an almost universal beverage among both sexes and all classes of the community, and seems to be equally acceptable at any time of day or night, either in town or country. For my own part I certainly could not endure it, though I was constantly obliged to try. Up the country in every shepherd's hut where a traveller stops to rest himself and his horse, the good woman of the house instantly retires to make *matè* for the new visitor, who would be considered something of a barbarian if he declined the delicacy; so I used to make up my mind quietly to burn my lips with the *bombilla*, or by awkwardness of suction to fill my mouth with boiling chips, and then return the vessel to the señora with as much grace and apparent freedom from painful inconvenience as I could simulate for the occasion.

A handsome new Bolsa, or Exchange, was nearly finished when I left the country; but the old one was certainly a very shabby affair. It was a curious sight, however, in the busy time of day to see some scores of horses waiting about in the street, while their masters were transacting business in the building. The trained horses of the River Plate will generally stand perfectly quiet, with the bridle merely thrown over their heads and trailing to the ground; but sometimes the *manéas*, or leathern hobbles, are used for greater security. At all events, nobody pays a boy to hold his horse, and it is very rare to see the animal walk off out of patience with his owner.

Here, in the Bolsa, the great drawback to the prosperity of the country soon becomes manifest; and the Yankees especially might learn a useful lesson as to what will be the speedy fate of the almighty dollar if they trifle with it.

Forty years ago, a dollar meant a dollar of rather more than four shillings in the River Plate as well as in North America, but in an evil hour the bank of Buenos Ayres was nationalised, and came very soon so completely under the control of the government as to be compelled to afford almost any accommodation they required. 'The consequences were soon apparent,' remarks Sir W. Parish; 'the wants of the government increasing, the bank was obliged, in order to provide for them, to increase its issues, which ere long reached an amount obviously out of all proportion to its real capital. The aid of the legislature was again called in, the notes were declared a legal tender for their nominal value, and the bank was relieved by law from the obligation of paying them in specie on demand; its credit fell to the lowest ebb, and its notes became proportionably depreciated.' The downward progress was remarkably rapid; and in the first three years of the experiment, from 1825 to 1828, the dollar was reduced in value to one shilling, thus losing seventy-five per cent. of its value. The war with Brazil then terminated, and the pining dwindling dollar made an attempt to rally and look cheerful: for a time it succeeded in keeping itself up to the value of two shillings, but this was merely a hectic smile. It faded away to sixpence, and at last was considered to look pretty well at 2½*d.* sterling. In the excitement of last year's war, when I was at Buenos Ayres, the go-ahead party sternly demanded more money for the annihilation of the Urquizista faction, and it was determined that, in the sacred cause of progress and liberty, the poor, wretched, fainting dollar should be squeezed and bled again. Several large emissions of paper took place, and the silly

Radical newspapers bragged and crowed as if they had discovered a gold mine. In the latter part of the year they were so pleased with their success that they asked for 50,000,000 more; but the doctors who understood the case felt the pulse of their old friend, and gravely said he was so exhausted that he could bear no more. In fact, the paper dollar, which is the universal currency in Buenos Ayres, is now worth *less than twopence,* and it was felt that a further emission of such notes would probably reduce them to no higher value than that of the paper they are printed upon.

The evils of such a currency are manifold: one is that people naturally become careless about small sums. It is almost impossible to count the bundles of dirty scraps of paper that are put into your hand, and sums corresponding to shillings are soon thought scarcely more of than pence in England. But the injury to commerce is enormous, from the rapid fluctuations in value which take place with every event of public importance. The gold ounce, or doubloon, is generally worth about 66*s.* English, and is used as a standard. The price of ounces, that is their value in paper dollars, may be considered as a political barometer in a very stormy climate. 'How are ounces?' is the first question one man asks another in the street. And the violence of the fluctuation in times of excitement may be judged of by the fact that, during a single month at the latter part of 1861, while I was absent in Entre Rios, the price of the gold ounce ranged between 390 and 440, giving an extreme difference of fifty paper dollars on each! Under such circumstances, no one can wonder that many respectable men, not daring to move a step in regular trade for the time being, are reduced to that of speculating in ounces on the Bolsa. Crowds of small brokers and outsiders, little more than betting men, hang about the neighbourhood of that establishment, while the greater chiefs are within; and the art of inventing shaves and *canards* is carried to an unblushing perfection which would astonish even Capel Court.

Later accounts from the River Plate inform us that the Buenos Ayrean government, anxious to retrace the evil steps of their predecessors, are about to inaugurate a system which will by degrees restore their currency to a sounder and more substantial basis; and, among the many steps they are wisely taking for the developement and improvement of their country and its resources, this probably will be one of the most useful. Meanwhile, I had the opportunity of changing English sovereigns at the rate of 125 paper dollars each, the latter being thus reduced to one twenty-fifth of their original value.

One very satisfactory feature in Buenos Ayrean life is the complete religious liberty that prevails. The cathedral and the many handsome principal churches in the city are, of course, monopolised by the Roman Catholics; but the priests do not appear to have the slightest influence or control over those who absent themselves from the flock or prefer the guardianship of other shepherds. There are no religious processions in the streets, and it is rare even to see a priest in public. Such devotion as there may be appears principally confined to the fair sex, the most devout of whom dress in black, with black mantillas, and perfume themselves so strongly with pastilles or incense before going to church as to make the air for some distance redolent of the odour of sanctity. A proof of ancient superstition still exists in a number of round black patches on the towers of the church of St. Domingo, which are said to be the cannon balls fired by the heretical English under General Whitelock, and rendered powerless by the sacred nature of the edifice. On certain grand fête days Church and State combine their pomps and vanities to impress the minds of the multitude with processions and genuflections; but the warmth of the *entente cordiale* is of short duration. I do not mean to accuse them of quarrelling, but each goes his own way. The priests minister to congregations of women, and the government looks after its own affairs. There is probably scarcely a country in the world where the Church has so little opportunity of putting spokes into the wheels of the State.

Perfect liberty of conscience is given to foreigners. The English have a capital church and an excellent chaplain; the Irish emigrants submit their judgment and their consciences to the opinion and keeping of a priestly fellow-countryman; and I believe the spirit of liberality is universally applied. The Protestants of various nations have as excellent a cemetery as could possibly be desired at the extreme west of the city; it is well planted with Paradise trees, and the vaults and graves are kept up in European style.

But one of the most curious and interesting places to be seen in Buenos Ayres is the Recoleta, or burying-place of the Catholics, whether natives or foreigners. It is a very large piece of ground in the northern outskirts, and is completely surrounded by a high wall pierced with loopholes, which would enable a small body of soldiers within to hold the road against an enemy. It is entered by very handsome iron gates, close to which is a chapel for the performance of the burial service. The poorer people are buried in the remoter parts of the ground, in the simple ordinary graves of Europe; but the central part is divided by numbers of paths into narrow streets of vaults and family mausoleums. The latter are for the most part built of white marble, and look like small temples, generally covered with a dome; an iron-grated door permits a view of all the coffins of the family, arranged on shelves or ledges round three sides of the interior, and decorated with *immortelles* and artificial flowers. Many of the principal inhabitants have spent very large sums of money upon these structures, and the general effect is remarkably good. Seen from the surrounding neighbourhood, the large collection of white cupolas and turrets, rising high above the wall, would make a visitor believe that he saw an Eastern city in the distance.

I often wandered about this Recoleta, studying the epitaphs in many languages; and one day, close to where an English Catholic had buried his wife, and graced her tombstone with the familiar 'Affliction sore long time she bore, &c.,' I found on a tall obelisk the most concise and terrible inscription I am acquainted with. It was this:

DON FRANCISCO ALVAREZ,
ASESINADO POR SUS AMIGOS,
1828.

'Assassinated by his friends!' Struck by this extraordinary epitaph I made enquiries about the subject of it, and found that a party of young men from good families of the place were in the habit of gambling together, till Alvarez won heavily from all the others. They determined to pay their debts by getting rid of their creditor, and enticing him to a lonely place they deliberately murdered him; they put his dead body in a coach that was ready, and threw it down a well in the neighbourhood. They had laid their plans so that detection seemed impossible; but by an extraordinary chance there was a witness to the crime, who denounced them. Great efforts were made by family influence to save them, but in vain; they were executed, and the brother of the murdered man erected the obelisk to his memory. In another part of the Recoleta was a dreadful hole, into which the victims of the tyranny of Rosas used to be precipitated wholesale; but those times are happily over, and no trace of them remains except in the memory of the Buenos Ayreans.

Not far from the Recoleta and in the most agreeable suburbs of the city was the Quinta, or country-house of my cousin, Mr. Parish, where I had the pleasure of finding a good welcome and delightful quarters during my stay at Buenos Ayres. We were nearly two miles from the centre of the town, completely out of the way of all noise and bustle, close to several friends' houses, some of which were exceedingly handsome in general appearance. But the great charm of the place was its situation. We were close to the edge of the high land, from which the ground descends in a very steep incline to the level of the river. The house was approached by an avenue of huge olive trees, which grow there with great luxuriance, though nobody seems to take much trouble about collecting the fruit. The garden was full of flowers, European and American, and roses bloomed remarkably well; but they required to be surrounded with a saucer of water to prevent the attacks of the ants. Violets, geraniums, and many of the usual European flowers, were there in perfection, and an excessively sweet verbena, called the *Margarita*, was one of the most fragrant. Figs and peaches were in abundance, and a huge *ombù* tree afforded its dense shade to a garden-seat looking over the wide-spreading river. The sloping land between the Quintas and the river was principally covered with *alfalfa*, or lucerne, which grows there with remarkable vigour, and seems capable of producing good crops in seasons where the ordinary grasses of the country dry up from want of rain. The alfalfa fields were divided from one another by hedges made of cactus, aloes, and wild fig trees, mixed with a great variety of flowering plants and shrubs, one of the most brilliant of which had the elegant leaf of a mimosa, but the flowers were in bunches, something like immense heads of amber honeysuckle ornamented with very long and protruding crimson stamens. The cactus of the river Plate grows to a great size, and makes impenetrable hedges of twelve or fourteen feet high, but as a general rule it is not seen to advantage: the flower is small, and the stems are much damaged by the ravages of insects. The fig trees offer a delicious shade and grow luxuriantly, but the aloes were my especial delight. They are truly magnificent, and with flower-stems of from twenty to thirty-five feet they form splendid rows of natural candelabra. I have measured a single leaf, which was more than ten feet long, and the branching flower-stems of some were like young fir trees. The *ombù* is a very peculiar tree; its rapid growth and dense foliage make it invaluable in a land where good trees are extremely rare, and shade for man and beast is often beyond all price. In the open country there is hardly an estancia-house, a *pulperia*, or a post-house, without one or more, beneath which you can tie up your horse or smoke your pipe according to your taste and circumstances. All blessings to the ombù as a friend! Human creatures are far too ready to sacrifice their human friends when tempted by motives of ambition or cupidity; but the ombù is better off. He is a friend whose life and prosperity are infinitely more useful than any possible results of his downfall or death; his huge trunk is absolutely good for nothing, the wood being little better than elder-pith, and the bark very like the hide of an elephant; the good which he does in his life is indisputable, and no one looks out for a legacy at his departure; the consequence is that he lives universally beloved, and when he falls to earth under the blast of a Pampero he dies, really universally lamented. Happy ombù!

These Quintas, white as snow, and surrounded by trees and gardens, ornament the ridge of the *barrancas* or cliffs for a considerable distance on the north side of the city, and have a very pleasing effect when seen from the river, parallel to which is a fine broad road that is used as the fashionable promenade for riding and driving: it is indeed the Rotten Row of Buenos Ayres. The most ubiquitous tree in my acquaintance is the weeping willow, called here *sauce*, and large numbers of them were planted to ornament the space between the road and the river. Unluckily, in one of the civil wars, which are the curse of the country, the greater part of them were cut down by the party in the city, as they were supposed to afford too much shelter to hostile skirmishers; but they are now recovering their original beauty. One of the great disadvantages of a river, enormous in width but deficient in depth, is its liability to suffer from the effects of violent winds, which at one time raise the water to an extraordinary height, and at another drive it several miles away from its natural banks. A few months before I went to Buenos Ayres there had been a dreadful gale from the south-east, which forced the mass of water up to a most alarming height, and I saw the carcases of good-sized ships high and dry among the willow-groves, and close to the high-road, left where they had been driven by the hurricane. At another time I walked out nearly two miles over the natural bed of the river, the water of which had been forced away by a furious Pampero from their channel; and I found quantities of fish large and small, which were left to die on the sand by the rapid retreat of the river. It is even on record that the Buenos Ayreans once went out over the deserted bed of the river, and with horse, foot, and artillery, attacked a blockading force of ships rendered helpless for want of water.

These Pamperos are sometimes accompanied by dust-storms, and their fury is then terrible almost beyond description. During the residence of Sir W. Parish at Buenos Ayres one of them occurred, in the course of which a constant thumping was heard against the closed doors and windows; and when the storm with its attendant darkness had passed away, the courtyard was found occupied by turkey buzzards, which had been whirled along by the gale and stunned against the building. The following description is extracted from a letter which was soon afterwards sent to him:—'Yesterday we had another of those awful dust-storms which you have previously witnessed: it came on at about a quarter past twelve o'clock. The rapidity of its approach and its awful opacity alarmed the whole population: in an instant, as it were, there was a transition from the glaring ray of the meridian to the most intense darkness. Immense flocks, or rather one immense flight of birds preceded it, and in fact, however incredible it may appear, commenced the obscurity by their numbers.

'The whole time of its duration was eleven minutes and a half; the time of total darkness eight minutes and a half, by watch, observed by Dr. S—— and myself by candle-light. It was accompanied by loud claps of thunder, but no lightning was visible, though the thunder was by no means distant. After eleven minutes and a half the rain began to fall in large black drops, which had the effect upon the white walls of making them appear, when the sun again showed itself, as if they had been stained or sprinkled with ink. I never witnessed a more majestic or awful phenomenon. The consternation was general, everyone rushing into the nearest house and struggling to shut their doors against their neighbours. I have heard as yet of no accidents, although doubtless there must have been many. The wind of course from SSW.'

In the neighbourhood of these Quintas are some excellent market-gardens, which supply fruit, flowers, and vegetables to the city. The orange trees were as large as our full-grown apple trees, and covered with ripe fruit, but the species is bitter and of inferior quality; the *naranja dulce*, or sweet orange, which is cried all day long in the streets, comes generally from Paraguay and other districts up the river. The love of flowers amounts to a passion with the fair ladies of Buenos Ayres, and there is a very large demand for the choicest and handsomest bouquets that can be found, to the great profit of the gardeners. Most of the European vegetables are grown successfully, and I observed a curious plan which the gardeners employ to protect young plants from the possible ravages of a Pampero. They take the huge leaves of the aloes, cut them into lengths of about two feet, and fix them into the ground on the windward side and close to the plants, each of which is thus provided with a good and efficient shield. The soil and climate are wholly unsuitable for ferns, but in the brickwork of the open wells in these gardens I was much interested to find that three species had established themselves and were growing luxuriantly.

About a mile farther to the north, and close to the Palermo Road, was the English cricket-ground. This important institution is maintained at Buenos Ayres with as much vigour as in any other part of the world where a moderate number of Englishmen congregate together; and I helped in several very good matches. The ground was not quite so smooth as might be wished, and was often excessively baked by the sun, the consequence of which was that swift bowling was apt to inflict wounds. One day a party of men from H.M.S. Ardent and Curlew came up to play, and the astonishing coolness with which they allowed their unguarded legs to be battered inspired me with fresh confidence that they would not flinch from cannon-balls. Practical cricketers will admit that the excitement of 'lost ball' is vastly increased by the fact of its being lost in a hedge of American aloes and gigantic thistles. During the last siege the besieging force of Urquiza was between the city and this cricket-ground; the Englishmen were very much disgusted at the prospect of losing an intended match, and had the assurance to ask if they might pass through his lines. Permission was granted, and the game was played; but it was a very risky proceeding for a few men to spend the day surrounded by such characters as might be expected in the rear of Urquiza's army. One day as we began the game our noses were assailed by an intolerable stench, of which the 'fons et origo' was discovered to be a dead horse. The poor beast had strayed into the cricket-ground to die, and had been treated after the custom of the country. No one takes the trouble to provide cat's meat in that part of the world, but he had been very carefully skinned by the first finder, and then left to pollute the air: the effect was disgusting, and we could do nothing till we found a man who tied a rope to his legs and galloped away with him. I have seen horrible carcases in this state used to stop a hedge-gap close under the noses of a country family; and at all times they are found extremely useful in helping to fill up a *pantáno*, or mud-hole, in the suburban roads. Between this place and the river is a wide range of marshy lands, where, in spite of holiday-making French barbers and cockney sportsmen, snipe and ducks are still to be found, and where for the first time I saw with astonishment and delight the great rosy-winged flamingo.

The climate in general appeared to me particularly agreeable, though the changes of temperature are now and then exceedingly abrupt. The north wind, which is hot, moist, and relaxing, is detested by most of the inhabitants, who say that it exercises a strange influence both upon mind and body. It is even recorded that some individuals have pleaded the north wind as the only excuse for murders committed by them, declaring that they were not then responsible for their actions. I cannot say that I was ever reduced to such a state as that; but I certainly once suffered from an abominable species of head-ache, which seems especially prevalent during the continuance of this wind. It lasted several days, and was very troublesome. One day the pain changed its quarters, and took possession of my back; I tried a hard gallop for some hours, and drove it into my head again, worse than ever. Next I was wheedled into trying a native remedy, the simplicity of which may create a smile, though it is firmly believed in by all the inhabitants. A dry broad bean is split down the middle; the inside surface is scraped with the teeth and moistened with the tongue, and each half of the bean is then applied as a plaister to the temples. I have frequently been greatly amused by the appearance of negro-women profusely ornamented with these white patches. The charm had no effect upon me, however, but a little castor-oil was completely successful; and I am happy to say that this trifling inconvenience was the only attempt at being unwell which I experienced during my whole absence from England.

The moisture of the north wind is sometimes very great in the neighbourhood of the river, and everything that can turn rusty or grow mouldy does so; but I never found these disagreeable effects in the open country. There, as far as my experience goes, it is impossible to wish for a more delightful climate.

I had the advantage of an unusually dry winter, which made riding about the country much more practicable and pleasant than it often is at that time of the year. Sometimes it was really cold in June and July, and in the first week of the latter month for three or four nights running we had very sharp rime-frosts, which left the ground perfectly white till ten o'clock in the morning, and made ice about the thickness of a crown piece.

With August the heat increases, and after a few months of deliciously temperate weather, it becomes at Christmas decidedly hot, the thermometer ranging frequently at about 90°, and sometimes reaching 100°. These, however, are the exceptionally hot days, after a few of which the pampero generally returns with a fresh stock of invigorating influences.

CHAPTER IV.

THE NEIGHBOURHOOD OF BUENOS AYRES.

VISIT TO A SALADERO — DRIVING IN CATTLE — THE SLAUGHTER — RAPID DISAPPEARANCE — JERKED BEEF — BUENOS AYREAN BUTCHERS — VILLAINOUS DOGS — FRENCH SPORTSMEN—THE 25TH OF MAY — POLITICAL DISTURBANCES — ANOMALOUS POSITION OF FOREIGNERS — OUTBREAK AT SAN JUAN — THE NATIONAL GUARD —BALL AT THE PROGRESO CLUB — DISPLAY IN THE PLAZA — JUGGLERS AND FIREWORKS—SAFETY IN THE STREETS—STEAMERS SEIZED—A VISIT TO MONTEVIDEO—M. BUSCHENTHAL'S QUINTA—AMATEUR CONCERT.

A FEW days after my arrival at Buenos Ayres, I was taken by a friend to see some of the *Saladeros* and *Barracas* a little beyond the southern extremities of the city. The saladeros are enormous establishments in which the cattle are slaughtered for their hides and tallow, and their flesh is converted into jerked beef: the barracas are store-houses for produce. On approaching this district there were plenty of indications of the trade in dead beasts. In one place was a vast heap of what I at first imagined must be gigantic mussel-shells, but they soon proved to be hoofs: a little farther the land was protected from the encroachments of the Riachuelo river by a wall composed of thousands of skulls of cattle patched with sods of turf. Large and fierce dogs in great numbers lurked about in corners, licking their lips after some dainty bit of offal surreptitiously walked off with, and looking as if they would soon take to the legs of a visitor if their natural supplies were curtailed. Countless seagulls, surfeited with their filthy breakfast, were lazily trying to digest it on the land which they whitened with their presence, now and then whirling about for a few moments, as if shaking themselves to make room for a fresh supply of garbage. Presently we saw a mighty cloud of dust, whence came a sound like muffled thunder, mixed with screams and wild yells. Stand clear! get out of the way! here comes a drove of about a thousand cattle from the country to be slaughtered at the saladeros. Not with the decorous march of Smithfield come these devoted beasts — quite another style of thing, and well worth seeing.

Four or five *peons*, or drivers, in brilliant *ponchos* of red, blue, and yellow, ride in front at full gallop, cracking their whips, and screaming to one another while you gladly draw up near the wall to get out of the way as they charge towards you. Close at their heels comes the whole herd, heads down and tails up, going at their maddest speed, encouraged thereto by more peons at their sides. On they go, thundering through the cloud of dust, and at last the mad line is ended by another set of peons all shouting and urging on the wild race in such a state of whip-cracking excitement, that even a calm spectator feels the spell, and is almost ready to give up his soul to the possession of the galloping ghost of Mazeppa.

Half-stifled with dust, we went on our way to the saladeros, where we were to see the completion of bovine destiny, and arrived there about a quarter of an hour before the slaughter commenced. About 800 beasts had been driven into a *corral* or enclosure, made of strong posts nearly a foot thick, one side of which towards the yard tapered off into a kind of funnel about six feet wide, which was crossed by a strong bar with an iron pulley in it. This was approached by a small tramway, upon which travelled a truck large enough to carry two of the animals at the same time, and running parallel to the slaughtering platform, which was of great size, and gently inclined towards the gutter made for carrying off the blood. Groups of dark-visaged men and lads were chatting gaily as they sharpened their knives, and the chief executioner stood by his post, somewhat raised over the bar and pulley. The pulley was traversed by a rope of the customary raw hide, one end of which terminated in the lazo or noose running on a ring of iron, and the other end was attached firmly to two horses standing saddled in the open yard. The time had come: two gaily dressed peons, with the unfailing cigarette in their mouths, jumped lightly into the saddles of the two horses, casting a Parthian glance behind to see if all was right; the infantry were ready, knife in hand, and the work of death began. The butcher-in-chief gathered up his lazo, and with practised eye selected two beasts whose heads were in sufficiently close proximity to be entangled in a single cast. He swung it two or three times round his head, and in a moment the four horns were firmly gripped with unerring accuracy. At a signal from him the two horsemen spurred their steeds into a plunge forwards for about twenty yards with the other end of the rope, and instantly the two poor brutes were dragged forwards till their heads were jammed hard against the bar with the pulley. Then the executioner stoops, and with two quiet thrusts of his knife divides the spine a little behind the horns; he casts loose the noose from their heads, and two corpses fall heavily on the truck which is ready to receive them; the truck is rapidly wheeled to the platform, and another rope attached to a horse is fastened to a fore-leg of each; a touch of the spur, a violent jerk, and the bodies are twitched off the truck and deposited on the platform with their heads close to the gutter, while the truck is sent back for more victims.

Two men seize on each, and cut their throats; the hide is taken off with inconceivable skill and rapidity; knives glance, and with light, but marvellously accurate touch, the head and limbs disappear. In about five minutes the animal has literally gone to pieces, vanished, almost before he has done kicking. The hide is hung up in one place; the legs are on different hooks; the good meat is hung in huge slabs to cool upon long railings; and the bony structure is carried off to the steaming vats. Meanwhile the fatal lazo is thrown again and again with horrible monotony, and the whole platform is covered with animals flying to pieces so quickly that you cannot follow the operation. In a moderate day's work the whole eight hundred will be disposed of in this way. I never saw so disgusting a sight, and could not help thinking as I watched these wild-looking men, how quickly they might have turned us into unrecognisable jerked beef and candles for exportation. I was soon glad enough to cross the yard and see the less horrid parts of the operations of a saladero. The beef is spread out over a large floor covered with a rough kind of salt, and is heaped up to the roof, layer upon layer, with salt between; in due time it is taken out, dried in the sun, and piled up in huge round masses, like wheat-stacks in Cambridgeshire. It is miserable stuff, and is only exported to Brazil, Havannah, and the slave states and islands for negro consumption. Such is jerked beef. One of the latest improvements, however, in the Rio de la Plata is a process for improving jerked beef so far as to make it palatable to and valuable for the poorer classes in Europe, and specimens sent from Montevideo to the International Exhibition were favourable enough to have been consumed by tasters. A little further improvement may render the flesh of millions of beeves an available and important article in our markets. Meanwhile the bones and remains of the victims are steamed in huge vats to draw off the grease. The fibrous parts are then taken out and subjected to great pressure to extract the last particles of grease, after which they are dried, and used as fuel to warm the pot for the next batch. Nothing in nature is lost: the last atoms are made useful. The hides are carried off to other establishments, where they are prepared according to the fashion of the markets for which they are intended—the main difference of treatment being, that for the English and German markets they are stretched so as to be as long as possible, while for Spain they are made so broad and short as to be nearly square.

Vast quantities of mares are slaughtered for the sake of their hides and grease; but the method of execution is different, as they are killed with the blow of a heavy hammer on the skull. Nobody in the whole continent would think of riding a mare, so all are killed except those required for the purpose of breeding. Thousands upon thousands of seagulls fatten on these scenes of slaughter, and find a paradise in what must be the infernal regions of the noble quadrupeds.

On the northern and southern sides of the city are the chief places for slaughtering animals to supply the inhabitants with food. A large piece of ground is surrounded by strong pens or enclosures, in which the cattle are shut up till a buyer comes. He comes, like all the rest of the South American world, on horseback, and selects his beast, which is then driven out into the open space: the mounted butchers pursue it at full speed; whizz goes the fatal lazo; the animal is instantly cut up where it happens to fall; and its mortal remains, disjointed in a way that would astonish a Briton, are carried away in a cart. The fowls of the air and the dogs of the field quarrel for the offal with herds of loathsome swine; and the horror which I conceived for pork brought up upon these independent principles was so great that I can hardly yet look upon English dairy-fed with anything like complacency. Little urchins resort to these places and practise upon the seagulls with the national weapon of the *bolas*, consisting of three balls connected by strings or strips of hide, which when whirled skillfully entangle the legs or wings of the beast or bird against which they are directed: and I have seen a couple of filthy negro-women squatting on the blood-soaked ground, and chattering like magpies over the disgusting operation of scraping every atom of grease from the intestines, which are left in all directions to the protection of Providence, and these loathsome harpies.

The dogs which are brought up on these latitudinarian principles are, as might be supposed, extremely dangerous; and no prudent man would think of walking or riding without a good whip or stick for his protection. I suppose it would be impossible to see anywhere else such a strange collection of mongrels of every size and shape. Many of them are large and ferocious; but little brutes of every description are to be met with in all directions. Perhaps the most disgusting are small bluish hairless curs, like sucking-pigs in a partial state of decomposition, which are used by women of the lower orders to keep their feet warm in bed—the absence of hair being a security against vermin. In the country, every house and hut has its own troop of dogs; and if an unlucky passer-by forgets the custom of the country, which compels him to pull up his horse on approaching a habitation, they rush out at him with a fury which soon reminds him of his want of politeness. The plague of dogs, if left to themselves, would soon be quite intolerable, and at certain seasons the police have regular battues to keep them within reasonable limits.

Amongst the motley collection may now and then be seen a good pointer or setter, belonging probably to a French barber or shopkeeper, who, after the fashion of his countrymen in Europe, takes advantage of every Sunday and holiday to take a gun into the suburbs, and there immolate every winged creature he can meet with, provided generally that the wings are not in motion. Long strings of little innocents of all sorts and colours, many of them smaller than larks and sparrows, hanging in the shops of the market-place, testify to the skill of these sportsmen, who, however miserable their game, like, if possible, to be accompanied by a *véritable* pointer.

I found the Buenos Ayreans in all the bustle of preparing to celebrate their great national festival, under circumstances of more than usual excitement. The 25th of May is their Independence day—the day on which they justly glorify themselves for having thrown off the dominion of Old Spain; and it is generally commemorated by every kind of festivity. On the present occasion, however, the general hilarity was tempered by a gloomy feeling of coming evil. There was every prospect of their tranquillity being disturbed by the outbreak of another civil war. It would be a long and thankless task to attempt to drag a European reader through the mazes of intrigue which form the main occupation of the low politicians who seem to flourish peculiarly in American republics, devoting themselves to the pursuit of personal aggrandisement and profit under the guise of lofty patriotism and republican purity. A very able article in the 'Quarterly Review' of October 1862 shows how the administration of democratic governments naturally falls into the hands of needy adventurers, whose only qualification for their office is excessive 'smartness.' Political lawyers are the chief bane of the North American States, and men of very much the same description do nearly all the mischief in South America also. Disraeli, I think, says somewhere that 'being in power means receiving 1,200*l*. a year, paid quarterly, and being in opposition means having the desire to receive 1,200*l*. a year, paid quarterly.' However hard this may be upon European politicians, very few would doubt its application to those of America; and it is common enough to hear that the mere receipt of their official incomes is by no means the limit of their pecuniary ambition.

Buenos Ayres, with its capital of the same name, is one of the thirteen provinces of the Argentine Confederation, which comprises the immense territory extending from Brazil to Patagonia, from the Uruguay to the Cordillera of the Andes. The city of Buenos Ayres, with its population of 140,000, a large proportion of whom are Europeans, and its constant communication with European politics and commerce, is very much more advanced in civilisation than any other part of the republic; and if its leading men would confine their attention to developing its resources and opening up fresh communications between this nucleus and all the outlying provinces, the arts of peace and civilisation would soon spread through the length and breadth of the land, and enormously increase the wealth and influence of the whole country. But the unquiet spirit of these intriguing *doctores* is not content to let nature work in her own fashion: they imagine, or pretend to imagine, that they have a holy mission to redeem the provinces from barbarism, and are engaged in continual intrigues for the humiliation and defeat of the *caudillos*, a term which corresponds pretty nearly with that of military Tories, the great bugbear of fervid Radicals all over the world. Many of these *caudillos* are undoubtedly rough and violent men; and with the bloody remembrance of such men as Rosas in their minds, the Argentine Liberals may be excused for great animosity against any system of policy which could admit of their being tyrannised over by semi-barbarous military chiefs; but, unfortunately, their tactics have too often given some appearance of justification to the cruelties of men who are much more ignorant than themselves.

One great difficulty in the country arises from the anomalous position of foreigners. A very large proportion of the business of the city is conducted by English, French, German, and Italian firms; and an Englishman especially is sure to meet his fellow-countrymen in all the principal streets. Again, very many of them hold under good titles hundreds of thousands of acres of the soil itself, covered with countless sheep, cattle, and horses, and gallop as undisputed lords over possessions which are equal in extent to many English counties. Foreigners of all kinds keep the greater part of the shops; and among the lower orders, it is remarkable that even the most thoroughly national occupations are passing from native into other hands. The picturesque water-carriers, and the curiously-mounted bakers and milkmen, include a very large proportion of Basques.

But all these, whether high or low, rich or poor, unless born in the country, are politically nothing but strangers in the land which has in many cases become their permanent home. No matter how large a stake they may have in the welfare of the country, they have no voice in the administration of its government; they have nothing to do with the rights or the responsibilities of citizenship. The German or the Irishman who emigrates to New York is entitled by a short residence to become a citizen of the States, but it is not so in the Argentine Confederation. There wealthy merchants and owners of *estancias*, like principalities, are cut off completely from public affairs, and remain citizens of their respective countries. The man born in the country can be compelled to serve in the national guard, or his horses may be seized by a government which dares not take a dollar's worth from the wealthiest foreigner, except at the risk of an immediate remonstrance through the agents of his government. This separation of interests is the cause of a total want of public opinion in any way proportionate to the collective wealth and strength of the inhabitants, and enables the professed politicians to intrigue at their leisure.

Unless some great change of feeling arises on both sides, it is not easy to see how this state of things is to be changed. It is doubtful if the native Argentines would concede citizenship to others, but it is not doubtful that many foreigners would decline it. They for the most part prefer having the strong arm of a European government to fall back upon for the protection of their interests, instead of adopting a South American nationality, with the constant risk of disturbances and revolutions, which past experience has induced them to anticipate for the future. There is much reason in such an argument; but at the same time I must add that I heard the contrary opinion from one or two old residents in the country. It must not be forgotten that a grand union of the representatives of the whole property of the country would be a greatly increased security for its preservation, and the greatest check against anarchy and disturbance. 'In the multitude of counsellors there is wisdom,' but under the present system Buenos Ayres suffers from the want of a large and sound public opinion.

At present this question appears a very difficult one; but its solution will very possibly be brought about by the results of the undoubted fact that the foreign population is increasing at a very much greater rate than that of the natives. Emigration from Europe is now largely in demand among the territories of La Plata; and when the excellence of the field is more generally known, the call will doubtless be well responded to. Railroads and the extension of commerce will soon call into existence a much larger population than the native stock can supply; and a country in which the majority of the inhabitants are not citizens would be indeed a strange anomaly.

In the beginning of the year 1861, and only a very short time before my arrival in the country, the Liberals of San Juan had got up a revolutionary disturbance in that distant province. The provinces being united in a Federation, the Federal government is, of course, in times of internal peace everywhere supported by the National or Federal forces, which were then commanded by General Urquiza, with the grandiloquent title of Captain-General of the Forces by land and sea. The outbreak at San Juan was speedily put down by the troops under the command of one of Urquiza's officers, named Sáa, who, not satisfied with restoring order, appears to have acted with great brutality, and was reported to have allowed the massacre of about 400 men who had taken to flight. I afterwards heard that this number was a great exaggeration; but, at all events, the facts were bad enough to cause the most intense indignation of the Liberals at Buenos Ayres, who saw in the result of this affair the entire destruction of a party which they counted upon as a valuable nucleus for their schemes of progress in the West. The name of Sáa was naturally branded in the newspapers with every term of opprobrium of which the Spanish language is capable; he had at once established his reputation as the darkest monster of the River Plate. He was execrated in public, and children were terrified into obedience by the whisper of his name.

Under such circumstances as these, imagine the indignation with which the Buenos Ayreans received official intelligence that Sáa had been formally thanked by the Federal government, which was at that time established at Paranà! It was considered as a sure indication of an intention on the part of the National Government to crush the vitality of the whole Liberal party, by destroying them piecemeal in the provinces, as a prelude to an advance upon Buenos Ayres itself.

About the same time, another galling insult was perpetrated by the Federal party: the deputies sent by Buenos Ayres to the Congress at Paranà were rejected, and sent back contemptuously, on the ground of an alleged informality in their election. It is extremely doubtful if there was any informality at all; the elections appear to have been conducted in the form which had been agreed upon, and the people of Buenos Ayres naturally looked upon the conduct of the National Government as insulting to the last degree. Their anger was doubly roused by knowing that the most bitter opponents of their liberal views in Congress were a knot of renegades from their own camp, unscrupulous men, who, finding themselves defeated and powerless in their own city, devoted all their energies to the service of the *caudillos.* High words arose, and while the Captain-General Urquiza was preparing his forces to punish the Buenos Ayreans as rebels, the latter called out their National Guard and threatened open war. Recruiting and negotiation went on together, and with every additional thousand men to either side, the violence of its language and the extent of its demands increased in proportion. The Buenos Ayrean papers hounded on the Government of their State to resist the National authority, and used ridiculously-inflated language in their endeavours to excite the languid population, which consisted, for the most part, of men who cared for neither parties or principles of policy, provided the country were left to pursue a course of peace and prosperity.

Thus it chanced that the strength of Federalism was being tried to the utmost in North and South America at the same time; and it was proved contemporaneously that, though perhaps a good system in calm weather, it is not to be trusted in a storm. In each division of the New World a great federation was threatened with dissolution; the difference being that, while in North America the slave States determined on seceding, in the Argentine Confederation the province of Buenos Ayres, trusting to her wealth and numbers, stood out alone against the rest, not condescending to secede and declare her own independence, but determined to make the rest of the nation submit to her ideas of what the republic should be. This was the real meaning of the war which was now impending.

On my first Sunday in the city, I found myself among a crowd of people assembled to see the return of the National Guard from a review. Their number was about 4,000, but I think they were the most motley assemblage of troops that I ever beheld. The men were of every shade of colour — white, yellow, whitey-brown, rusty-brown, and black. Some companies wore regular uniforms, some wore blouses, and some wore Garibaldian shirts; while others contained a mixture of all. I saw one company of men chiefly in blouses, commanded by an old grey-wooled negro in uniform, who looked amazingly contented with his own share in the exhibition. Sometimes, a gentlemanly-looking man was commanding some of the shabbiest of the troops; and, close behind, the next company presented the reverse of that picture. Drums beating and flags flying increased the excitement, and the review had at least two results, one of which was expected, and the other was not: the newspapers produced glowing articles on the heroism of Buenos Ayrean troops, and an unfortunate spectator was shot through the head.

Meanwhile, wise heads and sober men of business looked with anxiety upon the symptoms of impending war, and the May festival was not so lively as usual. I was present at the ball given by the Progreso Club in its own handsome rooms; but, though no pains were spared to make it a complete success, yet there seemed to be a want of the spirit and enthusiasm which such an occasion would usually call forth. The Governor, General Mitre, was present, with his wife, and was the observed of all observers, who would gladly have guessed his opinion of affairs by the expression of his countenance. He is a tall handsome man, of very elegant appearance, with a fine forehead and thoughtful face; he is a poet and scholar, and looks altogether too refined and gentlemanly to be mixed up with the dirty doings of second-rate politics. On the present occasion, he certainly looked anxious, and well he might; for he not only had to preside in the councils of the State, but, in the event of war, would also have to take command of that motley army in the field.

Buenos Ayrean fashion requires that no one should go to a public ball of this kind before midnight; and on arriving about half an hour after that, we found ourselves almost the first in the room. This is the more remarkable, because five o'clock is the usual dinner hour, and ladies who intend to dance are obliged to go to sleep for two or three hours before dressing for the ball. The rooms were beautifully decorated and ornamented with flowers, the band was powerful and perfect, and everything exceedingly handsome. The ladies are justly celebrated for their beauty and elegance, and made the rooms of the club so brilliant with their presence that an Englishman could not help thinking of the effect that might be produced by an occasional introduction of such gaieties into the stately halls of

Pall Mall. Promenading, however, seemed much more popular than dancing in the lively fashion of Europe; and, though the ball-room was very fairly filled, yet it was not uncommon to find only two or three couples dancing, while the band was exerting itself to the utmost with a popular waltz. There was, however, an atmosphere of somewhat stately solemnity about the Progreso, which does not affect the agreeable vivacity of the Portenians in private life and domestic *tertulias*.

Two days afterwards came the 25th of May, the great national holiday. The whole space of the Plaza de la Victoria was covered with people, who had come together to see the display of soldiers and fireworks. Church and State kiss one another with every appearance of respect on this occasion; the Governor and Ministers, accompanied by a crowd of minor officials, and such foreign representatives as may choose to accept the formal invitation, go to the cathedral in procession, and listen to the ceremonies of the Church. The Pontifex Maximus having completed his task, Mars assumes the duty of escorting Cæsar back to the Cabildo. All the troops that could be got together were marched round the Plaza, to the great delight of the crowd; and the artillery presented a rather formidable appearance, clustering round the beautiful pillar of Liberty in the middle of the square. The sun was brilliant, the sky intensely blue, and the air pure and invigorating beyond description; the soldiers marched off to their barracks, and the crowd circulated on the dusty parade which they had left; the orange-sellers drove a lively trade, and the attention of everyone was concentrated upon a stage where rope-dancers, tumblers, and jugglers were to perform in the open air for the amusement of the people, the expenses being, I believe, paid out of the proceeds of a government lottery. Some of the performances of these native artists were very amusing, and a clown, in sky-blue garments with a white-peaked cap, was not only 'a fellow of infinite jest,' but an astonishing acrobat into the bargain. Nothing, however, seemed to delight the mob so much as the production of a man apparently suffering from the agonies of swelled face and toothache; the clown took him in hand with a crowbar, and, after the fashion of our pantomimes, very skilfully extracted a wooden tooth about six inches long, and wide in proportion.

Fire-balloons of strange form are very popular in South America, and one of the largest on this occasion discharged a large number of very pretty parachutes as it sailed away across the river. But the most amusing one I ever saw in Buenos Ayres, was a huge effigy of a woman in full dress, with an immense crinoline and Bloomer appendages, who, dropping parachutes from her pockets, was carried by a fresh breeze out of sight in the direction of the Banda Oriental. The evening was devoted to a grand display of fireworks, which were really magnificent, but many of them were allowed to burst among the dense crowd so recklessly that I was surprised at not hearing of serious accidents. Large numbers of rockets were also let off during the day, bursting with loud explosions, and sending small white clouds of smoke drifting across the blue sky. Rockets by daylight are, however, very common in South America, and are especially used to announce by their sharp bangs the intention to have a performance at the theatre. The May festivities lasted altogether three days, and, to the great credit of Buenos Ayres, I can truly say that, though I was moving constantly about the town by day and night, I did not see a single case of drunkenness or any kind of disorder in the streets during the whole time. I heard of no cases of robbery among the crowds, or in the houses of those who had left home to see the amusements of the evening; and I very much doubt if there is a single city of Europe, where, under similar circumstances, such a good character could be given to the inhabitants. Indeed, I may as well say, once for all, that in the course of many a dark night's walk between the Quinta and the city, I never heard a disturbance or came into collision with anybody —excepting on one occasion, when a *sereno* or watchman had so far relaxed his vigilance as to sit down on a door-step with his lantern hidden behind him: he had fallen asleep with his legs at full stretch across the path, and as the night was as dark as dark could be, I stumbled against them and nearly measured my length on some rough stones. I recovered myself in time, and abused him; he returned the compliment with a sleepy grunt, and I went quietly on my way. Let this state of things be compared to the present condition of London, which, with all its boasted civilisation, was for a time given over to the rascally army of garotters! This, however, is a great improvement on the *ancien régime* of the city.

Meanwhile the probability of war was every day increasing, and the process of seizing passenger steamers, to be used for military purposes, commenced with great vigour on both sides. The principle was 'catch as catch can.' The Federals kept what they could at Paranà, and the Buenos Ayreans seized all the vessels they could lay their hands on at their own end of the river. None were safe except those which sailed under a foreign flag. The Paraguay steamers continued to run twice a month up the river; the 'Montevideo' was safe under the flag of Uruguay; and a huge Yankee steamer, called the 'Mississippi,' made a very good thing of it, being almost large enough to carry on all the necessary traffic between Buenos Ayres and Montevideo, till unluckily she was blown on shore in a heavy gale. When the Government took possession of a steamer, they set to work to strengthen and repair her as well as they could, to mount a few guns, and, through the agency of crimps, to get sailors from foreign ships in the port. Every *hijo del pais*, or man born in the country, whether of native or foreign parentage, was compelled to enrol himself in the National Guard, or to find a *personero* (substitute), to be victimised in his place.

The price of substitutes rose rapidly with the increased probability of actual fighting, and at last they could hardly be got for love or money. Many of those liable to service avoided it by escaping to Montevideo and elsewhere; but the precautions against this possibility were made more stringent continually.

About this time a good friend who had business at Montevideo, kindly asked me to go down with him in the 'Mississippi,' and I was very glad to have the benefit of his company and guidance. This immense vessel was splendidly fitted, and built, like all the North American river-boats, to combine great speed with little draught of water. The saloon was splendidly furnished, and nothing could exceed the comfort and neatness of the sleeping cabins. A very good dinner was served in *table d'hôte* fashion soon after we started, and early in the morning we found ourselves anchored at Montevideo. There were plenty of boats ready to take people on shore, and after walking up to the Hotel Oriental we breakfasted with a friend. In the course of the day we made a number of visits and saw a good deal of the city, which, though much smaller than Buenos Ayres, is built upon the same plan of squares and long straight streets. Its picturesque appearance is increased by the greater numbers of *miradors* or high look-out terraces and towers, from which the view of the city and sea is always interesting and animated. Next day I was taken to see the quinta of M. Buschenthal, who is a kind of Rothschild in the River Plate. We had a pleasant ride of about five miles, which gave me an excellent idea of the general appearance and position of the city. Instead of continual plains, the land rises immediately in a system of long undulations, from the crests of which we had charming views of the harbour filled with shipping, and the long peninsula covered with the snow-white buildings of Montevideo, all brilliant in sunshine. The hedges were, like those of Buenos Ayres, composed of cactus and aloes; but it appeared to me that the plants were even larger and finer than those of the latter place. We passed many very pretty country-houses, surrounded by gardens full of lovely flowers, and plantations of huge orange-trees loaded with fruit. Fig-trees also reached a great size; but the country has not yet recovered from the destruction of wood which took place in the nine years' siege by Oribe, before 1851 —in the course of which almost every tree in the neighbourhood was cut down for fuel by the soldiers, who spared none but those which were useful for the fruits which they produced.

I was more pleased than I had even expected with the appearance of M. Buschenthal's Quinta. He has spared no expense in filling his grounds with trees and flowers imported from all parts of the world, and has paid special attention to the cultivation of gcod fruit. The approach to his house was by a broad path bordered by shrubberies and Australian gum-trees, which, though young, seemed to be growing wonderfully fast, and showed that a large importation of them would be of great advantage to the countries of La Plata, where, as a general rule, want of wood is one of the most serious defects. The house itself seemed perfect as a summer retreat in a warm climate, ornamented with works of art and surrounded by gardens, while a magnificent *ombù* in front afforded cool and impenetrable shade. The grounds were kept in high order by a staff of French gardeners, who very civilly answered our questions. Most of the European fruits were produced here in large quantities, but the secret of the success of many of them seems to consist in keeping the trees small by close pruning; the sap has then a shorter distance to travel, and is consequently less likely to be dried up by the excessive heat of a Montevidean summer. This hint may be useful to many who may wish to cultivate European fruit in warm countries. Long winding walks led among luxuriant masses of flowers and flowering shrubs, and orange-trees growing in all directions to add colour and fragrance to the scene.

After a very pleasant afternoon we returned to Montevideo, where a feast awaited us. The landlord of the Hotel Oriental had honoured my friend by procuring an *anchoa*, something like a salmon, and by far the best fish in that part of the world: like most good things, however, it is not always to be met with. We were fortunate; and when the banquet was finished, with a dish of Alpine strawberries and a bottle of Burgundy, we felt that we had dined indeed, and were in a contented frame of mind for returning that night by the 'Mississippi' to Buenos Ayres, where we arrived at about six in the morning. Before parting with the 'Mississippi,' I ought to say that she was provided with an ingenious instrument for registering the number of revolutions made by the engines. There were six square holes in a row, and tables of figures behind were so disposed as to mark the correct number. Every stroke of the piston added one to this by making the necessary changes in the figures, which would thus go on increasing up to 999999, when they must begin again.

A few days after this a grand amateur concert was given in the Colon Theatre, for the benefit of the sufferers by the earthquake at Mendoza, which afforded a good opportunity of observing the beauties of Buenos Ayres, and their taste for music. The large and handsome theatre with its open boxes presented a charming spectacle; enormous prices had been paid for places, but every seat was occupied; beauty and fashion were most ably represented, and the concert itself was admirably conducted. The stage was occupied by a full chorus of ladies and gentlemen, who, as well as the solo performers, were strictly amateurs. Everything went well, but one of the most brilliant successes was a triple duet on three grand pianos, with two young ladies at each. The national hymn was sung, and sung well; but in spite of the exciting times it produced very little enthusiasm: two or three people said 'Bravo,' but even this seemed more as a compliment to the singers than anything else. As usual there was plenty of 'Libertad,' &c., but no one seemed to care very much about it. Altogether the concert was a grand success, and produced a large sum of money; and though it lasted till one o'clock in the morning, I think everyone in the audience was heartily sorry when it came to an end. I find that such a large number of English people cannot divest themselves of the erroneous idea that society in the cities of the River Plate is semi-barbarous, that, in remembrance of the many charming acquaintances I made there, it is a peculiar pleasure to attempt to disprove the popular view. Another fact will, perhaps, aid me. A brilliant bazaar was got up two years ago, for the purpose of assisting to build an English hospital. English ladies were supported by their Spanish friends, and the result was a contribution of 1,500*l.* to the hospital fund. Aided by liberal subscriptions from individuals, and supported by the goodwill of the Buenos Ayrean Government, this hospital was in full working order before I left the country, and in a state to reflect the highest credit upon its founders. Such works as these in a distant country are worthy of all praise, and are alone sufficient to vindicate the territory of La Plata from the unfounded supposition of semi-barbarism.

CHAPTER V.

VISIT TO THE CAMP.

PANIC ABOUT URQUIZA — SEIZURE OF HORSES — SCARCITY OF LABOUR — REVIEW IN THE PLAZA — DOUBTS ABOUT CORDOVA — AN INTERCEPTED DESPATCH — GENERAL MITRE MARCHES WITH HIS ARMY — EXPEDITION TO MONTE GRANDE — TIRU-TEROS — BISCACHOS — PAMPAS OWLS — PANTANOS — WILDFOWL — STORES— EVENING—THE RECADO—BRIDLE, BIT, AND SPURS—THE REVENQUE —MANRAS AND SILVER ORNAMENTS.

ABOUT this time we had fresh news from Entre Rios, where it appeared that Urquiza had been collecting his troops, and was quite ready to cross the Paranà with the Federal army, which had been excited to fever-point by the well-known principle of giving them no pay till they could get it for themselves by the plunder of the enemy. The excitement increased daily; some people thought that Urquiza would take the initiative, and come down the river without a moment's notice, and others argued that he would let the Buenos Ayreans march out to meet him; that he would give them a sound thrashing in the field, and then bring all his hungry hordes for the sack and pillage of the city. Either of these alternatives was enough to strike the good citizens with well-founded panic; and gold ounces increased rapidly in value, in proportion to the increased feeling of public insecurity. Vigorous measures were taken to drill the National Guard, and penalties were strictly enforced against those who neglected their duty in attending. A considerable part of the regular troops was sent forward towards Rosario, with a force of artillery, and fresh troops were brought in to supply their places. Draught horses were in great request for wagons and artillery, and very harsh measures were adopted to procure them. In some cases, the authorities even stopped water-carts, which are among the most important institutions of Buenos Ayres, and took away the horses; thus robbing the luckless owners of their little fortune and means of living, and giving them the poor consolation of receiving the regulation price of about 2*l.* sterling for what had been to them worth 20*l.* Contracts for horses at 150 paper dollars, or about 25*s.* each, for government purposes, of course, encouraged horse stealing to a very great amount; in one night about forty were carried off from a *potrero*, or meadow, near the Boca. The audacity of agents assuming the authority of government was so great that even carriage horses were occasionally threatened; and I remember one night, when some of our neighbours locked up their favourite steeds in halls and dining-rooms for protection. It was very unsatisfactory to an owner, after taking incredible pains to recover his stolen horses, to find them at last with their ears cropped, by way of indisputable proof that they belonged to government! The excitement became very great; there were frequent consultations of treaties which secure foreigners from being compelled to render military aid or munitions of war to the government; and strong expostulations were made to the ministers.

Foreigners made good their position by the intervention of their representatives; but the unlucky natives had no remedy. Forced into a war which they did not provoke, to carry out the schemes of men whom they had no respect for, they had no alternative but to submit to the arbitrary orders of those who had led them into the scrape. In South America the phenomena have been much the same as in the so-called United States; in short, if anyone wishes to see tyranny triumphant, and the rights of individuals trampled under foot by irresponsible governments, he must turn his back upon the effete monarchies of poor old Europe, and visit the republics of the West upon some occasion of political excitement.

Labour became very scarce, men of all kinds being pressed into military service; and happening one day to be riding past the great slaughtering places at the north of the city, I saw a number of the *gaucho* butchers reluctantly obeying the angry summons of a bugle. They came up very leisurely to the muster, and when I observed that they were well mounted, a friend told me that men who were compelled to serve in the cavalry, and bring their own horses, preferred bringing their best, as these were naturally the most suited to help them in running away! It is not that these men are more cowardly than others, but they detest being forced from their ordinary occupations to fight for a cause which has no interest for them. The poor devils may well be excused when we remember that they have everything to lose and nothing to gain among the miseries of civil war.

On the 30th of June, General Mitre had a grand review in the Plaza, and made a glowing speech to the troops whom it was expected that he would shortly have to take command of in the field. He paid the most flattering compliments to those of the National Guard who had come forward and enrolled themselves for the defence of their country; and he spoke with withering scorn of the cowards who disgraced their 'Argentine mothers' by keeping out of the way. This phrase, '*madres Argentinas*' sounds very well, and reminds one of the barbaric virtues of Rome and Lacedæmon; but in these degenerate days, Argentine, as well as other matrons, generally prefer keeping their sons at home to assist in supporting the rest of the family, unless under the strong pressure of foreign aggression. The General reminded them of the glories of the Argentine flag—the conqueror in a hundred fights—and called upon the troops to follow him to victory; forgetting, however, to say a word about who was to be their enemy or what they were to fight for.

Meanwhile, reports of the most contradictory nature were set on foot by the Liberals on one side and the Federal partisans on the other. One morning we heard that Cordova, where the Liberals thought they had a strong party, had gallantly refused to admit Derqui, the Federal President, within its walls; the 'Tribuna' newspaper was in ecstacies for two days, at the end of which it was obliged to eat dirt, and confess that Derqui had met with no resistance. Some cool heads hoped that this discouragement of the advanced party might very likely conduce to peace; but the first piece of favourable news undid the work of the other, and big words became the order of the day.

A few days later, a great excitement was created by an intercepted letter from President Derqui to Pedernera, his acting representative at Paranà. In this epistle the terms of peace laid down were such as could only be offered to a defeated enemy, and the Buenos Ayreans were naturally furious at finding that the President would make no terms with them, except on the condition of their abandoning all the points they contended for. He required their submission to the Federal government, the nationalisation of the custom-house, the surrender or neutrality of the important island of Martin Garcia, the surrender of their ships and the reduction of their army; adding, by way of final insult, that they should pay the expenses of the Federal government in preparing for the war! In case of resistance, they were informed that the army of Urquiza would be marched down into the province of Buenos Ayres, there to support itself by the spoliation of private property. Derqui from this time was honoured with the soubriquet of '*Ladron de vacas*,' or bullock stealer, and was looked upon as much worse than Urquiza himself.

There were great doubts about what should be done with the National Guard. Without this body, the Buenos Ayreans would make but a poor show in numbers, when compared with the National or Federal army, and yet it was a serious question whether they ought to be taken out for a campaign. Some said they ought not to go for two reasons: 1st, that they were only intended for the defence of the city; and 2ndly, that no one could compel them to take the field. Others said they ought to go and fight the enemies of liberty, independence, &c., wherever they might be found; and a third party suggested pretty plainly that the National Guard would refuse to march if ordered to do so, and that any attempt to coerce them would lead to a revolution in the city itself. It was certainly a very hard case for the members of that body; ten times as bad for them as it would be for the volunteers of London to be marched off to Lancashire and Yorkshire under similar circumstances. They marched without tents in the winter, and though, of course, even in winter, there is no very severe cold in Buenos Ayres, they had every prospect of being drenched with heavy rains, which they would have to endure as best they could in the open plains, without even the excitement of a foreign invader to contend against.

The political barometer indicated stormy weather, the gold ounce rising in two days from 380 to nearly 400 paper dollars. The city was declared in a state of siege, and great numbers of men were employed to surround it with a complete system of fortifications, which consisted only of a deep and broad ditch and embankment, studded here and there with small forts mounting two or three guns of various sorts and sizes. After several delays and postponements, General Mitre at last marched with the greater part of the army in the direction of Rosario, and it was understood that Urquiza was moving his troops across the river from Entre Rios at Diamante.

In spite of all the pleasures of society in such an agreeable place as Buenos Ayres, I was longing for the first opportunity of going into the camp, as the country is generally termed. I was also getting tired of the constant gossiping rumours of war and peace which entirely occupied the attention of the citizens.

The opportunity soon occurred. Among my chief friends were the sons of Mr. Fair, one of the first of the active Englishmen who laboured for many years in developing the resources of the Rio de la Plata, and opening up new channels for the enterprise of Europeans. He is the proprietor of large *estancias* in the Banda Oriental and the province of Buenos Ayres, and my first visit was to one of the smaller of these, called Monte Grande, only twenty miles to the south of the city. I started one morning with Mr. Frederick Fair, taking guns and materials for a week's shooting. A pair of saddle-bags contained a change of clothes, ammunition, and a few creature comforts, such as brandy and tobacco; we wore long boots, equally suited for riding and wading in the swamps, and we carried our guns in our hands. I was strongly recommended not to use a gun-sling, because it is a common thing for horses to fall suddenly on putting a foot into a *biscacho*-hole, and the danger of an upset is considerably greater with such an object as a gun strapped to one's back. I only once tried a sling, but it broke as I galloped along, and I never had it mended; in fact, though at first a gun in the hand is a great impediment to riding, a little practice makes it very easy.

No one, except doctors and officials, may gallop in the streets of Buenos Ayres, and as trotting is unknown to the horses of the country, we had a long and solemn march at a walking pace, till we got out to the suburbs. Here we passed one of the huge slaughter grounds, bathed as usual in blood, and containing as many disgusting sights as could well be produced in the same space. Pigs, seagulls, and negro-women were contending for the last scraps of the departed oxen, and the pigs seemed to me to have been degraded by their mode of life into the most ugly and revolting race imaginable. The stench was powerful, but not nearly so bad as I should have expected, and it is asserted by the natives to be peculiarly wholesome! A few miles from Buenos Ayres we crossed the Riachuelo by a bridge, where a small toll is paid, and we began to feel fairly in the country. For a few miles farther, however, a good deal of the land is enclosed by wire fences, a modern innovation which greatly annoys the thorough-bred *gauchos* who have from time immemorial been accustomed to gallop by day or night in any direction, and as far as they please. Presently this sign of civilisation disappeared and the road ceased; the open boundless Pampas were before me, and with a feeling of indescribable joy I inhaled the delicious and invigorating breeze. Away and away we went, galloping over the short turf towards a distant landmark on the horizon, which was to be our guide. The want of rain was being felt, and we found the camp so hard and dry that there was evidently good reason for the general expectation of a *seca*, or drought. Here and there a damp place had its snipe and snippets grubbing for worms, and flying startled from almost under our horses' feet. The *tiru-teros* or horned plovers strutted about the plains, rising with their strange wild cry, and screaming 'tiru-tero,' as they whirled over our heads. The *biscachos* were asleep in their holes, according to custom, and we knew we should not see one of them till sunset; but the lovely little Pampas owls were on duty guarding the approaches to their subterranean friends. There they sat staring at us solemnly, not moving a muscle except those which were necessary to turn their heads horizontally, and not attempting to stir unless they found we should ride over them; in which case they flew in a gently indignant fashion, and with a soft flapping motion, for twenty or thirty yards, after which they silently perched by the side of another burrow to stare at us again.

Presently we came to a small *arroyo*, hardly wider than a broad ditch. An English horse of the mildest description would have jumped it instantly, but though the South American horses have amazing powers of endurance, they have not the slightest notion of jumping—and are, with some reason perhaps, extremely suspicious of muddy *arroyos*. There is not a particle of stone or gravel in those vast plains, and nobody can judge certainly from the appearances what may be the depth of mud in a Buenos Ayrean stream or *pantano*. Scores of horses are continually being lost in these places, which sometimes let them in at once over the saddle; and scores of clean picked carcases, with buried legs, mark where these catastrophes have happened, If you are travelling with a troop of horses nobody cares a straw for the loss of one: if you have to depend for the day upon the beast you are riding, too much caution is impossible.

This was one of the first lessons taught to me, and I never forgot it. On the present occasion we looked about for the best place we could find, and passed safely with no inconvenience but a little mud-splashing. Away and away again, by the *banado* or swamp region, where large shallow *lagunas* were concealed by tall sedges and rushes, till we were close upon them, and a mighty rushing sound announced the alarm of innumerable wild-fowl. Ducks of various kinds, teal and widgeon, were mixed up with clouds of a species of water-hen. Storks, *mirasols,* cranes—some handsome, some foul and uncouth, rushed into the air, trailing their huge legs under them for a short ungainly flight, and dropping sleepily into their native mud as soon as we had passed them. We walked the horses for awhile, and in the stillness on the soft turf we heard the clear ringing scream of birds, slowly whirling round and round at such a vast height above us that they were difficult to see. These were the great turkey-buzzards—unclean carrion-lovers, which sometimes alight in such immense numbers on the plains that I have mistaken them at a distance for a flock of black sheep. A little way farther we came to a broader river connected with the lagunas, and I was for following its banks till we came to a narrower place; but the experience of my companion said 'No,' and he at once rode through, followed by myself: we found the water only up to our girths, with pretty good bottom, as he had predicted; but I had great difficulty in forcing my horse over; he was very hot, and I had a strong suspicion that he meant to get rid of me by rolling in the middle of the river. About a couple of miles before reaching the house, we entered the large wood from which the place takes its name of Monte Grande—the word *Monte* being applied to woods as well as mountains. There were no fine trees, however, and the greater part of them were *tala*, half shrub and half tree, which seldom grows larger than our whitethorn, and is anything but graceful. The grass was longer than in the camp, and many cattle and horses were wandering up and down. Here and there a cloud of hawks, kites, *coranchos*, &c., rose screaming as we disturbed them in the act of picking the bones of a dead bullock; and now and then large flights of ducks crossed on their way to the lagunas. We had no intention to shoot till next day, but the ride was made delightfully exciting by the variety and immense numbers of the birds which form so large a part of the inhabitants of South America. Latterly, we had more leisure to admire them, for the great heat of the day, added to our heavy loads, proved very trying to the horses, and they required a good deal of encouragement to get them beyond a walk. Heavy saddle-bags and guns make a considerable addition to the ordinary weight of a man; and the poor beasts must have been uncommonly glad when they got quit of us at the house. As soon as they were unsaddled we got water and hay for them, leaving them for the night fastened to a post by one of the hide ropes of the country. Then we looked after our own interests. An old Scotchwoman, who had acted as housekeeper there for many years, was very much surprised to see us; the house is not regularly inhabited, and I thought she contemplated the subject of stores with some anxiety. However, several very useful things were discovered when we began to search the cupboards: sardines, pickles, and a case of most delicious preserved lobsters, which proved to have kept their full flavour and freshness ever since they were caught at New York. Then we discovered a few bottles of wine, and playing-cards, also very useful things, as we found on the first wet day. Bread is a very rare sight, except in the towns, but there is always an abundance of the usual biscuits of the country, which, though sweet, are so excessively hard that it requires a strong hand to smash them against the corner of the table. We were surrounded by thousands of sheep, and knew that we should have plenty of mutton, so we began to put things to rights, and prepared to enjoy ourselves, trusting to ducks and partridges for the improvement of the larder.

The house consisted, as usual, of only one floor, with a flat roof, approachable by steps. The rooms were comfortable, and a verandah in front, and another one behind, offered plenty of fresh air, combined with shade and shelter. At the back was an enclosed piece of ground, which was once upon a time a garden, when the house was used as a residence. At a little distance in front was a row of buildings, which accommodated the agent and the *capataz*, or head man; and a little farther off the peons used to roll themselves up in their ponchos on the floor of a long shed, where, with a proper allowance of *matè* and beef, they were perfectly happy and contented. The corrals were close at hand for both sheep and horses. Even in a small establishment there must always be a considerable number of the latter; for where everything is done by hard riding, and sometimes the men are kept all day in the saddle, they must change their horses now and then, or the whole would break down, in spite of their wonderful powers of endurance.

We bustled about to aid the preparations of good old Mrs. Macdonald, and presently we announced dinner for ourselves. The dishes were not numerous; but good sweet mutton and rice, followed by part of the never-to-be-forgotten preserved lobsters, made feast enough for any man of well-regulated mind and body. I know we enjoyed it intensely after our hot ride; and when the feeding was over, we strolled out to smoke our cigars in the open air. The sun was just setting in a cloudless sky, and I watched its huge bulk sink beneath the boundless level of the plains with almost the same effects as are produced by a sunset at sea. And then the day's work was done; the last peon came galloping in from a distant station, tossed off his saddle, put his horse into the corral, and prepared to join his comrades in cooking their beef and chattering over the red glare of a wood fire. We could no longer see flights of ducks passing swiftly overhead, and even the scream of the ever-watchful *tiru-tero* ceased. The *biscachos* awoke from their sleep with the very last rays of the sun, and cautiously peeped from their holes to satisfy themselves that he had really set before they ventured to begin their supper. The stars came out in all their glory, shining through the pure air with a brilliancy which reminded me of many a night among the high Alps, where the stars indeed shine like lamps in heaven. The dogs at a sheep-station howled for a moment in the distance, and then all was still—buried in that wonderfully impressive silence of solitude which almost enables the mind to realise to itself the eternal silence of infinite space.

Next morning we got up betimes, and I need hardly add that I was in high spirits at the prospect of being initiated into the wild delights of a new life. A pair of oven-birds were 'saluting the morn' with their loud rattling note just outside my window. These birds are excessively sociable, and seem to enjoy building among the haunts of men. They are about the size of a thrush, of a reddish-brown colour, and make their nests of clay, fixed to walls, trees, or posts—I have even seen them select a tall post to which horses were being tied up all day just outside the house.

Very little time is required for the toilet when the dress consists of merely a strong pair of trousers, a light shooting-jacket, a flannel shirt, a pair of boots and a wide-awake hat, so were soon out in the exhilarating air of the morning. The sun, just above the horizon, shot its long rays across the vast plains, and preparations were being made for the day's work. A peon had been down to a neighbouring pond with about a score of horses, and he was now driving them back in a mad gallop to the corral, where they would have 'to wait till called for.' Breakfast is usually late at an estancia, and I have known Englishmen imitate the example of the gauchos, and do a very hard day's work without any breakfast at all, contenting themselves with cigarettes at short intervals, till they take a heavy meal at the end of the day. I certainly think this an unwholesome practice, and always made a point of eating a good breakfast, if it could be got; whilst it was preparing, we took our guns, and walked to the *monte* to look for a partridge. We only got a brace, but were lucky enough to fall in with a quantity of small doves; they were rather less than ringdoves, and of the same colour, but they were very fat, and proved to be delicious morsels. I also knocked over a *corancho*, whom I surprised among the remains of a dead horse. These powerful birds are justly hated by the shepherds, for they never lose an opportunity of picking out the eyes of a lamb, if it strays away from its mother. We also added a brace of *tiru-teros* to the bag, though we greatly doubted if they were fit to eat. These horned plovers are very pretty birds, about the size of a pigeon, and have the singular appendage of a short sharp horn, blood-red in colour, attached to the end of the pinion, which I believe they use as a weapon of defence. They are very tame, and seldom rise till a passer-by is within twenty or thirty yards of them, when they whirl overhead with a loud and constant repetition of the peculiar cry which is represented by their name. We found them very tough, and soon gave up shooting them for the table; but I am afraid we often killed them out of mere revenge for their abominable habit of screaming at nothing, and frightening ducks which we had been stalking with the greatest care. They are the most restless birds I know, and at night many a shepherd has been warned by the cry of 'tiru-tero' that something unusual was stirring in the camp.

After breakfast, we prepared for a start to the lagunas. I was not much accustomed to horses, and soon found that I had plenty to learn; there are no grooms or stables at the estancias of South America, and 'gentleman riders' must saddle for themselves. We took our horses down to the water, and then saddled and bridled at the door of the house. This operation is a serious business with those who use the *recado*, or native saddle, but we followed the English fashion. To the gaucho his *recado* is all-important, but it is a complicated and troublesome machine, consisting of a great number of coverings and belts, some for use and some for ornament. The tree is double-peaked, and on the top of all oomes a kind of rug, which makes a soft seat, though a very hot one. The whole concern is very cumbrous, and often weighs forty pounds; but we must remember that, when taken to pieces, it makes a pretty comfortable bed, whilst an English saddle is only good for a pillow. Rich men are fond of very handsome *recados*, with elaborately-stamped leather, and even a moderately good one is an expensive luxury. As compared with the English saddle, they certainly give a more comfortable seat; but, on the other hand, they are very hot and very heavy, besides being troublesome to put together. For the hard work of the country, however, they contain a necessary element which could not be used with an English saddle: this is a girth of strong hide, and about nine inches wide, which goes completely round the horse and saddle, the ends being fastened together by very tight lacing through two rings. This girth contains on one side a strong iron ring, firmly worked into it, to bear the whole pressure of the lazo. Skillful as the gauchos are with this instrument, they could do but little service if they depended only on the strength of their hand to hold it when entangled in the horns of an animal going at full speed; but with the other end made perfectly fast to this ring, the weight and strength of the horse are thrown into the scale. This arrangement is attended with only one inconvenience, which is that he cannot get rid of his lazo, even if he wishes, when it has once been fixed on the horns of a bull: he must follow every motion of the animal, turn as he turns, and avoid him if he charges, but he cannot get rid of him till, with the help of his companions, he throws him to the ground, to be branded or killed, according to the requirements of the case.

But whatever difference of opinion there may be about the comparative merits of the saddles, I think that, without doubt, the native bridles and head-gear of plaited hide are infinitely better than our own leather straps. The strength of their raw hide is immense, and plaiting fine strips of it is an art in which the gauchos excel peculiarly, and show very good taste. The best bridles are made of this work in short lengths connected by strong rings of pure silver, and the beauty of the workmanship makes them very expensive; but when once bought they last for ever. The native ring-bit is very powerful and punishing, and the fashion is to have it made also of pure silver; the same remark applies to spurs, which I have seen made of the same material, and weighing about three pounds each, the rowels being nearly six inches in diameter. In fact, the horse, with his accoutrements, is the grand hobby of South Americans, and they care not how much they pay for the latter in perfection. The horse himself is cheap enough in the country, and even in the cities 20*l.* sterling is considered a large price for a horse accustomed to town life, with no objection to shoes, which are entirely unknown to his brethren in the camp. The strength and durability of the raw hide, which is there universally used, form a standing proof of the falsity of the assertion that there is 'nothing like leather.' All the lazos and everything in the shape of a rope are made in the same way: a piece of hide is cut out as a spiral in lengths of 100 feet and upwards, and then made as pliable as a rope of silk by constant applications of grease. The *revenque*, or native whip, is made of the same material; the lash being about two feet long and an inch wide, tapering to a point, with a beautifully-plaited handle terminating in a large silver ring, through which hangs a narrow strap by which it is held on the wrist, so as to leave the hand quite free to use it only when necessary. In the middle of Entre Rios I picked up a very good specimen of the roughly-made country *revenque*, which had been lost by its owner; there is no plaiting on the handle, but there is a very heavy silver ring at the end, and the frame of the handle is of iron. This makes a formidable weapon of attack or defence, and I have been told that, armed with such a whip, a gaucho, finding his horse quite unmanageable, will stand up in his stirrups and kill the brute at once with a single blow between the ears, ready of course to transfer his *recado* and mount the next that he can find.

The taste for massive silver ornaments has always been carried to a remarkable extent in South America; and it is a matter of everyday life to find that in a country where a man pays for all the necessaries of life in filthily dirty paper dollars, he uses handsome silver coins, as large as English crown pieces, for his buttons. Bridles are sometimes loaded with silver; but I think that the progress of a practical age is rapidly diminishing the fancy for merely useless and even mischievous display: no one can deny the extreme inconvenience of spurs which are so heavy that it is impossible to walk in them, and nothing can be more unfair on a hard-working horse than to load his head with bars of silver. One of the most useful of the native instruments is a pair of *maneas* or hobbles, without which no one should go into the camp alone, for fear of losing his horse if he wants to dismount. With the *maneas* on his fore-legs no horse can move far, and very few ever attempt to.

Sir Francis Head, remembering the great advantages he had derived from these *maneas* in his South American adventures, has lately succeeded in bringing them into use among some of our mounted troops, and reports that they have proved invaluable.

Last but not least in importance among the necessaries of camp-life, is a long-bladed serviceable knife always worn at the back of the waist, and used for every conceivable purpose, from cutting a stick to revenging an insult.

CHAPTER VI

RIDING AND SHOOTING.

A COMING STORM — A FRIENDLY ROOF — ARMADILLOS — DUCKS— FLAMINGOES — BAD WEATHER — STILL WORSE — DEAD SHEEP — ELEY'S CARTRIDGES—POP AND THE NUTRIA—BISCACHO SHOOTING —THEIR FRIENDSHIP WITH THE OWLS — A GALLOP—VISITING IN THE PAMPAS — PACKING THE BULLOCK-CART — PEACHES AND FLOWERS—RETURN TO BUENOS AYRES.

WE were soon ready that morning; ammunition was put into the proper pockets, and precautions were taken to prevent it from being prematurely scattered by the jolting. We started away at a hand-gallop towards the north-west, gun in one hand and bridle in the other—an arrangement which is greatly facilitated by the fact that the horses are all broken to obey the rein on a principle exactly contrary to that which Europeans are more accustomed to. If you want to turn to the right, you must press the left rein against the neck of the horse instead of pulling the right, and vice versâ, which I think gives more independence to one hand, especially valuable to a novice.

The morning was exceedingly hot, and heavy clouds with distant growling in the north-east warned us of a coming storm. My companion, however, thought that it would pass away, as similar symptoms had frequently ended in nothing during the last few weeks, and everybody sighed hopelessly for rain. As we rode on I found I was right; the crashing of the thunder following soon after dangerous flashes proved that we were fairly in for it, and I thought it would be more judicious not to ride through the storm with guns for lightning-conductors in our hands. The lonely house of a fine old Scotchman was not far off, so we turned our horses to the right, and reached it just as the first heavy drops began to make large spots in the thirsty dust.

We were very kindly welcomed by Mr. Clarke and his wife and daughters, who supplied us in the first place with sheepskins to put over our saddles, and then asked us into the house. The rain came down heavily and the storm raged, while we sat down for a long chat about the old country, which is always the most interesting topic to an emigrant when he meets anyone freshly arrived from home. We talked also about the war, and found that the seizing of horses in the name of the government caused great alarm among quiet families, like that of our host. It is bad enough to be obliged to give up one's property to a regular official for a very poor consideration, but the system also encourages bad characters to rove about and rob without any authority whatever. Our old friend had all the courage and determination of his countrymen, and was fully prepared to shoot anybody who might attempt to take his horses from the corral. Many people were reduced to all kinds of artifices, such as turning their horses into the nearest *monte*, and showing nothing but a couple of screws to those who came to search the premises. Foreigners are protected by treaty from such outrages, but they do not always know this, and erroneously fancy that it is useless to appeal to the government for redress. The agents of the government in a crisis seize all the horses that they dare, without making very particular enquiries, and are often enabled to keep their spoil by the unwillingness of the owners to defend their own rights. The Argentine authorities are now fully aware that the great drawback to the success and welfare of their immense country is the want of foreign immigrants; they also know that this is owing to a deeply-rooted feeling of the insecurity of property; and they are generally desirous to act in such a way as to persuade the world that that feeling is erroneous, and that foreigners may claim and enjoy the full benefit of their treaties with the Republic.

The storm passed, and on going to the door we found the refreshing effects of the rain. All nature breathed again, and a delicious fragrance filled the whole air. At the back of the house was an enclosure, where pigs and peacocks walked in close proximity; pigeons and poultry shared the roof of the verandah, and two armadillos were in a tub, intended as a present for my companion. The armadillos are caught by boys, and give them plenty of trouble, for they dig their subterranean passages so fast, that even when their haunt is discovered, a pursuer can hardly overtake them by tearing up the ground. They are considered great delicacies by the natives, but are too much like hedgehogs to be agreeable to an Englishman.

The sheepskins had kept our saddles dry, and we were soon mounted again, scudding away at full speed to make up for lost time. After some few miles we came to the first laguna, and found immense numbers of ducks and all kinds of waterfowl. Some were in the water, and some feeding on land, closely packed together in brown masses, so we determined to stalk them. This, however, was by no means easy, for the wildness of the weather seemed to have affected them. As soon as we got within about 120 yards, off they went in myriads, and we were obliged to content ourselves with single shots at stragglers. We certainly had great inducements to shoot for the pot, but consoled ourselves with the reflection that we were a very small party, and had killed enough to begin with at all events. Meanwhile we left our horses hobbled with the *maneas*, and on our return found them surrounded by a large troop of others, who spying them from afar, had galloped down to see who the strangers were. As I looked at them in their perfect freedom, I could have fancied they were laughing at rather than pitying their enslaved and saddled comrades, who looked very much like criminals fastened in the stocks. We left them to their reflections, and galloped on towards some larger lakes, on one of which was a perfect cloud of birds very like our water-hens; we might have shot any quantity of them, but thinking them worthless we reserved our fire for the ducks.

The natives who supply these delicacies for the Buenos Ayrean market are very stingy of powder and shot, but they get at them by what our old friend Sir John Mandeville would call 'this soteltee.' Birds and beasts of all kinds on those plains have no fear of a horse, but cannot understand a man on foot. The native sportsman, therefore, gets a trained horse, which walks slowly towards the army of ducks; he creeps along by its side, so as to be nearly hidden by its body and legs, till he gets almost close and kills multitudes of them with a single charge. A much more amusing trick is resorted to in Central America, where a man puts on his head a hollow pumpkin with two holes for his eyes, something like a diver's helmet. Thus armed he wades into the water up to his neck, so that nothing is seen but a pumpkin, which appears to be floating upon the surface; he soon gets among the ducks, catches them one after the other by the legs, pulls them under water, and fastens them to a belt round his waist. Their companions never miss them, and he goes on quietly in this way till he has got as many as he can stagger under.

We dared not attempt the horse-trick with our present steeds, for the report of the gun would have left us instantly without a mount, and many miles from home; but luckily we had in our pockets a few of Eley's cartridges, which made splendid practice. As we approached another laguna the surface appeared covered with large bouquets of roses, and when we got a little nearer I found to my astonishment and delight that we had come upon hundreds of flamingoes. Stooping a little I walked towards them. They did not move, and I got a little closer: presently they raised themselves screaming from the water, and flew *en masse* across the laguna, which was there not very wide. Never have I seen such a beautiful sight as that rosy cloud of huge birds, shaded gradually from the delicate pink of their necks to the deep red of their long wings, which were tipped with black. The beauty of the sight and the rush of their flight as they crossed that silent lake almost bewildered me for a moment; but the slaughtering instinct of man overpowered my better feelings as I remembered that I had a cartridge in my left barrel. I fired at the head of the column when they were nearly on the other side, and two of the foremost fell. The distance was nearly, if not quite, 100 yards, and I was astonished at its effect on such powerful birds. Returning to the horses we rode round to the farther side of the lake, where we found the dead body of one victim; the other had life enough to struggle into deeper water, and escaped us. It was indeed a most exquisite bird, not fully represented in colour by the African flamingoes in the Zoological Gardens. All the most lovely shades of pink and red that can be conceived were to be found amongst its feathers, and its long legs were of the colour of blood. I could hardly forgive myself for the shot, but it was a wonderful test of Eley's cartridges, and I consoled my conscience by vowing that I would never shoot another.

Meanwhile it was evident that the thunder-storm had broken up the fine weather for the present. The wind shifted to south and south-east, a very bad quarter, and came mournfully sighing over the plains, raising a raw mist with its cold breath: every moment it blew harder and harder, the birds seemed more scared than ever, and the horses which had come down to drink looked as if they expected a bad night upon the open camp; darkness came on fast with a murky sky, and it was high time to make the best of our way homewards for fear of losing our only landmarks. The flamingo and the ducks were tied to our saddles, and away we galloped as fast as we could in the teeth of the blast. Clarke's house was nearly in our way, and we agreed to call there and ask if his hospitality would improve the stores of our larder. He kindly gave us a large joint of pork, a bottle of splendid Hollands, and some fresh bread, which was a special luxury in that land of wooden biscuits. Fair's strong arm carried the pork tied by a towel to his bridle-wrist; the Hollands and the bread were disposed of in our pockets; we bade the good people a hasty adieu as the rain was already falling, and with the fading light to increase the danger of biscacho-holes, we galloped back to the estancia all safe—guns, pork, bread, Hollands, ducks, and flamingo.

It was indeed a bad night. We unloaded our stores, unsaddled the horses, gave them a feed of dry *alfalfa* or lucerne, and left them to take care of themselves in the yard. At first I pitied them for having such a finish to a good day's work, but I did not yet know the toughness of their constitutions. The wind and the rain beat against the house furiously, so we made the doors and windows fast, and kept up a capital wood fire all the evening till we turned into bed, and I was soon asleep. A strange tapping on my pillow at regular intervals awoke me. What could it be? Was it some unknown and perhaps direful insect? A few more loud taps convinced me of the cause. The excessive heat and drought had opened a crack in the roof, and the rain oozing through fell in heavy drips about six inches from my head. I found a basin, and squeezing myself as far as I could towards the wall, tried to go to sleep again; but the water falling into the basin made a noise even worse than before, and splashed me in the face about every other second; besides which I was presently attacked in the same way on the other side. I thought of that famous mediæval torture which consisted in letting water drip on a victim's mouth till it drove him mad: so I got up and moved the bed into a part of the room where by the most careful listening I could not detect the immediate presence of the enemy. Next day matters were worse rather th n better, for the weather did not improve, and Mrs. Macdonald came to report that there was no more dry wood. This was serious, but we found the frame of a large sofa uncovered, and somewhat dilapidated. Necessity has no laws: an axe was sent for, and after a little active exercise we found ourselves supplied with enough firing for the rest of the day.

On the third morning came the first symptoms of improvement, and the afternoon was perfectly fine, so we had a quiet ride about the estancia. It was ascertained that the Monte Grande flocks had not suffered much, but as we rode along the side of the arroyo which divided them from those of the next proprietor, we saw the bodies of dozens of sheep, which seemed to have crawled under the lee of the river-bank and died there, probably from being previously out of condition.

The next four or five days were among the happiest I have ever spent. The weather was perfectly lovely, and continual sunshine on ground moistened by the rain soon began to give a fresh green tint to the camp. We were out all day riding and shooting, and as I became more accustomed to the horses and the customs of the country under the tutorship of a first-rate companion, I found the delights of this kind of life increase every day. Once we took the *capataz* down to the lagunas with us, and found the birds, as usual, very wild, and moving in masses. Now and then, however, an unlucky straggler gave us a chance; and in about ten minutes I made three extraordinary shots with Eley's cartridges at single ducks flying at a good pace, certainly not less than ninety yards distant. One fell like a stone at seventy-five measured yards from my feet, though he was fully fifty or sixty yards above the ground when I fired. I never saw anything like the astonishment of the *capataz*, though I confess that it was hardly greater than my own as the ducks fell one after another with a heavy thump upon the ground. Anyone who did not know of the existence of that famous magician, Mr. Eley, would have been justified in thinking Der Freischutz had come out to the Pampas. We used the Royal cartridges, with No. 5 shot; and one of the ducks at this long distance was so smashed by the charge as to be hardly worth carrying home.

On another occasion I made a delightful excursion to Monte Grande and the neighbouring lagunas with Mr. Parish, when we hit upon a large reedy swamp, which absolutely swarmed with birds; the reeds were thick enough to afford hiding-places, and the sport was as good as could possibly be desired. Unluckily for me, I had left my long boots behind, and was obliged to content myself with outsiders, while my cousin, with his retriever, went into the mud and water nearly up to his middle. At the first shot there rose straight into the air a column of birds of strange ungainly shapes, mixed with others of the greatest beauty, and the effect was like that of a picture which used to charm our childhood—the explosion into the air of the miller and his men. Some had such massive pelican-like beaks that they could scarcely keep their heads and tails in equilibrium: some had such long legs and little bodies that all the tucking up in the world could not make them look decently comfortable; and among them came the lovely *mirasol*, a snow-white miniature of the heron. Some screamed, some whistled, and some croaked with twenty-raven power, as they hovered lazily for a few moments and descended to their wallow with a splash. All of them, after the first alarm, displayed the utmost confidence in us, and after a short inspection they settled down in the same places as before among the rushes. We might have shot any number of them, and perhaps formed a valuable collection, if we had been so minded; but our attention was concentrated on the ducks, who were much more unwilling to give us a chance than the creatures who seemed to know that they were not wanted. The consul, however, completely filled his bag with them before he emerged, well sprinkled with mud, from this magazine of wild-fowl, and, with a few that I contributed from the outside, the spoils made a very fair show. Fop, the retriever, had a little affair of his own. Just before we left the place there was a grand splashing and snarling in the rushes, and presently he came out with a *nutria* about as big as a hare, which he had killed in single combat. The *nutria* is something like a beaver, with a dash of the otter in his appearance, and is remarkable for two long front teeth of a deep red colour; the skin is used as an article of commerce, and far up the rivers it is common to see a boat full of men and dogs paddling in search of them.

We generally returned from our rides about four or five o'clock in the afternoon, both men and horses pretty hot. The best thing for the horse, if very hot, is, as soon as he is unsaddled, to pour a can of cold water on his back, and then let him roll on the ground and feed at his pleasure. Having thus made our animals comfortable, we used to dine at five o'clock, and then turn out on foot for an hour or two with our guns about sunset. Ducks of various kinds were generally passing in large flights at intervals of a few minutes, but high enough to be out of shot; as the evening dusk advanced they flew a little lower, and with the last of the light they sometimes gave us very good sport as they flew across the golden sky.

This was also the only time of day to see those droll animals, the *biscachos*. These creatures are, I believe, not very unlike the prairie-dogs of North America, but considerably larger. They reminded me of our Alpine marmots on a large scale, and are brownish in colour, with white throats; their heads are garnished with whiskers, and, excepting the ears, are very much like those of rabbits, though much broader and stronger, and armed with such powerful teeth that it is dangerous to touch one till he is perfectly dead. They live together in groups of families, burrowing deeply in the ground, and bringing out sufficient earth from their excavations to make a gently-rising mound of considerable size. They have an extraordinary instinct for accumulating all kinds of extraneous and apparently useless materials round the mouths of their holes, where sticks, bones, thistle-stalks, and other rubbish may be found heaped up. If anything is lost in the camp, there is always a good chance of finding it among the *biscacheros*; and there is even a story of a watch having been recovered in this way. It appeared to me that their object is to raise the level of their homes, that they may have a better look-out over the flat plains, and have less chance of being invaded by water in the event of very wet weather. I never saw one by any chance in the daytime, during which they lie in their holes, while their faithful friends, the little owls, seem as if they were keeping guard at the entrances. There is something wonderfully attractive in these pretty little creatures and their solemn ways. They never attempt to stir till you are within a few yards of them, but they watch every movement with a patient and apathetic stare. They do not seem to have anything to do, and, more often than not, they stand motionless upon the dry unprofitable ground which has been excavated by the biscachos, where no one could imagine there would be anything to eat. When a man rides nearly over one of them, the little fellow rises with a ruffled air, and after a very short but indignant flutter, turns round sharply and settles again, staring angrily at the intruder, like a man who has been almost run over by a cab.

I could never understand their precise relations with their big friends, the biscachos, or what were the terms of their joint tenancy of the burrows: it seemed to be a kind of 'Box and Cox' arrangement. The owls were certainly out all day, and apparently on guard, while it is equally certain that the biscachos slept all day and came out at night, but I could never ascertain if the owls then went in to keep their friends' nests warm. This is contrary to the nature of owls generally, but it is the only supposition on which we can imagine that they get any rest at all.

The biscachos swarm on some parts of the land, and nowhere more so than round Monte Grande, where they injure so considerable a part of the camp that their destruction is necessary. Their holes are so deep and so ramified that it is nearly impossible to diminish the race, except by a steady process of shooting. On one estancia that I visited, a man had undertaken to contract for digging them out, but he soon gave up the attempt in despair; for the same reasons, smoking them out is impracticable, and we determined to shoot a few of them at all events. For this purpose we repaired for several evenings to the principal *biscacheros*, and generally exactly as the sun set we used to see their dark heads and white throats sticking out from their holes. Sometimes they first attracted attention by giving vent to a peculiar sound: it was very like 'ugh,' delivered from the throat so as to be something between a sigh and a grunt. Whenever we could see any, and they seldom showed much more than their heads, we walked quietly towards them, and delivered our fire as accurately as we could in the dark; but they were so tough that, unless they were killed instantly, they got back into their holes before we could reach them, and there grunted at their leisure. If they afterwards die, they are carried out into the open air by their sorrowing relatives, and are soon picked clean by the myriads of *raptores* that range over the plains. We always bagged a few, but not more than once had any pretence at sport with one: I fired at him with my first barrel, and, instead of tumbling into his hole, he ran forward at full speed; I gave him the second barrel, which turned him over and over, but he had enough strength and toughness to run again. I ran after him, followed by the laughter of Fair, and in spite of the risk of breaking my gun, I killed him by a most unsportsmanlike blow with the stock.

When it was almost entirely dark I thought I saw another, though it only looked like a dark spot, and I did not like to fire at what might be the skull of a dead bullock. I watched him silently to see if he moved; he did not move, but he sneezed or grunted, and the noise was fatal to him. They were very heavy, and it was hard work to drag home one in each hand for a mile, with a gun tucked under the shoulder. The peons gladly eat them as a change from beef, and though we did not try the experiment ourselves, I was told that they are quite as good as the marmots which Alpine travellers have so often eaten under feigned names. It is remarkable, that though these creatures swarm all over the plains on the eastern side of the La Plata, they are never met with in the Banda Oriental.

Ostriches and deer are seldom to be found so near Buenos Ayres as the neighbourhood which I have been describing, and which is, comparatively speaking, well inhabited. Houses of small landowners and sheep-farmers are generally to be met with at intervals of two or three miles, and here and there a small shabby tenement contains a family of squatters with no ostensible means of supporting themselves, and with a reputation about as bad as that of the gipsies of Europe. Sometimes instead of shooting we would take our horses, and gallop through a round of visits to some of the neighbouring estancias. 'The world was all before us where to choose;' not a fence or barrier all around the plain; a dark spot on the horizon, with one or two *ombù* trees shading it, would mark the residence of the man to be visited; and not being bothered by roads and finger-posts, we had only to ride straight to our distant mark. *Vamos!* is the word, followed by a touch of the *revenque* which hangs from the wrist, and we are off at a gallop. Take what direction we may, the tiru-teros are sure to be screaming in the air, the owls gravely staring from the *biscacheros*, and the *coranchos* with their unclean companions picking the bones of the last dead horse. We pull up for a moment to find a good place for crossing the *arroyo*, and the ducks start from under the bank so close that we regret having left our guns behind. A short flounder in the mud, and then we are across the stream, again flying over the plains straight to the *ombù* tree, which begins to look a little more distinct, while the dark spot begins to resolve itself into a house and some outlying sheds. We pass the corrals, and the barking of a legion of dogs announces our arrival, warning us at the same time to bow to the custom of the country, and exchange the exciting and exhilarating gallop for a decorous walk to the house.

If the *patron* is at home we are invited to walk in, and a gossip is at once started about the state of the weather and the sheep. Cigars and *matè* are provided, if it is in the house of a native; probably a glass of brandy or *câna*, the white rum of South America, if the host is an Englishman. A visitor is always welcome, and sure to meet with help if he wants any. Being recent arrivals from the city, we were of course expected to know a great deal about the war, which was a subject of very practical importance to all in the neighbourhood of Buenos Ayres, as it was clearly understood that if Urquiza came down to besiege it with the Federal army, those warriors would be permitted to support themselves entirely on other people's property. Natives and foreigners might in case of invasion suffer equally, if they had horses to be stolen, or sheep to be eaten; and it would be difficult to get redress from the Buenos Ayrean Government for what they would consider as one of the calamities which are necessarily incident to a state of war.

Away and away again, with a fresh sweet breeze and a grilling sun, the most delicious combination of elements that mortal man could desire; away over the springy turf of a country like ten thousand Newmarket heaths put together; away for another *ombù* and another dark spot on the horizon. A few leagues more galloping, and rejoicing in the exhilarating air, now and then suddenly swerving to avoid a *biscachero*, and laughing at the discomposure of a placid little owl; starting at last homewards, and ending with a race as fast as the horses could lay legs to ground, we finished another glorious day of healthy excitement.

Such was life at Monte Grande, but after a time we were both obliged to return to Buenos Ayres, and look after the English mail. Early one morning we left the place with sincere regret, accompanied by a peon carrying the armadillos in a box on his saddle, and rode a few miles to one of the neighbouring houses, from which we knew that a bullock-cart was to be sent that day into the city. We rode up to the house through a peach wood, the trees of which were already breaking into sheets of spring bloom, and sheltering among their stems bunches of exquisitely sweet narcissus and white iris in full flower. We met with a hearty welcome, and enjoyed a lounge in the garden, while guns, saddle-bags, and armadillos were being packed in the bullock-cart. Then we said goodbye to our kind host, mounted our horses again, and had a delightful ride back to Buenos Ayres. It seems as if a few such weeks must add something to a man's natural life.

CHAPTER VII.

AN ESTANCIA IN THE BANDA ORIENTAL.

A VISIT TO THE BANDA ORIENTAL, OR REPUBLIC OF THE URUGUAY—LONELY ISLANDS—CONCEPCION—URQUIZA'S PROPERTY—PAYSANDÚ—SWIMMING A HORSE—WHERE IS THE PORT?—THE 'FOREST PRIMEVAL'—ROBINSON CRUSOE—THE RESCUE—THE LAND OF THORNS—VEGETATION—ARRIVAL AT THE ESTANCIA—PARTRIDGES—CATCHING OUR BREAKFAST, AND KILLING THE SAME—THE AROMA—THE LARGE PARTRIDGE—PARROT PIE—CAPINCHOS—JAGUARS—CRESCIENTES—ADVENTURES OF AN INVALID—THE FAITHFUL MURDERER—HOW TO GET HOME IN THE DARK.

HAVING had a most welcome invitation to visit a friend's estancia in the Banda Oriental, on the bank of the great river Uruguay, and nearly 300 miles from Buenos Ayres, I gladly accepted it, and on the morning of the 13th of August started in very good company. The party consisted of one of the owners of the estancia, with a bride and bridegroom and myself, all bound for the same destination, and another friend who was only going to Higueritas

We left Buenos Ayres at 10·30 A.M. in the steamer Montevideo, a vessel of high reputation in the river, though scarcely larger than one of those which ply between London and Gravesend. She travelled fast, however, and in a few hours we had crossed the broad estuary of the La Plata, and were running up the River Uruguay near the coast of the Banda Oriental. The difference in appearance between the two sides of the Rio de la Plata is very remarkable. On the Buenos Ayrean side boundless plains, with scarcely an undulation of a dozen feet, afford not a landmark except to the long-practised eye that knows the shape of each lonely *ombù* tree; but the Banda Oriental, though certainly not a mountainous country, is at all events hilly enough to make very picturesque outlines, and to afford a charming variety of scenery to the traveller who gallops over its splendid pastures.

The neighbourhood of Higueritas is extremely pretty, with fine steep banks to the river, profusely ornamented with trees and flowering shrubs. Thence, league after league, we threaded the myriad islands of this mighty stream, and I was never tired of watching the boundless variety of plants when we passed near enough to the banks to observe them. Had the water been of good colour, the style of river scenery would have been admirable; but, unfortunately for appearances, it is so dirty from the vast quantities of sarsaparilla in solution, that nobody can willingly bring himself to drink it till he is assured that in reality it is very different from the contents of the Thames.

The islands are frequently many miles in length, and none but old hands at such navigation could possibly tell whether at any time the vessel was in the right channel or the wrong. All of them, both great and small, are covered with a dense jungle of rushes, Pampas grass, passion-flowers and other creepers, over which rise forests of trees with an amazing diversity of leaves and blossoms. These are the haunts of the jaguar or South American tiger, and I was constantly in hopes of seeing one of these splendid beasts refreshing himself by the waterside. But scarcely a living creature appeared to look at us, except a few huge storks and herons that lifted their heads in silent disgust as the swell of the steamer disturbed the serenity of their fishing. Here and there a half-ruined hut showed where men sometimes come to cut wood, but we saw no occupants; and if anyone tried a permanent residence there he would certainly soon die of despair, if not previously carried off by the legions of mosquitos which infest the banks of the river.

Swiftly sped the Montevideo. A magnificent sunset was followed by a cloudless night, great part of which I spent upon deck in company with my favourite pipe and the chief engineer, who, as usual in all distant parts of the earth, turned out to be a Scotchman, and a very good fellow. Next morning before sunrise I found we were stopping at Concepcion del Uruguay, the chief town of the Argentine province of Entre Rios, and the commercial head-quarters of that dreaded bugbear—late

Captain-General of the Argentine forces by sea and land—Heaven save the mark—Don Justo José de Urquiza.

This terrible worthy is an excellent example of those violent military despots who are sure to appear in countries where the civilised element is not sufficiently strong to render the existence of such persons an impossibility, while the uncivilised element commits a sufficiency of evil deeds to afford some apparent justification for the employment of force and brutality. Beginning as a military adventurer, bold and daring, he achieved enormous popularity in Buenos Ayres by overthrowing the blood-stained tyranny of Rosas; and he was smothered with the kisses of grateful citizens who soon took the first opportunity of upsetting him in his turn, when they found that he had not only picked up, but was preparing to wear, the detested mantle of that illustrious fugitive. In the course of many subsequent ups and downs and sharp encounters, he completely terrified the Buenos Ayrean mind with the scarlet ponchos of his wild troops, till the tables were completely turned upon him in the campaign which happened during my visit to the country. Now that the long-dreaded King of the Gauchos has compulsorily retired into private life, people have ample leisure for observing that, whether he was right or wrong in his notions as to the propriety of throat-cutting, he at all events had a good eye for business, and proved himself a perfect master of the art of feathering his own nest.

By hook or by crook, he has possessed himself of an enormous territory in Entre Rios, difficult to estimate accurately, though I have generally heard it considered as upwards of 600 square leagues, or about 3,600,000 English acres, covered with countless herds of cattle and troops of horses. At Concepcion he has established a model *saladero*, where his cattle are slaughtered wholesale, and their hides are prepared for the European markets. This establishment is on a very extensive scale, and has the great advantage of being so situated that large sea-going ships can take their cargo on board directly by means of an elevated tramway from the centre of the premises. A very handsome English barque and a number of smaller foreign vessels were engaged in this way as we passed the place, and we amused ourselves with vain attempts at calculating the annual profits of the unselfish patriot. There was no time to go on shore at Concepcion, but we could see it at a short distance, the most conspicuous object being the white buildings of a college founded by Urquiza.

About 9.30 A.M. we reached Paysandù, a small town in the Banda Oriental, prettily situated just above where a bend in the river makes a kind of bay. There is no appearance of anything remarkable about the town itself, but the general effect was lovely, the place being completely embowered in groves of peach-trees in every direction, which were now, in the early spring of August, in full bloom; every white house shone out from its particular sheet of pink, suggesting delicious notions of sitting under one's own peach-tree during the scorching heats of Christmas. It seems dreadful to English ears, but the fact is that the great majority of these trees in the neighbourhood of the Rio de la Plata are only grown for the ignoble purpose of firewood. They are treated like copse in our own country, the different parts of each wood being cut down in rotation every four or five years; and they grow so fast that three or four years are sufficient to produce fine young trees covered with delicious fruit.

During our stoppage of half an hour at Paysandù, we were mightily amused by the manœuvres of a native gentleman and his Chilian horse. I ought not to have mentioned the horse last, for he was a noble animal, while his master was a disagreeable little man, who had been annoying us all the way by the shrill ferocity with which he discussed the depths and mysteries of Argentine politics. The horse had been a passenger on the foredeck, and the Don wanted to disembark with him and other chattels. His family and goods, including a very tipsy Gallego servant, were handed over the side into a large awkward boat, commanded by the Don in person, who stood up in the stern holding one end of a long rope, the other end of which was attached to the head of his steed. The horse was then compelled to leap into the river, with his clothes on, and when he rose to the surface, the Don in his barge commenced the operation of towing him as he swam. All went on well enough for a few minutes, when the horse cast a hasty glance at the line of country, and resolved to make for the nearest point of land; this involved his taking a course exactly at right angles to that of his master, who soon found himself being pulled out at the stern of his boat. His ejaculations and shouts were useless: he leaned over as far as he could, and held on by the last inch of the rope; but the horse was a strong swimmer, and, amidst the laughter of all beholders, the fierce little man was compelled to let go. The horse reached the point he aimed at, and had every prospect of clearing out into boundless space, but, unluckily for him, he landed on some boggy ground, where, after a short struggle, he was recaptured by the natives.

After this little diversion, we went ahead again at full speed up the river, and a very important question arose before long. We knew that the estancia for which we were bound extended down to the river side at about forty miles above Paysandù, and as there was no town or village within many leagues, it had been agreed with the captain that we should be landed at what is technically called *the port.* Now, a port of this kind is very different from Bristol or Liverpool, and only means a particular spot on the deserted bank which is approached by a narrow path through the neighbouring jungle, and is indicated to *habitués* by some tree or other landmark, though there is nothing whatever to attract the notice of a stranger. It soon appeared that none of the party knew where the port in this case was to be found; and the Captain, though most obliging and willing to land us at any point we might indicate, was naturally not in a position to find that point for us. What was to be done? The country grew more and more beautiful, and for the last few hours I had been feasting my eyes upon the long rows and waving groups of palms which fringed every hill, and plainly told us that each minute was taking us into a hotter climate. We knew that we were somewhere near our destination, but the hills were remarkably like one another, and so were the palm-trees: the bank of the river presented an apparently impenetrable belt of forest and jungle to cut us off from the interior; no habitations of men were in sight, and our expectation that some one would have ridden down to look for us was disappointed. Our traps were collected on deck in readiness, but we began to feel in a somewhat ridiculous position. At length, a small branch river appearing on our right hand was very confidently affirmed to be the Arroyo Malo, which we knew to be the most northerly limit of our friend's estate.

Going further was useless, for we had gone too far already, so the ship was stopped, and four sailors prepared to lower a boat.

'Where can you land us, Señor Capitan?'

He pointed to the forest-covered bank.

'Well but, Capitan, nobody can get through such stuff as that; surely you do not expect a lady to try it; she would be torn to pieces by thorns, and very likely by tigers.'

The sailor's heart was, of course, moved by the spectacle of a lady in distress, and the boat was ordered to take us back, coasting along the bank till a convenient place could be found. About a mile from the ship we ran the boat into a little bay, with muddy soil, but free from jungle. This was what we wanted; in a few minutes we found ourselves with all our traps high and dry in the Banda Oriental, while the boat's crew returned, evidently in high amusement at our appearance and situation. This was certainly ridiculous enough: we looked like a batch of Robinson Crusoes wrecked on the edge of the 'forest primeval,' and we did not know where we were any more than he did on his desert island. Our traps consisted of sundry portmanteaus, three gun-cases, three saddles and bridles, a large parcel of shears for the coming sheep-shearing, and a mighty bale of empty woolsacks: in case of our not being discovered by civilised beings, the only article of food would have been supplied from a small bundle of seed-potatoes.

After enjoying a hearty laugh at ourselves, we held a council of war, and decided that the bride and bridegroom should be left to take care of one another and the baggage while I and my bachelor friend should take our guns and march towards the interior, in hopes of discovering some *puesto*, or shepherd's hut. We loaded our guns with the view of shooting partridges by the way, to eat with the potatoes if necessary; and, bidding a fond farewell to our baggage-guard, we started in what we thought must be about the right direction. Luckily, we did not wander long before we heard loud shouts, and saw three wild-looking men galloping towards us at top speed. They pulled up their horses with a jerk, and the leader, a splendidly-built young Yankee, with a face expressive of the frank coolness which is generally characteristic of free and wild life, informed us where we were. We had landed about seven miles from the estancia house, and should have been a long while finding it if these men had not by the merest chance in the world been employed in cutting wood in the extreme corner of the estate, from which they could see the steamer stopping.

Here, then, was an end of our small troubles. The gallant Dick at once undertook to gallop to the house with orders for men and horses and a side-saddle, while his tawny comrades rode to the nearest *puesto*, in the hope of finding a bullock-cart for our effects. We soon found that the long grass near the forest, through a gap in which we had landed, proved splendid cover for the large partridges, which rose in all directions as we walked up to them; so we had no difficulty in amusing ourselves. In making an attempt to find one of these birds which I had killed as it flew over the wood, I got a very speedy proof of the mess we should have been in if the captain had put us on shore at the mouth of the Arroyo Malo. I could not stir a yard for the dense growth of underwood and creepers, among which the beautiful passion-flowers seemed the only plants not garnished with rasping thorns. And here I may observe that, from some mysterious cause or other, the tendency to develope thorns and prickles of every kind is exhibited in a most remarkable degree in the countries bordering on the Rio de la Plata. I don't know if this phenomenon is connected with, or only emblematical of, their politics; its existence is painfully evident to a stranger. Sometimes he has to deal with huge aloes and cactus hedges fifteen feet high; at another time he must pick his way through leagues of thistles higher than his horse's head, and armed with points so hard and strong that every touch is like that of a needle; or he may get into a wood, consisting of *espinilla*, *tala*, mimosa, and acacia, with the intervening spaces filled up by clumps of cactus and prickly pear. I cut off and preserved a few specimens of acacia thorns, some of which are six or seven inches long, desperately sharp, and about as thick as a drawing pencil.

After about two hours' sport we were disturbed by the arrival of the peons from the house, bearing the desired side-saddle, and driving horses before them for our accommodation. So we packed up our guns and saddled our horses: two men were left with the stores to wait for the bullock-cart, and away we went under the guidance of the *capataz*.

The appearance of the country delighted me. It consisted mainly of long undulating hills, something like our English downs, but not so high; the hollows between them being generally watered by *arroyos*, an invaluable advantage in a country where want of rain is more dreaded than any other calamity. One of the larger of these, our friend the Arroyo Malo, forms a very pretty river, running merrily to the Uruguay, between delightful belts of woods and huge evergreen bushes hanging over the water. Passion-flowers, and the lovely blossoms of creepers unknown to me, ornament the trunks of the trees, and air-plants hang from the branches like natural swings for the blue, green, and yellow parrots that scream and chatter all day in the exuberance of their spirits. As to ourselves, we should have been dull souls indeed if our spirits had not been roused to enthusiasm as we rode through such novel scenes, revelling in sunshine, and inhaling a fresh breeze which had danced over leagues and leagues of grass and flowers, without being contaminated by the busy haunts of man. As we cantered over the crest of hill following hill, something fresh was always ready for the eye. Here was an immense herd of wild cattle that would instantly charge anyone attempting to approach them on foot, though they have no fear of mounted enemies: there, again, was a noble troop of mares, glorying in their independence, and knowing that no human tyrant will ever dream of saddling them for his nefarious purposes; the only misfortune that can ever happen to them is that of being some day perhaps knocked on the head in a saladero, for the sake of their hides. Startled deer and ostriches fled before us, and scores of partridges hid themselves in the tufts of grass as we galloped close by them, over soft turf mixed with dazzling patches of that scarlet verbena which ornaments our English gardens. In its native beauty it seemed a sacrilege to tread upon it, but the crime was unavoidable.

In due time we arrived at the house, were duly stared at by the peons, and most warmly welcomed by our kind host and hostess. It appeared that they had been on the look-out for us two or three days before, when the steamer ought properly to have arrived; but finding that it did not appear they naturally concluded that it had been seized by the Government, or treated in some similar fashion; for it creates but little surprise when Republican ministers make free with the property of subjects in a way that would scarcely be tolerated under the most despotic of emperors.

The estancia house was considered only a temporary arrangement. Mr. Smith had not yet been long in possession, and he was planning a house in a more picturesque part of the property. Meanwhile, we had a good specimen of the rough but comfortable quarters which are all that one requires in the wilds. There was a square enclosure, on one side of which was the principal building, containing a snug sitting-room in the middle, with a bedroom on each side; on the opposite side was a shed appropriated to the peons, who cooked their beef and condescended to sleep there in bad weather, though on fine nights they very much preferred rolling themselves up in their ponchos on the open ground. Part of the third side of the enclosure was occupied by a building divided into three parts, serving respectively as kitchen, store-room, and bachelors' hall; and the fourth side was only a fence with a gate in it. These buildings were all made of clay and wattles, well thatched with the *paja*, or broad rush-like grass of the country, and there was also a shed with open sides and thatched roof, which was chiefly used as a saddle-room.

The bachelors' room interested me particularly, as I hoped to be located there for a week or two; but I could not help wondering how it was to contain three of us, when it appeared that another friend was staying there before the arrival of our party. However this was soon arranged: a few *catres*, better known in England as scissor-beds, were set up in the corners of the room, leaving very little space in the middle. A few boxes did duty as wardrobe and table, and what more can anyone want? I can very safely say that I never was more happy and comfortable in my life, and never left luxurious quarters with such sincere regret. There was a good deal of life and liveliness about the room too: the mice running along the tops of the walls under the thatch constantly brought down pieces of the dried clay, and sometimes when the cat made a midnight stampede among them we all three awoke in shouts of laughter at the volleys that came down upon our beds. The cocks and hens were remarkably sociable, and showed their taste by preferring our society to that of the rest of the establishment: whenever we went into the room we commenced operations by a battle to turn them out, and a dive under the bed was generally rewarded by a nice fresh egg, left no doubt for us as a testimony of grateful affection. Two handsome young tame rams with an extraordinary appetite for tobacco were also amongst our intimates, and generally looked out for us at the corner; if we had none of the favourite delicacy for them, they had a most amusing way of butting heavily at our legs *en passant*; and once, surprised by them in that way after dark, I had considerable difficulty in preserving the perpendicular. One bed was close to the door, which could be opened by its occupant without moving, and as the rising sun poured all his splendour across the boundless pastures, sweet from the refreshing breath of night, we had but to jump out of bed and salute him in his glory.

The general rule was to get up early and do what we liked till breakfast, at about ten o'clock; one or two of us generally went out with our guns, and as partridges swarmed all round we used to make large bags in a very short time. The native boys amuse themselves sometimes by riding round and round these birds in a constantly diminishing circle, which so stupifies them with fear that they can be knocked down with revenques. They afford very fair sport, however, for a gun; they will very often run and hide in the long grass rather than rise, but if you walk them fairly up they go right away like the English bird. In size and appearance they are something between an English partridge and a quail, and in shape rather more like the latter; the flavour is not remarkable, but in a part of the world where in general there is nothing to eat but beef and biscuits, we used to rejoice in seeing five or six brace of them piled upon a goodly dish, and were quite content to shoot for the pot.

One of the first mornings of our visit I had just returned from one of these early strolls with my pockets full of partridges, and feeling hungry, I asked at what time breakfast would be ready. I was informed that the peons had only just gone out to look for it, so I lighted my pipe and went out to see what was going on. The house standing on rather high ground I had a good view in all directions, and presently I saw three men at full gallop going towards the nearest herd. As they came up to them they selected an animal of promising appearance, and the foremost man threw the lazo over his horns; off went the rest of the herd, but there is no escape for the doomed one; a second horseman makes a dash to his side, and carefully avoiding the furious stroke of his horns, compels him to start in the required direction. If necessary, a third attacks him on the other flank; and in spite of all his roaring, bellowing, and plunging, he is driven at full gallop towards the house. On they came thundering over the turf, the three peons all shouting and yelling at the beast till they were so near the gate where I was standing that I fancied he was beyond their control, and was going to lead them smashing over everything. Not so, however. At the last moment one of the men at the side reined in his horse a little, and as the poor beast passed to the front he was suddenly and dexterously caught by the hind legs in a second lazo. A shout to the man in front gave him a Spanish 'All right behind;' he rapidly turned his horse to one side, and the hinder man to the other side. In a moment the bullock was stretched to his utmost length by the lazos pulling in opposite directions; moored fore and aft, he fell heavily to the ground only a few yards from the gate, and the first important work of the day was done—our breakfast was caught.

I had hardly a moment to admire the splendid horsemanship and skill of these peons, for the third man had thrown himself instantly from his saddle, and cut the animal's throat before I knew what he was about, and with an expiring bellow our breakfast was dead, almost before it had done galloping.

A few more peons now crowded like eagles round the carcass, which was skinned and picked clean in about five minutes. The Spaniard who did duty as cook trotted down and carried off for his master's table some of the daintiest parts of the beast, consisting of the tongue, the liver, and some good steaks. He knew breakfast was rather late, so he bestirred himself, and half an hour after that wild ride we were heartily enjoying its results. The peons divide the rest of the meat in proper proportions, and in the course of the morning each *puestero* or shepherd rides in from his outlying post, and carries off his supply of beef for the day. Every man in these establishments has regular rations of beef and matè, and they seem to despise all other food. When their day's work is done they cook their beef for themselves, and have a regular gorge; then comes màtè in any quantity, and then sleep till dawn. Generally speaking, they take no food whatever, except perhaps a little matè, till the evening, however hard their day's work may be.

Close behind the house was a grove of a species of mimosa, called the *aroma*. The trees were for the most part about twenty or thirty feet high, and were covered with bright yellow tufted flowers, which perfumed the whole neighbourhood with one of the most delicious scents I have ever had the good fortune to rejoice in; after breakfast we usually selected this retreat for a morning pipe. Then came more shooting or riding, according to taste. I particularly enjoyed a shooting party over part of the estancia near the Arroyo Malo, where we were always sure of a miscellaneous bag.

Before coming to the river we had to pass through a tract of long grass, dry and tufty, the favourite retreat of that charming bird, the large partridge. This bird has almost exactly the plumage of our hen pheasant, and is as nearly as possible of the same shape and size, with the exception of the long tail. There were great numbers of them on the ground I am now speaking of, but for want of a good dog we could get very few; they often lie so close in the coarse grass that unless they are trodden upon they will not rise; and even when we thought we had marked them down pretty accurately, on walking to the place they were not to be found. With a good pointer there would have been an endless amount of first-rate sport with them, and anyone who may be fortunate enough to visit the estancias of the Rio de la Plata would be well repaid for the expense and trouble of taking one out. Without a dog you must take your chance of a rare shot, for if they do not lie still they almost always run before you, hidden in the long grass, instead of rising; with a dog who is taught to draw on them as they run, the sport must be splendid. Mr. Parish Robertson, who was a resident in these countries for many years, thus describes it:* 'Of all the shooting I ever saw—grouse, woodcock, pheasant, blackcock, partridge, snipe, ptarmigan—there is none equal, in intensity of delight and excitement, to this of the large South American partridge. He is called, *par excellence*, *perdiz grande*, or large partridge. His scent is so strong that from the moment your dog comes upon it the agitation of his frame is all but hysterical. The bird, before he will rise, runs at a prodigious rate; and if your dog in coming upon him, as an English dog does when he has traced a covey, should stop or lie down, you would never get a shot. The bird is off the moment his quick ears or natural instinct has told him his pursuers are near; not off by flight, but by a race which commences in suspicion and fear, and terminates in absolute precipitation. So that for the chance of shooting your bird you are obliged to encourage your dog to go in upon him, to follow up yourself the game with unintermitting alacrity, and to pay with palpitating satisfaction, after perhaps a ten minutes' run, for the achievement of bringing down the goodly prize you have so breathlessly pursued. I shipped four of these birds, under the hope of introducing the breed into this country; but they lingered, notwithstanding

* 'Letters on Paraguay.' Vol. i. p. 236.

every precaution, in an unhealthy state when they came into a cold climate, and died in the Channel. Still, I think they might be introduced, and they would be a very great acquisition to the English sportsman.'

Old inhabitants, who do everything on horseback, have another plan, and a very exciting one too, for catching the large partridge. It has been ascertained by long experience that this bird will only rise three times. Mounted men take dogs with them, and, as soon as one of the birds is flushed, away goes the whole party in pursuit; the dogs are encouraged to their utmost speed, and so are the horses; every eye is strained till the bird is marked down; when they come up to him the same process is repeated: again he is marked down for the third time; swifter and swifter is the chase, and they run into the victim, who surrenders at discretion and gets little mercy.

Crossing the region of long grass we entered the *monte*, or wooded district, bordering the Arroyo Malo, where we were always sure of enjoyment and various kinds of sport. Here, shaded from the sun by handsome trees and tall evergreen bushes, we amused ourselves with shooting anything that came in our way. Sometimes a strong whirr told us that a partridge had taken to the wood, and betrayed the course of his flight; sometimes a sharp flapping overhead warned us that wood-pigeons were hovering about the tops of the trees;

and sometimes a clatter like that of angry Irishwomen in an alley announced the immediate neighbourhood of a flock of parrots. All these in turn fell victims, and were most sweetly and harmoniously combined into a mighty pie, the flavour of which I shall never forget, and which I can confidently recommend to anyone starting for the pastures of the Uruguay. If these pages happen to fall into the hands of some cold-blooded philanthropist or humanitarian, who objects to the name of sport, I beg leave to inform him that we never killed more than could be conveniently eaten in the establishment, though it must be confessed that, owing no doubt to the exhilarating atmosphere, our appetites were undeniably large.

An ornithologist would have been delighted with such a situation: we were constantly falling in with birds that we had never seen, and I remember especially one of the kite species, perfectly white with the exception of black tips to the wings, and marvellously elegant in general appearance.

A little lower down the Arroyo, the wood grew considerably thicker, and here we knew that the *capinchos* loved to dwell; so we resolved to pay them a visit, though as we had no rifles it could only be a complimentary call. The capincho, or capybarà, is a sort of river-pig, almost as large as a small bear, with a broad head and heavy muzzle, garnished with long whiskers almost as strong as a tiger's. He is a very shy animal and difficult to get at, so we crept carefully among the thick bushes near the side of the river. Now and then a loud grunting Ugh! followed by a rushing plunge into the water, proved that we had started a capincho down the bank, though the thickness of the jungle prevented our seeing where he came from or whither he went. At last, suddenly emerging upon a somewhat clearer place, we had the amusement of seeing one of them rush grunting into the river close to where we were standing. He swam strongly, and went right down the middle of the stream, carrying his ugly head well out of the water, like a young hippopotamus, and presenting a most tempting offer for a rifle-ball. I had hoped to see and shoot a specimen of the *pavo del monte*, or wild turkey, in every way an admirable bird, but I was disappointed, and it seems they are now nearly confined to the wooded islands of the main river. The same is true of the jaguars, which shut themselves up in these lonely retreats, where if a man wishes to find them he will have plenty of misery and trouble for rather problematical sport. The islands are pretty safe retreats till some great flood or *cresciente* comes; large pieces of them are then frequently torn off and go floating down the mighty stream with a cargo of snakes, tigers, and anything else that may have had the bad luck to be there at the moment. There is no chance for them unless their floating homes happen to stick themselves to the mainland or some other less volatile island; and Sir Woodbine Parish even mentions a case of four jaguars having been thus carried the whole way to Montevideo, where they landed, to the horror and astonishment of the inhabitants.

The hot weather was beginning to 'waken snakes,' and we often came upon them when out shooting. I never saw any of them on the estancia more than about four or five feet long, and those were not of a dangerous kind; but I always took care on these occasions to wear a high pair of buff-coloured boots, which I had procured before leaving England from Kerby of the Haymarket. As riding-boots they were perfect, and were so light that even in a hot climate I could walk with them in comfort, and was thus enabled to defy thorns, snakes, and insects of all descriptions. The light colour of the leather doubles the value of boots in hot countries, where you can use them easily all day in the face of a sun which would make black ones intolerably painful in a few hours. I had been told that the coral-snake is dangerous and even deadly. I never saw any in the Banda Oriental, but when I afterwards became better acquainted with them in Brazil I found that this is a popular error.

The young Englishman whom we found already in possession of the bachelors' room was named Roberts, and he gave me a very amusing account of how he had come into the country a few weeks before. He had made friends in England with a young Scotchman named Anderson, who was then on the point of going out to try sheep-farming in South America. Falling into ill health soon afterwards he was advised to try a change of air and life; he wrote to his old friend who was beginning life in the Banda Oriental, and proposed paying him a visit. After a very long and stormy voyage of nearly three months, he arrived at Buenos Ayres, where he was most injudiciously advised not to wait for a steamer, but to go up to Paysandù in a small native craft, hardly better than an open boat. He spent nine miserable days and nights in this wretched vessel, not knowing a word of the language of the sailors, and then arrived at Paysandù, a stranger in the land. Luckily he was relieved from his helpless situation by falling in with a man who spoke English, and told him that Mr. Anderson's location was about fifteen leagues distant, and that there happened to be a peon who had come over from there, and was then ready to ride back, so that he would have a guide and companion if he liked to start immediately. This was too good a chance to be lost; a horse was found, and away they went at the usual pace of the country, which in due time brought them to his friend's place, after a ride of forty-five miles by way of a change after the long confinement on sea and river.

The meeting of the two friends may be imagined, but no one could depict the astonishment of the new comer when he found that there was no house! Mr. Anderson was one of those lion-hearted men who rely on their own pluck and independence to carry them through everything, and thus generally succeed in defiance of all obstacles. He came out to be a sheep-farmer, so he invested his capital in a flock of sheep, and a piece of land for them to live on. That was all he wanted to begin with; other things might come in due time. His sole companion was a peon of very unprepossessing appearance, but staunch fidelity, who having distinguished himself in frequent quarrels by generally killing his man, now determined to devote all his energy and talent to the service of his gallant young master. They began by sleeping on the open ground, resting on their *recados*, and wrapped up in their ponchos; but in a few days prepared, with sticks and bundles of *paja*, a kind of wigwam, the furniture of which consisted of little more than what is common enough on the Pampas, a bullock's skull for a chair, with a spare horn for a friend. A stock of more convenient things was left at the estancia where I was staying, pending the construction of a better house in the regular style of wattles and clay, the side walls only of which were completed when the invalid visitor arrived from England. It was already late in the evening; the sun had disappeared for the day, and the sky was cloudy; but Mr. Anderson at once determined to take his friend over to Mr. Smith's estancia, where he was sure of shelter and hospitality. A short hour was enough for the ride in daylight, but darkness came on so fast that before they had gone half way it was very difficult to see anything. Mr. Anderson thought he was sure of going right, and only increased the pace; a daring and accomplished rider himself, he could not half sympathise with the sufferings of his friend, who, at the end of a hard day's work to which he was wholly unaccustomed, now found himself urged along in a mad gallop over uneven ground, in total darkness, and expecting every moment to be his last.

At length he felt he could hold out no longer. Mr. Anderson admitted that he could not find the estancia-house, but was not yet prepared to give up the search. He told his friend to sit still on his horse, while he himself rode round and round in increasing circles, in hopes of finding the house. The hoofs were heard thundering round the plain, and the two men kept up communications by shouting till Mr. Anderson returned in despair, saying he had no notion of where they were. It was now, of course, as impossible to find one place as another, and had they both been novices they must have spent the night where they were; but the young Scotchman was ready with a piece of craft worthy to be noticed, for the benefit of those who may not have heard of it. He girthed up both horses with all his strength, and as soon as the benighted friends remounted, their steeds, by a marvellous instinct, made keener by the unpleasant pressure of the girth, started of their own accord at full speed, and finding the way home for themselves, never stopped till they arrived once more at the wigwam from which they started. The night was passed as comfortably as circumstances admitted of, and next morning they presented themselves at the estancia, where we found Mr. Roberts on our arrival.

CHAPTER VIII.

LIFE IN THE BANDA ORIENTAL.

A RIDE TO THE PUESTOS—OSTRICHES AND DEER—IMITATING INDIANS—RESULTS OF CHARGING A BULL—A FIGHTING SERVANT—CHARACTER OF GAUCHOS—THEIR HOLIDAYS AND THEIR QUARRELS—THE KNIFE—MARKING LAMBS—MULE-BREEDING—RAVAGES OF ANTS—THE BICHO COLORADO—MOUNTING A COLT—AWAY TO THE URUGUAY—THE GOLDEN FLEECE—TREES AND FLOWERS—THE FOREST—RUN AWAY WITH IN THE FOREST—AN AGREEABLE EVENING—GREAT THUNDERSTORM—ARRIVAL OF LETTERS—RETURN TO BUENOS AYRES.

A FEW days afterwards our host took us for a ride to the eastern or inland side of the estancia, where we visited some of his *puestos*. In several we found the shepherd at home, sometimes seated with a half-Indian wife, while a few tawny bright-eyed balls of humanity were playing at the door of the hut. Some of the best and certainly the handsomest of these men are Basque emigrants, who, as a general rule, are one of the most valuable classes of the population. French Basques and Spanish Basques arrive in great numbers in the River Plate, and are a remarkably handsome and hard-working race. The women have frequently very good features, but their general *physique* is not in proportion to that of the men.

On these occasions of visits from the master of the establishment to his *puesteros*, the greetings are rather stately, and nothing but the excuse of haste would prevent a feeling of disappointment if the whole party did not dismount and sit down for half an hour's gossip. The woman, wife or otherwise, is called *señora,* and she asks, with much calm dignity, after the health of the *patron* and his family; she then retires into the background, and my instinct informs me that she has gone to prepare the matè, which I detest, and with which I shall presently be obliged to burn my mouth, for fear of seeming rude to the *señora* in declining it. Meanwhile the *puestero* himself, who is resting after a hard gallop in the morning, answers questions about the sheep in the usual cool and lazy way of his countrymen, and invites us to dismount. This we decline, saying we have far to go, and knowing by experience that if once we get fairly seated in a puestero's house we are not likely to get away in a hurry. Presently the dark lady emerges, and pushing out of the way the small imitations of herself, bears the matè to the *patron*, who rather likes it than otherwise—so does his brother, and then comes my turn. I have to bend in the saddle and take the matè-pot with every appearance of gratification; but, as I have never liked this national beverage enough to get accustomed to it, I burn my lips with the *bombilla*, and then suck so awkwardly that I fill my mouth with the chips, inwardly execrating the good woman for her politeness, while she doubtless looks upon me as an unfortunate creature unacquainted with the ways of the world.

We were soon off again, further and further to the east, and fording a river we reached a rather different kind of country. The undulations of the land were closer together, and the intervening hollows bore the appearance of a system of small valleys worn by water in former ages, all tending in the direction of the river which we had lately crossed. The palms were here a great deal more abundant, and we had a delightful ride among them, up and down the sides of the ravines, while a refreshing breeze swayed their plume-shaped crests with a sharp rustling sound. Partridges in multitudes rose at our sides, or nearly immolated themselves under our horses' heels; further off the deer bounded over the turf, and the ostrich strode away at our approach; onward galloped our horses, incapable of fatigue, and it seemed hard to turn homewards; but the sun was sinking towards the palm trees, and we had far to go. A little deviation enabled us to call upon Mr. Anderson, whom we found at the door of his new house, which was now nearly finished; and another hour's ride brought us home with only just enough light to see where we were going.

A few days afterwards, Mr. Anderson came over for a

visit to our party, when I had a better opportunity of making his acquaintance. Light, active and daring, he was the *beau ideal* of a man for the country in which he now found himself; and he took to its ways with an eager enthusiasm, which was now and then cooled down by experience. He amused me very much with the account of some of his early doings, and told his story with a quaint gravity that doubled the effect. He said that he had wished to do everything that the natives did, and hearing that the Indians could let themselves fall to the ground from their horses when going at full gallop, he determined to try the result for himself: he whipped his horse to full speed, and then threw himself off. The effect upon a novice may be imagined: he rolled over and over like a ball on the turf, and made up his mind to leave the Indians to enjoy the monopoly of their accomplishment. Soon afterwards, he was present at a cattle-marking, where a young bull was particularly savage, and for some time defied the efforts of the peons to brand him. Some one knowing my friend's daring spirit, challenged him to charge the bull; he instantly rode at the savage beast, but at the last moment his horse swerved from the danger. He was rather laughed at, as if he had thought prudence was the better part of valour; and, being somewhat nettled, he made a furious charge at the bull, who sent horse and rider flying over his head. Anderson had proved his resolution, but he also made a resolution that, having escaped this time, he would not again tempt bulls and Providence in the same reckless way.

His faithful attendant, the accomplished homicide already alluded to, struck me as being a character in his way, and may perhaps be considered as a type or model man of a certain class of the gauchos of the country. He had the tall upright figure of a European, and his movements showed an activity and elasticity which would make him a formidable enemy in a struggle; his complexion was swarthy, and his straight black hair and low forehead showed the remains of Indian blood in his veins. His bearing was bold and reckless, and I think he was rather proud of being pointed out as a man celebrated for concluding personal quarrels by taking the life of his foes. He had a sort of superstitious idea that he bore a charmed life, which was very strongly confirmed by the fact of his having once been led out to execution by Urquiza, and yet having lived to tell the tale of his almost miraculous pardon. He was serving his new master very well, and looking after his interests, especially in the matter of a certain bad character named Hopkins. This man was a Yankee, who had given great dissatisfaction in the neighbourhood, and been turned away by his employers; but he continued to hang about for any chance employment, and pestered our friend Anderson by blackguardly and mischievous tricks; a wrathful disturbance was the result, and the peon, drawing his knife and kissing the blade with a fervid piety which, with gentlemen of his kidney, means mischief, swore by the most pure and immaculate Virgin that, if he ever caught him there again, that moment should be his last. He was known to be a man of his word, and I have not the least doubt that he has kept it by this time, unless Mr. Hopkins kept prudently out of his way.

It is not, however, by any means to be inferred that a stranger runs more risk than usual in trusting himself among such men, provided he acts with becoming dignity and prudence. There are, of course, bad characters to be found in the camps of South America as well as in other places, and men who would not hesitate to commit any crimes; and it is necessary to be extremely cautious. I was even told that, if asked by a suspicious-looking fellow for permission to light his cigar by my own, it would be highly desirable to stick it into the muzzle of a pistol before letting him come too near on the pretence of taking it. Some years ago, it is certain that violent crimes were extremely frequent, and it was common enough to hear of a man being knocked down and half or wholly killed for no better reason than that he was a *gringo*, or foreigner.

The facilities for escape in a wild country of boundless extent no doubt favour the commission of crimes; but there is great reason to hope that the vast herds of sheep and cattle, and the establishments connected with them, which are rapidly covering the land, are exercising a most beneficial influence on the inhabitants by supplying great numbers of them with regular work; this, after all, is the most powerful agent in deterring a population from the commission of evil deeds. The large and constantly increasing admixture of foreigners accustomed to more orderly ways must also be doing a great deal towards cultivating and improving the rough old gaucho families, and restraining the worst of them.

It appeared to me to be unusual to hear of violent crimes committed by the gauchos, excepting under peculiar circumstances of passion or the desire for revenge. I do not remember hearing a single case of attacks for the mere purpose of robbery, and I have heard it very unkindly remarked that nobody robs except the Government! The gaucho, in his normal state, is generally a good fellow—somewhat staid and solemn, perhaps; not making acquaintance with a stranger so easily as Europeans; very undemonstrative, and a most complete adherent of the 'nil admirari' section of humanity. You may talk to him of the most exciting reports, you may tell him the most important or afflicting intelligence—the probability is that he will only, between the puffs of his cigarette, say, in a half-abstracted way, 'Quien sabe?' which means, being interpreted, 'Who knows?' but when qualified by his tone and manner, has a strong dash of 'I don't care' about it. But if you tell him to ride twenty leagues with a message, he says, 'Si, señor,' and is off like the wind. To say that he is a perfect horseman is as unnecessary as to 'gild refined gold and paint the lily;' but I believe that in his own mind he even judges of the worth of a stranger by the test of his riding powers more than by any moral, religious, or competitive process that could be devised by the whole Board of Education.

Most of them do a hard day's work very steadily without food till the evening announces the time of their rest; they loll or sit lazily about the fire where their beef is cooking, while the inevitable cigarette ornaments their sunburnt faces; and if I may judge by my own experience of estancias which I visited, I should say they pass their evenings remarkably quietly in their own *quartier* of the establishment, where they peaceably gorge themselves with beef and matè. When they get into scrapes, it is generally when they go, after working hours, to some of the lonely *pulperias*, or drinking-shops, which occur here and there at intervals of some leagues about the camp; or when they get a holiday and ride into town, which generally means a far distant village. Here they meet strangers and acquaintances, and imbibe caña. Then they indulge in cards, music, singing and dancing, and soon get excited by the strongest feelings of rivalry. A dispute easily arises about a hand of cards or the heart of a woman, and a sharp word is too often answered by a sharp knife. Sometimes even the sweet muses are the cause of battle, when two keen rivals try their *improvisatore* talents against each other to the accompaniment of a tinkling guitar. Verse after verse is poured out by them alternately, and the spectators take an excited interest in the contest of the bards, both of whom probably are excited by liquor. At last, one begins to sing at the other, taunting him that he can do no more and is beaten; anger increases the confusion of the failing poet, and, amid the jeers of the spectators, he is compelled to 'shut up.' Boiling with wrath, Apollo casts his lyre upon the ground, and transforms himself into the god of war. '*Caramba!*' he cries, 'you may beat me at that stuff, but try this;' long knives gleam in the light, and a deed of blood is done.

These things happen I admit, but there is not the slightest reason why any stranger should mix himself up in them, unless he is carried away by that over-powering curiosity which so often leads the sons of Britain into disastrous consequences. An *estanciero*, of whatever country he may be, will generally have his work well done, and live in perfect security as far as his own men are concerned, if he looks after them in working time, and does not interfere with their private amusements. These men are very frequently dangerous when drunk, but I believe it is no less true that they are rarely 'drunk on duty.' Drunken men are apt to quarrel in all parts of the world, but in England they content themselves with hard language and fisticuffs; Spaniards, Italians and South Americans have a vile habit of using the knife, and wise men will avoid disturbances with them, unless they are prepared to take to the same weapon. An Irishman in the camp is said to have adopted the latter alternative in hearty indignation. He killed those who tried to kill him, and is reported to have slain seventeen professed knife-men by striking fast while they performed the initiatory flourishes of a fencing master.

This has been an unpleasant digression. *Revenons à nos moutons.* Let us talk of the peaceful pursuits of the estancia where I had the pleasure of staying. It was not a busy time, but grand preparations were making for the shearing, which is, of course, the harvest-time of those who dwell among the sheep-folds. The marking of lambs had to be gone through in the meantime, and I saw the operation performed on the offspring of one flock. The whole of the ewes and lambs were driven into a large corral, and then the lambs were separated and driven into an inner enclosure. Peons were here in waiting, and each lamb was in turn caught and handed over to those who ruthlessly snipped off its tail, then shortened one ear, and cut the other into an elaborate pattern with just such a machine as the railway guards use to nick a return ticket. This is the master's *señal,* or mark, and the poor lamb is then handed over the fence to its mother, who is waiting to console it by licking and other refreshment.

We arrived just too late to see a very curious proceeding connected with the breeding of mules. Every one knows the parentage of the mule; but in the wild plains of South America, the mares being accustomed to do as they like, totally refuse the companionship of asses, and fairly kick them out of their society. To obviate this difficulty a crafty device has been hit on, and an instance of its application had given great amusement to everybody at the estancia. The opportunity is chosen when a mare and an ass have each added to their species, the foal of the latter being a male. The peons then kill the foal of the mare, and take off its skin, in which they dress the infant ass. After dark they take it to the mare, who suckles it under the mistaken idea that it is her own offspring; and from the time of this most ludicrous mistake the little beast grows up on terms of friendship with the herd of mares, who, but for the trick, would have utterly scouted him. The operation of putting the skin upon the young impostor was described as ludicrous in the extreme.

Immediately in front of the bachelors' bedroom was an enclosure which was surrounded by a neat fence. In a country where labour and cut timber are exceedingly valuable, I asked the intention of this place. Our good host, with an Englishman's dislike of the national diet of beef *pur et simple*, had contrived this as a kitchen garden, and planted it with vegetables that grow in such a soil and climate with the greatest profusion. But what had become of the vegetables? There was nothing to be seen but coarse grass and thistles several feet high. It seemed that they had started well, and grown apace, promising many a treat; but unfortunately the ants had an eye for the crops, and as soon as they attained a satisfactory size, those busy little enemies of the human race in hot climates took the whole place by storm, and in two days carried off every vestige of all that was worth having. Some of them also devoured part of my saddle, and spoiled the beauty of a pair of boots. I went to inspect the fortifications from which they had issued, the inmost recesses of which were no doubt stuffed with the remains of my friend's kitchen garden. There were large mounds, from which beaten tracks led in all directions, looking like the streets of London as seen from the top of St. Paul's, and marked as distinctly as the paths of rabbits in the grass. The vegetables had been disposed of some time ago, but long trains of the enemy were marching along, bearing pieces of leaves and flowers edge upwards, several times as big as their own bodies, and reminding me of nothing but the famous phenomenon of Birnam wood on its way to Dunsinane. In the same neighbourhood as that of the ants we also found that the advancing heat of the season had turned out the early broods of a most obnoxious insect, the *bicho colorado*. These are very minute, and of much the same colour as the cochineal insect: they fasten themselves into the skin, and produce a horrible irritation with their poisonous secretions. My host had not yet had time to devote to the ants, but in other parts of the country I have seen them entirely exterminated from gardens by pouring water on their nests, and then puddling the whole into a paste by means of a spade: the ants are thoroughly entombed, and the sun in a few hours bakes them, as it were, into an enormous brick.

During my stay we made up a strong party to ride down to the banks of the Uruguay, and look at what was supposed to be part of an enormous fossil, at a distance of seven or eight miles from the house. We were prepared to start, and soon found that the horses were prepared to start also, in more than one sense of the word. Mr. Smith was a perfect rider, and delighted in nothing more than managing an animal who would never let a man cross his back if he could help it. On this occasion, a young *potro* or colt, which had been scarcely ever mounted, was prepared for his amusement. The animal had been sufficiently broken to allow the *recado* to be put upon his back without making a violent disturbance; the difficulty was to get the rider there. Mr. Smith walked very slowly, almost imperceptibly, to his side, till he could take the reins in his left hand; he then raised his foot in the same creeping manner, but did not venture to touch stirrup with it till he had taken the animal's whole measure with his eye. Suddenly he sprang with such astonishing quickness and precision that though the beast jumped high into the air, kicking out in all directions at the first touch of the foot in the stirrup, yet he vaulted accurately into his seat, and the savage colt descended to the turf again to find himself firmly backed by a master whom nothing could get rid of. A few desperate plunges followed, and then finding every effort useless he gave up the struggle with a good grace, and was perfectly quiet for the rest of the day.

Fate had reserved for me a destiny much less graceful, but decidedly more entertaining to the spectators. My horse for that day was a very lively bay, and though by no means such a desperate character as the *potro*, he was evidently an active specimen of the Banda Oriental horses, which are generally rather wild, and insist on starting the moment you take up their reins and touch the stirrup. I jumped as lightly as I could into the saddle, but he instantly made a plunge towards me, the result of which was that my spring took me clean over his back, and I came to the ground on the other side in an ignominious manner, on one foot and one knee: as, however, I kept my hold on the reins, I was soon up again, and the second attempt landed me safe in the saddle, the animal being apparently satisfied with my first discomfiture. Away we all went, over the close turf, upon as glorious a day as ever gladdened the heart of man. We crossed the long undulating hills one after another at a hand gallop, till we all pulled up on the top of the highest of them, near a point where our host proposed building his new house. Here we enjoyed a magnificent view over many miles of the Uruguay, which glittered in broad glassy sheets under a cloudless sky. Long green hills, crowned with groves of palms, rose one after another on the Entre Rios side of the river; and islands of every size, all covered with luxuriant vegetation, seemed at a distance to break up the mighty stream into a lovely region of lakes. Far as we could see, no town, no village, no human dwelling met the eye, though everything to tempt the energy of man was before us. Our small party of Englishmen were silently looking over a vast extent of country capable of producing all that is necessary to man; a country which, after having been first explored by the marvellous courage and enterprise of Spaniards, such as Spaniards were three centuries ago, has since, by the folly of their descendants, passed through a long period of insignificance and degradation, but is yet destined to be the happy home of thousands from the surplus population of Europe.

The wondrous deeds of those old Adelantados and their devoted followers will live for ever in history, and so will their fate. They crossed the Atlantic and endured infinite sufferings in their efforts, by means of the Rio de la Plata, to reach the Peruvian land of treasure, the fabled El Dorado. The courage and endurance which they displayed surpass all belief; but the *auri sacra fames* has ever been an unfortunate passion. They left their descendants a sorry heritage till in these times it has been found to be the true abode of the Golden Fleece. Energetic men from all parts of the earth are beginning to cover those plains and glowing hills with flocks and herds of sheep and cattle, gaining wealth faster than races of gold-diggers; and in due time towns and cities must spring up in a country where not only the beasts of the field, but corn and cotton, amongst other productions of the earth, can, and, with proper care and attention, will flourish in perfection. The land on which we stood is every year rising rapidly in value: the flocks of sheep are for the most part doubling themselves every two years and a half; and there must be a prosperous future for the distant regions of La Plata. As we halted on the summit, with the glorious sun above our heads, and the sweet fresh breeze waving the long grass around us and rippling the broad waters of the Uruguay before us and below, I became enchanted with the scene, and indulged myself for a moment in a fit of musing upon the coming prosperity of that fair land.

But 'forward' was the word again: our host led the way, and we followed in Indian file down a very rough and steep descent, tangled with weeds and bushes which covered the treacherous stones below. Some caution was necessary, till after a short time we reached comparatively level ground, and found ourselves among the wooded region which divides the pasture-lands from the river. We took our bearings by the sun before descending, for we knew that when once in the forest we should find no other sort of assistance towards finding our way. The forest itself was in some places impenetrable, but by choosing the clearest openings we went ahead pretty steadily. Some of the trees were of great size, and some I should think must consist of very brittle wood, for there were an unusual number of those weird-looking trunks with broken out-stretched fiendish limbs, which supply such admirable backgrounds in a nightmare. Amongst them, however, were many in the utmost luxuriance, and others almost knotted into a lump by the continuous nests of the parrots, which delight in uproarious crowding. The main part of the wood was composed of acacias and mimosas of various kinds; one of the latter of which is distinguished by the beauty of its myriads of tufted purple flowers, though not possessed of the delicious scent of the yellow *aroma*. Air plants and passion-flowers hung from the branches, or climbed over the stems, and in spots where there were no other plants or trees the ground was generally occupied by the tall cactus or the quaint ungainly shapes of the prickly pear. My horse evidently had not been accustomed to the woods, and infinitely preferred the open country; he had an intense dislike to thorns, which was natural enough, though at the time I thought it very unreasonable; and as I pushed him along in the best places I could find he jumped and fidgetted about in a most uncomfortable way, evidently wishing to revenge himself for his own sufferings by pitching me into what would have been anything but a bed of roses.

At last we emerged on the margin of the river, and some of the party indulged in a bath, while the rest contented themselves with a cigar upon a shady bank. For my own part I certainly thought that the pleasurable sensation of cold water would be overbalanced by the misery of warm mud on stepping out of it. We soon remounted, and again began picking our way through the wood, but keeping as near as possible to the water-side, till we found ourselves close to the spot where the fossil was supposed to be. Here we picketed the horses, and began to scramble about on foot. The surface of the ground was very uneven and bare, the result apparently of the action of the river, which from time to time must have flowed over it, washing away the softer parts and leaving the remainder projecting. Among these was what appeared very like the long back of some monster, scarcely covered with soil, but sufficiently so to prevent the bones from being distinguishable. At one point, however, one of the horses had broken off a piece containing evidently part of a large fossil bone, which I put in my pocket, and afterwards showed to Professor Owen at the British Museum. He said it was undoubtedly fossil, and placing it by the side of the megatherium he pointed out the complete resemblance to part of one of its ribs.

We made no attempt to disturb any other part of the fossil, for at that time I fully calculated on again coming up the Uruguay later in the year with Captain Parish, of H.M.S. Ardent, armed with proper means and appliances for unearthing some of these monsters, and sending them properly packed to the learned Professor. There is little doubt that the place contains a great quantity of fossil remains, some of which may be as yet unknown, and we hoped to have had a very interesting expedition; but the 'dogs of war' were determined to spoil everything. The continuance of the war between Buenos Ayres and the provinces maintained constant alarm; for the Buenos Ayreans knew that a defeat of their army in the field would subject their city to the fearful risk of pillage and sacking by the savage troops of Urquiza, who had received no pay for some months, and were only kept in order by the prospect of plunder. Under these circumstances the foreign men-of-war were obliged to be in constant readiness for any emergency; they might at any time be wanted to protect the interests of their own nations, or to supply shelter and charity to some refugee president or defeated tyrant. Thus it was that month after month passed away without giving us any chance of digging for monsters; but there they are still, quietly resting by the side of the great river, and I have no doubt whatever that some day they will amply repay the trouble of an investigation. I should like to see how the eyes of some of our wise men would twinkle with delight if they could suddenly be dropped down into a garden of megatheriums and 'chimeras dire.'

Wandering soon afterwards to some distance I came rather suddenly through the trees to a very high and extensive bank of sand and gravel, considerably above the present level of the river, and containing countless numbers of agates and cornelians, very bright and beautiful in colour, but in my short search I did not find any large specimens. There would be no difficulty in filling a ship with them, were it worth while to do so. Loaded with a pocket full of brilliant pebbles and a handful of scarlet verbenas mixed with a variety of other flowers which were quite unknown to me, I returned to the rendezvous under a shady tree, where we stretched ourselves on the grass, sucking oranges and inhaling the fragrant weed, till we found it was time to return to home and dinner. My horse had with his brethren been indulging himself upon a good feed of grass, which seemed to have inspired him with fresh materials for mischief. I had learnt to mount pretty quickly, and was soon in my saddle; but at the first touch of the stirrup the brute had contrived to run his head into a bush, and I, unfortunately, had not taken up my reins so short as I intended. As he flung up his head suddenly the bridle caught against a thorn, and the off-side rein was jerked over to the near-side; at the same moment his tail encountered another bush, and he instantly bolted as fast as he could go. I was helpless, with both reins on one side of his head, which was stretched out so far that I could not by any amount of jerking and shaking put matters right again. The only result of all my efforts was to frighten him more completely than before, and he flew like the wind. Luckily I was perfectly firm in my saddle, and felt, as I fancy many people do, more cool than usual in the real hour of danger. Still the prospect was far from agreeable, as he rushed through the forest, every tree and branch of which threatened me with destruction. The trees, moreover, were of the usual thorny description, and in the almost certain event of a smash the softest thing I could there have been impaled upon was a prickly pear! By a desperate jerk at both reins on one side, and a most spiteful kick on the other, I steered him clear of a tree, which for a moment I thought would be the death of me; but it was only exchanging Scylla for Charybdis; I was fairly in a difficulty, when I fortunately remembered a hint which I had had from a friend who was run away with by a horse with a broken bridle. Keeping firm in my seat I stretched out my right hand till it passed between the ears of the beast, and grasped the head-stall with all my fingers. Half measures were useless, but rising slightly in my stirrups I put the whole strength of my body into one sudden and severe jerk upwards. The first touch of my hand only quickened his speed, if possible; but when he felt the sudden wrench which forced the punishing native bit into his mouth, with a violence which took him completely by surprise, he stopped as if he had been shot, and I must have been pitched over his head if I had not been prepared for such a catastrophe. Instantly dismounting, I found him trembling with fear; he was completely beaten. I soon put the bridle to rights, and jumping on his back again took him back as a humbled slave to meet my companions, who were coming after me in the full expectation of finding my remains on the ground, or spitted among the thorns of an acacia, and complimented me greatly on my successful method of taming a runaway. A few minutes afterwards I found that in about a dozen strides farther we should have been tumbled over a steep bank into the rocky bed of a dry stream, which was completely concealed by a mass of overhanging brushwood. I was well out of a dangerous scrape, and I mention the incident in the hope of supplying a hint to some one who might otherwise not know the best treatment under similar circumstances. We rode merrily across the hills again as the sun sloped down towards the palms of Entre Rios, and gilded the distant waters of the

Uruguay. The evening was passed very pleasantly; our kind hostess, with the taste which accompanies a cultivated Englishwoman into the remotest wilds, had ornamented her temporary home with a pianoforte, and many a familiar air floated through open doors and windows over the silent pastures of the Banda Oriental. Mr. Anderson added to his many accomplishments that of an admirable voice, and we could see the tall forms of the peons standing in the broad moonlight, and listening, half enchanted, to the strains of 'Goodbye, sweetheart, goodbye.'

During the last few days the heat had rapidly increased, but the weather though oppressive was still perfectly fine, and the sky was generally cloudless. But a change was at hand. Distant thunder growled, and masses of cloud ranged themselves all round us till at length they burst with a terrific uproar. For nearly three days and nights the storm continued with more or less severity. Sometimes, after several hours of continual thunder, lightning, and rain, we were able to go out for an hour or two and shoot a few partridges, while the black masses of clouds all round the horizon were incessantly pierced and seamed by the descending flashes. The noise of thunder was in our ears the whole time, till the very brain ached with the uproar and longed for a little repose. As a spectacle, this storm was magnificent in the extreme, and the effect of such a deluge of soft rain upon the parched earth was marvellous. I had particularly noticed a bush near the house which seemed a mere bundle of dry sticks, but in the third day of the rain it was covered with large green buds from which the new leaves were already springing. The *aroma* trees opened their flowers as if by magic, and were covered with bright yellow tufts breathing one of the most exquisite perfumes that can be imagined. All nature seemed gasping with delight. Swarms of fresh insects started into life; and, as we rode through the low grounds, we were pursued by thousands of a race which combined the attributes of the May-fly and daddy-long-legs, but of greater size and pertinacity than either. They clung to horses and men till we were perfectly black with them; they got into my ears and whiskers, and down the back of my neck; every cut with the *revenque* and every blow of the hand annihilated heaps of them without the least apparent effect on the others, who followed us as we flew before them like Tam O'Shanter. They were fortunately harmless, though very annoying; but I was not sorry to see the old laws of supply and demand assert themselves as usual. The same genial warmth which made the insects dance so cheerfully, brought out from their retirements a variety of fresh birds to devour them, and thus enjoy their share of the bounties of Providence.

In the middle of the bad weather an important event occurred: the post arrived. A peon is sent to Paysandù, about fourteen leagues distant, to meet the river steamer next after the arrival of the European mail at Buenos Ayres. The rain had swollen the rivers; and as it was known that our envoy would probably have to swim the Queguay and the Quebracho, we had some anxiety as to when and in what condition the letters would be delivered. He arrived looking very wet after his long ride, but was as undisturbed as his compatriots always are.

'Have you got the letters?'

'Si, señor,' he replied, untying a closely-knotted handkerchief with which he had contrived to keep them dry.

'Did you have to swim the rivers?'

'Si, señor.'

'Will you have a glass of wine?'

'Si, señor.'

This man was not the regular messenger, but considered himself something more of a gentleman, being in fact a species of policeman from Paysandù, who, wanting to come in our direction, volunteered to do duty as postman by anticipation, the steamer having arrived sooner than was expected. He was accordingly invited to sit down in the dining-room, where he sipped his wine in perfect silence, apparently quite puzzled at the situation in which he found himself. In answer to questions he never rose beyond 'Si, señor,' or 'No, señor,' and at last when he was satisfied he quietly remarked, 'Adios, señor,' and stalked heavily off to his horse.

Meanwhile, there was a rush to the contents of the handkerchief. 'Punch,' 'Illustrated News,' the last number of the 'Times,' only six weeks old, and a bundle of letters! The Pope seemed to be in a fright, the Emperor in a difficulty, and the Yankees rapidly getting accustomed to fratricidal slaughter; but what cared we for Popes, Emperors, or Presidents? The Pope might 'lead a happy life,' or the contrary; Italy might be united, or divided into cubic inches; it was perfectly immaterial to us who were roaming at our own sweet will among the delights of a wild country where the hills were spangled with verbenas, and where we could gallop after ostriches or make parrots into pies. But though it is true that public news loses nearly all its influence in passing through the medium of distance, and the 'thoughts that shake mankind' in cities are dissipated into thin air when they reach the remoter regions of the earth, how differently valued is the happy gossip of brothers and sisters and friends! No man has any notion of the value of a letter till he has feasted upon one far away from all his old associations in some wild halting-place among the forests or the plains. Then every word is sacred, and he dreads coming to the last page.

That evening we read and talked, and played at whist, while the storm raged round us more fiercely than ever. Mr. Anderson had made one of the party, and finding that there was no chance of the weather improving, he made up his mind to ride home, in spite of all remonstrances and the temptation of a comfortable sofa. He found his horse by the aid of the lightning, saddled and bridled him, and shouted 'Good-night,' as he rode off through the tremendous rain into utter darkness. He had about eight miles to ride, with nothing to guide him on such a night; and he had a river to cross which we knew was so swollen that, even if he found the ford, his horse would probably not be able to keep his legs, and anywhere else he must certainly swim for it. But storm and darkness, slippery ground and swollen rivers, had no terrors for him; he girthed up his horse tight, and reached home without any catastrophe.

My visit was now coming to an end; and after nearly a fortnight's very great enjoyment I was going back to Buenos Ayres with one of my late comrades. The steamer going down the river, on her course from Salto to Montevideo, was expected to pass the estancia about eleven o'clock in the morning, and when all was ready we rode off towards the river, with two or three peons carrying our baggage on the front of their saddles. We passed by one of the *puestos* on the top of a hill which overlooked the river, and there hoisted a large union-jack as a signal for the steamer to stop. A little way farther we came to the place where we ought to have landed on our arrival; and, after waiting nearly an hour, our old friend the 'Montevideo' arrived and pulled up for us. A boat was sent ashore, and in a few minutes we were descending the river under the care of the Scotch engineer. There had been no rain for a couple of hours, so we were quite dry, but very soon after we got on board our vessel the storm returned to the charge; it lasted all the afternoon, and at night the thunder and lightning became so tremendous that the captain resolved to wait at Fray Bentos till the weather improved. Early in the morning we moved on again, and at Higueritas took in some half-drowned passengers, one of whom proved to be a great friend of mine. About noon we arrived at Buenos Ayres, full of grateful recollections of happiness in the Banda Oriental.

CHAPTER IX.

GAUCHOS AND WAR.

FORTIFICATIONS OF BUENOS AYRES — TRAINING OF A GAUCHO — HIS INDEPENDENCE — LONG RIDES — THE RASTREADOR AND VAQUEANS — GENERAL RIVERA — CIVILISATION AND THE SWORD — GENERAL URQUIZA — EL CAÑON TIENE LA PALABRA! — RAILWAY TO MERLO — PEACH WOODS — PRODUCTIVENESS OF CORN — SOLEMNITIES AT THE CATHEDRAL — QUESTION OF PARAGUAY — HIGH PRICES — ALARMING REPORTS — CALMNESS OF HERNANDEZ — VICTORY! — PRISONERS — GENERAL GLORIFICATION — RESOLVE TO RETURN TO BRAZIL.

WHEN we returned to Buenos Ayres, wars and rumours of wars were still in the ascendant, and it was interesting to watch how in an immature country such matters are managed. A state of siege was maintained, and the fortifications had been progressing. Every man and horse that could be got at was pressed into the service and sent into the field; but the question which naturally suggested itself was how, with only a few troops and national guards left in the city, it would be possible to man the works that extended round a place of such dimensions. Large issues of fresh paper dollars were voted by an enthusiastic Sala, and high wages were paid to hundreds of men employed in the construction of the forts. The trenches and embankments were completed, and one of the most curious little forts ever seen was established on the side of the Palermo road, scarcely a quarter of a mile from the quinta in which I was staying with the Consul. It was a thorough toy: they patted it smooth, covered the outside with plaster to look like stone, and arranged turfs very neatly on the top of it. Two guns were mounted, one apparently a 12-pounder and the other about half that size; a solitary sentinel paced up and down, and when some heavy rain set in they built a sentry-box for him; a small gipsy-tent on the other side of the road contained three or four other soldiers to relieve guard: and this was called a fortification.

Some of the works at the opposite end of the city were rather more imposing, and had the advantage of a very commanding position; but no European could look at them without wondering how they were to be manned or defended against a determined foe. The fact is, however, that they were in all probability quite sufficiently strong to resist any enemy that was likely to be brought against them. The greater part of such an army as Urquiza could bring into the field would consist of gaucho cavalry, to whom the trenches, slight as they were, would be an insuperable obstacle, while a few round shot thrown judiciously among them from the occasional forts would deter them from attempting the task of entering by even the most favourable approaches.

In fact, a gaucho army is in all probability too wild and undisciplined to maintain such a continuous and energetic effort as would be required to storm the simplest of defences. The red ponchos and long lances of Urquiza's horsemen inspired terror in the open field, but the Buenos Ayreans had an infinitely better chance with a trench in front of them.

One day in the camp, seeing something moving in an unusual manner we turned towards it, and found two little ragged urchins, about eight years old, who hid themselves suddenly in a hole in the ground, but seeing they were discovered they came out again; they had been skinning a cow—which we will charitably hope had died a natural death—and then, harnessing two dogs to the hide, they were driving it home in that fashion across the camp, looking highly satisfied with their prize, lawful or unlawful. We amused ourselves by trying to frighten them with questions about it, but the swarthy imps boldly said it was their own property, and we left them with a laugh.

Such are the materials from which the full-blown gaucho is developed in perfection. These half-wild urchins ride almost as soon as they can walk, and their highest ambition is to be tall enough to catch a horse by the mane, which is all they require for mounting him; they are on his back in a moment, and he must be a very clever back-jumper if he can get rid of them. Saddle or no saddle, it is just the same to them, and they ride with a gusto and keen sense of wild enjoyment which is very inspiriting to a spectator. They practise with the *lazo* and the *bolas* on pigs and fowls; they ride round and round the partridges till they are near enough to knock them down with the whip, and make a profound study of the use of the knife. With these accomplishments they are considered ready for the life of a peon or servant on a farm or estancia, where they soon get accustomed to managing sheep and cattle, and where by good conduct they may be pretty sure of obtaining promotion on the establishment. From men trained in this way the greater part of the army is extemporised: they are taken suddenly from their occupations and their homes; and though they have no objection to using the knife in a disturbance among themselves, they detest being compelled to fight in masses for some object which they do not understand or care for. No wonder that numbers of them throw down their arms and run away at the best speed of their favourite horses. They abhor discipline, and are distinguished by a haughty and independent dignity. If they do not like their master or their position they ride away, perfectly sure of suiting themselves somewhere else, and would generally do anything rather than take to soldiering.

Their endurance on horseback is wonderful, and they think nothing of riding hard all day, before touching a morsel of food. In actual distances however,

I doubt if they have ever surpassed some of the feats of our own countrymen. I remember an Englishman in the Banda Oriental who rode 55 leagues, or 165 miles in one day, with a *tropilla* of horses from Montevideo; and great as was this exertion, I think it is surpassed by Sir Francis Head's exploit of riding 900 miles between Buenos Ayres and Mendoza in eight days. Many years' experience, however, are required before a foreigner can hope to rival the skill and address with which a true gaucho manages his horse in all circumstances as if it were a part of himself. To ride a certain number of hours is a mere matter of endurance, but to catch a bull with the lazo and then drive him over the plain in any direction required, turning and winding to avoid the stroke of his horns—to do this requires the hand and eye of a master.

Mr. Darwin relates that once upon a time a South American army elected its general by the following trial:—A troop of unbroken horses being driven into a corral, were let out through a gateway, above which was a cross-bar; it was agreed that whoever should drop from the bar on one of these wild animals as it rushed out, and should be able without saddle or bridle not only to ride it, but also to bring it back to the door of the corral, should be their general. The person who succeeded was accordingly elected, and doubtless made a fit leader for such an army. This extraordinary feat has also been performed by General Rosas.

Many of these men have extraordinary powers of following a track, and of finding their way at night or in unknown parts of the country. I have before me a curious little Spanish book by Don Domingo Sarmiento, the governor of one of the Western Provinces, who gives some marvellous stories of these faculties. 'Once upon a time,' he says, 'I fell in with a path crossing that from Buenos Ayres, and the peon who was my guide fastened his eyes upon the ground, as usual. Presently he said, "Here goes a dark mule, a very good one—it belongs to the troop of D. N. Zapata—it is saddled, and has a very good saddle too—it passed yesterday." This man came from the Sierra of San Luis, the troop was coming back from Buenos Ayres, and it was a year since he had last seen the mule whose foot-print was mixed up with those of a whole troop in a path of two feet wide. This, which may appear incredible, is nevertheless a common kind of knowledge: the man was a common peon, and not a professional *rastreador* or tracker.

'The tracker by profession is a personage of grave and circumspect appearance, whose assertions are believed in the inferior tribunals. The consciousness of the knowledge which he possesses gives him a certain reserved and mysterious dignity. . . . A theft has been committed in the night—they run to find a foot-print of the thief, and when found it is covered with something to prevent the wind from effacing it. Then they send for the rastreador, who sees the track and follows it, looking only from time to time at the ground as if his eyes saw in relief the footprint which is invisible to another. He follows it through the streets and across the gardens, enters a house, and pointing out a man whom he meets, he coolly says "That is the man!" The crime is proved, and it is seldom that a delinquent resists this accusation. To him, even more than to the judge, the deposition of the rastreador is convincing evidence: to deny it would be ridiculous, absurd. He submits then to this witness whom he considers as the finger of God denouncing him.'

My legal friends will probably agree in thinking that this would be a very dangerous kind of evidence to receive in a court of justice, nor do I suppose it would be considered conclusive in Buenos Ayres. It points, however, to a very singular state of society, and a certain Calibar, who was personally known to Sen. Sarmiento, and who is said by him to have practised the profession of a rastreador with the greatest distinction for forty years, must have had many opportunities of revenging himself on an enemy if he were so disposed.

To be a good guide, or *vaqueano*, is a very important qualification for life in the Pampas, and many of the gauchos are marvellously skilful in that way. Don Domingo goes on to say that an accomplished *vaqueano* can find his way by methods inconceivable by other men: he observes trees and bushes, and knows them all by heart; in utter darkness he dismounts from his horse and tastes the herbs or grasses, or tries whether the water is fresh or salt. He can inform a general in what direction an enemy is approaching by the course taken by ostriches and deer; he observes the dust, and states the number of the foe. By the manner in which the crows and condors whirl in the air, he can tell whether they are hovering over a party of men, or only a dead animal.

He adds: 'Will this be thought an exaggeration? No. General Rivera, of the Banda Oriental, is a thorough vaqueano, who knows every tree in the whole Republic of the Uruguay. The Brazilians could not have occupied it without his assistance, and without him the Argentines could not have liberated it. . . . . General Rivera began his studies of the country in 1804, and in making war against the authorities as a contrabandist, against the contrabandists as an *employé*, then against the king in the character of a patriot, afterwards against the patriots as a brigand, against the Argentines as a Brazilian chief, against the Brazilians as an Argentine general, against Lavalleja as president, against President Oribe as a proscribed chief, and lastly against Rosas as a general of the Banda Oriental, he had plenty of time to learn something of the trade of a vaqueano!'

That is a singular history of an old-fashioned chief: no doubt Sarmiento is right in saying that he must have learned something in the course of such varied and distinguished services. Probably he was really fond of fighting, but that is not the general feeling of the country gauchos.

Urquiza kept his men together with an iron hand and by the promise of plunder, but they must have been sadly disappointed at the result of the campaign. This is a dangerous game to play: when the Captain-General was defeated and compelled to fly back to Entre Rios, it was said that he would find no greater enemies than those of his own party.

The Rio de la Plata, with its countless branches running through an immense and fertile territory, ought to secure wealth and prosperity to a very large number of inhabitants. There is room for hundreds of thousands to live happily in its delightful climate, but the progress of the Argentine Republic has been always retarded by the feeling of insecurity which has been firmly implanted in the European mind by its disturbed politics and frequent wars. It is true that the circumstances which have unfortunately given rise to this want of confidence have been greatly exaggerated, and that the amount of ignorance which generally prevails in Europe with respect to those countries is very great; but still it must be granted by their best friends that the misconception has not been altogether without reason.

Under the galling yoke of Old Spain her colonies were governed by a blind and narrow-minded tyranny, which exerted all its power to convert their means and resources to the sole benefit of the mother country. When, after a series of struggles, they proclaimed and maintained their independence, the reaction seems to have been at first too violent; and it is true that, according to the laws which generally assert themselves in periods of revolution, the Republics of South America have been frequently subjected to military tyrannies forced on them by adventurers who from time to time have been enabled to assert the power of the sword over that of law and civilisation. The most disastrous consequences have ensued, and the confidence of the world has been withdrawn from countries which, if the real feelings of the mass of their inhabitants could have made themselves better known, would be found more worthy of it than is generally supposed.

The Buenos Ayrean politicians and newspapers, finding that the Congress at Parana, presided over by Derqui and dictated to by Urquiza, was inimical to their interests, adopted a tone of defiance and bluster, which brought down upon them the retort that they were rebels and traitors to the Confederation. This was theoretically perfectly true; but they determined to carry matters with a high hand, to beard the Congress, and draw out the old lion from his den in Entre Rios. They made up their minds to beat him, and have done with him for ever; and, finding that he did not come out so readily as they expected, they assailed him and his friends with violent and abusive language, after the manner of hunters who throw squibs and crackers into the cave of a wild beast. To say the truth, he had every reason for remaining quiet in his own province, where he was surrounded by immense possessions and where his influence was entirely paramount. But the Federal party could do nothing without him, and in compliance with the wishes and necessities of his old friends he prepared once more to bring the terrible red ponchos into the field.

Mr. Thornton and M. de Bécour, the English and French Ministers, exerted themselves to the utmost for the preservation of peace, and when their mediation was accepted, great expectations were entertained by the general public of a favourable issue to the conferences that ensued. They had an infinitely difficult task, and at length the passions and intrigues of the contending partisans proved too strong for all better influences: it was found that the quarrel must be settled by the sword, and '*El cañon tiene la palabra*' was the expression of the day. Sober men, wealthy merchants, and thinking men of the world, all those whose opinions ought to be entitled to the greatest weight, were disgusted at seeing a state of things which they were powerless to prevent. In South America, as well as in North America, it is abundantly shown that the Republican form of government suffers from this very serious drawback. Where all assume equal rights to talk, to act, and to govern, it is scarcely possible that any but the noisiest should be heard, or that any but the most intriguing and least fitted for good honest government should rise to the head of affairs. Under such circumstances the best men will not and cannot come forward, and in moments of danger or difficulty the national ship tosses grievously on the waves for want of good pilots and commanders.

If the silly and excited newspaper editors, who hounded on the war-party, had devoted a little calm, longheaded calculation to the subject, they would have found that the whole question in dispute could have been compromised by a few concessions to the Provincials for a much smaller expenditure than that which even a successful war must infallibly involve; whilst, on the other hand, a defeat would have been followed by the most ruinous and disastrous consequences to the whole province. They preferred to rush into war, madly thinking to cure all the evils of the State by boundless issues of inconvertible paper money; they did not consider the infinite injury they were about to inflict upon their country by still further depreciating the pining, dwindling dollar, and offering to Europe one more proof of the folly of their government: 'No surrender! No compromise! *El cañon tiene la palabra!*'

The hardest part of all this is that the whole country gets the undeserved reputation of turbulence and ferocity. All the mischief is brought about by a few violent men on one side, and a few clever but unscrupulous intriguers on the other. I frequently heard it observed that the elimination of twenty or thirty unquiet spirits would secure the tranquillity of the Republic.

In the middle of all the excitement I went out to spend a few days with my friend, Mr. Harry Smith, on his estancia at Merlo, about thirty miles from Buenos Ayres. This short journey gave me a delightful specimen of what civilisation has done for the country, and enabled me to judge better than before of what a satisfactory prospect there is for the future. Merlo is a station on the railway which runs westward from the city, so we took tickets at the terminus in the Plaza del Parque. The price was very small, the carriages clean and airy, and passengers in plenty were going into the country for business or pleasure.

The generally level nature of the country offers the greatest possible facility for railway-making: there is nothing to be done but to lay the rails over any extent of land that may be required, and your railroad is ready, without cuttings or embankments so high as your knee. As the train emerged from the city, after quietly travelling down the middle of a street, it soon became evident that the railway was producing its natural effect. Stores and mills were growing like mushrooms in its neighbourhood; pretty villas were springing up near the stations; and *cafés* with pretty flower-gardens were tempting crowds of Buenos Ayrean cockneys to spend their Sundays and holidays as Englishmen do at Richmond or at Gravesend. I know no place where there is a greater want of something of the sort; for Buenos Ayres itself has no public gardens or parks like those which ornament the European capitals; and though I believe the native-born inhabitants are for the most part satisfied with the sociable ways of town-life, yet there is an immense foreign population of English, French, Germans, and Italians who are eager to grasp at any opportunity of getting a little of the variety which so pleases them in European ways. I think the South American railways will, for very many reasons, be highly successful, and pleasure-seekers will probably contribute considerably to the returns.

A wildly-picturesque boy, with a dash of the Indian about him, had brought horses to the station, so we had nothing to do but to gallop straight over the smooth turf till we came to the estancia house. The house was very agreeably situated by the side of a large peach-wood. These trees grow very fast, and the crop of peaches is generally enormous; but sometimes one of the great hailstorms of the country will destroy the whole. Farther up in the interior vast quantities of peaches are split up and dried for sale; and, though in appearance they are not more tempting than bits of leather, the flavour comes out well when they are cooked with rice like Normandy pippins.

The ants had been very troublesome in the garden, and great efforts were being made to exterminate them; but they had got under the house, and after a great deal of digging and smoking they were still in possession when I left. The early spring was bringing the flowers into bloom, and I was particularly pleased with an avenue bordered with masses of a large and very beautiful iris, perfectly white, and possessed of a delicate perfume. We had a delightful ride about the neighbourhood for some hours, passing a very handsome country house of the Alcorta family, and we visited what was considered a great curiosity in the camp. Some enterprising Frenchmen had built a large flour-mill on the side of an arroyo, and by damming up the stream had obtained a powerful head of water to turn the wheel. The cost must have been very great, and the machinery was in high order.

Where the land is so admirably adapted for sheep-pasture, the cultivation of corn has been greatly neglected, but the advantage of transport to the city which is supplied by the railway will no doubt draw more attention to it. The Montevideans sent some specimens of wheat to the London Exhibition of 1862, which were highly remarkable for the immense productiveness of the seed. There were 135 fine ears from a single grain.

When we went to take our places back to Buenos Ayres, a day or two later, the station-master told us that the news was very bad: the city was placed in *asamblea,* meaning under martial law, and things were supposed to be going all wrong. The armies were known to be close together in the neighbourhood of San Nicolas, and every hour was expected to bring tidings of a bloody battle. We found great gloom in the city: shops were not allowed to open till the fire of a gun at nine o'clock, and were compelled to close when another gun was fired at four in the afternoon. Payment of debts could not be enforced, and some people were delighted to take advantage of that commercial phenomenon.

The 11th of September being considered a lucky day for the arms of Buenos Ayres, it was supposed that Mitre would, if possible, give battle on that day, to encourage his troops. To add solemnity to the occasion the aid of the Church was called in, and it was announced that a solemn service would be held in the cathedral and other churches on the morning of the 10th, to invoke a blessing on the army. I went, like many others, to see what was to be seen at the cathedral, and to observe the conduct of the people on such an unusual occasion. The editor of the *Tribuna*, departing from his usual line, had called on all good patriots to go and listen to the church through the medium of its bishop, and had declared Urquiza guilty of sacrilege, in addition to all his other crimes, for daring to invoke the favour of the God of battles on behalf of the other side of the question.

I found the whole body of the building filled with ladies and women of various ranks kneeling on the marble floor, while the aisles were occupied by men quietly promenading and commenting *sotto voce* on the ladies. The mass, followed by a sermon from the bishop, made a very long service, and the fair devotees evidently suffered from kneeling on the hard floor, which compelled them sometimes to turn and assume a very graceful half-sitting posture. The men went in and out as they pleased; and one of them, on being asked by one of my companions what it was all about, merely remarked with a shrug that he believed it was some piece of '*religioso fanatismo*.' Certainly it is only justice to the taste and beauty of the belles of Buenos Ayres, to say that the clouds of incense floated over a rare collection of lovely faces and exquisite *mantillas*.

My own plans and arrangements were greatly hampered by the state of public affairs. My heart was set upon crossing the Andes into Chili as soon as the summer melting of the snow should make the passage of the Uspallata pass practicable, but I was told that this could not be till near the end of the year. To fill up part of the time, I determined to take my passage by the steamer to Asunçion, the capital of Paraguay, about 800 miles from Buenos Ayres; and having been kindly furnished with valuable introductions, I intended to start by the 'Salto de Guayra' on the 16th of September. The suspense about the expected battle, which would determine the fate of Buenos Ayres for some time to come, became more intense every day, and I did not like leaving my kind friends and relations in the city at a crisis in which it would have been my pleasure as well as my duty to assist them in case of need. Had Urquiza gained the day and brought his undisciplined troops into the city, every bullet might have been useful, and I should have been sorry to be absent on such an occasion.

Seeing an advertisement that a Brazilian steamer, the 'Marquis d'Olinda,' would sail two days later than the 'Salto de Guayra,' I gave myself the benefit of this extra time to wait for the great event. The people seemed to be more and more oppressed by gloom and uncertainty: no definite news could be obtained, but reports multiplied at an astonishing rate. It was said that parties of *dispersos* or runaways were already scouring the country, and had actually come into San Isidro, only five leagues from Buenos Ayres itself. This circumstance, if true, would indicate that the popular army had been beaten in the field, and that the arrival of the pursuing enemies was a mere question of hours; but lies of every description abounded. In great uncertainty I went to the office to which I was referred about the 'Marquis d'Olinda,' and found that that vessel was only going as far as the Guazù mouth of the Paranà, not far beyond the island of Martin Garcia, at which point the passengers, if any, would be transferred to a small steamer which was to make the first regular trip up the river to Cuyabà, in Brazil. The smallness of this vessel, and the uncertainties of such an experimental trip in what I expected would be like a travelling tea-kettle in the coming hot weather, were so many additional reasons for deciding me against the expedition. I afterwards was very glad to have arrived at this decision, particularly when I heard that the 'Marquis d'Olinda' was stopped by the authorities at Martin Garcia.

As the crisis approached, the price of necessaries was greatly increased. Hay, or dry *alfalfa*, rose to about 16*l*. English per ton; and the butcher declared that beasts cost him nearly four times as much as usual, owing to the number of peons who had been compelled to join the army, and the consequent difficulty of bringing the necessary quantity of animals into town. This may have been partly true, and partly owing to the fact that butchers, like bakers, are animated by much the same principles all the world over. Milkmen may safely be put into the same category; and those of

Buenos Ayres are fully equal in resources to their brethren in Europe. The greater part of the milk is brought into the city by mounted *lecheros*, who squat upon the top of a sheepskin saddle, garnished with large vessels of tin on both sides. They are so exceedingly given to the admixture of water that scarcely a month passes without the police making a general raid upon them as they come into town, and fining them all round for adulteration; but the process is so lucrative that they pay the fines cheerfully, and continue their nefarious practice.

Things came to a head on the 19th of the month. The government was pretty sure of getting certain news in the course of the day, and about 10,000 rockets were said to be ready at the Plaza del Parque, in hopes of being able to announce a victory. In the middle of the day a sprinkling of weather-beaten deserters rode into town, declaring, as is usual with such men, that it was all over with the army, and faces grew proportionably long. In the afternoon, at a house where I called to pay a visit, I found a very lively discussion going on among a large party of ladies. One section declared that there was a complete *derrota* or rout of Mitre's army, and the other said it was perfectly certain that Urquiza was in full flight. They were of opposite political principles, and in each case 'the wish was father to the thought.' Matters looked rather serious, however, and the ladies gravely doubted if it were safe to sleep in their suburban *quintas*. They were persuaded to be tranquil; and before going to bed I went with the Consul to ask the last news from our friend Sr. Hernandez, the chief of the northern section of police. He was calmly smoking his cigar, puzzled as much as any of us by the conflicting rumours, and patiently waiting the result with the dignified tranquillity of a Spaniard. In due time I went to sleep, and was awoke about two o'clock in the morning by a peculiar bang, which I instantly recognised as proceeding from one of the detonating rockets. I jumped out of bed, and saw the sky alive with these victory-announcing meteors, streaming up among the stars in every direction. Presently an infinite variety of reports proved that weapons of every description, from pop-guns to 12-pounders, were being fired all round us; and having satisfied ourselves that matters were all right, we went to sleep again, though the noise and uproar were continued till after daylight.

Next morning we found the streets all strewed with the remains of fireworks, and it appeared that a *chasque* or government courier had ridden in with the joyful news of a complete victory. Nearly the whole of Urquiza's artillery with many prisoners had been captured, and the redoubted Captain-General himself had ridden at full speed with a few officers of his staff to Rosario. People were wild with joy, even though it soon transpired that the Buenos Ayrean cavalry had run away as usual before the red ponchos of the Federals, and that a great part of Mitre's baggage had been captured. Before long, however, it turned out that the runaway cavalry had succeeded in taking some of the baggage of the other side, and the extraordinary spectacle was presented of a good hard infantry fight having been well maintained and completely gained by the Buenos Ayreans, while the cavalry on both sides had got round to their enemy's rear. Mitre's infantry, and especially an Italian brigade in Garibaldian costume, had captured the artillery of Urquiza in a really brilliant charge, and we were told that a batch of guns, prisoners, and standards would soon vouch for the reality of the victory which had been gained on the banks of the Arroyo del Pavon. The total spoil announced in the official despatch consisted of 37 guns out of 42, 10 standards, 1,600 prisoners, and no end of ammunition and stores.

Two days later I formed one of an immense crowd assembled on the mole to witness the reception of the standards, which were sent down in charge of a few officers on board the 'Montevideo' steamer. The same vessel brought 96 prisoners, said to be officers, but it was not judged advisable to land them till the crowd had dispersed. The standards were carried in a very undignified way, being strapped into a bundle and carried on the shoulders of a couple of sailors, just like a dead man on a stretcher.

The honours of a public reception were reserved for the following day, which was Sunday. The population turned out *en masse* to witness a very brilliant display. All the troops and national guards remaining in the city were marched through the principal streets to receive the trophies of war and escort them to the Government House. The day was gloriously fine, and the people showed as much enthusiasm as the Spanish disposition is capable of. Myriads of rockets banged away in the clear blue sky, and the evening terminated hilariously. There was indeed plenty of cause for rejoicing: Buenos Ayres had passed through the peril of a neck-or-nothing encounter with her most dreaded foe, and had come out undeniably victorious. I cannot, however, help thinking that surprise was mingled with delight. The sober mind of Europe can hardly appreciate the wild and explosive spirit which headed the official account of the battle as follows:—'*Viva la Patria! Viva Buenos Aires vencedora sobre el caudillaje! Viva el valiente exercito de Buenos Aires, cubierto de gloria en los campos de Cañada Rica! Viva el jòven y patriota General Mitre! Viva el gobierno!*' 'Long live our country! Long live Buenos Ayres, victorious over the provincial tyrants! Long live the brave army of Buenos Ayres, covered with glory in the plains of Cañada Rica! Long live the young patriot, General Mitre! Long live the government!'

The immediate crisis was over, but the campaign

was not at an end. Colonel Gelly, the war minister, aided by the valiant editor of the *Tribuna*, went out to collect the scattered cavalry, and it was supposed that their task would be greatly facilitated by the fact of Urquiza's men having been once beaten. Meanwhile we enjoyed comparative repose, and had some capital cricket-matches in spite of the sun. My expedition to Paraguay having been abandoned for the present, I turned my attention once more to Brazil; and, considering that I had seen very little of that lovely part of the world, I determined to take advantage of the season, and see all that I could in the next two months among the Organ Mountains.

CHAPTER X.

RETURN TO BRAZIL.

START IN THE 'MERSEY'—STRANGE COLOUR IN THE WATER—LAND-BIRDS BLOWN OFF SHORE IN A GALE—HEAVY SEA—ENGINEERS FROM PARAGUAY—A MAN BURIED AT SEA—ENTRANCE TO RIO —WANT OF HOTELS—JENNY THE MONKEY—OFF FOR PETRO-POLIS—MAUÀ RAILWAY—BEAUTIFUL ROAD—CLIMATE AND ELEVATION OF BRAZIL—HISTORICAL SKETCH—HUGUENOTS AT RIO JANEIRO—THE HOUSE OF BRAGANZA—DOM PEDRO I.—CON-STITUTIONAL EMPEROR—DOM PEDRO II.—THE SLAVE-LABOUR QUESTION—ATTEMPTS TO IMPORT COLONISTS FROM EUROPE—CONDITION OF SLAVES.

ON the 27th of September the 'Mersey' dropped down the river, and anchored at Montevideo early in the next morning. According to regulations we waited there for two days; and at noon on the 30th Captain Curlewis with his usual punctuality gave the order to go a-head. The weather was delightful, and we started with as good a prospect of a pleasant voyage as could be expected on that uncertain coast.

Early in the morning of October the 1st we passed through two very large patches of reddish-brown water, which contrasted strangely with all around it. No one on board had ever seen such a thing before on that part of the coast, and the captain stopped the ship to see if, by any possibility, we were going over an unknown shoal. The lead, however, gave twenty fathoms water, so we went on our way wondering what cause could have so completely discoloured several miles of sea.* Some one suggested that it might be a set of fresh water on the surface, but on hauling up a bucketful we found not the least diminution of the usual saltness. Whether it had anything to do with the weather I cannot say, but on the following morning all pleasant symptoms had departed. A heavy gale was blowing right a-head, and a furious sea was flying in sheets of spray and water from one end of the ship to the other; the deck was so flooded that the scuppers could not carry off the water, and the engines were eased to prevent her driving through it too heavily. The cape pigeons and the stormy petrels screamed and whirled in our wake, caring nothing for the savage blast as they steadily fulfilled their destiny, and swept monotonously over the foaming crests.

Next day two shore-birds came on board, having been blown away by the fury of the gale, and seeming very glad to find something which they could hold on by. One was a lovely little creature, pure crimson in colour, and the other was a kind of butcher-bird, which is the most constant and sociable frequenter of the

* They were probably shoals of minute confervæ, like those observed by Mr. Darwin higher up on the coast of Brazil.—*Voyage of the 'Beagle,'* p. 14.

Buenos Ayrean gardens: it is called in Spanish '*bien te veo*,' or 'I see you well,' from a cry resembling those words. Their favourite position was in one of the ship's boats, and when disturbed they made very short flights, taking good care to keep close to the ship. They kept company with us all day and all the next night, soon after which they were captured by the sailors, and added to the menagerie which Jack generally likes to have in the forecastle. I dearly love stormy weather at sea, and for two days I had a good opportunity of enjoying myself in that way. It was a grand sight to watch the long hull of the 'Mersey' dipping down the side of a huge wave, and then rising with a joyous shake of the head, which sent sheets of spray and broken water flying sometimes over the foreyard. The possession of a sound stomach makes one rather unfeeling under these circumstances towards the sufferings of weaker brethren; and I am conscious of having upon this occasion behaved in a way to justify the criticism, though the cause may perhaps be held to justify me in return. The doctor and I were smoking a pipe in the driest place we could find under shelter of the bulwark, when an unlucky Brazilian staggered past us, and, making for the first door he could see, prepared to pour his sorrows into the bath-room! There was no time for gentle remonstrance, but we made a rush at him with loud shouts, accompanied by violent shaking and vituperation. The sorrow-stricken look of the poor wretch almost made me regret the harshness; but what else could we do?

The ship behaved nobly through the gale, though I was obliged to stop the continuance of my journal for a couple of days. Sitting and standing were feats of skill, but I would have defied Blondin himself to write a letter in the ridiculous positions occasionally assumed by the chairs and tables of the cabin. Though I could thoroughly enjoy the weather in the daytime, yet the long night passed in one's berth during a gale of wind is hardly so pleasant as on shore: the combination of groaning, roaring, shaking, bumping, rattling, and quivering, accompanied by the various noises of pails, plates, chairs, and glasses flying from their proper place, makes sleep almost impossible; and on the third day we all rejoiced to find a glorious sunshine and a gradually subsiding sea.

Among our passengers were three working engineers, on their way home to England after completing a contract for three years with the government of Paraguay; and I learnt a good deal about the state of things in that very out-of-the-way part of the world. President Lopez was doing everything in his power to promote the progress and developement of the country. He had imported a staff of English engineers, who were well paid and well treated; a railway and various public works were progressing favourably. These men had been receiving monthly 16*l.* sterling, with free quarters, and 4*l.* more for provisions. They complained of the climate being fearfully hot for three months in the year, and excessively changeable during part of the southern winter. One of them said he had often been utterly exhausted by excessive heat, and reduced to that state in which Sydney Smith said 'he should like to take off his skin and sit in his bones,' only a few hours after being compelled to warm himself against the side of a boiler. English doctors have also been in request among the Paraguayans; and one of the pleasantest of my fellow-passengers from England was an assistant-surgeon in our army, who, after serving through the Crimean war, had been induced by handsome pay and the prospect of gratifying his sporting propensities to form one of the medical staff of the Paraguayan troops. He was particularly interested in cases of tetanus, or lockjaw, and I understand he has had a great many cases of it to deal with. It is certainly true that for some reason or other this fearful malady is much more common through a great part of South America than in other parts of the world, and often results from the most trifling wounds. A member of the club at Buenos Ayres died of it after running a small splinter of a skittle-ball under his nail. I am informed that one of my medical friends in that city has lately succeeded in curing two cases by constant use of chloroform—lasting in one instance for, I think, eight days.

A quarrel with President Lopez had been the cause

of suspending diplomatic relations with the British government; but individual Englishmen seem to have lived pretty comfortably in Paraguay. On his death, which happened quite recently, his son General Lopez began to reign in his stead; and it is supposed that the interests of Englishmen will be favoured by the circumstance that the honours of the presidential throne are shared by an amiably-disposed Englishwoman. The diplomatic quarrel has been adjusted, and it is said that there is very much that is curious and beautiful in Paraguay; but at the same time I must be permitted to doubt the fulfillment of the late Mr. Mansfield's fanciful idea, that it would be the chosen and the choicest home of the migratory Anglo-Saxon.

But I am forgetting the good ship 'Mersey.' A hopeless invalid from H.M.S. 'Curaçoa' died in the middle of the voyage and was buried at sunset. The wind was abeam, and the ship rolling in the swell left by the gale as we came on deck to attend at the ceremony. The poor fellow's body was laid upon a narrow sloping plank, and the captain read the service as we stood bare-headed in the breeze. When he came to the words, 'We therefore commit his body to the deep,' and a heavy plunging sound told that the sailor's corpse was being swallowed by the waves which he had so long triumphed over, I thought it the most affecting sight that I had ever witnessed: it was one that could never be forgotten.

The next day was lovely, but in spite of steam we could not make up the time lost during the gale. Late in the evening we approached the lighthouse island near Rio Janeiro, but were obliged to anchor for the night in a heavy swell outside the entrance to the harbour. Early in the morning of the 6th I came on deck to watch once more the exciting operation of running through the swell, as it broke in walls and towers of foam upon the granite rocks which guard the entrance to the most famous harbour in the world.

As soon as we had got through the usual formalities with the officials, I went ashore with the captain, and landed among the usual picturesque combination of fish and fruit, heaps of bananas, and crowds of the gaudiest negro women. A powerful darkie whipped up my portmanteau as lightly as if it had been a pocket-book, and we marched away for the Rua Direita. In the only two decent hotels I found there was not a room to be got till the next day, when the English steamer was to sail, and I received another proof that the busy crowded city of Rio Janeiro, with its 400,000 inhabitants, is worse off in the matter of hotel accommodation than any place with which I am acquainted. The Emperor is doing wonders in the way of roads and railways, and a thriving English company has taken in hand the drainage and purification of his capital; but there is scarcely a tolerable place for a traveller to lay his head in, and, considering the wealth and importance of the city, I should think it must be difficult anywhere to find a better opportunity for starting a model hotel on a really large and handsome scale. On the second day I thought myself fortunate in getting a very small room at M'Dowell's, which was approached by a narrow passage through a perfect chaos of boxes and packing-cases, among which the only redeeming feature was a charmingly sociable little monkey, whose grand delight was to be half-suffocated by tobacco-smoke. I always stopped to talk to poor Jenny, and at the mere sight of a cigar she used to curl herself up in an attitude of delight, and almost entreat me to puff the whole smoke into her face. Peace be with Jenny! But I could hardly have imagined anything so bad as the hotel system at Rio, and I shall congratulate any speculator who may take advantage of my hint. He will probably make his fortune before long, and I might find respectable accommodation if I go there again. Rio is about the most expensive place I ever saw. The shopkeepers pay almost fabulous rents in the principal streets, and of course their customers are charged accordingly.

Here I found my friend Mr. Malet, the attaché to the British Legation, by whom I was introduced to Mr. Baillie, the Secretary of Legation. The city was abominably hot already, and I was anxious to be off to the hills; so I gladly accompanied them to Petropolis, as soon as they had concluded their business for the homeward mail. Our traps were carried down to the pier by negroes for a few dumps—the elegant name for a penny in Brazil — and at one o'clock we started in a small steamer to cross the lovely bay. The heat was intense, but as the deck was covered with an awning, we fared very well. We passed the dead body of a man floating on the surface, but no one seemed to care who he was or how long he might have been there. He was evidently, however, beyond the possibility of human aid.

Our course was right across the bay in a nearly northerly direction, and towards the end of it we passed among a number of curious little rocky islands, some of which seemed nothing but a collection of huge loose boulders, like the *blocs perchés* of the ancient glacier districts of Europe. At first it was difficult to imagine how they got there, surrounded, as they were, with deep clear water, and poised so delicately, that, to all appearance, they could be upset by the slightest touch. The truth, however, I believe to be that, the granite being very coarse-grained and liable to destruction, huge blocks, at first only fissured by cracks, have been weathered down to the appearance of boulders. Wherever the islands were large enough to have accumulated a little soil of their own, they were ornamented with palms and cactus in abundance.

Two hours of pretty fast steaming carried us nearly

twenty miles, at the end of which we ranged alongside a small pier, within fifty yards of the railway carriages that were waiting to take us to the foot of the Organ Mountains. The whole fare for the journey to Petropolis, a matter of more than five hours, was only eight *milreis*, or about seventeen English shillings, including the steamboat across the bay, the railway for about twelve miles, and carriages for about two hours and a half up the steep zig-zags of the mountains. The guards and porters were chiefly negroes, and when one of them called out 'All right!' in good English, we rattled away for about half an hour; this brought us to the foot of the Serra, towering overhead in lofty summits, the upper part of which was veiled in dark clouds that promised us a damp reception. We were soon transferred to small carriages, built low to diminish the chances of an upset; and, to prevent the passengers from picking and choosing among the vehicles, each man's ticket consigned him to a particular place. The carriages were each drawn by four mules, almost the universal propelling power in Brazil, and after a little plunging and kicking we soon started up the winding road at a jogging pace, which in spite of the steepness was seldom allowed to reduce itself to a walk. Every bend revealed some new beauty in the scenery; magnificent trees were above us and below, and between their huge trunks and marvellously green foliage we enjoyed infinitely various views of the harbour of Rio, which I had never half appreciated till the increased elevation began to give me a worthy idea of its beauty and extent. The vegetation astonished me, and I did not know which to admire most, the stately trees with their dark wide-spreading branches, the graceful festoons and clusters of palms and bamboos, or the masses of ferns, lycopodiums, and brilliant flowers which clustered round their feet, and drooped over the road. All were new to me in their wild state, but every moment showed me some fern or flower in which I recognised an old hot-house friend. There was a wonderful charm in climbing up a sort of St. Gotthard pass with such gorgeous fringes instead of barren rocks.

About half-way up we stopped for five minutes at a small roadside inn, to rest the mules, and let the passengers enjoy a cup of coffee or a glass of caña. Then we climbed on again, higher and higher, and soon got into the cloud which cooled the air with a light drizzling mist. Just before we entered it, we had a very remarkable view: under the black canopy which hung over our heads like a pall, we looked down across slope after slope of mountain and forest, all glowing in brilliant sunshine, till the eye rested on the broad silvery sheet of the harbour 2,000 feet below, and the long line of purple mountains stretching out to the Atlantic beyond it. Truly a magnificent contrast of light and shade! As we reached the top of the Serra, the mist settled into a steady rain; but the mules were whipped into a lively gallop, and a few more miles over a pretty level road brought us to Petropolis, where I was deposited at the door of a clean-looking inn called the Hotel Oriental, which I intended to make my head-quarters for some weeks.

Before entering into a more minute description of the lovely district in which it was my good fortune to spend some time, I wish to make a few general remarks on Brazil which may perhaps afford some information to those who have not visited it, and which may assist them in understanding why it may be considered a particularly delightful region to a traveller.

One of the most interesting works on the subject is the joint production of Messrs. Kidder and Fletcher, two American missionaries who have spent many years in Brazil, and who have given the results of their experience in a book which is as agreeable as it is instructive.* To them I am indebted for many observations which the shortness of my visit and the limited extent of my Brazilian excursions rendered it impossible that I should make for myself. One of these writers speaks as follows:—

'Those whose Tropical experience has been in the East Indies or on the West Coast of Africa can have no

* *Brazil and the Brazilians*, by Rev. D. P. Kidder, D.D., and Rev. J. C. Fletcher, Philadelphia, 1857.

just conception of the delightful climate of the greater part of Brazil. It would seem as if Providence had designed this land for the residence of a great nation. Nature has heaped up her bounties of every description: cool breezes, lofty mountains, vast rivers, and plentiful pluvial irrigation, are treasures far surpassing the sparkling gems and rich minerals which abound within the borders of this extended territory. No burning sirocco wafts over this fair land to wither and desolate it, and no vast desert, as in Africa, separates its fertile provinces. That awful scourge, the earthquake—which causes strong men to become weak as infants, and which is constantly devastating the cities of Spanish America—disturbs no dweller in this empire. While in a large part of Mexico, and also on the western coast of South America—from Copiapo to the fifth degree of south latitude—rain has never been known to fall, Brazil is refreshed by copious showers, and is endowed with broad flowing rivers, cataracts, and sparkling streams. The Amazon—or, as the aborigines term it, Parà, "the father of waters"—with his mighty branches, irrigates a surface equal to two-thirds of Europe; and the San Francisco, the Parahiba do Sul, the vast affluents of the La Plata, under the names of Paranà, Paraguay, Cuiba, Parahiba, and a hundred other streams of lesser note, moisten the fertile soil and bear their tributes to the ocean through the southern portions of the empire. Let any one glance at the map of Brazil, and he will instantly be convinced that this land is designed by nature for the sustenance of millions.'

This moisture and fertility is supposed to be chiefly caused by the trade-winds which sweep across the Atlantic from the north-east and south-east, charged with vapour that condenses against the lofty sides and rarefied temperature of the Andes, to descend again to the ocean in the shape of mighty rivers.

The author from whom I have already quoted remarks that—'No other tropical country is so generally elevated as Brazil. Though there are no very lofty mountains except upon its extreme western border, yet the whole empire has an average elevation of *more than seven hundred feet* above the level of the sea. This great elevation and those strong trade-winds combine to produce a climate much cooler and more healthful than that of the corresponding latitudes of Africa and Southern Asia. The traveller, the naturalist, the merchant and the missionary, do not have their first months of pleasure or usefulness thrown away, or their constitutions impaired, by acclimatising fevers.

'The mean temperature of Brazil—which extends from nearly the 5th degree of north latitude to the 33rd degree of south latitude—is from 81° to 88° Fahrenheit according to different seasons of the year. At Rio de Janeiro, according to Dr. Dundas, the mean temperature for thirty years was 73°. In December (which corresponds to June in the northern hemisphere), maximum,

89½°; minimum, 70°; mean, 79°. In July (the coldest month), maximum, 79°; minimum, 66°; mean, 73½°. I can add, from my own observations for several years, that I never saw 90° attained in the summer time, and the lowest in the winter (June, July, and August), was 60°, and this was early in the morning.'

These figures are, no doubt, correct in the main; but when I passed through Rio, in January 1862, the thermometer stood at 98°; and a few days later, when close to Bahia, the water which was brought up from the sea for the morning's bath showed a temperature of 80°, according to the statement of the chief engineer. The highest of these points, however, is not much greater than may occasionally be found on a very hot day in the south of Europe: what the European feels most in a tropical climate is the steady continuance of the heat, day and night, for weeks and months together. Places near the coast get the benefit of the afternoon sea-breeze, which is one of nature's most beautiful and welcome instruments of compensation. The air on land becomes so heated by the morning and mid-day hours of an almost vertical sun, that it rises rapidly, and the cooler air rushing from the sea to supply its place makes a breeze that brings fresh life and animation to exhausted nature.

Over a great part of the interior of the country, the very considerable elevation of the land which has been mentioned already has a powerful effect in moderating the intensity of the heat, and the hill-climate of 2,000 or 3,000 feet above the sea is generally delightful, though it must be admitted that the pleasure of out-door amusements is too often interfered with by excessive rains.

Under these circumstances, it is natural that the highlands of Brazil should present unrivalled attractions to a visitor. In a few hours he can transport himself from the city of Rio Janeiro to a region where mountains of fantastic shape, with magnificent forests, rapid rivers, and the infinitely beautiful forms and colours of tropical vegetation combine into scenes of unimagined beauty, under a climate not too hot for their enjoyment.

History-writing certainly forms no part of my present intention; but I hardly like to say anything of so interesting a country as Brazil without alluding briefly to the circumstances which have led to a far greater political prosperity than that of other South American States, and mentioning a few curious matters connected with the olden time.

Brazil may be said to have been born in disputes and grown into tranquillity. To begin with, there was a grand dispute in the year 1500 between Spain and Portugal, each of whom claimed possession of the land by right of discovery. It so happened that a Spanish and a Portuguese explorer had landed on different parts of the coast within less than three months of each other, and the latter had fixed upon Vera Cruz for the name of the country. The Pope had the cutting or untying of this knot, and decided in favour of Portugal.

The next disagreement was about the name of the country. When some of the earliest ships returned to Europe, bringing home as the most valuable part of their cargo the red dye-wood which before the discovery of America had been called brasil-wood, on account of its resemblance to *brasas* or coals of fire, the land whence the new supplies came in such great abundance was termed the 'land of the brasil-wood.'* This appellation was shortened to Brasil, or Brazil, and completely displaced the name of Vera Cruz. The change, however, was not received unanimously. According to Dr. Kidder, 'One of the *reverendissimos* declared that it was through the express interposition of the devil that such a choice and lovely land should be called Brazil, instead of the pious cognomen given to it by Cabral. Another, a devoted Jesuit, poured forth a jeremiad on the subject, concluding with emphatically stating what a shame it was that the cupidity of man by unworthy traffic should change the wood of the cross, red with the

* I happened lately to find the following passage in Evelyn's Diary showing that the Dutch made criminals useful: 'Here (at Amsterdam) we went to see the Rasp-house, where the lusty knaves are compelled to worke, and the rasping of Brasill and Logwood is very hard labour.'

real blood of Christ, for that of another wood which resembled it only in colour!'

France next tried to establish herself on the new continent. Rio Janeiro, then called San Sebastian, was chosen in 1555 for the experiment of forming a colony, which, under the support and patronage of the famous Admiral Coligny, was to form a home for the persecuted Huguenots. Three vessels started under the command of Villegagnon; and on arriving at Rio Janeiro, the colonists were so well received by the native tribes, who had already begun to detest the Portuguese, that the French began to believe that the continent would be their own, and they called it La France Antarctique.

This promising scheme was brought to an end by the treachery of the leader, and France lost a good chance of important possessions in the South. Thenceforth Portugal held her own against all comers, and governed the country by viceroys, upon a system of extreme political, commercial, and religious intolerance. Spain governed her colonies in the same way, both nations looking upon these invaluable possessions as merely mines wherein to dig wealth for the mother countries, and taking every precaution to prevent the colonies from raising or benefiting themselves. But the day of reckoning came; and a few years of struggling deprived Spain and Portugal of the whole continent of South America.

Brazil differs from all the other colonies in the immense advantage of having established a constitutional empire. The independence of the country virtually dates from September 1822; Dom Pedro I. was soon afterwards crowned as 'Constitutional Emperor and Perpetual Defender of Brazil,' and an assembly of delegates was convoked from the provinces to draw up a constitution. Ultimately the completion of this task was entrusted to a commission of ten, who drew up an admirable constitution, which was sworn to by the Emperor, March 25, 1824, and which has ever since been maintained to the great benefit and advancement of Brazil in peace and civilisation.

The empire has been a great success, and deservedly so; for the government being monarchical, hereditary, constitutional, and representative, combines all the elements which experience has shown to be most conducive to the welfare of a state. Brazil has been constantly progressing, while the Spanish American colonies which exchanged the yoke of the old country for republican government have been continually distracted and torn to pieces by the intrigues of politicians, and the violence of military adventurers. Some of them are no doubt improving, and much may be hoped for the future of Chili and La Plata, but many valuable years have been lost.

Under a good system of government, with an honest man at the head of it, no one need be surprised at finding that the peace-loving people of Brazil have made immense advances in all the elements of material prosperity. Europeans generally complain that the Brazilian ideas of religion and morality do not altogether agree with their own standard; but we must remember that Brazil is almost entirely between the tropics; and I fancy that, in spite of the opinion of enthusiasts to the contrary, the world will some day be compelled to acknowledge that religion and morality are considerably tempered by geographical position.

Dom Pedro I., the darling of the people, proved at length a little too independent for them. In 1831 they called upon him, in a manner that was something more than pressing, to dismiss the ministry which had just been appointed, and to reinstate that which had been disgraced. Dom Pedro, however constitutional he may have been, did not forget that he was also an Emperor, and very gallantly exclaimed, 'I will do everything for the people, but nothing by the people.' He who nearly ten years earlier had given to the people of Brazil their favourite watchword of 'Independence or Death!' feeling himself in the right, now declared that he would suffer death rather than submit to the dictation of the mob. Though he was determined not to yield to their demands, he was far from desiring bloodshed; whatever may have been his faults, he acted at the critical moment like an honest gentleman, and abdicated in favour of his son, rather than sacrifice his own convictions.

Dom Pedro II., the present Emperor, succeeded to the throne, and a long period of peace with foreign nations has been accompanied by great prosperity and continual progress. The Emperor himself is a man of very high attainments, and gives every encouragement to the advancement of science and art. He is a distinguished historian and linguist, and holds wide and liberal views for developing the wealth and importance of his vast country. English, French, and German engineers have been carrying the skill and experience of Europe across the Atlantic; admirable roads, railways, and bridges testify to their success, and are yearly adding to the commercial progress of the empire.

The grand difficulty of Brazil is the labour question. In abandoning the slave trade out of deference to the prejudices of Europe, the Brazilians deprived themselves of their usual supply, and they have found it difficult to remedy the deficiency. I was told on very good authority that the rich coffee proprietors of the southern, and consequently cooler, parts of the country, are constantly buying up at high prices slaves who have been employed in the equatorial districts, where it is much more difficult for white men to do any hard work. The withdrawal of slaves from the regions where they are most necessary, and where it is most difficult to find substitutes for them, must of course produce a very serious derangement and deficiency in the labour-market. It is notorious that free blacks will not do more than just enough to earn a bare subsistence for themselves; and white men cannot do the work of sugar estates. In the more temperate districts Europeans can and do thrive pretty well, but the difficulty of procuring land deters the great mass of emigrating whites from trying their fortunes in Brazil. The government has tried many colonies of Swiss and German labourers with very indifferent success; the best of the land is in the possession of large owners who will not part with it, and there is a great tendency to deteriorate among white men, when they are engaged in the same pursuits with slaves. They learn fresh vices in addition to their own, and are too apt to degenerate into the condition of their companions; to become, in fact, nothing but white slaves. In some cases the colonising experiment seems to have been carried out with good effect upon a new system, the credit of which is attributed by Kidder and Fletcher to the intelligent mind of Sr. Vergueiro of Ybecaba.

He conducts his immense coffee estates by means of free labour, and has brought Swiss and Germans to displace the blacks. His plan, according to their authority, is either to pay the emigrant's passage money beforehand, the emigrant agreeing to repay it afterwards, or to let each man pay for himself. On arriving in Brazil, the colonists are conveyed to the plantations at the cost of the proprietor, who furnishes each head of a family with a house and so many thousand coffee-trees, according to the size of the family, and he agrees to supply all with provisions and clothing at wholesale prices. The expenses and profits of the plantation are shared equally between the master on one side, and the labourers on the other. Each man has, therefore, a direct interest in the success of his labours, and these gentlemen found the colony in a very thriving and happy state, some of the colonists having already in five years gained from 5,000 to 7,000 *milreis*, or rather more than from 500*l.* to 700*l.* sterling. This is a model estate, and if such a system is widely extended in Brazil, there may be an ample field for some of the superfluous labour of Europe. The plan appears to be as satisfactory to the master as to the men, and in all probability slavery will gradually die out in the cooler parts of the empire. It remains to be seen, however, if free labour can take the place of African slaves in the hottest work of the Amazonian regions.

As far as the slaves themselves are concerned, few men could visit Brazil without being convinced that in all matters of material comfort they are, generally speaking, better off than the lower orders of agricultural labourers in Europe. No one can look for a moment at a party of them without seeing that they have no cares: they are always merry and laughing, whether bustling about the streets as porters, or trying to persuade you to patronise their boat. They have great facilities for making money for themselves, and purchasing their freedom if they desire it, and the great ambition of a liberated negro is to have slaves of his own. From all I could hear and see, they are generally very well treated in their working days, and when they get old or feeble they are not tormented by the fear of the workhouse. An English gentleman of large experience assured me that not only were the slaves in Brazil in every way, morally and physically, much better off than the free blacks of the West Indies; but that many of those who had actually bought their freedom, and gone to Africa, were so disgusted with the savagery of their native land, that they came back to Brazil of their own accord to offer themselves again for the service of their old masters.

Let not my reader imagine that I am going to drag him into a discussion about the great question of slavery. Nowadays it is the fashion for almost every one who has not seen 'the institution' at work upon its own soil, to pour out the strongest language at his command in wholesale condemnation of slavery, and all connected with it; but it is equally true that almost every one who has ever visited a slave country has felt himself compelled to hold the contrary opinion. I have no intention to dogmatise about such a knotty point; but I may venture to remark that we must judge all things by comparison. Most people would agree with poor Sambo that it is much better to be compelled to carry coffee in Rio Janeiro than to assist at a custom of the throat-cutting King of Dahomey. He has a strong idea that a live donkey is better than a dead lion.

CHAPTER XI.

SCENERY OF THE ORGAN MOUNTAINS.

PETROPOLIS — HEAD-QUARTERS WITH THE TURK — A BRAZILIAN GARDEN—THE PRESIDENCIA—FERNS AND LYCOPODIA—BAMBOOS, ORCHIDS, PALMS, AND BANANAS — BURNING FORESTS — BIRDS AND BUTTERFLIES — CLIMBING ANTS — THE FALLS OF ITAMARITY — RAIN — FROGS AND TOADS — FIREFLIES — THE ALTO DO IMPERADOR — MOUNTAINS AGAIN — BEWARE OF INSECTS — SNAKES — A SEVERE REMEDY — CARAPATOS AND JIGGERS — YANKEE EXPERIENCE.

PETROPOLIS is one of the most successful results of foreign emigration to Brazil, and a comparatively flourishing town now occupies the place of a miserable little village called Corrego Secco. Don Pedro I. obtained all the land in the neighbourhood, with the view of establishing a German colony there, and the present Emperor has carried out his father's scheme. Being only six hours' journey from Rio, and situated in a lovely position among the Organ Mountains, Petropolis had very great advantages. The Emperor has built a beautiful palace there, to retire to in the hot season, and most of the foreign ministers and fashionable Brazilians are very glad to avail themselves of such a delightful situation; the town is studded with good houses, and there is employment for tradesmen and artisans of all countries and of all sorts.

The town is about 2,500 feet above the level of the sea, and is completely embosomed among mountains, which are covered with luxuriant forest, except where the colonists have made way for their patches of maize. From the centre of the town numberless roads struggle away among the mountains in all directions, dotted with houses, and cottages, and gardens, till the verge of cultivation is reached, and the paths lose themselves in impenetrable forests. One thing which I have no doubt is very conducive to the salubrity of Petropolis is a stream of running water, which has been diverted into several channels so as to pass through the principal thoroughfares. A road is carried along both sides of it, crossing it at proper intervals, over excellent bridges for carriages; besides which, others are provided for foot-passengers only. There is a hospital, and schools which are doing good service for the rising generation of Petropolitans; some very fair cafés and billiard-rooms are ready for the delectation of idlers; and Petropolis altogether may be, in some respects, considered as a combination of happy valleys.

The Hotel Oriental, my particular head-quarters, was an establishment both peculiar and polyglot. The landlord was an elderly Turk, named Said Ali, who, having accompanied a distinguished nobleman about the world in the capacity of valet, had feathered his nest thereby, and then settled down as proprietor of the hotel. He was, and I hope is still, a right good fellow. I certainly did not understand the languages of the shining Orient, and my knowledge of Portuguese was, to say the least, imperfect; so I liked him all the better when I found we could get on together in French, which was tacitly agreed upon as our corresponding medium. The only waiter was a Portuguese—quiet, and by no means a genius; but possessed of inexhaustible good-humour, and a partial knowledge of the French tongue. The chambermaid was a bare-legged daughter of Deutschland, great at scrubbing, and a most persevering enemy of the dirt and insects which are too commonly the pest of tropical countries. The fourth and last element in the household was the 'boots;' a young negro of unprepossessing exterior, but very amiable disposition, who was always ready to make himself useful upon the slightest provocation. I had been told that the Turk rather objected than otherwise to the incursions of visitors, because he felt bound to exert himself in the department of cookery; but that he felt it was his 'kismet' to keep an hotel, and he kept it accordingly. Whether his taking a personal fancy to me, or the paucity of visitors at that season of the year, made the endurance of his kismet more tolerable than usual, I know not; all I can say is, that everything was done for me in a manner that ought to satisfy all but the most unreasonable of men. If I got up earlier than usual in the morning, I was sure to find Said Ali smoking his cigar, and carefully pounding a beefsteak to the maximum of tenderness, or skilfully manipulating a fowl which had just been decapitated by the attendant 'boots.' His cooking was admirable; and this circumstance, added to pretty good powers of digestion, enabled me at all times, and in the hottest weather, to enjoy everything he put before me, and to leave the house after a stay of several weeks without having had a single hour of any kind of bodily discomfort. I had a perfectly clean bedroom, with new furniture; and close by me was a very pretty public sitting-room, with a pianoforte for those who understood the mysteries of that instrument; and though I was for the greater part of the time the sole guest in the house, every Saturday brought a few who, exhausted with the heat and bustle of business at Rio, came up to enjoy their Sunday among the cooler beauties of Petropolis.

At the back of the house was a small garden, with a profusion of the lovely flowers of the country mixed with others of a hardier race, most conspicuous among which were the giant orange and red Gladioli which are so popular in England, and which, whatever may have been their original *habitat*, appear to arrive at unusual perfection in the hill-gardens of Brazil. Close behind this rose up a hill, the greater part of which was still covered with noble trees, feathering palms, rich clusters of bamboos festooning into natural bowers, and tree-ferns in all the beauty of their bright green fronds, 7 or 8 feet long. Underneath was a mass of tangled ferns, creepers, and lycopodiums—all new to the European, except those which he might have known in hothouses at home, and so beautiful in their variety of form and colour, that when I took my first morning climb up a zigzag path among them to a point which overlooked the chief part of the town and the countless hills of equal beauty around me, I almost felt glad that my solitude prevented the disturbance of a charm which was increased by silence.

After breakfast came my friend Mr. Malet, from the British Legation, which he was occupying during the absence of Mr. Christie, the minister, and away we went for a walk, armed with the conventional umbrella, which is almost indispensable in a country where it may be at any time wanted as a defence against excessive sun or rain. We followed one of the winding valleys for a little while, and then took a branch road leading rather steeply up among the hills. The view increased in beauty and extent as every moment's ascent revealed some new summit, delicately blue with distance, and contrasting exquisitely with the rich colouring of the nearer hills, which were separated from us by deep glens of the forest stretching below towards Petropolis.

A turn in the road brought us to a large house called the Presidencia, which, I believe, was for some time kept by an Englishman, and used as a sanatorium. Certainly it would not be easy to find a better situation for one. The view from it was remarkable, even among the host of beautiful objects round Petropolis; the great peculiarity of it being that the wooded hills on both sides, fringed with palms and forest giants standing out against the brilliant sky, approached each other very nearly, and were only separated by a deep ravine which became purple in the middle distance, while far above it rose up range after range bathed with a glorious light, in which at last they seemed to lose themselves. About noon the heat was very considerable, in spite of our elevation of about 3,000 feet above the sea; and in an attempt to sketch the scene under the shadow of our umbrellas, we found that the colours dried almost as fast as we could put them on the paper. In the course of the ramble I began a collection of ferns and lycopodiums, which were continually delighting my eyes and arresting my progress.

One of my chief objects in going to Brazil, was to see the tropical ferns in their wild state, and I never can forget the intense enjoyment of realising my wish. I had taken with me a large stock of botanical paper, and made additions to my collection in every expedition round Petropolis and other districts of the Organ Mountains. Sometimes I came home laden with a bundle of them large enough to make me look something like Jack-in-the-Green, on the 1st of May. The natives could not understand such extraordinary conduct, and the honest Turk looked on with that placid bewilderment which prompted one of his countrymen to ask why on earth Englishmen took the trouble to play at cricket, instead of making somebody else do it for them! It was a constant source of amusement to me; but unfortunately I found that the greater part of my treasures were much too large for botanical paper, and I was obliged to confine myself to the smaller species, or look for very small specimens of the larger kinds. The tree-ferns, when not more than 10 or 12 feet high, are amongst the most lovely creations of the vegetable world: standing under one of them is like being covered by a huge umbrella, consisting of drooping fronds, about 6 or 8 feet in length, of the most exquisite green that can be conceived, and moulded into lace-like forms by the delicate hand of nature. Many of them appeared to be 30 feet high; but I thought that the great length of stem took something off from the beauty of their proportions. An infinite variety of smaller species ornamented the ground, and seemed to fill up every corner that was not already occupied by some more powerful vegetable brother. Great clusters of the beautiful silver-fern were among the most common by the roadside, and nearer the streams were frequent masses of a fern which in size and general appearance resembled our common bracken, or *Pteris aquilina*, but whose fronds proved to be divided more like the *Osmunda regalis*. There were several *Osmundaceæ* of remarkably graceful form, and others grew into such tangled masses of branching fronds, that none but a fern-lover would have distinguished them from the more ordinary shrubs as he passed on his way.

Vast bowers were formed by the festooning bamboos; and winding about their feet, or drooping over a bank, were creepers of various colours, chief among which were the long-petaled scarlet passion-flower, and a magnificent ipomœa. Now and then came a tall fuschia, 20 or 30 feet high, contrasting its crimson blossoms against the bright green background of bamboos; and again, a more than usually moist place was pink with hundreds of begonias. High above rose the rustling palms, and the hardwood monarchs of the forest spread their dark green boughs across the sky to shade the many-coloured orchids which clustered about their stems or hung from their branches. Such were a few of the beauties upon which I feasted my eyes among the mountains of Petropolis.

I was very glad to find that the profusion of flowers with which nature had blessed the country had not the too common effect of making the people neglect them. The better houses were for the most part ornamented with pretty gardens, the hedges of which were made of pink and white cluster-roses, so thick with blossom that it was difficult to see the leaves. The gardens of the Emperor's palace and the chateau of the Baron Mauà were in a blaze of beauty; and even in the outskirts of the town many of the poor German cottages were surrounded with roses as well as bananas. I have seen the pigs fattening themselves into a most desirable rotundity upon wreaths and clusters that would have been invaluable in a drawing-room. The orchids and air-plants are brought by negroes from the forests, and some of the inhabitants have beautiful collections of them. The rarer kinds are, however, very expensive, and the chief gardener in the place did not scruple to ask from *5l.* to *10l.* sterling for a single plant.

It was a cruel sight to see the process of destroying these lovely forests for the purpose of cultivating the land. Sometimes in our rides or walks we were warned by clouds of blinding smoke that we were approaching the conflagration, and a sudden turn round a corner displayed columns of fire destroying all before them, while the German agents of destruction screamed to one another through the clouds of smoke, with voices that could scarcely be heard for the roaring of the blaze and the bursting of canes and bamboos. When the work was over, nothing would remain but the blackened trunks of the largest trees: the lovely palms and bamboos, and all the flowers of the forest, had disappeared to make way for maize. The gaunt trunks remain for a time, grimly mourning over the departed glories, and then they fall, rotten from the effects of the heat and moisture, soon to be converted into vegetable mould. The terror of the lawful inhabitants of the forest — birds and beasts, snakes and insects,— may be imagined, and a regular stampede is the result.

A day or two after my arrival, Mr. Baillie, who was always ready to fill up the intervals of his diplomatic duties by walking, riding, and sketching, accompanied us in a delightful excursion towards the falls of Itamarity. We followed the old Minas road for several miles, and then turning sharply to the right, took a very narrow footpath along the side of one of the tributaries to the Parahiba. The river was bounding merrily over its rocky bed with all the life and animation of a Scotch salmon-stream, but with the indescribable advantage of tropical luxuriance as a setting to the picture. The mountains all around were shining with a perfect glory of warm light, and dark thickly-leaved trees overhung the greater part of our path, shading the masses of trailers and parasites which drooped towards the laughing water, and met the unnumbered ferns and flowers clustering on its banks. Gorgeous butterflies, purple and red, fluttered among the bushes, and the wild rattling note of the *iniambù* resounded through the forests which mixed with the granite rocks above us. Now and then the last wriggle of a tail and a rustling over the dry leaves showed where a snake was running away from the intruders; and once in this exquisite valley an *iguana*, the eatable lizard of Brazil, apparently nearly four feet long, skimmed across our path to hide himself in the jungle.

At last even the narrow path seemed to come to an end, and we scrambled among some huge rocks which stretched out into the middle of the river; hence we had a perfect view of the sunlit mountains in the distance, while we sat under the shade of trees whose overhanging boughs almost embraced across the rushing waters. A scarlet-blossomed creeper hung in wreaths by our side, and the stem of the nearest tree was ornamented with masses of a fern whose long green fronds drooped gracefully for 4 or 5 feet from the hollow in which they grew. I soon filled my vasculum with specimens close round me, and then amused myself by watching the movements of a colony of ants. They must have had reasons of their own for preferring the leaves of a particular tree, the branches which overhung the river; for a continuous stream of them was descending by the long shoot of a trailing plant which led from the upper boughs to the neighbourhood of their own abode, each one laden with a piece of leaf from the tree. They were evidently aware that caution was required to pass this narrow suspension-bridge hanging over the torrent; and travelling as it were upon a single line of rails, they avoided the risk of collision by only moving in one direction.

The fresh ants ascended by another route; and each having cut off as large a piece of leaf as he could carry, began the descent with great caution and apparent safety over this perilous rope.

We were so enchanted with the beauty of this spot, and my companions were so well occupied with sketching, while I amused myself with hunting for ferns and watching the ants, that we did not move till the approach of evening warned us to turn our steps homewards; but a few days later Mr. Malet and I retraced the path, and followed it up to the Falls, in the heart of the Serra da Estrella. The name of Itamarity is said to signify in the Guarani or Indian language, 'the rock which shines;' and the glittering appearance of the rock between the two falls in the engraving, caused by the trickling water, may have originated it. The only way to see the Falls well from below was to force a way through the ferns and bushes which guarded the precipitous side of the river; after which, by a narrow winding track, we climbed to a point where the water emerged from a darkly-shaded retreat in the forest, and took the upper plunge over a wall of granite. Between this and the lower fall, a large and somewhat hollowed shelf in the rock formed a basin in which the water paused for a moment before taking a greater leap into the gulf below. Above the upper fall it was easy, by jumping from stone to stone, to cross the stream, and return to Petropolis by another route.

The weather had been excessively hot; and, shut in as we were by hills and forests, we had felt it more than usually. In the evening, however, a thick mist settled down upon the mountains, and was followed by many hours of heavy rain. The rain in these highlands is more frequent and enduring than down at Rio Janeiro, and it is no uncommon thing to be shut up at Petropolis or Theresopolis for several days together; but it does not appear that any part of Brazil suffers from such continuous wet as that of the rainy season in India. Generally speaking, through all the year round, brilliant sunshine alternates pretty equally with nourishing moisture; still it must be admitted that one of the great drawbacks to travelling in Brazil is the frequently excessive rain. All this luxuriant vegetation must be fed upon something; and though orchids, air-plants, and epiphytes may boast that they can live without earth, it is certain that they imbibe a monstrous quantity of water. In soft dripping weather the country roads become almost impassable, and my favourite resource was to sit still and read Tennyson or Longfellow; but the studies of a novice in Brazil on a wet evening are strangely interrupted by the extraordinary proceedings of frogs and toads of all sorts and sizes, which testify their exuberant joy by the most discordant noises. Croaking is no name for it. Some of the milder and quieter kinds may perhaps be said to croak, but these are soon silenced by another tribe, whose name is Legion, grunting, snorting, and almost shrieking like a railway train at full speed; and when they stop for want of breath, the 'wondrous song' is taken up by larger numbers of other detestable batrachyians, which keep up a frantic revel of rattling and clattering such as I have never heard equalled, except by an intoxicated chorus of May sweeps.

Some of the toads are enormous. In one of my mountain rambles I suddenly spied a very beautiful lycopodium growing in large quantities on a moist bank, and, without looking at my feet, sprang across the path to gather a specimen. I stumbled over something very hard and immoveable, and nearly measured my length in the mud; but I seized the lycopodium; and then turned round to look at the obstacle. It was a monstrous toad, nearly a foot long, with great yellow pits round its spiteful eyes, and as ugly a brute as ever I saw. He did not make the least attempt to move, and seemed to be chuckling over the fact of nearly upsetting a traveller. A friend of mine, however, told me that he had been offered a still larger specimen as a present, which he had declined to accept on the ground of ferocity. He said it was as big as a hat, it opened its mouth like an oyster, barked like a dog, and flew at his legs! A nice pet to keep in a strawberry-bed!

But, if a wet night at Petropolis was not agreeable, who shall describe the glories of a fine one? The balmy breath of nature reposing after her encounter with the sun: the moon rising behind the crest of a palm-crowned hill; the sky blazing with stars more brilliant than in the frigid north, and great Orion saluting the Southern Cross through the ether; the air sparkling with swarms of fireflies, some skimming along a hedge of roses, some shooting downward, and others darting upwards with their intermittent flashing light—the remembrance of the whole is that of a 'thing of beauty,' and a 'joy for ever.' The intermittent light of the fireflies in motion on a dark night has a very peculiar effect: it is often easy to trace the course of one of them in the same direction by the bright flashes which alternate with the few seconds of darkness in which the insect has advanced some distance; and I could not help thinking now and then of the famous question raised by Thomas Aquinas, as to whether an angel who wished to go from one point to another is obliged to pass through the intervening space.

A view which I imagine can hardly be equalled in the whole world, is that from the Alto do Imperador, to which Mr. Baillie escorted me. A walk of about seven miles from Petropolis, among the winding mountain roads, ended with rather a sharp pull up a hill, where the trees so completely overshadowed the way that the effect of the heat was somewhat counteracted. Suddenly, as we turned a corner and reached the summit, the whole scene was before us, never to be forgotten. Right down from our feet stretched endless masses of forest, glowing with the lustre of mid-day sun, and clothing the tops of the pyramidal mountains below us. Beyond these were the long undulating plains between the Serra and the water; and then came an almost complete panorama of the harbour of Rio, with its narrow entrance from the Atlantic, nearly 40 miles from where we stood. A little white speck marked the Fort, and the Sugar Loaf was diminished into a blue molehill. On the right the sharp peak of the Corcovado and the mountains of Tijuca looked down upon the city, now indistinct in the distance; and the long island of Gobernador stretched for miles across the glassy waters of the bay. Memory and imagination filled up the details of the glorious picture. Did I not know that those distant spots upon the surface of the mirror were islands most lovely to behold? Had I not sailed blissfully amongst them, peering into fairy-like retreats among palms, and aloes, and bananas, as the sweet sea-breeze made the water lap against the over-shadowed rocks? Had not the oars skimmed lightly past the groves where—

> 'Slides the bird o'er lustrous woodland, droops the trailer from the crag;
> Droops the heavy-blossomed bower, hangs the heavy-fruited tree —
> Summer isles of Eden lying in dark purple spheres of sea?'

And did I not know that, in spite of all its seeming smoothness, the sea was rolling its long swell through

T. Picken, lith. Day & Son, Lithrs to the Queen

HARBOUR OF RIO JANEIRO FROM THE ALTO DO IMPERADOR.

that gateway from the Atlantic, and bursting against the cactus-covered hills.

A few days later we rode to the Paty d'Alferes, a more distant point among the mountains, where the path, winding steeply up through the forests, was suddenly carried round the side of a precipice to an open place, whence we saw range after range of hills, all purple and gold, rising beyond the sea of forests at our very feet. One side of the path was so precipitous, that the green crests of the trees below were only on a level with our eyes, temptingly displaying the rich flowers of the orchids which hung upon their branches. On the other side was a rising bank leading up to still higher forests, and densely covered with ferns and flowers, among which I found a very beautiful crimson *amaryllis*, and a fern of which I never saw another specimen in Brazil. I saw some enormous fuchsias in the course of that day's ride, one of which could hardly have been less than twenty-five or thirty feet high, and immense quantities of passion-flowers in full blossom. On our way home we were obliged to make our horses push on as fast as they could through the smoke of a blazing forest, which was doomed by civilisation and the wants of man. To judge by our own sensations, I should say that it must be cruelly hot and suffocating work to the men engaged in it, and excessively alarming to the snakes.

Such were our walks and rides about Petropolis. In

every direction some new charm was found, some new and unexpected view was ready for the eye. In bad weather the mountain roads became almost impassable, and we were often forced by stress of mud to confine ourselves to the house or to walk upon the main road, which is macadamised. Generally, however, I contrived to be out for a great part of the day. Half-past six or seven o'clock was the usual hour for dinner, when, thanks to the hospitality of my friends, I was not very often alone. Generally speaking, I got through a little reading and writing in my own room before going to bed, but was never tempted by the coolness of the night air to open my windows to the invasion of insects. I had not forgotten a lesson which I heard some years before from one of my relations who arrived at Rio with his family and three or four English maidservants. He took a house, and consigned the maids to a large room in the upper part of it. Before midnight he was aroused by fearful screams which proceeded from that quarter of the house, and on opening the door of the maids' room he found a scene of horror. With the superstition common in their class, they resolved not to sleep in the dark in a strange place; and as they found the heat very different from what they were accustomed to at home, they went to bed with the windows open. The lighted candles soon attracted all noxious things that fly by night: mosquitos and other enemies of the human race took possession of the room, and stung the poor girls almost into madness, while their pain was raised to terror by the sight of tropical bats and vampires careering about the room. *Hinc illæ lacrymæ.* Their master found them rushing frantically about, and screaming violently, in their nightgowns.

I was very much afraid of snakes in my first rambles, and kept a good look-out if I wandered among the jungle; but I afterwards found that they were not nearly so numerous or so dangerous as my ignorance imagined, and I seldom saw anything but the latter end of a fugitive. The coral-snake had been described to me as poisonous; but the doctor in charge of the hospital at Petropolis assured me that this is not the case, and added that, out of the many accidents coming under his care, the cases of serious snake-bites were comparatively uncommon. He said, however, that a species of rattlesnake—*un serpent qui crêpe*—inflicted a wound which generally proved fatal in half an hour. It is said that some years ago a crotchet-monger asserted that the horrible disease of elephantiasis, so common among the negroes of Rio, could be cured by the bite of a rattlesnake. A patient was discovered who found life such a burden from this disease that he had no objection to a 'kill or cure' remedy. A cage was brought with the snake, and the man's arm was exposed to the bite: the snake seemed rather to shrink from him, but at last delivered his bite in the little finger.

The disease apparently retarded the effect of the venom, but the man died within twenty-four hours.

The enemies most to be dreaded in reality are those which escape notice by reason of their small size. The tick, or *carapato*, and the jigger (a corruption, I suppose, of *chigo*), are plagues indeed. *Carapatos* frequent the low brushwood, but on the first opportunity exchange that habitation for the human skin. Getting into a snug corner, the loathsome beast buries its head under the cuticle, and his body grows fat upon your misery. It is a difficult task to eradicate him; and if the least bit is left behind, it produces a serious sore.

Jiggers appear to be even worse; but fortunately, by taking great care of my feet, I escaped their attacks. They generally insinuate themselves under the toe-nail, or into other parts of the foot, and, burying themselves entirely under the skin, deposit a little sac of eggs in the cavity which they have made. A bad wound is soon formed in hot countries, and it is no uncommon thing for the loss of toes to follow the attack of this minute tormentor. Negroes are peculiarly skilful in the delicate operation of extracting them; and as the Africans have the credit of having originally introduced them into the western world, their experience no doubt is very ancient. They suffer terribly from this cause; and when a banjo-bearing darkie sings

> 'Rose! Rose, coal-black Rose!
> I wish I may be *jiggered* if I do n't love Rose,'

you may depend upon it that he speaks feelingly, and means to invoke a heavy malediction on his feet.

A very amusing Yankee, with whom I afterwards travelled from Rio Janeiro, gave me a graphic and characteristic account of his sufferings in this way.

'By the bye,' said he, 'have you had jiggers?'

'I 'm happy to say I have not,' was my reply.

'Well, I guess I have. One day I felt something itching like fits under my great toe, and I could n't see what on earth was the matter, but I scratched away when I could get a chance. Next day it got a deal worse, and I found that scratching did no good; so I sent for the doctor. "You 've got jiggers," said he, "and bad ones too." So he brought out his knife, and *whittled* away at my toe till there was precious little left but the bone, I can tell you, sir; and that 's a fact.'

They are an abominable nuisance, and I always took particular care not to move with bare feet, if I could avoid doing so.

CHAPTER XII.

VISIT TO THERESOPOLIS.

START FOR THERESOPOLIS—WALLETS AND HOLSTERS—BOOTS AND UMBRELLAS—ALOES, ARAUCARIAS, AND DATURAS—CORREA—GIGANTIC FIG-TREE—MULES AND COFFEE—A MOUNTAIN-STREAM AND FLOWERS—THE CASTOR-OIL TREE—A HORSE BREAKS DOWN—SUMMIT OF THE PASS AMONG THE ORGAN MOUNTAINS—THE SHADE OF THE FOREST—STUCK IN THE MUD—ENGLISH BEER—HOSPITABLE RECEPTION—THE ORGAN PEAKS—THE CABEZA DEL FRAYLE—HEIGHT OF THE ORGANS—'JOLLY HEATH'—GUIDE, PHILOSOPHER, AND FRIEND—ACTING CHARADES—A MOTLEY AUDIENCE—THE RETURN—A ROUGH LUNCHEON—A WET GALLOP BACK TO PETROPOLIS.

AFTER a day or two of very heavy rain, the north wind came one evening to our assistance, and blew away the clouds to sea. I and my friend Mr. Malet had been kindly furnished by Mr. Tupper, of Rio, with a letter of introduction to his wife and family, who were residing at his *fazenda*, or country establishment, at Theresopolis, close to the highest peaks of the Organ Mountains, the distant view of whose curious forms had often struck me with astonishment. We were very anxious to avail ourselves of such a pleasant opportunity of seeing that part of the country, and we thought the change of weather favourable for an immediate start.

The usual way of reaching Theresopolis is by a steamer across the harbour, and then by a somewhat rough road up the mountains. We did not, however, wish to descend to the level of the sea, unless it were absolutely necessary; and having heard of a path by which we could reach our destination in a long day's work, without leaving the mountains and forests, we determined to go by this overland route. The grand difficulty was to find the way, which did not seem to be known to many of the inhabitants, and we had to send eight miles for a man who was warranted to be a good and trustworthy guide. This involved the loss of a day; but on the 16th of October the weather was still finer than the day before, and we were in high spirits at the prospect of our expedition. At six o'clock in the morning I breakfasted with Mr. Malet at the Legation; the guide came up with three horses and two dogs, and we soon completed our preparations. Mr. Malet had an admirable set of wallets and holsters made by Peat, of Bond Street, and our saddles had been fitted so as to receive them. Each wallet carried a change of clothes, and was fastened at the back of the saddle; and the holsters, containing spare boots, with a revolver and a flask, were adjusted in the usual fashion. The guide had to carry a sketch-book, a bottle of sherry, and some light refreshments, as we knew we should have no chance of getting anything else to eat till we arrived at Theresopolis.

We wore long buff riding-boots, fitting loose above the knee, and very thin light-coloured ponchos, which, with their fringe and border of red, blue, or green, are picturesque as well as comfortable. Umbrellas are indispensable in Brazil, and, by way of economising implements, we determined to make them also do duty as whips. About seven o'clock we fairly started; the dogs barked for joy, the guide looked resigned, and none of the party, except the horses, could have dreamed of anything but a pleasant expedition. We filed slowly out of the town, and, passing the beautiful rose-hedges of the Baron Mauà, we followed the new road towards the province of Minas Geraes. Close to our side was a small but rapid river, tumbling merrily over its rocky bed, and sometimes hiding itself under the overhanging mass of trees and flowers. About two miles from Petropolis a sudden turn in the road showed us in the distance some of the mountain group towards which we were bound, and the river banks formed an admirable foreground to the picture. Sloping down to the river on our right, now some hundred feet distant, the ground was covered with characteristic vegetation. Huge *araucarias*, most truly named puzzle-monkeys, raised their dark heads and stiff-looking branches to the height of apparently sixty or seventy feet; clusters of aloes fringed the road with their lofty candelabra-like spikes of flower; and the river below was overhung by masses of *datura,* filling the air with the sweetness of their long white bells.

A few miles further we left the macadamised road, and crossed the river at Correa. Here are a few stores and immense *ranchos*, or stabling-sheds, for the mules, which make this one of their halting-places in the journey to and from the mines and plantations. Close to the bridge was a noble clump of trees; the trunk of one of them was enormous, and at a height of about sixty feet from the ground it was ornamented by a fine orchid of very unusual size. A considerable part of the open space near the *ranchos* was completely shaded by a celebrated wild fig-tree, the branches of which are said to extend to a circumference of four hundred and eighty feet. This, for a single tree, was a tolerable approach to the 'boundless contiguity of shade' so ardently desired by the desponding Cowper.

We were now on the old Minas road, and the change from the new-fashioned Brazil to the old was remarkable. In place of the admirable Macadam, which I shall have to say more of hereafter, we had for the rest of the day to deal with the lumpy ground and quagmires of that ferruginous soil which makes the worst of roads, though it is eminently well adapted for showing off the green glories of the vegetable world. It was cut into deep narrow tracks by the troops of mules continually passing in their wonted fashion, and we met multitudes of them coming down laden with the treasures of the interior. Each is furnished with a substantial packsaddle, peaked like the roof of a barn: their heavy loads of coffee are piled upon this in bags, and drawn together by a rope of hide, tightly twisted with a stick which is used like a tourniquet. They march in Indian file, following their leader, turning when he turns, or crossing the road when, for reasons best known to himself, he chooses to do so. They insist upon going their own way, and if a traveller in the opposite direction attempts to divert them from their course, he will very likely throw the whole troop into inextricable confusion. Some will break away from the road, and get entangled in the bushes, and others will stop in a sulky fit and roll with their burdens on the ground, in which case they often have to be unloaded before they can get up again.

We had followed this road for about an hour among a charming variety of beautiful scenery, when our guide suddenly turned up a narrow pathway to the right, and started us upon a track which none but a man who was thoroughly acquainted with the country would have thought of following. Sometimes it was so narrow that a horse could scarcely pass between the tall bamboos and creepers that interlaced over our heads; sometimes we dived into deep glens with difficult streams at the bottom, and narrow foot-bridges so rotten that we were obliged to dismount and drag our horses over them. Then would come a heavy up-hill pull over a path slippery with moisture collected under the dense shade of an overhanging forest; and presently we emerged upon the side of a steep mountain, round which the narrow winding path led us between ferns and bamboos and scarlet passion-flowers, giving us occasionally a splendid view of forest-covered hills before us and around.

The heat became excessive, and on coming to a stream my horse made up his mind to drink with a determination not to be resisted. The water was clear as crystal, and rippled over a pebbly bed like a Cumberland trout-stream. A huge tree with giant *arums* clinging to its stem shaded the ford: close on my left was one of the largest *daturas* I had seen, not less than ten or twelve feet high, with its long white trumpet flowers drooping towards the water, by the side of a passion-flower, hanging in festoons from a group of the freshest bamboos. No enjoyment that my horse may have derived from the water could have equalled my own as I dropped the bridle and took my fill of gazing at that lovely spot. Then I pushed up the steep bank and rejoined my companion. At about half-past eleven we came to a lonely deserted hut, where we determined to halt for a while and enjoy our luncheon. We tied up our horses to a castor-oil tree, and left them to bury their heads in the shade of its broad leaves whilst we made the most of a light repast, and followed it up with the pipe of tranquillity.

Half an hour later we extricated our unwilling steeds from their castor-oil umbrella, and mounted at noon under an almost vertical sun. Before us were two lofty mountains connected by a magnificent saddle, or *col*, as my Alpine brethren would call it; and, though my knowledge of Portuguese was not enough to enable me to hold much conversation with our rather stolid guide, I soon discovered that our path lay over it. He led the way with perfect confidence on his small horse, and I brought up the rear as we began a very steep ascent, which wound round the side of a tolerably steep mountain. The path was very slippery from the late rains, and not much wider than a sheep-track; I was the heaviest of the party, and my horse, not being the strongest, soon began to show symptoms of distress.

Several times I pulled him up when nearly on his nose; but at length he seemed determined to carry me no higher. He flung out all his legs at once, and dropped on his belly in the miry path. I had nothing to do but to extricate myself quickly, for fear of being rolled down the steep side into the jaws of a possible ounce or the folds of a boa-constrictor. The beast picked himself up, but mounting him again was impossible in such a narrow path, with a steep slope on each side of me. I yielded to my destiny, and, seizing the bridle, began towing him up the pass, in the hope of finding some more convenient locality. It was not to be done, however. The track became narrower and narrower, steeper and steeper; and masses of bamboos and a thousand plants closed upon it so completely that it was sometimes difficult to force a way. Moreover, the brute displayed an unconquerable passion for eating the bright green leaves of the bamboos, and half my strength was exhausted in tugging at him. The dense jungle shut out every particle of the light breeze, and I never felt the effects of heat so intensely as in the hour which elapsed before I got to the summit of the pass. My companions had kept their saddles; but we were all rather done, and let our horses eat what they liked while we threw ourselves upon a bed of ferns and again enjoyed the blissful weed.

We were in a position which commanded the whole of the surrounding scene. We looked backwards over a great part of our morning's work, and forwards to a new view of surpassing beauty, through which we were to pass to our evening's rest. On our right rose a huge truncated cone of bare granite, in one clear unbroken precipice, smoothly rounded like the *roches moutonnées* of the glacier-world, seemingly more than a thousand feet higher than our own position, which I suppose to have been not less than four thousand feet above the sea, though we had no means for taking accurate observations. I had never seen anything so marvellous in its way as this mass of rock, and the singularity of its appearance was increased by thousands of huge yucca-like epiphytes, which clung to every cleft around its base. Its bare grey head soared into the blue sky under a sun which seemed hot enough to split it.

In the descent we were all obliged to lead our horses for three-quarters of an hour, and a difficult task it was. At one moment it was impossible to tear them away from the fascinations of a delicate bamboo, at another there was a long *glissade* in wet clay, and at a third the difficulty was to make them jump down a steep rock without falling on our heads. At last all these difficulties were passed, and after halting for a few minutes on a lovely little knoll, we girthed up all fast and mounted again.

A few miles further, on turning round, we had a wonderfully fine view of the pass which we had crossed, and of the extraordinary mountain which towered above it to a greater height than we had imagined. As the afternoon advanced, and still not a cloud appeared, the whole air glowed with light and warmth. A hazy golden lustre enveloped earth and air, mountain and forest, with a beauty that seemed not of this world, but the work of an enchanter. For some time we had fancied that we saw the highest peaks of the Organs rising through the luminous atmosphere; but at another bend in our course we were undeceived by the reality. A much higher chain came into view, towering above the rest, and we knew that we now were not very far from our destination.

Having been grilling in the sun for several hours, and almost dazzled with the splendour of the scenery, we could hardly be sorry when we dived once more into the recesses of a dense forest. The path descended steadily, and the difference of elevation was soon marked by the enormous size of the bamboos, eighty or a hundred feet high, instead of the dwarfed specimens in the upper regions of our journey. The ferns in this moist shade were more luxuriant than I had elsewhere seen them, and I observed many species which I had never met with on the Petropolis side of the mountains. As we approached the Theresopolis road, which we knew was not far below us, the path became worse than could be easily imagined. Some people were employed in cutting timber, which was being dragged down by bullocks. These animals had poached up the soft wet soil till tbe way was impassable, and then an attempt had been made to mend it by laying down short timbers, like railway sleepers, to form a corduroy road. The bamboos were so thick and close on both sides that it was impossible to get out of the path, and the horses' legs sank deeper and deeper between the timbers. At a point where the jungle was a little thinner, I forced my beast into it, but was soon compelled to return, and presently he sank up to his belly in a filthy mud-hole. I thought I should never get him out again, and in his struggles I had the greatest difficulty in keeping my seat. To dismount, however, was to put myself into a hopeless mess; so I held on by my knees, and by dint of kicking, shouting, and encouraging with the point of my umbrella, I forced him to a final effort, which brought us out pretty well covered with mud. My companions were not much cleaner, and we found a lively amusement in laughing at each other.

Soon after this our troubles were over, and at about half-past four we found ourselves upon a tolerable road with a clear stream running by the side of it. Our first care was to march the horses into the water, so as to wash them and our boots at the same time. The guide ascertained from a passer-by that we must turn to the right to reach the *fazenda*; but we rode about a league in that direction without seeing more than a few small scattered habitations. We were getting rather disgusted, when we arrived at a small imitation of an inn; a woman came to the door, but our limited knowledge of Portuguese prevented a good understanding, until it occurred to me to try her with German, which, from the number of Swiss and German colonists in Brazil, is more often useful than any other foreign language. The old lady was highly pleased, and told us that she came from near Strasbourg, and her husband was a Frenchman. Summoned by her he appeared, and, finding we were Englishmen, he at once began speaking in our native tongue: he was rather drunk, but assured us that many years ago he had been a French cook on board an English man-of-war. We had a polyglot conversation while a few bottles of good English beer were produced. Our day's work had been a very fair one for a hot climate; and if the beneficent Bass could have known how our thirsty throats were at that moment doing honour to his production, I think it would have rejoiced his heart. The worship of Bass and Allsopp is a very popular cult in Brazil, and even in lonely places it is by no means uncommon to find *Cerveja Inglesa.*

We found that Mr. Tupper's *fazenda* was hardly half a mile farther, and about half-past five we rode up to the house in such a dirty condition, that we almost hesitated before presenting ourselves as perfect strangers to the lady of the house. I soon found that I had under-estimated South American hospitality. We were received most kindly, and assured by our hostess that we had been expected for several days. Negroes were ready in abundance to carry off our horses and our guide to proper quarters; and a good-natured negro woman, who introduced us to our rooms, was very particular in repeating that if we wanted anything we were to be sure to ask for Florence, the fair name of this sable beauty.

As soon as we had got rid of our muddy garments, dinner was ready, and never was that meal more thoroughly appreciated than it was by ourselves after our long ride. We passed a delightful evening; and as the stars with marvellous brilliancy lighted up the faint outlines of the Organ peaks, and the fireflies danced among the palm-trees, we turned into our beds well disposed for a sleep.

The house consisted, as is usual in Brazil, of several buildings ranged round the garden. The main block contained the principal sitting-rooms and bed-rooms, and close by the side was another, which was appropriated to ourselves. Next came a large room, called the billiard-room, containing a billiard-table, a pianoforte, and a library; and various other tenements were intended for servants, negroes, and stables. The lovely Florence had made all things comfortable in our rooms, and we slept without need of rocking.

In the morning we had a good opportunity of looking at all around us, and as far as natural beauty was concerned, we might say—

'And oh! if there is an Elysium on earth, it is this.'

The garden ended in a deep glen, through which a shady path led among rocks and natural bowers down to a bath made in the hollow of a clear stream and overhung by luxuriant vegetation. The rocks were covered with masses of ferns and flowers, and here and there were magnificent bunches of the crimson *strelitzia*. To the left of the glen was a hill covered with palms and forest, and on the right rose up the granite precipices of the Organ peaks, separated from us by several miles of forest stretching upwards to the base of the highest rocks. It will be seen by the accompanying illustration that the form of these peaks is very singular, the most remarkable being the second from the left. It is called the Cabeza del Frayle, or Monk's head, from the likeness to a long draped figure, with a stooping head, formed by what appears to be a detached block on the very summit. How or why that ancient granite grew into so strange a shape must remain a mystery: at all events no man is likely to climb the peak and examine it for himself. If the hardiest of my Alpine friends succeeds in reaching the crest of the Matterhorn, let him not despair of finding fresh difficulties to master. I confidently recommend him to go to Brazil, and find out how the Monk's head is fastened upon his shoulders.

A little farther to the left, but in such a position that I could not introduce it into a sketch with the other peaks, is the Finger mountain—an extraordinary pillar of granite, exactly in the proportions of a human finger, rising vertically to a vast height above the surrounding forest, and seeming, like the finger of Time, to hold out a cold grey menace to the beautiful world. The fantastic forms of this group, when seen from Rio, reminded its first visitors of the pipes of an organ, and gained for the whole range the name of Organ Mountains.

Though the most remarkable in form, they are not, however, so high as some of the summits a little to the east of them. Dr. Gardner, the botanist, after much labour, succeeded on his second attempt in reaching the highest top, where, with the thermometer at 64° in the shade at noon, he found water boil at 198°, and thence estimated the height of the mountain to be 7,800 feet above the sea. The rule of Professor Forbes is, that each degree of diminution in the boiling-point of water corresponds to about 550 feet of elevation; and if we multiply 550 by 14—the difference between 198 and 212—the result is 7,700 feet, or very nearly the same as that of the Doctor's observation. It must not be imagined, however, that the difficulty of climbing up such tropical mountains is in any way proportioned to their comparatively small height. Many of us who have enjoyed the ascent of Mont Blanc and Monte Rosa would be exhausted by the task of cutting and forcing a way, for days together, through dense jungle and pathless forests, climbing in the stifling temperature of a hothouse, and lucky now and then to come upon the track of a tapir leading in the right direction. For my own part, I never suffered any serious inconvenience from the heat of the sun, provided there was a sufficient amount of open air; but whenever I wandered away from paths to look for a fern or a flower in the thick jungle, I found the close heat very oppressive.

The day after our arrival we found a supply of horses ready, and started with the two daughters of our hostess and their governess for a delightful ride among the mountains on the other side of Theresopolis. On our way we paid a visit to Mr. Heath, an Englishman, who is one of the chief notabilities in the place. He is the son of a Kentish farmer, but has been nearly forty-five years in Brazil without once leaving it, and seems as hearty and flourishing as if he had remained on the paternal acres. For a long time he kept a boarding-house at Constancia, not far from his present quarters, where, by his good arrangements and many excellent qualities, he seems to have fairly earned his soubriquet of 'Jolly Heath.' He has long been the Nimrod of the neighbourhood, and has slain innumerable ounces, tapirs, and other animals. He accompanied Dr. Gardner in many of his expeditions, including the ascent which I have just mentioned, and always has the greatest pleasure in doing the honours of Theresopolis to a stranger.

We were fortunate enough to find him at home; and, after showing us his house, he took us into the garden, of which he is justly proud. Three years ago the land had been covered with virgin forest, and now here was a large garden in perfect order. Geraniums and roses, violets and heliotropes, fuchsias and lilies, camellias and Cape jasmines, flourished in company with the flowers of the country. The elevation of Theresopolis above the sea is about 3,000 feet, which enabled many of the European fruits and vegetables to grow to perfection; and peas, beans, cauliflowers, and strawberries, were especially flourishing. Mr. Heath's gardeners were negro women, who, as he said, worked remarkably well, and took a real interest in the results of their labour. He gave the young ladies a magnificent bouquet in a basket, which was consigned to the care of their servant, and he showed me, with great delight, a copy of Kidder and Fletcher's book, in which he is very pleasantly remembered. He appears to be the general confidant and counsellor of the neighbourhood, and doctor besides, being thoroughly acquainted with local complaints, and specially skillful with snake-bites. Could we have stayed longer, and had a continuance of fine weather, we should have seen more of that excellent fellow, 'Jolly Heath,' and perhaps have had the benefit of his guidance in some new mountaineering expedition.

That day's ride, the merry party, and the splendid view of the mountains, were things to be remembered as sunny spots in an existence; but after a short walk next morning the weather changed, and we had an uninterrupted deluge of rain for thirty-six hours, during which it was impossible for anything except amphibious animals to enjoy themselves out of doors. We were, however, by no means dull: the whole party adjourned to the billiard-room, and spent the day with music, billiards, reading Dickens aloud, and reviving half the games of the old country. In the evening, a grand discovery was made. Mr. Tupper, during the Crimean war, had made a journey to Europe to see Sebastopol, Constantinople, and Greece, whence he had brought a huge chest full of national costumes. These were disinterred. I was soon dressed in a burnouse and a huge turban, Mr. Malet was arrayed in the stiffly-folded petticoat and jacket of a Greek officer, and the two young ladies were brilliant in scarlet velvet jackets with gold lace and sundry ornaments. One of the rooms was turned into a theatre, and the greater part of the establishment, negroes and all, were admitted as audience and spectators, while we performed various charades to their infinite delight and astonishment. It was a treat to see the faces of dark Florence and her brethren.

We should have found it difficult to tear ourselves away from the lovely Theresopolis and the cordial hospitality of our kind friends; but business sternly intervened. My companion was obliged to return to Petropolis, and do his share in preparing the despatches for the French mail; and one fine morning, about seven o'clock, our guide, with the three horses and the two bridled dogs, which had been fattening on good cheer, presented himself at the door. There was nothing left for us but to bid an unwilling adieu, and we started homewards, not without being loaded with good things for our march.

We returned by our former route, and the weather

seemed very promising; but we expected that the late heavy rains would make the road even more difficult than before. In this foreboding we were agreeably disappointed; for the country is so mountainous, that the water had soon passed off, and carried a great deal of the hateful mud along with it. At a lonely *fazenda* among the mountains a man was standing looking at us, who, to our great surprise, proved to be an Englishman. He had very seldom seen a countryman passing that way; and when we told him we were going to Petropolis, he said that the weather was changing, and we should have a rough time of it over the mountains. Unfortunately he was right. When we arrived at the foot of the high pass, the air was filling with a driving Scotch mist, which soon settled into steady rain. We were obliged to lead our horses all the way up, and the path was detestably steep and slippery. It was hard work; and our boots, which were intended for sun rather than rain, were soon wet through. We descended the other side with very cautious steps, and were sufficiently cold and miserable when we arrived at our halting-place in the middle of the journey. We did justice to the ample luncheon which had been sent with us, and shared it with a negro, who was so wretched and deserted that I concluded he had lost his master.

We fortunately had a little brandy, which in some measure counteracted the evil effects of wet and cold, as we rode for the next two or three hours, generally at a foot-pace, on account of the slippery state of the steep paths. At last we joined the main road again at Correa, and, with the hope of getting a little warmth into our feet and legs, we galloped over the remaining four or five miles as fast as we could make the horses go under the combined influences of persuasion and umbrella-points.

Soon after five in the evening we reached the abode of the friendly Turk at Petropolis, wet through and covered with mud — a spectacle for London friends to gibe and sneer at. This state of things was, however, soon remedied, and we dined together in the best of spirits, and in a high state of satisfaction with our successful expedition.

As a matter of finance, and for the benefit of those who may be fortunate enough to follow in our steps, I may state that each of the horses cost us six *milreis*, about thirteen English shillings, and the guide three *milreis*, for each day of our absence. Our joint daily expense was thus twenty-one *milreis*, or rather more than two guineas. Of course, anyone who might wish to make a very long journey in the interior, or to stay in the country for a considerable time, would buy horses or mules, instead of hiring them; but the latter is the pleasantest and least troublesome process if animals are only wanted for occasional expeditions.

CHAPTER XIII.

EXPEDITION TO JUIZ DA FORA.

DRYING FERNS — BEAUTIFUL BIRDS — JOURNEY TO JUIZ DA FORA — A FINE BRAZILIAN ROAD — SWISS PASTOR — THE CONDUCTEUR — MACADAM IN BRAZIL — ECCENTRICITIES OF THE MULES — UNHAPPY STONEBREAKERS — LIFTING THE VEIL — GERMAN TOUGHNESS — THE HALF-WAY HOUSE — VIRGIN FORESTS — COFFEE PLANTATIONS — TRAINS OF MULE-CARTS — KEEP THEM STRAIGHT — DISASTER OF A COUNTRY GENTLEMAN — MR. WELLER ABROAD — ANACONDAS — A NEGRO GENTLEMAN — FIREFLIES AND MUSIC — BEAUTIFUL FLOWERS — CHANGES OF TEMPERATURE — FAREWELL TO THE TURK — START AGAIN FOR BUENOS AYRES.

THE next week or ten days were spent at Petropolis, with a very good share of fine weather, during which we had several new walking and riding expeditions, and I again visited the Presidencia and the Falls of Itamarity. Sometimes we made up a party of three or four, and sometimes I wandered about by myself with the tin case which always came home full of ferns. In such a moist climate the process of drying plants is troublesome, and I was constantly obliged to steal an hour or two on the hottest days to change all the papers, and bake them thoroughly in the sun. Everyone has heard of the brilliancy of the Brazilian birds, but I was agreeably surprised to find that some of them were very tolerable songsters. Besides the harsh screams of toucans and parrots and the wild rattling of the *iniambù*, it was not at all uncommon in remote places to hear notes not much inferior to those of a thrush. Outside show is, however, their prevalent characteristic: some were of pure red, and occasionally I saw one of the colour of the most brilliant emerald flashing through the air.

I had settled so comfortably into my quarters with Said Ali, and was so delighted with the infinite variety and beauty of the surrounding country, that I was in no hurry for the next change. Having been, however, strongly advised to travel by the new road to Juiz da Fora, in the province of Minas Geraes, I determined to do so on the first favourable opportunity. Another burst of bad weather detained me for a couple of days, during which it was almost impossible to move from the house. The ordinary roads are composed of the red earth which lies below the vegetable soil, and their state after a few hours' rain is filthy in the extreme. The Brazilians are fully aware of the vast importance of making better roads, not only for the comfort of travelling, but also for the more safe and expeditious transit of their valuable productions from the interior to the coast.

The province of Minas Geraes is one of the most important in the empire, on account of its mines of gold and diamonds, and its still more valuable treasures of coffee. It was determined to open up a communication between this part of the country and Rio Janeiro by means of a first-rate road, to be made available for wheeled carriages and wagons in all kinds of weather. A company was formed with the support of the government, and a few months before my arrival at Petropolis the new road had been opened as far as Juiz da Fora, about a hundred miles distant. It was spoken of as a miracle of good work, which was not only well worth seeing for its own sake, but would also take me through some of the finest scenery in Brazil.

The cost of constructing this road through a mountainous country was necessarily enormous, and with the purchase of mules, coaches, &c., amounted, as I was informed, to about 1,200,000*l.* sterling. Every morning and every night one coach started from Petropolis and another from Juiz da Fora, while a fifth relieved the others in rotation. The coaches were sent out from England, and are exactly like those which were the glory of our school-boy days, except that they are not so high: this difference is intended as a precaution against upsetting. The outside fare was nearly 2*l.* 10*s.* English, which is not too much for a hundred miles, considering the expenses of the company and the novelty of the experiment.

At six o'clock in the morning of October the 30th, the swarthy 'boots' walked with me to wait for the coach at the corner of Baron Mauà's, carrying a very small allowance of baggage in a hat-box, together with a waterproof coat and a stout poncho, for I was by this time much too experienced in the changes of weather and climate to trust to favourable appearances. The driver kept time punctually, and I was in a moment perched on the seat behind him and the conductor. Away went the four mules at a slapping pace, which greatly increased the effect of the morning air in our faces. There was a raw fog, positively cold and very disagreeable. The driver and conductor were well wrapped up, and I soon slipped on my own good poncho. Thinking my neighbour looked very miserable, I gave him my waterproof, venturing a remark in German, for I thought he had been pointed out to me a few days before as a Swiss missionary. I was right: his countenance lighted up as he expressed his thanks in the same language. I soon found that he had lately been sent out from Europe to look after the spiritual welfare of his countrymen somewhere in the interior of Brazil. He was a good-natured rustic, who had been educated at the University of Basle; and, though he did not look a very promising subject, yet I hoped to have some interesting conversation. To my utter disgust it turned out that he had never been so far as Berne, and hardly knew what was meant by the high Alps. This appeared downright treason, 'flat burglary,' in my eyes; but before I had recovered my surprise he turned the conversation towards his theological opinions upon the state of the world in general. I saw I should speedily be drawn into the direful vortex of Calvinism, and felt it was now my turn to withdraw from the conversation. For the rest of the day we confined ourselves to occasional remarks upon wayside objects.

Luckily I discovered that the conductor was a lively Frenchman and a capital little fellow; very well informed and as sharp as a needle. He had left his country in disgust at what he called the 'canaille' of Imperialism, but seemed quite contented with living under the constitutional empire of the west. An exchange of cigars cemented our acquaintance, and in the course of the journey he supplied me with much amusement and information. He was armed with a whistle and a brass horn, and I soon saw that he had no sinecure. These instruments were continually called into play to warn the drivers of mule trains and wagons to get out of the way, our mules being so skittish that a sudden pull up or jerk to one side would very likely throw them all into confusion and perhaps upset the coach. This kind of accident appeared to be not unfrequent, according to the conductor, but very few people had been seriously hurt.

The road is admirably made throughout the whole distance, and I can truly say that I never saw its equal in any part of England or Europe. The greater part of it is carried through a mountainous country, where an inexhaustible supply of gneiss and granite is to be found on the spot; and hundreds of men, black, brown, and yellow, are constantly employed in blasting the rock, breaking it up, and mending weak places in the road. This is not done in the slipshod English fashion of throwing down vast quantities of broken stone across the way and then leaving the unhappy public to smooth and pulverise it as best they may. The Brazilian labourers fit in every piece almost as if it were for a mosaic; pails of water are then poured over all, and an enormous roller drawn by a dozen mules pounds it down into a firm floor. The road thus made was perfectly sound and smooth.

So far, so good: the mules are the ticklish part of the matter. These beasts are the most amusing fellows in the world, and if their pranks were not so very serious, they would be a source of unmitigated mirth. They are small, but well-bred, and beautifully formed; they are very fast, and are kept to a pace of twelve miles an hour without much apparent effort or distress. The conductor told me that the company keep three hundred for the service of each of the five coaches, besides a large number for running between Petropolis and the railway; and as they cost, I believe, on an average, nearly 40*l.* apiece, it is clear that they must be a formidable source of expense. When all goes right, it is very pretty to watch the little team well settled down to work, and going at such a pace as to leave no possible excuse for the whip: but sometimes, when they are going on as steadily as clockwork, the sight of a novelty is too much for their nerves. The driver hopes they will pass it; the conductor is ready to jump down in case of a catastrophe. Just as we think they are all right, they suddenly begin to shy in all directions, and it requires great skill and heavy flogging to get them together again without overturning the coach on a bank.

On the day of my journey they had a considerable number of young mules, and, though there were no accidents, our escapes were quite narrow enough to be eminently exciting. At one point in the road we suddenly came upon a mule drawing a cart of heavy stones and led by a sun-burnt boy, who instantly tried to draw on one side: the mule, however, was determined to dispute the way against his Imperial Majesty's mail, and refused to move an inch. Our driver was a stolid young German, whose coolness and strength qualified him particularly for the management of lively mules. He slackened speed without stopping, the great object being to keep the team moving, and the active Gaul was on his feet in an instant; he rushed at the cart-mule, found he could not move it to one side or the other, seized it by the bit, punched its head as if he were the illustrious Sayers, forced it backwards till he upset the cart in a ditch, spattered the boy with kicks and execrations, and jumped to his perch again without having let go his cigar. A desperately steep slope on our left led to the river, which was thundering along some hundred feet below us, so that it would have been an awkward place for a serious battle with our teams.

Later in the day we caused confusion among a gang of stone-breakers. The heat was tremendous, and most of them had contrived a little shelter for themselves by sticking up a branch or two so as to shade the place where they sat at their work. Others had planted three sticks and hung their shirts and coats on the top, thereby making something between a gipsy-tent and a scarecrow. My friend the conductor had no objection to the branches, because the mules are accustomed to them, but the scarecrow arrangement with a red waistcoat made him furious. The pace was again slackened, while he jumped down and rushed forward against the enemy. The unlucky object of his wrath was quite unconscious of committing a crime against Don Pedro; he came forward to meet the Gaul with a smile, offering him a light for his cigar; but the latter brushed him out of the way, knocked down the obnoxious construction, and kicked it over the steep bank amidst a torrent of abuse. The poor fellow was altogether taken aback, and looked helpless with dismay and astonishment. 'Voilà!' said the Frenchman, resuming his seat and shaking his fist at the discomfited enemy, while he explained to me that nothing would have induced one of our leaders to pass that waistcoat if she had seen it.

The chilling fog in which we had started did not last

more than an hour. A few gleams partly breaking through the mist then warned us of the sun's approaching victory, and in a few minutes more nothing remained of it but a few fleecy puffs curling over the sides of the palm-crowned hills, which, in all their luxuriance of flower and forest, were now suddenly revealed to us as if by the uplifting of a veil. Truly it was a glorious sight. From that moment the heat rapidly increased, and for several hours in the middle of the day it was impossible to sit long without the shelter of an umbrella. The effect of the mid-day sun was greatly increased by the fact of our travelling down hill all the morning and reaching the Parahiba river, which was the lowest point in our journey, exactly at the hottest part of the day. The blazing sunshine and the white dry roads made my head whizz, and everybody else seemed to suffer except the young German coachman, who, with nothing but the smallest of caps on his head, seemed utterly unconscious of inconvenience. Sometimes I used to wonder what these Brazilian Germans could be made of. At Petropolis in the hottest weather I have seen their flaxen-haired children playing bare headed in the sun, just as actively as if they were still on the banks of the Rhine. Even the wiry Frenchman tied up his head in a handkerchief under his hat, but the German winced not for a moment. Our inside passengers were two or three of the large coffee planters in the country through which we were going, one of whom was an elderly man, looked upon with much reverence by the conductor, and always called Monsieur le Comte. He very good-naturedly made acquaintance with me, and hospitably insisted upon my trying various refreshing compounds which he recommended. He and his friends being nearly stifled with heat inside the coach, joined us on the top for an hour, but after the next change they crept into their old quarters rather than face the burning sun.

About noon we came to the half-way station near the junction of the Parahiba and Parahybuna rivers, almost at the same moment as the return coach arrived from Juiz da Fora. Here we dined tolerably well and not expensively, but the heat was too great for excessive hunger, especially as we were obliged to contest every morsel with a legion of flies, in spite of the activity of the negroes who were especially devoted to keeping them in order. They filled the plates and dishes, and it was difficult to eat without swallowing them. I was glad to escape from the table and sit down in a shady balcony to admire the magnificent scenery of the great Pedro de Parahybuna, and the river rushing by its feet. There was something marvellously grand in that vast mass of rock, rising precipitously almost from the roadside to so great a height that the palm trees on the summit looked mere specks against the sky.

The variety of scenery which we had passed through was very great, and its beauty was immensely increased by the river, which was our companion nearly all the morning, thundering through rocky falls and rapids, or swirling more quietly through the recesses of the virgin forests. Here the trees were infinitely finer than any I had seen near Petropolis; and where the broad road was carried through the midst of them, so that whilst we travelled in their shadow we could enjoy all the beauty of the vegetation, it would be difficult to imagine anything much more delightful. A true monarch of the virgin forest is not only a tree — it is a garden. Gigantic arums and drooping masses of ferns cling about its stem, and orchids display their brilliant colours and fantastic forms upon the branches; rope-plants hanging to the ground form natural ladders for innumerable creepers and climbers to raise themselves towards the sky, and trailers stoop to meet them as they rise. The only ungraceful tree that I used to observe in Brazil is the *sumambaia*, or sloth-tree. The boughs are stiff and ungainly, and the chesnut-shaped leaves only appear in tufts at the extremities. Sloths abound in the forests, and climb these trees to eat the leaves, of which they are remarkably fond; but I suppose they find that the task of getting at their favourite food is difficult, for having once got into the branches they remain there till every leaf has been devoured, and nothing remains but the skeleton of a tree.

For many leagues we travelled through some of the coffee plantations, which produce such a large share of the wealth of Brazil. The contrast was very striking as now and then we emerged from one of the magnificent forests which I have attempted to describe, and found ourselves surrounded by hills which had been entirely cleared of wood and jungle, and covered with the stiff lines of coffee plants, looking something like Portugal laurels grown in the shape of small poplars about 7 or 8 feet high and 2 or 3 feet thick. They look very well in flower, the pure white star of the blossom being well set off by the extreme darkness of the foliage. I observed that in many places the leaves looked thin, and Monsieur le Comte told me that they were suffering from the attacks of an insect which by destroying the leaves would have a very injurious effect upon the fruit.

This region was full of bustle and activity; large numbers of people were at work in bringing new soil into cultivation, and long trains of loaded mules and waggons streamed along the road, to the constant peril of ourselves. In the careless fashion of English waggoners, the drivers were generally chatting among themselves, while their charges went quietly along the middle of the road, which wound about among the mountains so that we could seldom see much of it at once. The moment a train was seen the horn was put into requisition and blown furiously by the conductor; and veryamusing were the battles that began at once between the obstinate mules and their drivers, who tried pushing, punching, and kicking with all their might to clear the way for the coach. The mule is, as far as I have been able to observe, a quaint, but at the same time a sociable beast, with a strong disposition to fraternise with strange brethren on the road; so that all the skill in the world, aided by hard thumping and whipping, could hardly prevent collisions. We were generally going at full gallop, often having a river or a precipice at our side, and at least a dozen times in the day I thought we must be upset by the heavy waggons, which seemed on the very point of running into us. But a vicious blow of a heavy whip at the very last moment enabled us to pass, and to my surprise we got through the day without accident.

Each team was, upon an average, driven about ten miles. The stations were new and clean buildings, something in the châlet-style; at some of them a toll is taken, and large supplies of spare mules are kept. On driving up to one of these we always found the negro or German hostlers ready, and the gallant little animals were led off to their *rancho*: there was no hurry in bringing out their successors, and driver, conductor, and passengers all enjoyed themselves for at least ten minutes. M. le Comte and his friends insisted on being hospitable, and proved to me at one of the hottest moments of the day that nothing was so wholesome and supporting as a glass of *caña,* with plenty of sugar, filled up with the nearest approach to cold water that could be got. Fresh cigars were lighted, and then came preparations for a fresh start, which was more exciting than pleasant till we were pretty well used to it. The wheelers are with some difficulty forced into their places, and then all the passengers are compelled to take their seats: another fight ends in the leaders being put-to at the same moment that the driver mounts to his perch. Two negroes hold the heads of the leaders, and all is quiet for an instant till the driver gives the signal to march by a furious crack of his whip. An explosion of the team follows immediately: one jumps in the air and another to the side, and on one occasion I saw the wheelers squatting on their tails and staring wildly at different sides of the road, while the leaders kicked out right and left, and tried to shake off the men who held them. The driver answered with tremendous blows from a whip almost as thick as a rattle-snake, and they all plunged forward a little with heads on high: the negroes could hardly keep their hold till a shout of 'Larga, larga!' gave the word to them to get out of the way. The team rushed towards the river on the right, and I was preparing to drop off, when the sturdy German smote the off-siders with such might that they charged across the road and tried to wreck us against a steep embankment; but again the heavy thong successfully asserted its power, and before the phlegmatic Jehu could take another puff from his cigar, the whole team surrendered at discretion, and settled down into a fast hand-gallop, which they kept up for the whole stage. It was a practical illustration of 'Ce n'est que le premier pas qui coûte.'

The most amusing episode of the day was our meeting with a country gentleman travelling after the manner of his fathers, and in a direction opposite to our own. Our team was going at full speed when we met a very different kind of conveyance. A heavy kind of palankeen or sedan-chair advanced towards us, not carried by men, but attached by its shafts to two gaily-caparisoned mules, one before and one behind. A native lady lounged at her ease in the interior, and the slaves in charge kept the mules very steady as we passed. So far, so good; but about fifty yards behind them rode 'paterfamilias' in all the glory of the old style, mounted on a showy mule, with gaudy trappings for both man and beast. Not thinking of danger, and seeming to contemplate us with dignified contempt, he advanced at a foot-pace till he was abreast of our leaders, when his mule was either panic-stricken or seized with that irresistible love of mischief which appears to me to be a strong feature in the mule disposition. The animal turned sharply round, almost unseating its astonished owner, and galloped away ahead of us as fast as it could go. Now and then the poor man turned his head, shooting Parthian glances of rage and despair at us, and now and then he made a fruitless effort to induce his mule to turn again and face the coach. It was not to be; his situation was ridiculous in the extreme, and as an Englishman I could not help thinking of the famous Johnny Gilpin. M. le Conducteur, as the representative of modern progress, enjoyed the joke extremely, and urged our driver to 'make the running;' so away we went in a mad gallop after the unwilling fugitive, whose career was only terminated by his running to earth in a narrow cross-path through the forest, after a sharp chase of about a quarter of an hour. What must have been the feelings of the lounging lady and her slaves, as they saw the strange disappearance of the head of the family!

Never in Europe have I seen anything to compare in its way with the excitement of this Brazilian coaching; and even the immortal Mr. Weller might have envied the skill and boldness of his representatives in the land of the sun. Blow the whistle—sound the horn—out of the way, you niggers—clear out with your mules—clear out, clear out, in the name of Dom Pedro Segundo!

We spent nearly an hour in the mid-day halt, and then prepared once more to face the heat, which increased in intensity till about three o'clock. The Frenchman tied up his head so effectually that nothing was to be seen of it except the ever-watchful eyes; and we all felt as if we had been consigned to an oven. We crossed the broad river Parahiba by a magnificent iron bridge, which had been sent out from England; and thence, having passed our lowest point of elevation, we began to rise again during the greater part of the afternoon till we reached Juiz de Fora, which is about the same height above the sea as Petropolis. I saw a great many snakes in the latter half of the journey, some of which seemed large, and a particularly fine specimen of the handsomest snake in the world, the coral-snake, crossed the road immediately in front of us, as if expressly for the purpose of showing off his splendid blood-red rings to the greatest advantage. This 'beautiful devil' seemed to be about five feet long; it wound itself gracefully up a steep bank and disappeared in the jungle. Near this part of the Parahiba, Mr. Caldcleugh, a former traveller, saw a boa constrictor of sixteen or eighteen feet in length playing in the foliage just over his head, which frightened his horse so excessively that, though the snake retreated at once, it was only with the greatest difficulty that he could be induced to pass the place in a trembling state.

The common boa constrictor is, however, nothing in comparison with the anaconda, or *sucurujù* of the Indians. Dr. Gardner, when at Sapê, in the province of Goyaz, saw one of these monsters which had just been found dead in the fork of a tree, where it had been left by the retreating waters of a flood, when in an inert state and incapable of motion. It measured

37 feet in length, and when opened, was found to contain the bones of a horse in a somewhat broken condition, and the flesh in a half-digested state. The bones of the head were uninjured, and there is little doubt that the horse had been swallowed whole. Dr. Kidder received from an Italian physician in Brazil an account of the way in which the anacondas swallow their food, from which it would appear that, though they undoubtedly gulp down whole cows, after breaking their bones by compression, yet they do not attempt the deglutition and digestion of the horns; he said that they get over this difficulty by beginning with the tail and hind legs, and allowing the horns to protrude from their mouth till they fall off from decay. Dr. Kidder does not vouch for this as his own experience, but it appears very probable, when we remember that these brutes remain for a long time in a state of inaction after indulging in a gorge.

Those who visited the Brazilian department of the late International Exhibition, may have seen some fine skins of these large snakes tanned and ready for use; the leather is soft and very popular for boots in the interior of the country. One of those exhibited was swung horizontally like an immensely long hammock, and was nearly wide enough for a man to sleep in. The scales are defined as those of the living snake.

This has been a digression from our journey. About

four o'clock the heat began to moderate, and as we were pretty constantly ascending, matters became much more tolerable. Two hours more of winding among hills and forests, and coffee-plantations, through constant scenes of beauty and magnificence, brought us to Juiz da Fora, the terminus of the new road. This place was described by Mr. Caldcleugh forty years ago as a small spot, with two or three huts, called 'the Juiz da Fora,' the chief inhabitant being a justice of the peace. It is now a flourishing place containing, as I was informed, nearly 4,000 people, and sure of a large and constant increase from the extension of commerce and the improvement of communications. There are many excellent houses, which being almost entirely white give a bright and cheerful appearance to the town; but its chief ornament is a very beautiful Italian villa, built for the director of the road, surrounded by a flourishing garden and decorated with excellent taste.

The coach pulled up at the company's station, close to the small hotel which they have provided for travellers. It was not yet quite six o'clock; so we had done a hundred miles in rather less than twelve hours, out of which more than two had been spent in stoppages at the various stations: not bad work in a mountainous country, on a blazing day, in the tropics. The pace could not be kept up, if the road were not so skilfully engineered: the gradients are very easy; and in one place I observed that a small hill, only about 50 feet high, had been cut through to avoid the sharp pitch that would be necessary to cross it.

Hat-box in hand, I walked through the little garden in front of the hotel, and met at the door an 'African gentleman' of gigantic proportions. He was dressed in European fashion, with a Panama hat; and, from his way of looking at me, I fancied he must be the master of the house. While I was hesitating what I should say to him, he opened the conversation himself, by asking, with the peculiar gutturals of his race—'Are you English?'

Satisfied on this point, he looked as stately as the Emperor Soulouque, and said—'Ah! it is well. Vary few peoples spik de English; I spik it some. What will you?'

He led me into the house in a patronising way that I was obliged to submit to, and then handed me over to the landlady—a very pleasant and intelligent German woman. She and her husband, M. Bartels, did the honours of the little place; and, about an hour after our arrival, I and a few other passengers were served with a comfortable *table d'hôte* dinner and excellent wines. The dark gentleman turned out to be only an amateur, who derived his principal amusement from watching the arrival of the coach, and smoking the evening cigar under the shade of some magnificent cocoa-palms in the hotel garden.

After my long ride I was glad to stretch my legs

for an hour before dinner, and strolled about to get a general view of the place, which has a tolerably open situation, in the midst of a hilly rather than a mountainous country. The sublimities of the Organ range have long been left behind; and the scenery, though very pretty, is of a much tamer description. Everything that I saw was suggestive of progress and activity; and the people looked perfectly aware of the great things which would result to them from the opening of the road which I had just been travelling over. Seldom have I felt dinner more welcome than on that evening; and when it was over I turned out into the garden to enjoy a quiet cigar on the black gentleman's favourite seat among the palm-trees.

I was utterly enjoying the coolness and tranquillity of the evening; the sky blazed with stars, and the air was alive with fireflies darting in every direction and entangling themselves in the palm branches, which they illuminated by their presence; the host and hostess came out to have a little chat in German about their old country, and to wonder that I had travelled so far for mere pleasure; a few people were pacing up and down slowly to cool themselves after the labours of the day; and all nature seemed luxuriating in rest: when a well-trained German band of about twenty young men marched out from a neighbouring building, to prove that the Germans carry their love of music wherever they go. These lads were in the habit of practising together regularly, and twice a week they turned out in strength for the benefit of the small public of Juiz da Fora. I listened with delight to well-known airs of Meyerbeer and Mozart, and to Mendelsohn's Wedding March, while thousands of fire-flies danced wildly to the music.

I had neither time nor inclination to travel further in this direction, and visit the mining districts of Villa Rica. I had only wished to see the road to Juiz da Fora, and the magnificent scenery which it passes through. After a long and very pleasant evening, the tranquillity of which was all the more appreciated after the heat and excitement of the day, I went to bed about midnight, and got up again about five o'clock in the morning for the return journey to Petropolis. M. Bartels and his wife soon had a good breakfast ready for me. I paid a bill of eight milreis, about seventeen English shillings; and at six o'clock we started with a lively team of mules, and the Frenchman's horn in full play. I enjoyed the second day's journey even more than the first. It was, if possible, hotter; but then, on the other hand, I was more accustomed to the style of thing, and had more leisure to look about me. I observed two conspicuous plants which were new to me, but could never find either of them near any of the places where we stopped. One was a large white *Ipomea*, and the other a flowering shrub of from three to twelve feet high, completely covered with Magenta-coloured blossoms, which, at a little distance, appeared of much the same size and shape as those of the azalea.

We had no particular adventures that day; more plunging mules, more cigars, more dust, more heat, and more amusement with the Gaul, accompanied us through the greater part of the journey. In the middle of the afternoon the closeness of the heat became very oppressive, and the black clouds quickly forming, though they veiled the blaze of the sun, yet did not make the temperature more comfortable. A storm was brewing, and would evidently burst upon us in a very short time. We arrived at Petropolis, and as I walked up to the abode of the Turk, a huge drop of rain made a splash upon my hat-box almost as large as an oyster, by way of a prelude to a terrific thunderstorm, which raged for two hours. After turning the streets into rivers, it effectually succeeded in cooling the air, and the remainder of the evening was deliciously pleasant. These changes of temperature are sometimes excessively great. Mr. Caldcleugh, in his 'Travels in South America,' says, that one day when 'the land breeze continued until four o'clock in the afternoon, the air became intolerably oppressive and resembled the hot wind of India. At five o'clock the storm began, and an immediate fall took place in the thermometer, which soon after daylight was found to have registered highest 120°, lowest 56°, a difference of 64°!'

The effect of the present storm was delightful in the

extreme; all nature seemed refreshed, and in the course of the next few days, I had some very agreeable walks and rides, making many additions to my collection of ferns. I made another expedition to the Alto do Imperador, and impressed for ever on my mind one of the most perfect scenes in the world. On another day I had the pleasure of escorting two strangers to the falls of Itamarity, and began to think myself a cicerone in the familiar neighbourhood of Petropolis. But all these things were coming to an end. The 'Mersey' was due from the Rio de la Plata on the 5th of November, and it was expected that she would go for a few days into the new dry dock just opened at Rio. I had intended in the meantime to devote the spare days to another stay in the capital; but an old friend of mine at Buenos Ayres, coming up to Petropolis before leaving for England, declared that the dry dock was occupied by another ship, and the packet would therefore return at once. After spending a pleasant day with him I packed up my goods, and with sincere regret paid my bill and bade farewell to Said Ali. Peace be with him! may his shadow never be less, and may all his guests have as much pleasure in his house as I had!

Early in the morning of the 7th my friend and I started for Rio; a fresh burst of rain had set in which made things look thoroughly miserable among the mountains. Before noon, however, the sky had again cleared, and in the hotter regions near the level of the sea I found that five weeks had made an astonishing difference among the vegetable world. The southern summer had fairly set in, and that which I had formerly admired was now a scene of still more gorgeous beauty. Huge trees covered with purple flowers to the very summit contrasted with others which appeared like masses of golden bells, illuminating the dark shades of the evergreen forest. Fresh creepers were hanging in bright festoons, and multitudes of orchids had opened into blossom. Once more we passed among the lovely islands of the bay, and reached Rio early in the afternoon. The city had been cooled and refreshed by the heavy rain of the morning, and the commercial world was in full activity for the departure of the packets. We amused ourselves with a few hours of strolling about the streets and shipping, and then consigned ourselves to the care of the negro boatmen, whose strong arms rowed us away to our respective ships. I felt some disappointment at losing the expected stay at Rio; there was nothing to do, however, but to go on board the 'Mersey,' which was to start early in the morning for Montevideo and Buenos Ayres.

CHAPTER XIV.

LA PLATA AND PARANÀ.

SOUTHWARDS AGAIN—STORM AND BUTTERFLIES—LIGHT CARRIED AWAY—H.M.S. 'ARDENT'—FLIGHT OF DERQUI—GALE IN THE RIVER—WATERSPOUTS—COURAGE OF EARLY EXPLORERS—THE 'SEIBO' TREE—OBLIGADO—WATERFOWL—EVENING ON THE PARANÀ—SAN NICOLAS—ROSARIO—BUENOS AYREAN ARMY—THE GENERAL—VICTUALLING THE TROOPS—THE COLONEL AGAIN—RAILWAY PROSPECTS IN THE ARGENTINE TERRITORIES—PROBABLE INCREASE OF COMMERCE—THE TWO SQUADRONS—A SOUTH AMERICAN ADMIRAL—'DEFENDEMOS LA LEY FEDERAL JURADA'—CHANGED APPEARANCE OF LAND—ARRIVAL AT PARANÀ.

SOON after breakfast on the 8th of November, we steamed down the harbour, and ran through the heavy swell rolling into the entrance. Next day we had a strong wind and following sea behind us: the weather was fine, but distant lightning in the south was the prelude to a change. A heavy squall struck the ship about 2 o'clock in the morning, accompanied by incessant thunder, lightning, and torrents of rain, making 'night hideous' and sleep impossible. At breakfast-time all was quiet again, but the squall had left behind it a very curious effect. Though we were about 150 miles from land, thousands of moths and butterflies had been blown on board, and were being caught in all parts of the ship. The largest which I saw was handsomely marked with blue and brown, and measured six inches across the wings. Everybody was surprised at the phenomenon, for it is difficult to imagine how these delicate insects could survive such a long journey amidst all the dangers of tempestuous wind and rain.

About noon the ship was stopped for a short time for the purpose of securing a rickety float in one of her patent wheels. We were in deep water, and had a better opportunity for observing the colour of the sea than we could have when in motion. It was of the deepest ultramarine, verging upon purple.

All was made fast just in time. The wind suddenly flew round to the south-west, and by 3 o'clock a savage Pampero was tearing the sea into ribbons and raising a sort of fog with the scud. Every half-hour added to its violence, and by nightfall it was not easy to stand on deck. The 'Mersey,' however, is especially well-behaved in a head sea, and I wanted to see how she would go through it; the other passengers had long ago turned in, hoping vainly for sleep, when I put on a waterproof and went on deck. I joined the officer of the watch, and stood near the companion to observe the effect of the sea striking the ship. About midnight we were trying hard to look through the darkness and the spray which swept along the deck, when a tremendous sea struck the port paddle-box, and nearly blinded us in a sheet of foam; but through the roar came a shrill cry from the look-out man, and the officer, rushing forward, found that the port light was carried away, smashed to atoms. The strong brass frame and immensely thick plate-glass were as completely flattened and destroyed as if they had been pounded with a Nasmyth's hammer. Had I not seen it, I should not have believed that a sea could produce such an effect on so small and strong an object.

Soon after this the two men at the wheel, not being strong enough to hold it, were sent spinning over and round it; one of them was considerably hurt by being squeezed between the spokes and the deck, while the other, being thinner, passed safely under. Four men were then sent to this duty, and there were no more accidents. Meanwhile, I began to think I had had enough of it; and, finding that my waterproof coat did not prevent streams of water from entering at my neck, and effectually cooling my back-bone, I at length retired to my cabin. Next day the wind shifted to the south-east, which made the ship roll heavily, and on the day afterwards it followed what appeared to me the general rule of that stormy coast: it worked round by east to north and west, and then settled into the south-west again, though the Pampero was very much lighter than that which we had lately fought against. It must be a plaguy coast to sailing-vessels.

As usual in this voyage, the wind went twice round the compass in the week, blowing more or less violently from every quarter.

Early in the morning of the 14th, we anchored once more in Montevideo, where, to my surprise and pleasure, I found H. M. S. 'Ardent,' commanded by my cousin, Captain Parish. I had thought she was far away up the river, but it appeared that one result of the Argentine war had been the flight of President Derqui, the arch-enemy of the Buenos Ayreans. He found that his game was lost; and, dreading the consequences of falling into the hands of those who might have been tempted not to temper justice with mercy, he had asked the protection of an English man-of-war to convey him and his family to the neutral ground of Montevideo. The Buenos Ayrean authorities at Martin Garcia requested that he might be given up to them as the ship passed down the river, but they only received from her captain the appropriate answer, that it is not customary for English men-of-war to deliver up political refugees. He had been landed at Montevideo the day before our arrival, and, as the 'Ardent' was going back at once to Paranà, I gladly accepted my cousin's invitation to accompany him to that place. He sent off his boat, and I was soon transferred with my goods to the deck of his ship: at 11 o'clock we started up the river, and reached the outer roads of Buenos Ayres next morning before daylight.

After breakfast we went on shore, and found that the stormy weather we had suffered from at sea had done immense mischief in the river. Vessels had been blown from their anchors, and many accidents had taken place, the chief of which was the driving on shore of the monster American steamer, 'Mississippi.'

There had been no more fighting of any consequence, but it could by no means be said that peace was yet established. The storm of war had rolled away from the neighbourhood of the city, but the clouds in the horizon were black. The Buenos Ayrean army, under the command of General Mitre, was still in the field at Rosario, ready either to meet the possibility of Urquiza renewing the struggle, or to march westward for the subjection of the refractory provincials. The so-called squadrons were watching one another near a point up the river called Diamante, and had been doing so for a considerable time, without either of them hazarding an attack. Meanwhile, the depreciation of the paper dollar was continually increasing, and trade was in every way greatly interfered with.

The progress of nature, however, had been much faster and more satisfactory than that of the politicians. The garden was in summer beauty, though we had not yet passed through November. Roses and geraniums were in full perfection: the peaches were swelling apace, and the figs were fast ripening above beds of exquisite violets that lay at their feet. The long-tailed brownish magpies of the country hunted for insects in the upper branches of the ombù, which was now covered with dense foliage and tails of blossom like those of our sycamore. The oven-birds had not built their nests without reason, and the exquisite little humming-birds flashed gaily among the roses.

Instead of passing our evenings in the house, often not disdaining the comfort of a fire, the fashion now was to arrange ourselves after dinner in cool cane chairs under the long verandah, and let the fragrance of the havannah mix with the sweet breezes of the River Plate.

I hoped, by going up the river, to obtain some better information about the actual condition of the country, and the chances of crossing to Mendoza and Chili, the passage of the Andes being still my cherished scheme. A couple of days were spent among my good friends at Buenos Ayres, and on the 17th we went on board the 'Ardent,' accompanied also by Mr. Boyd. Next morning at 4 o'clock we were in motion, and went on steadily till it became necessary to buoy the channel to Martin Garcia, the old buoys having been, as it was alleged, lost in the late gales. The operation was slow, for the channel is very difficult to find and dangerous to miss: the ship drew 13½ feet of water, and at one time there were only 6 inches to spare under her bottom. Heavy masses of cloud were discharging thunder and lightning around us; and we saw several waterspouts, one of which was very large. It burst, as far as I could guess, about two miles from us, and might have been a very awkward visitor to a ship underneath it. Before the boat's crew had finished the work of buoying the channel and picking up the buoys again, they were thoroughly drenched by one of the heaviest thunder-showers that I have ever seen, after which the weather soon settled into 'very dry.' The clouds rolled away, and I hardly saw another in the course of the next month.

We passed the island of Martin Garcia, and entered the Paranà Guazù, the Paranà de las Palmas not being deep enough for any but small vessels. The navigation of these rivers is so difficult, the multiplicity of branches and channels so great, and the general appearance of the banks and islands so similar, that it is a marvel to me how the pilots can learn them as they do: that the old Spaniards should ever, in spite of such dangers and difficulties, have succeeded in exploring the intricacies of the Rio de la Plata and its mighty affluents, is only to be accounted for by the fact that they were supported by an imaginary magnet of gold. 'Auri sacra fames' is invincible; and no sufferings were able to damp the energies of men who firmly believed that the Paranà was the highway to El Dorado.

When we had left the river Uruguay on our right, and fairly entered the Paranà Guazù, we found ourselves at last in a river which was narrow enough to permit of our seeing both banks at once. The land on both sides was low and marshy, for the most part covered with jungle and a great variety of trees, the haunts of jaguars, capybaras, and snakes. The most conspicuous and abundant of the trees was the *seibo,* which I now saw for the first time in bloom, covering the banks with sheets of brilliant crimson. Some of them were very large; but the wood is pithy, and as useless as that of the ombù: the flower is papillonaceous, about twice the size of the garden pea; and few objects in the vegetable world can be more splendid than their crimson bunches of laburnum-like tails hanging among leaves of the brightest green. For many leagues together they were the constant ornaments of the scenery.

Buoying the channel had delayed us some time; and when, rather late in the afternoon, the ship was anchored for the night, we had not gone so far as had been expected. However, it would have been too great a risk to navigate the ship after dark, in a river teeming with shoals dangerous to all but small craft; and, besides this, the pilot had to be considered. He never left the paddle-box or bridge while we were in motion, and human endurance has its limits, even with the strongest of men. Next morning, at 4 o'clock, the 'Ardent' got under weigh again, and in due time passed San Pedro, where we found the firm land of the province of Buenos Ayres on the right bank of the river, rising in precipitous *barrancas* or cliffs to a height of apparently about 100 feet. The low ground of Entre Rios formed the left bank, scarcely rising above the water, and affording shelter to myriads of aquatic birds.

At Obligado, eleven miles beyond San Pedro, the river narrows for a time to less than half a mile in width; and here, when Rosas wanted to close the navigation in 1845, he constructed a battery and threw a chain across the stream. The combined force of French and English, with a convoy of merchantmen, determined to force the passage; after a gallant fight, with considerable loss, they succeeded in cutting the chain and silencing the battery, and then proceeded up the river with their convoy.

All day long the sun blazed upon us like a furnace, but the motion of the ship created a light breeze, which added not a little to our comfort. The smart crew of blue-jackets looked smarter than ever, in their summer costume of white trousers and white caps. The huge river shone all day like a sheet of glass under the fiery sun, and the many strange birds which we passed floating on the stream seemed too lazy even to turn their heads and look at us, the 'masters of the deep.' Preparations were made for rigging up mosquito-curtains in the cabin, as the mosquitoes of the Paranà have the character of being most truculent gallinipers; and I was told that they were certain to make a feast of me, as a new comer. However, I have always had the good fortune of being disliked by insects, and in many continental experiences have come off better than my fellows. On the night of my first landing at Buenos Ayres some months before, I was ornamented by the mosquitoes with about a dozen red knobs on the face; perhaps they reported unfavourably of me, but certain it is, that during the rest of my stay in South America I was very rarely bitten again.

League after league of monotonous *barrancas*; island after island, gorgeous with the blood-red blossoms of a thousand seibos; green masses of willows, among which tall cranes and herons fished quietly in the shade; and channel after channel of marvellous intricacy, were passed; and then, just before the sun sank below the boundless Pampas of the west, we anchored a few miles south of San Nicolas. Down came the pilot, half scorched, from the paddle-box; there was to be no more heaving of the lead: 'Oh! rest ye, brother mariners,' for the evening!

And those evenings on the Paranà were indeed never to be forgotten. The moon shone brilliantly over our heads as the 'Ardent' lay quietly at anchor, bathed as it were in light: not a ripple disturbed the glassy surface of the river; not a sound broke the silence of the surrounding scene, as we clustered round a 32-pounder in the enjoyment of tranquillity. Then came the Muses. A word to the Quarter-master summoned the band, and for an hour we listened to many a well-known air, and heard the famous chants of Old England performed with all the enthusiasm of the British tar. Terpsichore followed; and the white-trousered sons of Neptune, jumping to their feet from various corners of the forecastle, danced as if their sweethearts were present in the flesh, till the band retired, and nothing but the customary fiddle remained to lead the ever-glorious hornpipe. Ah! how I pitied my London friends, who were then in the middle of their November fogs! How devoutly I wished I could suddenly transport a few of them across 'the vasty deep' to inhale the pure atmosphere of that delicious climate!

At 5 o'clock in the morning of the 20th I came on deck to see San Nicolas, which we were just passing, about 200 miles from Buenos Ayres. It appeared to be a small place, with a snug port, containing a considerable number of country vessels. Soon afterwards we passed the confluence of the Arroyo del Medio, the boundary of the provinces of Buenos Ayres and Santa Fé; and a little later we came to that of the Arroyo del Pavon, the scene of the late battle in September. About 1 o'clock we anchored at Rosario, where there are fifteen fathoms of water nearly close to the edge of the river. Here we were to land, and, if possible, to pay a visit to the Buenos Ayrean army, which was known to be encamped in the neighbourhood.

I went ashore with the captain and Mr. Boyd to call upon an American merchant, who was also performing the duties of consular agent to the United States. We found him at home, and, after a little conversation with his son, he kindly made arrangements to send us out to the camp. A pair of horses were put into one of the queerest vehicles I ever saw, though I must say it was light and very well adapted for the purpose of getting about a country without regular roads, in our sense of the word. It was open at the sides, and had a flat roof supported on stanchions, so that, while sheltered from the sun, we had the full benefit of the lively breeze.

In a short time we started, the young gentleman evidently disposed to make the most of our time by driving furiously, and occasionally encouraging the horses with 'Now, then, get along, old hoss, you have not got father behind you to-day!' The suburbs of Rosario are rather pretty, and the proximity of the camp had given an unusual appearance of bustle and activity to the whole place. Soldiers and civilians were riding backwards and forwards; strings of heavy bullock-carts sometimes nearly blocked up the road, which was deep in dust, except at some half-dry ditch, or muddy ford of a stream, which no genuine son of the soil would think of improving by a bridge. We had some very rough jolting in these places, and once I fully expected that we should follow the example of a bullock-cart, which had stuck hard and fast, and was being dug out by a large party of natives. Our charioteer proved himself quite equal to the occasion, and charged up and down all obstacles with a skill and gallantry which deserved the highest praise.

A drive of about six miles took us to the camp, and we went through the middle of it without being challenged or asked any questions. It was a strange sight. The heroes of the Pavon were encamped in a fine situation on the high grassy plains, commanding an extensive view of Rosario and the river below, with the long *barrancas* running out like a promontory towards a group of islands nearly opposite to the town. There was, however, nothing fine about it excepting the situation. The tents, if they could be called tents, were pitched irregularly, and were of all sorts and sizes; the greater part of them being mere pieces of sacking supported on a few muskets or sticks, so low above and so open at the bottom as to combine the minimum of protection with the maximum of discomfort. From underneath most of them a row of swarthy, gipsy-looking heads protruded, stolidly staring at us, and resting on their chins, while the outstretched bodies of the owners were concealed under the canvas. A large proportion of them were smoking the inevitable *cigaros de papel*, or cigarettes, and some were chatting to one another in an under-tone. They are a singularly undemonstrative race, except under the influence of extraordinary excitement; and the army was now at rest. As far as I could see, sentries were considered perfectly unnecessary, and we had the greatest difficulty in finding the quarters of the Colonel commanding one of the regiments, who was an acquaintance of our American friend.

At last the Colonel was discovered, and we dismounted in front of his tent, where he received us very politely. An officer of the same rank in Europe would be mightily surprised if he were invited to lodge under a strip of canvas just large enough to cover a small truckle-bed and a box by the side with his saddle on it. The Colonel, however, took all his discomforts in a most good-natured and gentlemanly way; he smiled apologetically as he asked his visitors to sit down on the end of the bed, and sent for matè, the universal favourite and chief consoler of the native Buenos Ayrean. We all tasted this beverage in turn, and conversation lasted for about half an hour, during which we were patiently stared at by a dark-featured gaucho, in charge of the Colonel's beautiful Chilian horse.

We left the carriage here, and walked up the centre of the camp to the point at which we were told to look for General Mitre's tent. We picked our way among a seeming chaos of wretched tents, full of recumbent and motionless figures: rows of dark faces watched us silently, and the expression of many was unpleasant in the extreme. Not a word of greeting or of challenge came to us, and at last we found ourselves close to the tent of the Commander-in-Chief.

We hesitated to advance, thinking it might be an intrusion to invade the privacy of the great man; and as a man, apparently an officer, was passing by, we asked him if General Mitre was at home. He neither asked us what we wanted, nor did he offer to introduce us; but passed on his way, remarking only, with perfect unconcern, 'Si, señor.' As no one appeared to bar our way, we walked boldly up to the door of the tent, where we found the General, in plain clothes, smoking and talking with the war minister, Colonel Gelly y Obes. He was already acquainted with Captain Parish, and received us very politely into his spacious tent, where a pretty fair show of really good furniture afforded a remarkable contrast to everything else we had seen in the camp. He is a handsome man, with the decided stamp of intellect upon his forehead, though it is somewhat disfigured by the scar of an old wound. The last time I had seen him was in a brilliant ball-room at Buenos Ayres, where every one remarked his eminently quiet and elegant manners; and I could not help thinking how much he must have endured in the course of the last six months, condemned to the command of an undisciplined army and the banishment of a camp on the Pampas. In spite of his successes in September, he had an anxious, melancholy manner; the army was to march that night or the next morning, and perhaps he felt heavily the responsibility of its future movements.

After a short conversation we withdrew, and found our way back to the quarters of our friend the colonel. I observed a great want of cleanliness in the camp: bones and offal were frequently to be seen lying about in the blazing sun, but the extreme dryness of the climate prevents such things from being so noxious as they would be in Europe. After a very short period of corruption, the drying process follows; and even the dead horses and cattle, which are found in numbers upon the plains, and skinned by the finder, after presenting the ghastly object of a blood-red carcase to the passer-by, soon become comparatively inoffensive under the scorching influence of the sun, aided, no doubt, by the greedy efforts of predatory birds. The number of men in the camp was, as we were informed, between eight and ten thousand, only about half the force of the original army of the Pavon: probably, however, the greater part of those who 'skedaddled' on that occasion had never been induced to return, and many more must have died from wounds and sickness. The process of victualling the army was very simple, beef and matè being the only food. Large droves of cattle are sent into the camp, and there slaughtered after the fashion of the country. Each beast supplies about forty men for the day, so that rather more than two hundred fell daily for the consumption of the army. They are quite independent of kitchens and cumbrous establishments, for every man in the country has been accustomed from his boyhood to cook his own beef in his own fashion. Bread and vegetables, and many other things which we consider necessaries, being entirely unknown to the common people, many difficulties are removed from the commissariat; and the trouble of transport is reduced to a minimum where the staple commodity of bullocks is marched to the scene of consumption upon its own legs. I saw a few fish which somebody had brought up from the river; but that was quite an exceptional case.

The irregular arrangement of the camp, with its various kinds of shabby tents spread about the plain, the artillery, bullock-carts, and ammunition-waggons drawn up on the higher ground behind, and the wild looks of the gipsy-like, undisciplined gauchos, gave a very picturesque appearance to the whole scene, and I was extremely glad to have had such a good opportunity of seeing a South American army in the field. The weather was, to my mind, delightful; the burning sun shone all day without a cloud, but a fine westerly breeze blew across the heated earth, laden with the pure essences of a thousand miles of Pampas. In the neighbourhood of the roads cut up for the service of the army, the dust was certainly very trying, and I had many opportunities of seeing fine specimens of whirlwinds, loaded as it were with dust, careering over the plain in immense dark pillars of from 50 to 200 feet in height, and apparently large enough in bulk to overwhelm any one who could not get out of their way.

At last we said farewell to the colonel, and, hoping he would get successfully through the disagreeables of breaking up the camp and moving his men towards Cordova, we were driven back to Rosario as fast as the lively steeds and active whip could do it. Just as we left the camp, I met my old friend and fellow-passenger from England, the soldier-like Garibaldian colonel. He had been induced by his fighting instinct to join the Buenos Ayrean army, and was a distinguished member of the Italian brigade which captured Urquiza's artillery at the battle of the Pavon. He had since been very ill, and bore traces of suffering, though his eagle eye and erect figure made him look every inch a soldier as he rode leisurely into the camp. The chief novelty that I observed among the wild flowers was the abundance of a lilac verbena, instead of the scarlet species that was among the chief ornaments of the more southern plains.

We returned to Rosario by a different road, and I had a better opportunity of seeing the town. It is one of the most thriving and progressive places in the Argentine Confederation, being the chief point at which the produce of the upper provinces is shipped for Buenos Ayres, Montevideo, and so to other parts of the world. The population has increased very rapidly to about 16,000, half of whom are foreigners, and new buildings in all directions testify to fresh enterprises. The great thing, however, for Rosario will be the railway to Cordova and the interior, by which the resources and wealth of the provinces will be immensely increased and developed. Rosario will be the terminus at which their productions will be shipped, and there will be nothing to prevent those productions from being almost infinite as soon as a good communication is made for their transport. At present every article of commerce from Cordova, Mendoza, San Juan, Santiago, Salta, Tucuman, &c., must be brought for many hundreds of miles in lumbering bullock-carts, placed on high wheels, like those of bathing-machines, to help them through rivers and ditches; and made so heavy, to secure the requisite strength, that their pace is reduced to the slowest crawl that is consistent with motion. To travel for 800 miles with a train of these conveyances must be a severe trial of patience to those in charge of them; but, fortunately, that is one of the virtues of a country where no one is in a hurry.

In the province of Mendoza, among the first approaches to the Cordillera of the Andes, and also in the province of La Rioja, excellent wine is made; but with such means of transport as bullock-waggons for more than 700 miles to Rosario, who can wonder if it is little known? It can be made, however, in enormous quantities, and even now is sent over from Mendoza into Chili; though, to get there, it must be carried on muleback over a pass of about 13,000 feet above the sea.

Cotton can be produced in any quantity in the

provinces on both sides of the Paraná; and I have even been told that the first stock of cotton planted in North America came from the neighbourhood of the Argentine city of Cordova. It is hoped that this will be an important article of trade with the River Plate, and a considerable quantity is already being grown; but at present more labour and improved communications are required. The territory of the Confederation extends through eighteen degrees of latitude, and there is, consequently, a great variety of climate in different parts of it: and, as there are also great differences of elevation between the level of the Pampas and the slopes of the Andes, nearly all the necessaries of life are produced between its boundaries. The one great want is railway communication, and the Government are now in a fair way to supply the deficiency.

The country is probably the easiest in the world for carrying out such undertakings. For hundreds of miles there is hardly anything to do but to lay down rails upon the plains. Two smaller lines are already opened out of Buenos Ayres, one to the north and the other to the west; and a third, which will extend from the capital to Chascomus on the south, is now, I believe, in course of construction. But the grand work will be the line from Rosario to Cordova, which has long been talked of, and now seems pretty certain of accomplishment. It will naturally extend itself to all the important cities of the interior, and a proposal has even been made to carry it over the Andes, and bring it into cooperation with the railways of Chili.

When the minerals of the Cordillera, the fruits and wines, the cotton and the tobacco, the hides and fleeces of the interior can have a safe and easy transit to the Paranà, the world will see how important a country has remained thus long in comparative obscurity. The benefits will be manifold. One of the greatest will probably be that many of the cleverest men in the country will find new and profitable fields for their energy. It may fairly be hoped that many will abandon the unfortunate practice of damaging the best interests of their country by petty intrigues and trumpery politics, and by prattling about their holy mission for the establishment of universal liberty, while they lose the substance of it. True liberty was never established by mere theorists; but it is the natural reward of honest, hard work.

Before leaving Rosario, our American friend shewed me over his establishment, which consisted of a large courtyard, nearly surrounded by storehouses, or *galpones*, as they are called. Here were piled up heaps of hides, bags of raisins and dried peaches from Mendoza, tierces of *yerba*, and sacks of *alfalfa* seed. Ponderous bullock-wagons were coming and going, and lazy groups of peons were loitering about the gates in gawdy ponchos, and staring at us with their customary expression of utter indifference to all things human and divine.

Some of them were evil-looking knaves, and my host told me that it was often very hard work to manage them; but perhaps one ought not to expect much from men who pass their existence in goading bullocks across boundless plains at the rate of about two miles an hour.

The good people of Rosario had suffered a great panic two months before our visit. When Urquiza fled in hot haste from the battle of Pavon, and arrived at Rosario, the inhabitants not unnaturally feared that the rest of the defeated army might fall back upon their town in a frame of mind which might induce them to commit every kind of plunder and outrage in revenge for being disappointed in their expectation of sacking Buenos Ayres, which had been their only inducement to serve willingly in the war. Many ladies and children were received by Captain Paget, on board H.M.S. Oberon, and the greatest excitement prevailed. Fortunately, no harm was done, and the victorious army of Buenos Ayres was pushed forward to Rosario as quickly as possible.

We had another delightful evening on board, and soon after four o'clock next morning started once more up the river. Two or three hours later we passed San Lorenzo, conspicuous by its fine old church and convent, and amused ourselves by taking long shots at a freshwater seal when he came to the surface.

In the afternoon we came up with the Buenos

Ayrean squadron, whose persistent inactivity had been frequently the object of invidious remarks from the Federal party in the city. This fleet consisted of six steamers and a sailing brig, the steamers being ordinary passenger-vessels, seized by the Government, and armed with such guns as they could muster. The average size appeared to be about that of a Margate boat, and the whole could have been destroyed in less than half an hour, by the most moderate fire of a small battery on shore, if there had been one. We stopped for a short time to let them send off a boat for some letters and papers which we had brought up for them. The boat came alongside, and the letters were handed down to the officer, who was greatly obliged. We were rather struck with the smart appearance of two or three of the crew, who looked very like Englishmen, and the suspicion was soon confirmed. The officer gave them the word in Spanish, and one of them at once remarked to the man next him, 'Shove off, Bill. All right!' No doubt they had been victims to some of the Buenos Ayrean crimps, who liked nothing better than inducing English and American seamen to run from their ships. If they liked idleness better than anything else, they were probably satisfied, as they had not weighed anchor for many weeks. If they expected to get a pleasanter set of messmates by the change of service, they must have been lamentably disappointed.

The vessels were anchored in line, and just as we

came alongside of the headmost, a broad reach of the river enabled us to see the hostile squadron of the Federals over the low ground of the next corner, scarcely more than a league distant. This magnificent armament consisted of nine steamers, of which, however, at least one or two were not larger than a Thames tug-boat. To any one accustomed to see the powerful fleets of Europe, there was something ridiculous in the idea of these two squadrons being ecstatically puffed by their respective partisans, and assuming the pretensions of naval forces; but, say what one may, all things are great and small by comparison, and these collections of cock-boats were, at all events, sufficient to frighten one another; they had remained for weeks together without either party venturing an attack.

Being perfectly neutral, we stopped for a short time near this squadron of Urquiza's as we had just before done by that of Buenos Ayres; and on looking at the crews, I could not help thinking that, in the event of a fight, the latter ought to have had much the best of it. The decks of the captain-general seemed to be chiefly occupied by gangs of that gaucho cavalry whose scarlet *ponchos* and *chiripàs* inspire terror in the minds of the southern soldiery, but who would of all men be the most useless on board a ship. A boat came off, but returned when it was announced that we were going to anchor for the night just above them, and we were led to expect a visit from the admiral.

Soon after four in the afternoon, the 'Ardent' anchored about two miles ahead of the Federal fleet. A strong breeze was blowing down the river, and we soon saw that a boat was pulling hard against wind and stream towards us. It was curious to watch the faces of our noble blue-jackets standing ready to receive the admiral, as soon as the gipsy-looking, mongrel crew could put him alongside. At last he stood upon our deck. Sure such an admiral was never seen! The poor old man was an Italian, and a brave one too, who had fought at Montevideo in the same cause with Garibaldi, when the hero of the red shirt was a lesser man. In one of the fights at that time he had lost an arm at the shoulder, and he now looked lean and haggard. His long, iron-grey hair had a wild and greasy appearance, as it hung over his shoulders from under a dirty cap, and his clothes were shabby in the extreme. Still he looked a gentleman, and bowed politely in answer to the attention with which he was received by the English officers.

He was accompanied by the commander of one of his smallest ships, the son of a distinguished officer in the United States navy, who had some years previously done good service by his explorations of the Paraguay and Paranà. Round the cap of the commander was a ribbon which had once been red, inscribed in dirty-white letters with the Urquizista motto, '*Defendemos la ley federal jurada, son traidores los que la combaten*;' meaning, 'We defend the sworn federal law, and those who resist it are traitors.' Considering the deeds which have been done in South America to this tune, one is sorely tempted to compare the conduct of the Mexican brigands who, before the French occupation, assumed the character of 'defenders of the church,' and in that capacity robbed the Vera Cruz *diligence* whenever they could find an opportunity.

The chief engineer of the squadron—as usual, a very sensible and intelligent Scotchman—also came on board the 'Ardent,' and from the united testimony of these officers we discovered that the defenders of the Federal law had a most miserable life of it. Not a man or officer, from the poor old admiral downwards, had received a farthing of pay for six months, with the solitary exception of the engineers, who, under the guidance of their able chief, had secured the payment of their dues by clearly explaining to the captain-general of the forces that, unless their assistance was properly paid for, the fleet could not and should not move under any possible circumstances.

A comfortable meal and a little rational conversation on board a British man-of-war seemed to do them all good, and the party returned to their ships apparently highly gratified. The chief engineer, however, remained on board, for it was agreed that he should be allowed a passage to Paranà on leave, as we were now not many leagues from that place. I do not know by what precise feelings the admiral was influenced, but we soon afterwards heard that he had abandoned his charge and coolly retired to *terra firma*, probably disgusted with the whole affair.

The sequel of this naval campaign remains to be told. Some weeks after our visit the Urquizista party appear to have felt that their chance was gone, and their squadron went up to the town of Paranà to disarm. The Buenos Ayrean squadron, which had never ventured to give them battle, waited their opportunity; and when Urquiza's ships were nearly disarmed and partially deprived of their crews, they went through the farce of capturing them, which was magnified by the Buenos Ayrean commander into a great naval victory, and made the subject of a grandiloquent despatch. Such were, in the year of grace 1861, the squadrons of the two contending factions in a South American civil war!

We were lying off Diamante, formerly called Punto Gorda, near which a great change takes place in the appearance of the country. The high land and steep *barrancas*, which extend the whole distance from Buenos Ayres on the eastern or the right bank of the river, now cease; and without any important deviation in the general course of the stream, the high land appears on the other side. At Diamante there is a fine headland, and thenceforward to Paranà the coast of Entre Rios appeared to be from about a hundred and fifty to two hundred feet in height, breaking off suddenly in precipitous *barrancas* at the water's edge. The Federal ships were lying in a very pretty situation, near the Entre Rios side, under shelter of the lofty headland and wooded banks of Diamante, just at the point which Urquiza selected for crossing the Paranà with his troops.

About five o'clock in the morning we started again, and three hours later all care and attention were required to get the 'Ardent' through a difficult and tortuous channel where there was scarcely water enough for her to float. All the difficulties, however, were safely passed. Before long the shining white buildings of Paranà appeared above the heights, and at ten o'clock we anchored opposite the landing-place, or Bajada.

CHAPTER XV.

PARANÀ AND SANTA FÉ.

PARANÀ—THE HOTEL DE PARIS—THE SIESTA—BEDS OF FOSSIL OYSTERS—PRETTY ENVIRONS—THE NOGOYÀ DILIGENCE—EXCURSION TO SANTA FÉ—ALLIGATORS ON THE BANK OF THE SALADO—ORIGIN OF SANTA FÉ—ROUGH-LOOKING SOLDIERS—BREAKFAST AT THE FONDA—VISIT TO THE CHURCH—VIEW FROM THE TOWER—DUST AND DECAY—THE OLD FORT—THE SCARLET PONCHOS—AFFAIR OF THE CARCARAÑA—THE POSTMASTER OF SANTA FÉ—A CIRCUS—'SIC VOS NON VOBIS'—AGREEMENT TO START FOR NOGOYÀ.

THE city of Paranà is about four hundred miles higher up the river than Buenos Ayres; and, though by no means entitled to be considered an important place in itself, yet it was selected by the provincial majority of the Congress as the official capital and seat of government of the Argentine Confederation. Here sate the Congress which had proved so obnoxious to the real capital, the head-quarters of the wealth and intelligence of the country, that the wrathful Buenos Ayreans had taken up arms for its destruction. The course of the last few weeks had been marked by the flight of Derqui, its president, and the downfall of his party. It was certain that one main result of the war would be the change of the capital; but the foreign Ministers had not yet removed from Paranà.

I had been fortunate enough to make the acquaintance of the English Minister, Mr. Thornton, when I was at Buenos Ayres some months earlier; and, on hearing that I had come up the river in the 'Ardent,' he kindly offered me a room in his house during my stay. I therefore sent my goods on shore, and prepared to follow them. My friend, Mr. Boyd, landed at the same time, and for the first time we touched the soil of Entre Rios. The bank of the river was dry and shingly, with a considerable mixture of loose sand, which was disagreeably hot in the middle of the day. The *barrancas* are of a very considerable height, apparently nearly 200 feet; and, where not covered with grass or bushes, are white, like chalk cliffs, from the vast quantities of shells, which are being worked for lime. A road from the port to the town is carried in zig-zags up the most practicable part of the cliffs; and finding there were no horses on the spot, we agreed, in consideration of the heat, and partly for the fun of the thing, to enter Paranà in a bullock-cart, which was hanging about in charge of a young negro.

We climbed into this vehicle, and amused ourselves by conversing with our charioteer while the bullocks crawled up the hill with their accustomed solemnity. He was very much puzzled about the 'Ardent,' and very anxious to know which side we had come to fight for. Poor fellow! he was disgusted with the war, and groaned over the idea that in a few days he would be compelled to join the Federal army. Near the port are a few scattered houses, and on the highest part of the *barranca*, to the north, is situated a colourable imitation of a fort. Its position is admirable, and if well manned and well armed it could entirely bar the passage of the river; but, unfortunately, it is neither the one nor the other. After arriving on the high ground, we were carried about a mile farther over a very white and dusty road into the heart of the capital, where my companion took up his residence at a *fonda*, or inn, which was dignified by the name of Hôtel de Paris. The proprietor and his family were only partially dressed, and did not seem in a very accommodating or lively humour, which was probably caused by our having disturbed them before their siesta was quite finished. The building consisted only of a tolerable courtyard, with a few dirty rooms on each side of it: the brick floor of that which was destined for my friend was partly taken up, and things looked in general confusion; but we were assured that all would be *muy bien*, or quite right, before the evening.

Every day since leaving Buenos Ayres, the heat had been gradually increasing as we approached nearer to the tropic; and while I was at Paranà the thermometer was generally from 86° to 90° in the shade. A few weeks later, however, this temperature was considerably increased; and Mr. Thornton, who kept a careful account of observations during his whole residence there, informs me that in February it rose to 102°. The inhabitants of all classes and ages consider the midday heat quite incompatible with exertion, and generally shut up their doors or windows for a quiet sleep of several hours. In Santa Fè, Paranà, and the other towns which I visited in Entre Rios, the streets during the whole middle of the day were almost entirely deserted, like those of some city of the dead. I believe I was considered half mad for disregarding this institution; but I must confess that I dearly love sunshine, and I never hesitated to take my fill of it. This was, perhaps, partly because one has very few opportunities of ever seeing real sunshine in many parts of Europe, and its glory is, therefore, more completely appreciated; but it is also true that, as a general rule, those who are spending their first season in a hot climate can bear it much better than those who have been there for several years. They carry out from their more temperate regions a stock of vigour which lasts some time before it is exhausted or appreciably diminished. One man may hold out longer than another; but in the long run very few resist the influences which draw them into adopting the customs of the country. In the meantime, I thoroughly enjoyed day after day of blazing sunshine and deep blue skies which were seldom sullied by a single cloud. There was almost always a light air which was very agreeable, but occasionally a heavy wind driving dense clouds of dust made it difficult to breathe or see. The dust of a soil where there is no stone becomes fine as flour, penetrating into every corner, and sadly destructive of clothes. This is probably the chief drawback of Paranà.

Under these circumstances the dinner-hour was four o'clock, and the evenings were devoted to riding or exposing ourselves to the probable contempt of the inhabitants by condescending to walk. The town is not large and only contains a few thousand inhabitants. There is the customary *plaza,* or square, in the centre, containing the public buildings and sundry insignificant shops; a few churches, of which the exterior is the most imposing part; and the regular chess-board system of streets at right angles. The houses look remarkably white, but not even an enthusiast could find much to admire in the place itself. The immediate environs, however, are remarkably agreeable, and a few minutes are sufficient to reach the open country and pure breezes of the Pampas. The people seemed very quiet and peaceable, and there were many picturesque outlying cottages rejoicing in the shade of the ombù, and ornamented with the brilliant clusters of the seibo. The most curious feature that I observed was the enormous quantity of fossil oyster-beds. In many places the soil had been furrowed by torrents, the steep banks of which presented the appearance of walls composed entirely of these shells; and sometimes the earth was split open by chasms exactly like large crevasses in a glacier. Their depth appeared to vary from 10 to about 30 or 40 feet, and their perpendicular sides were composed almost entirely of gigantic oysters. The small Rio de las Conchitas in the neighbourhood, takes its name from similar shells which form the principal characteristic of its banks.

One of my principal objects in coming to Paranà, was to cross the interior of Entre Rios with my friend Mr. Boyd, and, if possible, reach the estancia of his father-in-law, which we knew was not far from the town of Gualeguay. The question was how to get there. The estanciero generally travels with his own peons and *tropilla* of horses; when one horse is tired he changes his saddle and mounts another; the tired one is compelled to keep up the gallop with the rest of the *tropilla*, and in this manner very great distances are accomplished in a single day. We could not, however, arrange anything of this kind at Paranà, and as we were not expected at the estancia, no preparations could be made for meeting us. On making enquiries, however, we were informed that a *diligencia*, or omnibus-like conveyance, made the journey to Nogoyà at certain periods, one of which was near at hand; in fact, if all went well, the coach would start in two or three days. We were referred to an address where we could make further enquiries and take our places if we so wished.

With some little difficulty we found the place indicated, and entered a huge yard, covered with rubbish and confusion, the chaotic premises of a South American coach-builder. On one side was the battered frame of a *galera*; on another side a loose heap of old wood and iron, apparently intended for the repairs of a small vehicle, which I should have thought was past all recovery; remains of bullock-carts and broken wheels strewed the ground in all directions, and there did not seem to be anything worth half-a-crown in the place. I thought of Dickens's delightful story of the decayed mail-coaches, as I looked about in wonder for the object of our search. At last a fat and grimy man emerged from a shed: my companion asked him where the *diligencia* for Nogoyà was to be found.

'*Aqui, Señor*' (here, sir), said the man, pointing out to us one of the most dilapidated wrecks in his establishment.

'That the *diligencia*!' we both exclaimed.

'*Si, Señor.*'

'Well; but we thought it was to start to-morrow or the day after, and it is all in pieces.'

'It will be ready, *Señor.*'

'But half one side is gone, and half the bottom; it has no seats, no windows, no coach-box; the lining is torn to atoms, and it has only one spring!'

'All will be ready, *Señor, mañana.*'

We knew that *mañana*, though literally meaning to-morrow, is practically a very indefinite word in the mouth of a Spanish American; so we resolved to pay no money for places till we saw matters in a little more advanced stage, and proposed to call again. Next day an iron support was added to the weakest side of the wreck, but there were no other signs of progress, and we resolved to make an excursion to Santa Fè, a little way up the Salado river.

Very early in the morning a country carriage was ready to take us down to the port, but we found ourselves obliged, as a preliminary step before leaving the province, to procure passports from the local police. This was of course a mere excuse, perhaps excusable, for extracting a few dollars in return for an extraordinary document surrounded by mysterious emblems of commerce; our names, hurriedly taken down from our own *vivâ voce* statement, were distorted by the authorities more outrageously than I could have thought possible: I figured as Señor Xequel, and my companions fared scarcely better. At eight o'clock we went on board one of the smallest steamers ever seen, charged with the task of towing a clumsy government horse-raft, which was intended for the conveyance of Federal cavalry. The Salado debouches into the Paranà through a channel of very considerable width, up which we made pretty fair progress. The high lands and white *barrancas* of Entre Rios were soon left behind as we steamed between the low and marshy banks of the ever-narrowing Salado. Marshes and lagunas, lagunas and marshes, were the chief features of the scenery; and many a quaint ungainly bird soared lazily from the reeds, as our paddles disturbed the water where they were reposing. Even if there were no other evidence to support the belief, a sportsman would immediately see from the appearance of the surrounding country that, by paddling about those retired lagunas which communicate with the river, he would have an immense variety of wild-fowl shooting.

A few alligators showed themselves on the banks, and the steam-boat captain, a very pleasant Italian, amused himself by suddenly clutching a musket and firing at them. We could not see any material effects, but perhaps he may have tickled one of the scaly monsters, for they rushed incontinently into the water. There was a very amusing and intelligent man on board in the person of the captain's uncle and money-taker. He was a Genoese skipper, who had for many years navigated a vessel of his own in the Mediterranean, till an unlucky gale wrecked him on the coast of Spain and stripped him of all his little fortune. He was a very pleasant old fellow, who had seen the 'cities and customs of many men,' had learned something of their languages, and gained in a very high degree the invaluable art of not yielding to adversities.

About half-past ten o'clock a small grove of masts appearing over a corner of the land showed that we were near our destination; another turn was made, and presently we came to anchor among a crowd of small schooners waiting for cargoes of produce from the interior. A boat of the Norwegian pattern took us on shore, and we landed at the highly interesting town of Santa Fè.

The early Spanish adventurers in the Rio de la Plata suffered greatly from the want of friendly ports, of which there had been an entire deficiency from the mouths of the river to Assumption in Paraguay, since the abandonment of the settlement of Buenos Ayres in the year 1535. Under these circumstances De Garay in 1573, selecting a neighbourhood where the Indians were more friendly than those of the southern part of the country, commenced the foundations of Santa Fè de la Vera Cruz on the right bank of the river, and about the latitude of 31° south. In 1651, the inhabitants moved a little farther south, and established themselves in the present city at the mouth of the Rio Salado. Santa Fè has thus been for a considerable period of high interest and importance as a half-way station between the mouths of the Paranà and the capital of Paraguay.

We were quietly stared at on landing by a few idlers, but no one troubled us with questions; so we wandered past the few houses near the water-side with the hope of reaching the principal part of the city, and discovering some establishment where we might get the breakfast of which we began to be in need. The place looked poor and thinly built over, but with the usual system of long streets intersecting one another at right angles we had no difficulty in finding our way to the Plaza, which we knew must be pretty near the centre. It was scarcely eleven o'clock yet, but many of the people had composed themselves for the siesta, and many sleepy faces looked at us languidly through half-open doors, wondering apparently what new kind of madmen we could be.

At last we saw some chance of refreshments, and turned into a very small and dirty establishment, which called itself the Hôtel de la Republica. Some rather savage-looking soldiers were hanging about the place, lazily leaning against the walls of the court, and smoking in rather a sulky fashion. Their many-coloured pouches and wild appearance were exceedingly picturesque, but they had a dangerous look, and did not seem at all in the humour to be trifled with. We walked past them into what I suppose must be called the coffee-room, where we ascertained that one of the Federal generals had made his head-quarters in the house.

A remarkably dirty waiter in due time brought us some tolerable imitations of *filets de bœuf*, which, though rather redolent of garlic, were by no means despicable, with some fried potatoes and Carlon—a red Spanish wine generally drunk in the country. We thought we had breakfasted well, and soon afterwards we walked out to see what we could of the town. By this time everybody in the place seemed to have gone to sleep; and, though we were anxious to make the best use of our eyes, we certainly had very few opportunities of observing the inhabitants. We came to the Plaza, which was merely a burnt-up lawn intersected by a few paths, but we saw no living creatures except a couple of dogs sleeping against the wall of a house. The heat of the sun was certainly very great, but it appeared to me that the action of a light breeze made it much more endurable than the conduct of the inhabitants would have led me to suppose.

The tower of the church attracted us towards it, and we strolled through thick dust to the entrance. The principal gate was closed, but we found a little door at the side, leading into a cloistered enclosure full of peach and orange trees. We walked in, but there was no one to be seen: Santa Fè was like a city of the dead. Through a window opening into the cloisters, I saw a tolerable large collection of very old books, some very bulky and black with age; and I have no doubt that many of them would be found of great value as choice works brought out by the early Jesuits. We peeped into all kinds of holes and corners, and presently found that at one corner of the cloister there seemed to be a way to climb the tower of the church. We were preparing for the ascent, when a boy appeared with a can, in which he seemed to have been carrying refreshments for some sleeping saint. Thinking that perhaps he belonged to the place, we asked him if we might go up and explore for ourselves. '*Si, señor,*' he replied, and vanished.

It was too hot for hurrying, and we climbed leisurely by an old and battered staircase. After some time this ceased, and the remainder of the ascent was completed by means of steps and ladders among the ancient timbers of the tower. From the summit we had a complete view of the whole town, with lagunas and immense plains stretching out into the distance. The Salado river glittered in the sun, twisting and turning in its course to the Paranà; and beyond it rose the distant hills of Entre Rios. On one side was the expanse of the Pampas, with the road to Cordova and the provinces of the west; on the other was the great river, the noble Paranà, waiting to carry their undeveloped treasures to all parts of the earth; and here at our feet was nothing but a slumbering city! Looking from that lofty tower over the surrounding country, I could not help thinking of the gallant old Spaniards who built it long ago. What eager ambition must have nerved the arms of those who, not contenting themselves with the slow course of a colonisation which penetrates by gradually advancing its settlements, pushed at once boldly into the heart of a new continent, and established their cities in the teeth of hostile Indians! What faith must have possessed those pious men, who determined, in the face of all obstacles and difficulties, to carry the religion and civilisation of their fathers into these distant regions! What high hopes and aspirations must have animated the founders of Santa Fè, and how greatly would they be disappointed if they could revisit the scene of their labours! Faith is dead, and El Dorado was a fable.

My thoughts, however, soon travelled from the past to the future; and it was not difficult to foresee that the rapid multiplication of mankind with their ever-increasing necessities, the spirit of progress and railways, and the improvement of government with the advance of common sense, must soon combine to bring into those wonderful regions a much larger proportion of the human race than has hitherto been enabled to enjoy them. More immigrants are wanted to labour themselves, and to arouse the energies of the natives. Other things will follow in due course. Railway communication especially must have a good centralising effect in a country whose greatest misfortune has been the establishment of a Federation. The Federal system is, as Mr. Markham correctly observes in his 'Travels in Peru,' 'entirely unsuited to a thinly-peopled region, without roads, and unprovided with a sufficient number of capable educated men in the distant provinces to undertake the local government. Power necessarily falls into the hands of any cunning adventurer; every little state becomes a focus of revolution, and an endless succession of civil wars is the result.' Let us, however, hope that Santa Fè and other places will awake and prosper.

The appearance of the city, as seen from our eminence, was extremely curious. The long streets, now entirely silent and deserted by the sleepy inhabitants, stretched away to the surrounding plains—the houses gradually declining in size and style from tolerably good and substantial white buildings in the central districts to mere huts on the outskirts; but a very large number of them, whether great or small, were ornamented with gardens or enclosures full of peach and orange trees, the bright verdure of which contrasted charmingly with white walls and red roofs in every direction.

After a long enjoyment of our airy perch and the pure breeze that blew around it, we prepared for the descent, in the course of which we discovered an old door that led into the organ-loft. I saw no organ, however, but there were several old-fashioned instruments of music. A few high-backed chairs, elaborately carved, and a few old books lying about in disorder, must have come from Spain, and had to all appearance been there ever since the church was built. The dust and dirt of antiquity lay thick in every corner, and the whole place gave me the impression of having never been touched or entered since the palmy days of the Jesuits in America. We could not get into the body of the building, nor could we find anyone to interrogate on the subject; but, as far as we could see from above, the whole appeared to be in an equal state of neglect and shabbiness.

We sallied forth into the streets again, and happened to find an Italian who had come with us from Paranà in the morning, and was now going to look after a small piece of property which he had purchased. He asked if we would like to walk with him, and, not being at all particular as to our direction, we were glad of his company and information. After inspecting his garden and house, both of which were terribly out of repair, we all strolled together towards the outskirts of the town, where the Italian said he would show us a relic of the olden times, the ancient fortress which was built to protect the early settlers from the attacks of Indians.

Getting clear of the streets we soon found ourselves upon the turf amongst a few huts ornamented with the crimson blossoms of the seibó. Ten minutes or a quarter of an hour more brought us very near the fort, which was a huge pile built of red *adobes,* the sun-dried bricks of the country, and was connected with a large walled enclosure, intended, I suppose, to protect the cattle and possessions of the people in case of need. We had hoped to explore this curious old edifice, but on coming up to it we were surprised to find a considerable number of soldiers hanging about in the much-dreaded red ponchos of Urquiza. Some of them were lying at full length asleep on the ground, some were smoking paper cigars under a species of verandah, and others were lounging sulkily with their backs against the wall, staring at us silently. The Santa-fècinos are considered the finest of the natives, and certainly these were the most formidable-looking men I have ever seen, with the exception, perhaps, of the Life Guards. Many of them must have been several inches over six feet, and there was an appearance of dangerous ferocity about them which was anything but pleasant. I saw that our Italian friend, who knew the country well, was not only surprised but greatly alarmed at finding himself in such company about a mile from the town: he whispered hurriedly that we must pass without taking notice of them, and turn as soon as we could. We passed many fierce faces, but no one said a word to us: we walked on, looking indifferent to their presence, and, contenting ourselves with only seeing the outside of the fort, we turned to the left as soon as we could do so without seeming to avoid these desperate-looking characters, and walked back to the town by another route.

It turned out afterwards that, in the night before, a part of the Buenos Ayrean army had attacked a body of Federals in the neighbourhood of the Carcaraña, not very far from Santa Fè. It was said that treachery had enabled them to surprise the position while the men were asleep, and that several hundreds of them were killed on the ground. It was very difficult to get at the truth in such a matter, but all accounts stated that a large number had been thus slain; and if, as was supposed, the party which we fell in with had only just escaped from the horrible fate of their comrades, there would be no ground for surprise at their looking dangerous and out of temper. We had no arms, but even if we had, they would have been useless against numbers; and I daresay the Italian had good reason for his panic. In fact we were all glad to find ourselves safely in Santa Fè.

After a good deal of trouble we succeeded in finding the house of the Post-office manager, who had been known to one of our party when at Paranà. He had concluded his siesta, and received us very politely, though still in *deshabille.* His room was a model of neatness, and was ornamented, to my great surprise, with sundry shells and cannon-balls, carefully mounted, and painted with certain dates and names of places. I found he was a sailor by profession, and had been for some time an officer of the Argentine navy. He spoke English, and told us that the missiles in question were trophies of various engagements in which he had been concerned, but Obligado was the only one of the inscriptions which I now remember. He did not seem at all satisfied with the administration of the government, and naturally remarked, that it was, to say the least, passing strange that the authorities at Paranà should fill their ships with cavalry soldiers, and put him, a sailor, in command of the post-office! He evidently thought he was not the right man in the right place. After visiting his garden, which was full of oranges and figs, and ornamented with Cape jasmines just coming into flower, we concluded an agreeable visit, and returned to the port.

The little steamer which brought us from Paranà was to return about four o'clock, and whilst waiting for that time, we refreshed ourselves in a small and dirty café near the water-side. It was kept by an Italian, with a handsome French wife, who did the honours of the house with all the animation of her race. She had the assistance of a very pretty sister, who had been married only two days before; and as the little world of Santa Fè had at last finished its siesta, several visitors came in to have a glass of wine and amuse themselves by joking with the bride, who certainly evinced not the slightest symptoms of shyness. The dresses of these young ladies were somewhat peculiar; they were made of very gaudy muslin, fitting quite tight to below the hips, whence they were suddenly distended by enormous crinolines. In due time we went on board our vessel, and had a pleasant run down the river, arriving at Paranà in time to have a very welcome dinner with the officers of the 'Ardent.'

About nine o'clock in the evening I went on shore with Mr. Boyd, and we wound up the day by going to a travelling circus, which was astonishing the good people of the town. A small payment admitted us to the performances, and we found ourselves in a place which could scarcely be surpassed in simplicity of arrangement. A pole had been planted in the middle of a square enclosure, which was surrounded by a wall, but not favoured with a roof. A hoop supporting about twenty common candles was suspended from the pole, and the stars above assisted the illumination. The performances were few and far between, and very much the worst that I have ever seen. The company stood round a rude ring, and the performers mixed with them very affably, till after a long effort of an abominable band, they mounted their horses and revolved in the circus. Many a gaucho would have beaten them in horsemanship, but the people seemed highly amused with the spangled dresses and the rough jests of a Spanish clown.

In the course of the next few days we made several visits to see after the state of the *diligencia* for Nogoyà. The progress was very slow and eminently unsatisfactory; but we were always told that everything would soon be ready, that we should have very good places, and that there would be only one passenger beside ourselves. One day, however, I heard that a native family wishing to cross the province had engaged six places, and I knew this would leave no room for us. Here was an end of all our care and watching. We had worried the coach-mender, and looked after the details of his work; but others were to reap the benefit. 'Sic vos non vobis nidificatis, aves!'

Highly indignant, I went to find my friend, that we might join in a grand remonstrance, but on the way I met our former companion, the Scotch engineer of Urquiza, who told me that he knew a certain Don Martin, who was going to Nogoyà with a Paraguayan gentleman in a private carriage, and would probably take us also for a moderate consideration. He showed the way to the premises of Don Martin, who turned out to be a very pleasant little man, and was the owner of sundry shabby vehicles of different descriptions. He took us across a yard, full of lumber and rubbish, and pointed out the carriage in which he proposed to carry the Paraguayan and his fortunes. It was a small and dirty affair, but he declared he could take us all. The matter of luggage was the most serious question; for the Paraguayan had an enormous box, which would monopolise the stern of the carriage, and leave no room for our portmanteaus. Finally, it was agreed that for thirty Bolivian dollars (about five guineas) we should have another vehicle for ourselves, all travelling in company as far as Nogoyà, which was said to be about thirty leagues distant.

I had spent a very pleasant week, and was exceedingly reluctant to leave behind me the kind hospitality of Mr. and Mrs. Thornton; but part of our plan was to go through Entre Rios, and my companion's time was more limited than my own. Many doubts were suggested of the prudence and safety of our expedition; and it was even hinted that if we fell in with any of Urquiza's soldiery, the least evil that might befall us would be the seizure of our horses, and our consequent abandonment in the midst of uninhabited plains! We took the best precautions that we could: Mr. Thornton gave us a good recommendation in Spanish, which would help us if we came in the way of any of the authorities, and we had pistols at hand to spoil the sport of more ordinary ruffians.

As the weather was exceedingly hot, it was arranged that we should start at four o'clock in the morning; and, therefore, after another delightful evening ramble among the pretty environs of Paranà, we bade farewell to our kind friends, and spent the night together at the fonda, in order to be ready for an early move. We had a good many little arrangements to make; and we found packing and sorting such hot work, even at night, and in our shirt-sleeves, that we advanced very slowly, and it was past midnight when the trunks were locked. We then sate down at an open window to cool our bodies with the night air, and to compose our minds with the assistance of a cigar. Both these objects were attained in the course of an hour, after which we stretched ourselves on our beds for a short repose.

CHAPTER XVI.

TRAVELLING IN ENTRE RIOS.

START FROM PARANÁ — WANT OF WATER — MUDDY PONDS — ARRIVAL AT NOGOYÀ — COUNTRY-QUARTERS — CHRISTIAN NAMES — THE GUALEGUAY DILIGENCIA — A ROUGH JOLTING — LETTERS FORGOTTEN — CHANGING THE TEAM — ROUGH DRIVERS — A DANGEROUS PLACE TO CROSS — DOWN THEY GO — THE COACH IS UPSET — MENDING A BROKEN LEG — A FRESH START — ARRIVAL AT THE ESTANCIA — 'OLD BOB' — BRICK MAKING AND HOUSE-BUILDING — CHOICE SHEEP — INCREASING VALUE OF LAND — A GARDEN — FERNS GROWING IN THE WELLS — GENERAL APPEARANCE OF THE LAND.

SOON after three o'clock in the morning, we were ready for Don Martin, who was rather behind time in coming for us. At last he came. Our trunks were firmly tied on a board behind the carriage; and, taking with us a bottle of wine and a piece of cold meat, we started through the silent streets a little before five o'clock.

Don Martin drove the first carriage, with the Paraguayan and his goods; the latter consisting of an enormous box and a grey parrot. The driver of our carriage turned out to be a Swiss, from the Canton of Berne, with whom, in the course of the day, I had a long talk about the beauties of his native country. Each vehicle had two horses, and a third was attached by a slack rope to the side, so that he could run free without doing any work, but would be ready to take the place of either of the others in case of their knocking up. This was considered quite sufficient for a journey of nearly a hundred miles, which was to be performed in one day, and without the chance of seeing even a village till the end of it.

As we drew out of the town we met a few country people riding in from the outlying houses with supplies for marketing; but in a very short time we saw the last of them, and did not meet another human being for about fifty or sixty miles. The road is merely a track, consisting of two light ruts upon the turf, which are made by the occasional passage of a bullock-cart or other vehicle, and were sometimes so faint as to be hardly visible. The dry weather had made the grass very brown; and the sun, rising in our faces like a ball of fire in a cloudless sky, promised another intensely hot day. On we went for hour after hour, at a steady pace of about nine miles an hour, over an almost completely level country; a sea of dry grass was around us, and for many leagues together not a tree or bush was to be seen. There was not a drop of water, not even a ditch of any description, and both ourselves and our animals were beginning to look out rather eagerly for it, when suddenly, about half-past nine, the quick eye of Don Martin detected a green spot near the road. We drove up to it, and called a halt by the side.

A kind of crack or crevice in the ground, about two feet wide, and extending for a few yards, contained a little clean water, tolerably cool withal, from its surface being about a foot below the level of the earth. Its effects were visible for some little distance on both sides, where green grass and a few fresh flowers made a very welcome oasis. Having done justice to the refreshing water, we unharnessed the horses and brought them down for their share of the treat. Whilst they ate and drank at their leisure, we threw ourselves upon the grass and produced our provisions. Don Martin had an uncommonly good roll of stuffed beef; and with the help of our own supplies, and a cup of wine and water, we thought that we had fared sumptuously. About a quarter of an hour after our arrival at this spot, the faithless *diligéncia* overtook and passed us at a quick pace; but, as we reclined at our ease on the turf, we congratulated ourselves upon not being jammed in with the native family.

The Paraguayan gentleman made himself very companionable, though he seemed rather a victim to the dreamy, lotus-eating manner of his country. He spoke Spanish in a very subdued tone, and with the soft pronunciation of the Guaranì; but he seemed to be enjoying himself in his own quiet way.

At last, after about an hour's halt, little Don Martin

rose to his feet, and said that we must march. The horses were harnessed as before, the spare ones being not yet thought necessary, and away we went again over the hot plains. Groups of deer and ostriches were startled every few minutes by our approach, but it did not appear to me that the partridges were so plentiful as in the Banda Oriental. The deer were very much like our English fallow deer, both in size and colour, and it was delightful to see them bound away to the side and then turn to look at us with astonishment. The South American ostriches are, as is well known, quite different from the African species. They are smaller, and their plumage is grey, without the beautiful side-feathers which are the glory of the African. They have, however, an exceedingly graceful way of expanding their long drooping feathers, which, when they are picking their way through long grass, makes them look at a little distance something like a mixture of lace and crinoline.

After pushing on for three or four hours longer, we approached a series of small ponds, and turned off the road in hopes of finding refreshment for man and beast. It was no small disappointment when we discovered that the water was scarcely better than hot mud, of about the same consistence as mock-turtle soup. It was scarcely a foot deep, and had been poached up by horses and cattle into such a state that no one could have swallowed it, except in the most direful emergency. We went on from one to the other without any better result, and turned back in despair towards the road. We took out the horses, who soon showed that they had no overpowering objection to the water; and, putting the two vehicles near together, we extemporised something of a tent, by stretching a couple of ponchos across from one to the other. Not far from us was the first tenement which we had seen since leaving Paranà, some fifty miles before. It was a mere hut, entirely alone upon the plains, but I saw some milch cows near it, which suggested the idea of sending the Swiss with an empty bottle for some milk. His mission was successful, and we rejoiced over a good substitute for the filthy water of the pond. Don Martin gave the horses a large feed of maize, and we returned to the attack upon our cold beef. As the blazing heat of the sun was kept off by the roof which we had contrived, and a sweet fresh breeze played freely under it, our pic-nic on the Pampas was a very enjoyable affair.

I thought we stayed here rather too long, but little Martin thought it would answer better, in the long run, to rest the horses well. At last we started; and went steadily on till nearly six o'clock, when we reached the *estancia* house of Don Manuel Leibe, who was a friend of Don Martin, and received us very politely. One of the horses was here changed for one of Don Manuel's, but the delay in bringing up the *tropilla* to choose from made us seriously late. We had still six leagues to travel before reaching Nogoyà, during three of which we were told that the road ran through woods, and it was seven o'clock when we left the house.

Night came on apace, and though the stars were bright, there was no moon. Every now and then we lost the road, and many times I thought we must certainly be upset in the rough hollows of dried-up water-courses. At last we came to the wood region, where, of course, it was more difficult than ever to see the track over the grass. The air was very chilly after our roasting through the day, and we were glad to wrap ourselves up in ponchos instead of sitting with our coats off. The horses were frequently pulled up by running into trees, but at last we came to a dead stop by the side of a large arroyo, evidently too deep to be forded. Martin had heard the dogs barking at a *rancho*, or hut, a little while before, so as we had evidently lost the road, he resolved to go back and ask the way, if he could find anybody. The furious barking of the dogs served as a guide, but just as we were close to the *rancho*, our horses charged into a stack of wood, and altogether we were in a mess that would have been highly ludicrous if it were not so annoying. The noise brought out a man, who explained the way to a bridge; soon afterwards, somewhat tired, but very hungry, we reached Nogoyà, and drove up to a small inn called the Hôtel de l'Union, at a quarter past eleven o'clock.

Our arrival created a complete sensation. The public

room of the house seemed to be frequented by the tradesmen and clerks of the place; who, after the heat of the day, came to enjoy the pleasures of a sociable supper and conversation. The unwonted sound of wheels drew them all from their tables; they seemed to look upon us as visitors from some distant planet, but when they found that we were English travellers, they volunteered every civility and attention in their power. To my great surprise, one young man had learnt English in some house of business on the river, and came forward to give us all the information he possessed about our intended route; not without displaying some natural curiosity about our movements. The people of the house, in spite of the lateness of the hour, exerted themselves for our comfort; and while a very satisfactory supper was being prepared, they produced sundry bedsteads of the country, and roughly fitted up a room at the back of the establishment for our reception. They produced some good English beer and Carlon wine, and about one o'clock in the morning we retired to our quarters, well disposed to sleep after a very long day's work.

The room was large, with a bare brick floor, and in three corners of it were the *catres* to be occupied by the Paraguayan, my companion, and myself respectively. The wall on one side did not reach the roof, and on the other side of it, as we rightly guessed by their snoring, the family which had arrived in the *diligencia* were peacefully reposing. We slept delightfully in these simple quarters, and were only aroused by the departure of the Paraguayan, with Don Martin, on their way to Gualeguaychù.

We had ascertained that a *diligencia* would leave in two days for Gualeguay, and we found, to our great satisfaction, that it passed the Estancia de las Cabezas, the very place which we wanted to reach. Under these circumstances, we had an idle day before us, and were quite content to breakfast leisurely at ten o'clock, the usual hour in the establishment. We then strolled out to see what we could of this small provincial town, which is nevertheless one of the chief places in Entre Rios. My companion being perfectly acquainted with the language and customs of the country, we heard of all that was going on by calling in at various shops and stores upon sundry pretences. There was not much to see in the way of regular sights; but I was pleased and surprised to find at Nogoyà, as well as in other remote towns of the Republic, an amount of intelligence and good manners on the part of the shopkeepers which, considering the difficulties entailed by their isolated situation, was really remarkable. I sincerely regretted that the scarcity of population cut them off from the much better position which they seemed worthy of. We listened incredulously to various reports that Urquiza was going to make a last effort in a few days, and once more to call out his troops, the greater part of whom had already returned to their homes. The result justified us in supposing that the Captain-General had had quite enough fighting for the present, and was glad to return to his acres and his beeves. The only attempt at military display which we saw was a small collection of National Guards in the Plaza, neatly dressed in blue uniforms and white trousers, listening to the music of a very tolerable band. We were in the heart of Urquiza's peculiar province, where I had expected to find everything and everybody rough and unmannerly; on the contrary, everything appeared to be peaceful and orderly in the extreme.

The siesta was maintained as rigorously as at Paranà; blinds were drawn and doors were shut for several hours, and in the hottest part of a very hot day we two were almost the only people to be seen in the streets of Nogoyà. In the evening the world emerged again, and we had an interview with Don Juan, the proprietor of the *diligencia.* He said he should start in the morning, about four o'clock, on the strength of which representation we went to bed rather late. He was an Italian, and a very good fellow. What his surname may have been I have no notion; everybody in that part of the world is known only by his Christian name. Whether you are Jew, Turk, infidel or heretic, you are to all intents and purposes Don Tomas or Don Antonio, Don Jorge or Don Diego. It is the same with the peons. I have stayed at an *estancia* where there were three Pedros; but they were not distinguished by their surnames, if they ever had any. They were Pedro el Grande and Pedro el Chico, or Peter the Great and Peter the Little, and the third was Peter the Basque.

I was aroused from my peaceful slumbers by the entrance of our stout friend Don Juan, bearing a lantern, with which he lighted a candle. I looked at my watch, and found it was scarcely past two o'clock. We both started rather crossly, and asked what on earth he wanted at that hour. He simply said that the day would be very hot, and he meant to march immediately. Remonstrance was useless, so we dressed as fast as we could, while the team was being harnessed. We paid a very moderate bill and climbed into a clumsy kind of a yellow omnibus, taking care to keep the two seats nearest the door. There were a few other passengers, including a Spanish woman with her baby, and as it was still quite dark, a candle in a common brass dish-candlestick was very considerately put in a vacant place on one of the seats. Baggage of various kinds was packed on the top, and with a smart whip-cracking to enliven the horses, we were off.

We galloped over the ground, and were soon out upon the open plains. Everything went on smoothly enough for a time; but presently we came to a standstill, and were requested by Don Juan to get out. It appeared that we were going to cross over the river of Nogoyà by a high bridge, which was not thought strong enough for a heavy load. All passed over safely; we returned to our seats, and again galloped on. Presently came a tremendous jolt; we charged down one side of a dried-up stream and rushed up the other side. I clutched the candlestick by my side to preserve it from the shock, but my intention was frustrated by circumstances: the baby was shot out from its mother's arms and precipitated upon the lighted candle, which it flattened and extinguished. The want of artificial light induced us to look to nature, and I never, not even in nights among the high Alps, saw so beautiful an appearance of the moon. It was in the thinnest possible crescent, but the reflected light upon the remainder of its surface was almost as bright as the full illumination presented in less transparent skies.

After travelling very fast for nearly an hour, we were conscious of somebody galloping after us at a still quicker pace. The rider reached us nearly breathless, holding in his hand the letter-bag, which Don Juan, in his hurry, had forgotten. At the end of four leagues we arrived at the first post, just as dawn was beginning to make things visible. The post-house was nothing but a very small and dirty hut, under the shade of an ombù-tree, from which emerged an old gaucho at the sound of Don Juan's horn. Jumping upon his horse in a moment, he rode off like the wind to bring up fresh animals for us, and returned in about a quarter of an hour, driving before him the *tropilla* of about thirty horses, which he had found feeding somewhere in the neighbourhood. These were forced, galloping, into the corral, where six of them were captured, one by one, with the lazo. The team consisted of four wheelers abreast, driven by a man on the front seat, and two leaders, fastened by chains to the end of the pole, and ridden by picturesque Murillo-like urchins, who laughed and shouted as they galloped along.

The horses were generally very wild at starting, which is not to be wondered at when we consider the way in which they had just been caught and handled; but neither driver nor boys seemed to care a farthing for kicking and plunging. The more a horse kicked, the harder they flogged him; if he refused to move, they whipped the others forward till the refractory beast was dragged on by the powerful majority of five to one. The old gaucho rode behind us or at our side, looking the *beau idéal* of his race—a perfect horseman: at the end of the stage it was his duty to take our horses back again to their own *tropilla*.

Such was the order of the day for several posts in succession. A fresh set of horses was driven into the corral, caught with the lazo, and harnessed amidst a wild accompaniment of kicking and shouting. The same ragged boys rode all the day; the farther they went the merrier they seemed to be, and, though the torn shirt of one of them was rapidly disappearing, he evidently enjoyed himself to the utmost.

With the exception of some tremendous joltings, we had no particular adventures for some time: at last, however, the coach stopped suddenly, and Don Juan said we must all dismount, as the load was too heavy to cross the dangerous place in front of us. Dangerous, indeed! So much so, that I could hardly believe they seriously intended to make the attempt. We were on the edge of the hollow formed by a river since dried up, about 30 yards wide and 25 or 30 feet deep; the sides were excessively steep and irregular; and the ground at the bottom was rough, from cattle having trodden in the clay. Don Juan intended to charge down one side of this with his whole team, trusting to the impetus for carrying him up the opposite bank. The worst part of the business was that the nature of the ground compelled him to turn sharp to the right on reaching the bottom, and so describe a difficult angle in his course.

We walked across and took up a favourable position for seeing the upset, which we considered quite inevitable. The driver gathered up his reins; Don Juan maintained his seat by his side, for the purpose of working a species of drag; and the boys, at a signal, moved their horses slowly forward. As the front wheels reached the edge of the declivity, and the ponderous machine seemed going to fall upon the horses, the whole team was whipped furiously forward, boys and driver shouting like maniacs, and the tremendous plunge was made. At the bottom they contrived to turn, and were actually half way up the other side, when, after two or three heavy lurches, the coach capsized with a crash, and the horses and boys were all rolling in a dense cloud of dust. Rushing to their assistance, we found the boys had extricated themselves instantly without injury: they slipped off the chain-traces, and the horses also jumped safely on their legs. The driver, who had been shot out in front, came towards me in sorry plight, covered with dirt and bleeding in the face. Poor Don Juan, however, was *hors de combat*, and could not move: a heavy box had fallen across his leg, and he lay groaning on his back. We cleared away the wreck from around him, propped him up with a portmanteau, and found his leg was broken in two places.

This was awkward. We were about forty miles from Gualeguay, the nearest place where a doctor could be found, so we determined to mend him on the spot, though we knew nothing of surgery. The luggage being scattered all about the place, we soon found a broken deal box, which seemed admirably adapted for splints; and our patient sat very quietly on the grass whilst we cut them as well as we could. The mother of the baby who had fallen into the candlestick supplied some linen and a bottle of Eau de Cologne, which refreshed him greatly. Mr. Boyd was chief surgeon, and the leg was set with the best splints and bandages we could make. To our great satisfaction, when we saw Don Juan a fortnight later in bed at

Gualeguay, he told us, with most abundant thanks, that we had set the limb so well that, though he had a rough journey before reaching town, the doctor had only applied rather finer splints.

The next thing was to set the coach upright: this also was accomplished after several failures by the united strength of men and horses; it was not seriously damaged, and with a lively hurrah! we landed it safely on the lèvel ground. We carried the patient in our arms and deposited him on the floor of the vehicle, sitting up with his back to the horses. All hands helped in bringing up the luggage, except some things which were so smashed as to be not worth carrying off the field of battle; the boys jumped on their horses as if nothing had happened, and away we went again at full gallop. Early in the afternoon we arrived at our destination without further accidents, and exceedingly surprised the good folks of Las Cabezas by our unexpected appearance.

Don Juan's misfortune elicited great sympathy from the peons of the establishment, who crowded around us; and some little time passed before I got my portmanteau down from the roof. I observed the countenances of these wild-looking men, and was especially struck with one, who was rather stout and elderly. He was very greasy, and seemed to have just come from some slaughtering business: his long grizzled hair and beard hung about his sun-burnt face, which was characterised by a devil-may-care kind of expression. I was just thinking that the old fellow with his greasy skin and long knife must be a good specimen of the rougher class of natives, when he caught my eye, and, to my utter astonishment, pointing to my portmanteau in the dust, he said, in the genuine language of Cockaigne, 'Well, I don't know who you are, but I suppose, if you're coming here, you want that thing taken up to the house: so look here, you take hold of one end of it and I'll take the t'other; that's all fair.' As there was a very humorous twinkle in his eye, I took rather a fancy to him, and laughingly fell in with his suggestion. We carried 'the thing' between us, and I could not help expressing my surprise at his being an Englishman. 'I was brought up in Smithfield, though you mightn't think so, perhaps,' he replied.

I afterwards came to hear and see a great deal of this 'Old Bob,' as he was universally called, and he was a very singular character. According to his own admission, he had been a great scamp in his young days in London, and by chance went out to Buenos Ayres about thirty years ago. His Smithfield tastes soon enabled him to get on with the gauchos, and in due time he entered the service of Mr. Black, the proprietor of the estancia, where I found him; there he worked for many years in the camp, till his drinking habits induced his master to get rid of him. It seemed, however, that about two years previously he had come back for a nominal fortnight's visit, and there he was still, a privileged character entrusted with the charge of the grease-house. Though the old fellow had lived for those thirty years entirely at home among the gauchos, riding, dressing, and living like the rest of them, and quite content to do so till death, yet I found that nothing gave him so much pleasure as talking about his old haunts in London: he would take me aside now and then and cross-examine me about all his favourite streets. He had an astonishing memory, and had forgotten nothing; he was sufficiently educated to enjoy reading anything he could find, and had a great deal of every sense, except that common sense which would have kept him out of his many scrapes. He was always ready with a jesting answer, and, if fate had destined him for the House of Commons, he would have proved a master in the art of repartee.

Meanwhile, poor Don Juan had been refreshed by a glass of cold brandy and water: we shook hands with him as he lay, and he declared, with the greatest gratitude, that he never should forget the kindness of the Englishmen. Fresh horses were supplied from the corral, and they galloped away with the *diligencia*, which had seven leagues more to accomplish before reaching Gualeguay.

Mr. Black was not at the estancia, but we were welcomed by one of his sons and two young Englishmen, who were there learning the business of a sheep-farmer.

One of them was very ingenious, and spent all his spare time in constructing various machines, which only brought upon him the laughter of the gauchos, who detest every kind of change and improvement upon their old ways: some one mockingly suggested that he should invent a machine by means of which a well-fleeced sheep should go in at one end and come out clean shorn at the other.

The house and other buildings, the cooking department, and the peons' quarters, were ranged round a large square enclosed with fences, and surrounded with paradise trees, near which was a large galpon, or storehouse for wool. The estancia contained about seven square leagues, or rather more than 40,000 English acres. There were 12,000 head of cattle and about 40,000 sheep, besides large numbers of horses. The corrals were on a large scale, and everything in first-rate order. The sheep were, as usual, divided into flocks of 2,000 or 3,000, each of which was under the charge of a shepherd or puestero, who lived with his flock in their own part of the camp. In the course of our visit, we went to all these puestos in turn, and found most of them very comfortable. Their construction is greatly facilitated by the nature of the soil: when a new flock is formed, and consequently a new puesto is required, the native brickmaker is sent for; he gallops over with a spade upon his knee, and dismounts occasionally to examine the ground. He soon finds a suitable place for the situation, where nothing more is required than to dig up the earth and let the sun dry it into bricks: the hole makes a well for the establishment, and the bricks are quickly arranged into a house; a small piece of ground is enclosed for a garden, and planted with maize, onions, and peach trees; a rough rancho is perhaps added, for hanging up dried skins or saddlery, and the puesto is complete. Each puestero is supplied with beef and maté; and, besides living rent-free, he gets, by way of capitation grant, a small sum for every lamb added to the flock, if it lives long enough to take care of itself.

There were altogether fifteen of these puestos on Mr. Black's estancia, and the aggregate of the sheep had doubled in less than three years. The stock was also being carefully improved in quality, and a number of beautiful Negretti rams, imported from Germany at a cost of 50*l*. each, had very soon raised a first-class flock. The value of the sheep depends, of course, very much upon the nature of the breed; but, judging from what I heard in various parts of the country, I should say that a man wishing to buy a flock of good average quality would give about 8*s*. or 10*s*. for each of them. The estancieros on both sides of the La Plata are making great efforts in improving their stock, and while I was in the country one of my friends gave 200*l*. for a choice ram from Europe.

The value of land in Buenos Ayres, Entre Rios, and

the Banda Oriental, varies greatly, according to circumstances and situation; but it has all been so rapidly rising of late that it would be difficult to say anything about it with precision. Good land, with river communication, was sold two or three years ago at about 2,000*l*. a league, containing about 6,000 English acres; but what I have lately heard leads me to suppose that it would now fetch nearly half as much again, and land which is conveniently near the city of Buenos Ayres is of course considerably more. As a general rule, it may be assumed that a young man fond of healthy life and climate, possessed of a few thousand pounds, and disposed to work, may with a good conscience try sheep-farming in the neighbourhood of the Rio de la Plata. He may buy land and flocks with every probability that his land will increase continually in value, and his capital in sheep double itself before long, the wool in the meantime paying him very handsome interest, if he has ordinary luck. I am of course presuming that he devotes a little previous time to learning his business, and that he works hard for himself: if he trusts to an agent he must be very sure of his man, and must of course lose a portion of the profits. There are various ways of managing these things; very commonly one man buys the land, and another stocks it, dividing in specified proportions the profits of the wool and the increase of the flock. Having never been in Australia, I cannot compare the two countries from personal experience; but it so happened that in South America I made the acquaintance of several men who had seen life in both, and they all expressed a decided preference for that of the River Plate.

My kind host at Las Cabezas was one of those clear-sighted men who always had an eye to improvements, and endeavoured to show that both the profitableness and enjoyment of the country might be greatly increased by constant energy, instead of lazily falling into the ways of the gauchos. One of the first proofs that I saw of this was a large garden which he had made in the open land, about 300 yards from the house. It was enclosed with a good fence, and full of fruit, vegetables, herbs and maize. An Italian gardener lived in a cottage at the corner, and kept it in perfect order with the aid of a good well: the ants had been destroyed; and every now and then, in the stillness of the evening, a sudden bang told us that Antonio was preventing the intrusions of a biscacho. The gauchos care for nothing but beef and maté: is it, however, reasonable, that 'because they are virtuous, there shall be no more cakes and ale?' The more wholesome and agreeable the country life is made by the proprietors, the more will other people take to it, and in the long-run the profit will be greater to all.

The mention of a well reminds me of what appears to me an interesting fact. Here in the middle of the plains of Entre Rios, and probably hundreds of miles from any likely *habitat* for a fern, I found three species of these plants on the damp sides of the wells. Two of them I had met with in the neighbourhood of Buenos Ayres, but the third I had never seen except among the mountains of Brazil.

The greater part of the estancia consisted of very good land, and it had the great advantage of the river Clè for one of its boundaries, thus securing water for the cattle and a certain quantity of fresh herbage even in dry seasons. The undulations of the land were very slight, and very little wood was to be seen, except in the immediate neighbourhood of the river, the course of which was marked by large and handsome willow-trees. The dry weather and constant heat had injured the grass in some places; but there were few thistles, and in some directions the ground for miles together was covered with long waving grass.

The house stood upon a slight eminence, so that, with its surrounding groves of ombù and paradise trees, it was conspicuous for a considerable distance across the camp. Large corrals for sheep, cattle, and horses were close at hand, and from the open door of the room assigned to the visitors we could overlook the proceedings of some of the peons. Old Bob fulfilled the duties of chambermaid to the best of his awkward ability, and generally came in to rouse us very early in the morning. Our room faced the east, and day after day we saw the huge ball of the sun rising in unclouded skies, and flashing its first rays across the level of the plains.

CHAPTER XVII.

LIFE AT LAS CABEZAS.

TROPILLAS OF HORSES — A PICTURESQUE BOY — VISITING THE PUESTOS — JOHN THE GERMAN — ROUGH FURNITURE — FAMILY OF THE GENERAL — CATTLE ON THE RODÉO — A FINE SIGHT — FISHING EXTRAORDINARY — A TAJAMAR — HUGE SPURS — RIDING TO BREAKFAST — GAUCHO HEAD-DRESS — HOOF-PARING — THISTLES OF THE PAMPAS — ANT-HILLS — KILLING A FOX — FRESH ARRIVALS — THE BARRANCOSA — A FEAT OF HORSEMANSHIP — CARNE CON CUERO — DELIGHTFUL EVENING AL FRESCO — A SICK GAUCHO — — A STRANGE FUNERAL — CROSSING THE RIVER CLÉ — LOST AMONG THE THISTLES — PREPARE TO LEAVE THE ESTANCIA.

THE morning after our arrival we were dressed early, and ready for our first gallop over the estate. Just as we walked round to the other side of the house, we found the peons driving into a corral the tropilla of horses from which we were to make our selection. The son of our host was reasonably proud of this part of the establishment, and was very particular about the tropillas, in some of which all the horses were of the same colour. It does not, at first, seem an easy thing to bring in horses which are at large upon these boundless plains; but the system adopted in the country does not leave any formidable difficulty.

After the first violent and cruel treatment of the *domador*, or horse-breaker, the animals are arranged in tropillas of any size that may be required by the establishment. Each of them is accompanied by a *madrina* or mare, whom they learn to follow under all circumstances. The peons know pretty well in what part of the camp to look for her, and when found she is driven to the corral, the others accompanying her as a matter of course. When they have all got into the corral the bar is dropped, and those who want horses walk in amongst them on foot, and either by coaxing or with the aid of the lazo, capture as many as they require. The bar is then removed, and the rest of the tropilla with a thundering rush start forth again over their native plains.

We had a tropilla of about forty or fifty roans to select from, three of which we led round to the house and saddled at the door directly after breakfast; but when on the point of starting, we were interrupted by the visit of a native gentleman who had ridden over about eight leagues for a morning call. He had an estancia in that neighbourhood, and was a very agreeable and well-informed man; but a boy whom he brought with him by way of a groom, I suppose, was one of the most picturesque little savages I have ever seen. His dark piercing eyes, with his sun-burnt face and bare legs, would have made a good subject for Murillo; and, though he could not have been more than twelve years old, he had all the bold and defiant bearing of a guerilla chief. His somewhat scanty clothes were shabby in the extreme, and for a saddle he had little more than a piece of old rug; but the stirrups were real curiosities. They consisted of nothing more than the heels cut off an old pair of boots, with holes bored through the middle to admit the strings by which they were fastened to the saddle. When he mounted, the string was held between the great toe and its neighbour, and he seemed perfectly satisfied with the contrivance.

Our visitor remained for an early dinner, and it was not till late in the afternoon that we could start for a ride. At last, we had a delightful gallop to some of the distant puestos, where we looked at the sheep and took maté with the shepherds, returning home with the last of the light. In the course of the next few days we paid similar visits to many of the other puestos, and I was much amused by the variety of character and of race exhibited by their occupants. Most of them were natives, grave, serious-looking men, and much given to taciturnity, though not ill-disposed. One was a merry Irishman, burnt to a colour which would astonish his friends in Tipperary, and cherishing a swarthy help-mate who would astonish them still more. We found him sitting under the doorway of the hut, quietly cooling himself after a hot day's work, and playing with a coffee-coloured baby, while the Señora prepared the beef for supper. About a couple of leagues distant another flock was tended by John the German. We jumped off our horses at his door, and found him at home with his German wife and a group of genuine fair-haired, blue-eyed, German children. John was a most worthy fellow, and set a good example of prudence and industry to his neighbours in the camp. He filled up all his spare time by working as a shoemaker, and in a place where everybody was twenty miles from the nearest village he naturally found plenty of occupation. By this means he had been enabled to save all his pay as a puestero, and was beginning to get a small flock of sheep for himself; so that, considering the rapid multiplication of these animals, honest John has a fair chance of making his fortune and dying an estanciero.

I was very much pleased with this family, and it was a great treat to see how all their faces brightened up when they found that I could talk to them a little in their own language, which they had probably not heard for many a long day, and could tell them something of what I had seen in their own country. The next puesto after this was occupied by a remarkably fine, handsome young Englishman; his whole appearance and manners were such that I could not help wondering what freak of Fortune could have reduced him to the position of a common shepherd. He was smoking a short pipe in utter solitude; but, though he had no furniture whatever but a truckle-bed and a couple of bullocks' skulls instead of chairs, he seemed perfectly resigned to his fate.

A day or two after our arrival, our host arrived from Gualeguay, and I saw a grand sight in the afternoon. A certain piece of the camp is called the *rodéo,* to which the cattle are driven on certain occasions, and where they are accustomed to stand quite quietly, however wild they may be elsewhere. There is no fence or enclosure; nothing but a large patch of ground trodden bare by frequent use. The peons had been at work for several hours driving in the cattle from wherever they could find them, and towards evening we mounted our horses and rode over to see the result. About six thousand cattle were already assembled on the rodéo, and the cry was, 'still they come!' Little smoke-like puffs of dust in the far distance grew in size as they approached nearer, and presently I could distinguish the gaily-dressed peons turning and wheeling as they galloped, and driving fresh herds thundering towards us over the plain. The new arrivals are quiet when they reach the rodéo, and the peons ride slowly round, forgetting the recent excitement of the chase in the soothing pleasures of a cigarette.

When all the vast troop was collected, the business of the day began, the object being to see if any strange cattle had strayed among them from the neighbouring proprietors, who were there with their own peons. We all rode at a slow walking pace in and out among the thousands of beasts, and when any one was found with the wrong brand, he was instantly driven out of the charmed circle and taken charge of by his master's peons. The contrast between the perfect quietness of the animals on the rodéo and the excitement of the various chases going on in all directions, to prevent the stragglers from returning, was very curious and interesting. Presently I found myself near the edge of the herd, watching the movements of two or three peons, who were walking their horses very slowly by my side. One of them pointed with his finger to a fine young bullock, the others said 'Si!' and in a moment they were transformed from dignified statues into excited maniacs. They drove out the luckless beast with wild shouts, and charged furiously after him as he rushed over the plain. Whizz went the lazo of the foremost man, and caught him by the horns: up came the others to drive him in the required direction; and as fast as legs could go, he was urged towards the house to provide the establishment with supper. It was a signal that all was over for the day: the stragglers were carried off by their owners; the party broke up, and we galloped homewards, well pleased with such a spectacle.

Next day we had a very unexpected change of diet. Mr. Hinde, one of the young Englishmen staying in the house, was returning from a ride towards the river, when he made a remarkable discovery. In former wet weather the river had overflowed its banks, but the water had retired long ago, with the exception of just enough to leave a piece of swamp. In passing through this place he saw something move, and, on dismounting, he found some fine fish, living half in mud and half in water which was not deep enough for them to swim in. After marking the place, he rode back for a basket and returned to the fish. He stuck his long knife into the first, which immediately began to kick and flounder furiously, splashing him all over with black mud. He was not disposed to give in for the sake of appearances, and succeeded in capturing nine handsome carp-like fish, in spite of all their struggling. After this specimen of fishing extraordinary he remounted and rode home with his prize, which was very highly appreciated, as a great treat for all the party. In another day or two they would have died a lingering death by the drying up of the mud, and would have been altogether lost to society.

Another of our excursions was to see some new works at an outlying part of the estancia. *Tajamares*, or dams, had been made across the bed of an arroyo, by means of which considerable ponds were formed in wet weather to supply the sheep with water during the droughts. A similar process would facilitate washing the sheep, which would be a great advantage, as dirt is now the principal drawback to the fleeces from the River Plate.

One day, on returning from a ride, we found that two visitors had arrived — Mr. Robson, an Englishman, and his native friend. They were dressed in the *gala* costume of the country, with such enormous silver spurs that they were obliged to take them off to make walking practicable. We had a very pleasant day, and before they left in the evening it was arranged that we should get up early next morning and ride over to breakfast at Mr. Robson's, about seven leagues to the northward.

Soon after four o'clock in the morning of December the 6th, we turned out to catch and saddle the horses, and about an hour later we started, four in company, with every prospect of a pleasant day. The heat was now always so great about the middle of the day, that all expeditions were arranged, if possible, for the morning or evening, and all residents in the country sacrificed about a couple of hours to the siesta in a darkened room. Several times, however, I rode through all the middle of some of the hottest days without feeling any inconvenience, after arranging my head-gear in the gaucho fashion. This consists merely of folding a pocket-handkerchief diagonally, and tying it very loosely under the chin, the remaining corners hanging over the back of the neck. The hat or cap is then put on, and a pleasant breeze is made by the flapping of the handkerchief. The substitution of a thin poncho for a coat and waistcoat is another great improvement, which I enjoyed very much in the heats of December.

The morning air was marvellously delicious, and we

rode away at a lively pace. One of the horses, however, stumbled several times, and it was suggested that his hoofs were too long. Turning aside to one of the puestos, a hammer and chisel were found; the horse was made to stand on a hard piece of ground, by way of a chopping-block, and he behaved very well during the performance of this rough operation. Shoes are utterly unknown to all the country horses, but the hoof, of course, wants occasional paring.

We passed the scene of our disaster with the *diligencia*, and pieces of the wreck were still lying about on the grass; soon after which we struck right across the country, passing amongst myriads of thistles. The thistles of the Pampas are among the most striking features of the country. There are two principal kinds, but, as far as my experience goes, they are not often found in company. The one is a very handsome plant, closely resembling our garden artichoke, with beautifully divided grey leaves, and throwing up very large handsome purple flowers to a height of about three or four feet; the other has a green leaf, and is double the height of the first, but the flower is much more insignificant, and the stalks thinner. Both are furnished with terrible spines, and men and horses are equally afraid of them.

On the morning in question we passed over several leagues covered with large quantities of the shorter but handsomer kind, and their purple flowers had a beautiful effect against the grey leaves. They were not close enough to prevent our riding among them pretty easily, and the perpetual starting aside of the horses to avoid them as we galloped past, afforded capital practice in horsemanship. In the latter part of our ride we passed through a region of ant-hills of about the size of many ancient barrows that I have seen in England; many of them appeared to be twelve or fourteen feet in diameter, and six or seven in height. Presently a fox was started, and away we went after him at full gallop; he was run to earth in a small hollow, and one of the party—tell it not in Leicestershire — dismounted, and shot him with a revolver! The slayer skinned him in a couple of minutes, tied the skin on his saddle to dry in the sun, and we were off again. I thought it not only a treasonable but also a cruel proceeding; he justified it, however, by saying he had probably saved the life of some of his lambs.

Soon afterwards, we crossed the bed of a small river, which was now nearly dry, but had eaten its way so deeply through the stoneless soil that we had some difficulty in finding a place where we could descend the bank and ascend on the other side. A large ombù tree came presently in sight, which was declared to mark our destination, and soon after seven o'clock we had dismounted at Mr. Robson's. Here we had a hearty welcome, and found two other Englishmen, who had ridden over to meet us. A famous breakfast was soon ready; and, after the siesta, we passed the afternoon in looking over the property. Nothing could exceed the kindness of our host in his exertions to accommodate so large a party, and the evening was passed delightfully *al fresco* on the grass, the sweet breeze playing across the camp, and the southern constellations brightly beaming over all.

Next morning, after breakfast, we rode away towards the north, a party of seven Englishmen, bound for another estancia, four or five leagues distant, which was also managed by Mr. Robson. The style of country was the same as that of the day before—sunny plains and tall thistles, with ostriches and deer. We were not long in reaching the house, the only particular feature in the ride being the Barrancosa river, running between very steep banks, which were ornamented with an unusual profusion of brilliant scarlet verbenas. A bold rider of the party, hearing me admire them, stooped from his saddle as he galloped along, picked a handfull and gave them to me, without stopping!

The great event of the day was to be a feast of *carne con cuero*, the chief delicacy of the country, for which purpose a choice bullock was killed. This dish consists of a large piece from the animal's ribs, roasted with the hide on, which preserves all the juice and essence of the meat in the highest perfection. The hide is, of course, spoiled, and, as this is by far the most valuable part of a bullock in the River Plate, it is only on especial occasions that such a luxury is indulged in.

The peons were busily roasting it over a wood fire, the smoke of which nearly stifled me on looking into their rough kitchen, and at length the feast was brought in. No dish was applicable or necessary, as the beef was about a yard square, and stood on its own hide upon a rough table. There was something Homeric in the entertainment; the heroes of the Iliad and the Odyssey must have eaten their beef as we did in Entre Rios, and I am not surprised at their thriving upon it. I had several opportunities, during my journey, of testing the admirable qualities of *carne con cuero*, and can safely say that the preservation of the whole goodness of the meat makes it the most satisfactory way of roasting that I am acquainted with.

Our dinner was very early; and, after the ensuing siesta, we mounted our horses, to see the cattle brought up to the rodéo. They were a remarkably fine breed, nearly all black and white, and had a very pretty effect when massed in large numbers, as we saw them. In the evening, we all had a very merry gallop back to Mr. Robson's: after tea, a guitar was produced, and as two of the party sang well, and all the rest were in high spirits, we did not go to bed till a very late hour. On the following day we were up early, and rode home in company to Las Cabezas before the great heat of the day had begun, astonishing 'Old Bob' by charging up to his boiling-house as if we had been a party of Urquiza's cavalry.

The beef diet must have a wonderful effect in hardening and strengthening the gauchos: they scarcely ever have anything the matter with them, and get over accidents with remarkable ease. One evening, however, just as we finished our day's riding, and hung up our saddles on the fence, one of the peons came up to Mr. Black, and told the 'patron' that he was ill. It appeared that he had some time since been badly thrown from his horse by the charge of a bull, and had never quite recovered: he now asked for some physic, and his master gave him a strong dose of castor-oil, with which he expressed himself much gratified. Next day, at the same hour, I again saw him come up and ask for some more. Mr. Black satisfied his request; and on the third day, to our astonishment, he declared that he must have another dose, as the two others had done him so much good.

Being a good deal struck with this specimen of a sick gaucho, I asked my host if he had ever seen a dead one. He said that one of two brothers working as peons upon the estancia was brought to him nearly dead from the effects of a similar fall. Having taken care to obtain the full consent of the man's brother, he attempted to bleed him, but no blood flowed, and in the evening he died. The surviving brother asked for leave of absence to bury him at La Victoria, many leagues away to the westward. His master gave the permission, and got up early to satisfy his curiosity as to the intended method of proceeding. The dead man was dressed and placed by his comrades in the usual position on his horse; his legs were made fast to the saddle, a forked stick was adjusted so as to support his chin; with the help of various bandages, all was made firm, and he sat exactly as in life. The brother then leaped into his own saddle; the horses were accustomed to travel together, and the living man rode all day across the plains with his dead brother, till he reached La Victoria, and piously buried him. There seemed to me something romantically wild and terrible in the idea, and I could not help picturing to myself the feelings of any one who might have encountered that strange pair in their ride — the contrast between the excited appearance of the galloping horse, and the pale face of the dead rider, must have been awful.

We spent a few more days in riding over all the surrounding country within our reach, and at last a party of four of us started for an excursion to the farther side of the river Clè. Not knowing where to cross the stream in the required direction, we called at the distant puesto of Patricio, and induced Patricio himself to act as our guide to the ford. A great part of the way was through tall thistles scattered here and there, but at last we came to the steep bank of the river. Patricio led the way down, and rode his horse successfully through the water, which was up to his saddle. Two of the party followed him across, but nothing would induce the two remaining horses to make the experiment. Another place, however, was found, and, in a short time, we had all passed over the dangerously muddy bottom and reached the opposite side in safety.

Patricio here left us, and we rode over gently rising ground towards the estancia of an Englishman. A considerable part of the land was completely covered with a species of blue borage, which I had frequently observed throughout the province of Entre Rios: it was in full blossom, and gave a beautiful colour to the plains. Some hours were spent in visiting the establishment, where there were some very fine sheep, and I was also struck with a kind of garden, where apples and pears, peaches, apricots, and figs were flourishing in good order, even though the trees appeared rather neglected.

A few miles of farther riding, on the same side of the river, took us to the estancia of a native, where we spent half an hour in conversation, accompanied with maté; and then, as the evening was approaching fast, we started homewards. One of the party declaring he knew a safe ford across the river, we were induced to ride straight towards the house, instead of returning as we came in the morning. In due time we saw the willow-trees which marked the course of the river; but, on approaching, we found that we were cut off from them by a belt of enormous thistles, which was apparently about half a mile wide, and stretched along the bank as far as we could see.

We forced the horses through a part where the thistles seemed rather thinner than elsewhere, and tried to get to the side of the river; but it was hard work, and my companions, not being armed with such good boots as myself, suffered considerably from the thorny spines. The thistles were so tall that I was obliged to use one arm to guard my face as I rode, though my horse was by no means short, and at a distance of a few yards we could only just see each other's hats. Finding after a while that we could not get through, we resolved to retreat and try for another place. He who had undertaken to act as guide was somewhat ahead, so we shouted to him as we turned our horses. We got out into the open ground and galloped along the edge of the belt for about half a mile, till we found a passage which had been forced by cattle going down to drink. Following this, we arrived at the river, and were looking for a likely place to ford it, when we discovered that our leader was missing. We shouted, but could hear nothing, and looked around, but saw nothing of him, and concluded that his horse must have thrown him in the tall thistles, in which case there was no chance of seeing either of them, and even if he were not seriously hurt, he would in all probability lose himself. We rode back as fast as we could, and followed our old track among the thistles, but could find no trace of him.

Then we thought that perhaps he had reached the river at a wrong place and been lost in the dangerous mud; so we again retraced our steps to the bank, and followed it for a long distance in both directions to look for him.

Still nothing was to be seen or heard: darkness was fast approaching; and, seriously alarmed for our friend, we agreed to ride to the house for further assistance. We succeeded in crossing the river at a tolerably good place, and galloped off to the house, where we found he had not been heard of. With the agreement that a gun should be fired if he returned by some other route, we returned to the search, and tormented ourselves among the thistles till it was perfectly dark. At last I declared I saw the distant flash of a gun, and we rode hard for the house. 'All's well that ends well.' There was the missing man, safe and sound. He had contrived to cross the river at another ford, and there was no harm done: it will be a long time, however, before I lose the lively remembrance of looking for a man among the gigantic thistles of Entre Rios.

We had now spent a fortnight in constant enjoyment and excitement among those magnificent plains, and I was getting so accustomed to the ways of the country that I contemplated with sincere regret the prospect of returning to the life of towns. Not only was our own party a very happy one, but we had made several agreeable acquaintances within a circle of a few leagues;

and it was to me exceedingly interesting to see this nucleus of Englishmen, full of health and energy, working at and improving this distant corner of the world; making fortunes for themselves, and opening up the country for others to follow in their steps. The splendid climate, the pure air, and the independent style of life, were exceedingly attractive to a stranger, and appeared to have a remarkably healthy and invigorating effect upon all whom I became acquainted with during my visit. The hand of friendship and hospitality was always ready; and, though we were in what some people call a state of banishment, which means being separated by a certain number of leagues from theatres and shops, yet I can remember very few merrier parties than some of those among the estancias in that part of Entre Rios. The work of civilisation is advancing rapidly, and increased facilities of communication will probably, before long, have most important effects.

The rough life and the extreme difficulty of travelling for a long time prevented ladies from going to live in the camp, and thus produced one of the greatest drawbacks to the country. Now that the main rivers are traversed by steam-boats, one great difficulty has been removed; the same advantage must be extended to some of their branches. Already it is not at all uncommon to find whole families comfortably settled down in the middle of their flocks and herds, and ladies from

Buenos Ayres or Monte Video often make visits to the distant estancias of their relations and friends.

The Gualeguay river is not yet favoured with a steam-boat, and our host made arrangements for us to go down to Buenos Ayres with him in a schooner laden with wool. He sent forward a bullock-cart with our goods and a stock of supplies for the voyage; and there was every prospect of our being amusingly initiated into the mysteries of river navigation under difficulties.

CHAPTER XVIII.

VOYAGE DOWN THE RIVER FROM GUALEGUAY.

DEPARTURE FROM THE ESTANCIA — GUALEGUAY — VISIT TO DON JUAN — THE POET — OUR SCHOONER — SCANT ACCOMMODATION — SNAKES IN THE HOUSE — GREAT HEAT IN THE EVENING — TOWING DOWN THE RIVER — THE PAVON AND YBICUY — WANT OF DISCIPLINE — A DANGEROUS CARGO — FORMATION OF NEW CHANNELS AND ISLANDS — MOORED TO THE BANK — GIGANTIC SNAILS — MUSQUITOS — THE NUEVE VUELTAS — PAMPERO AND PANIC — EXTRAORDINARY RISE IN THE RIVER — THE BOCA DEL CAPITAN — SAN FERNANDO — RETURN TO BUENOS AYRES — A HOT CHRISTMAS — SAIL FOR ENGLAND.

THERE had been no change in the weather since we entered the province: day after day, the same bright sunshine added another shade to our complexions; and on one of the hottest afternoons in the middle of December we said good-bye to our friends at Las Cabezas, and, with much regret, set forward to Gualeguay. Our host drove me over in his dog-cart, his son and Mr. Boyd accompanying us on horseback. A carriage of this description, built very strongly, and with wheels wide apart, is exceedingly useful in the camp: a friend of mine, Mr. Brittain, who was, I believe, the first to introduce one in that part of the world, used to travel immense distances in it, taking with him a couple of peons and a good tropilla of horses to relieve one another in turn.

The seven leagues were got over in little more than two hours; and we arrived at the town of Gualeguay in time to enjoy dinner at a fonda kept by an obliging but preternaturally fat landlord. It appeared, upon enquiry, that the schooner would not be ready to sail till the next evening; so we had the greater part of a day for making an exploration of the town. It appeared to be about the same size as Nogoyà, with no great signs of activity, though it is an important outlet for one part of the province.

Our passports for permission to leave Entre Rios had to be obtained, and with this object we entered a large courtyard surrounded by a colonnade, with the public offices on one side, and a barrack for soldiers on the other. The officials were very polite, and soon provided us with the necessary documents. The offices, however, were abominably untidy, and very little like the same class of rooms in most parts of Europe. It was, however, adorned by a huge picture of Urquiza, in full uniform, painted in the worst possible taste and style, which covered one of the walls, and seemed to threaten grim vengeance upon delinquent clerks.

We then paid a visit to Don Juan, who was still in bed with his broken leg, though he was mending rapidly. He was delighted to see us again, and overflowed with gratitude for the service which we had been enabled to render him. We walked about for some time during the middle of the day; but as every man, woman, and child were sleeping the siesta, we found it rather dull, and returned to the inn, where we followed their example. About four o'clock we dined together, and paid a short visit to the club, which consisted of a tolerably large room, with billiard-tables and other amusements, and was well filled with men who seemed enjoying themselves to their hearts' content.

All was at length reported ready, and we started for the port of Gualeguay, which is about three leagues from the town. The road was chiefly carried through a wooded region tenanted by large numbers of the red-headed cardinal-birds, and would have been very dangerous in the dark from the quantity of stumps still left standing to the height of several inches above the ground. We reached the port a little before sunset, but, as there was no wind, the heat was very great, and I certainly had qualms of anxiety as to what would become of us in such weather, cooped up in the little vessel which I now beheld. She was a neat schooner of about a hundred tons, but with very little draught of water, on account of the shallowness of the upper river. Her cargo was piled on the deck, which it entirely occupied, with the exception of about ten feet at each end of the ship. The wool was covered with hides, and rose up like a haystack, completely cutting off all communication, except by a difficult climb up one end, and a similar descent at the other. The cabin was approached by a descent like that into a Thames barge; but, as the ship was new, everything was fortunately very clean. It contained four very small berths, in a double row, upon each side, and one at the end, with a table about three feet square in the middle, and nothing to sit upon except the lockers at the foot of the berths. Our own party consisted of three; and when, to my horror, I found we were to have two gentlemen of Gualeguay as additional passengers in that small den, with the thermometer at upwards of 90°, I must own that I wished myself anywhere else, while my thoughts reverted dismally to the Black Hole of Calcutta.

Before starting, we went over a saladero close to the bank of the river, with the proprietor of which Mr. Black was negotiating for the sale of three or four thousand of his cattle. Then we had a conversation with the captain of the port, who made himself very agreeable, and told us several interesting stories about the country, describing particularly the effects of *crescientes*, or the periodical floods of the river-system. A remarkable feature of them is the alarm and flight of animals living on the marshy banks and islands; and he said that, three years previously, the lower parts of his house had been filled with snakes which had been driven by the rising waters from their accustomed haunts.

Late in the evening, we went on board the 'Maria Luisa' in a small boat; the anchor was weighed, and we began to float down the river, at the sluggish pace of the stream, towed by four men in the boat. Our two fellow-passengers also came on board, and we soon saw that one of them was very ill. He had had a touch of sun-stroke in his journey to the port from Gualeguay, and suffered intensely. I was beginning to contemplate the probability of his death, and the consequent alternative of either burying him in the river or carrying his body down to Buenos Ayres, which might be an affair of three days or as many weeks, according to the humours of wind and weather; but a severe fit of sickness relieved him greatly, and on going to bed he slept profoundly. We made tea, and climbed into our berths as the vessel slowly crawled down the river. I found that to get into my bed required a feat of skill, for the entrance was not much larger than a rabbit-hole; but repose was sweet, and I lay quietly for a few hours: the heat then became intolerable, and I rushed upon deck in my shirt, about midnight, just as a fresh breeze sprang up right ahead and compelled us to anchor. I then returned to my burrow and slept till morning.

About dawn the captain started again, and began the tedious process of beating down the river against contrary winds. We passed a schooner which had sailed before us, but had been unlucky enough to take the ground, where she stuck fast till they got her off by warping; and in the afternoon she passed us again, by dint of better sailing to windward. At last we came to the point where the Gualeguay river joins the Pavon, and, after many fruitless tacks, we succeeded in getting into the latter stream, where we had more water and a more favourable wind.

The captain and crew were, as usual in these vessels, all Italians, and got on very well with us and with each other till the occurrence of the slightest difficulty revealed their want of discipline. According to their system, all hands have a share in the venture; and, consequently, each thinks himself socialistically entitled to direct the motions of the ship. The cargo being piled upon the deck, the effect of a stronger puff of wind than usual was really dangerous to such a shallow vessel; and when she began to heel over more than they thought safe, the whole six men screamed, gesticulated, and yelled at one another with contrary orders, mixed with the profanest of language, beginning with 'Santa Maria!' and ending in a torrent of Spanish and Italian oaths, such as I should not like to commit to paper. Hard swearing cannot steer a ship; and amidst the horrid discord and utter want of discipline, I sometimes thought that the 'Maria Luisa' would really be capsized. As soon as the danger was past, their good temper returned, and they seemed to live happily at their own end of the vessel.

Thanks to the forethought of Mr. Black, we were

well off for provisions: he had sent on board three fat sheep and a batch of poultry, besides a good supply of wine and beer. One of the crew acted as cook, and acquitted himself very creditably, considering the smallness of the space at his disposal. As we could not anywhere find more than six feet of deck uncovered, all exercise was, of course, out of the question; and for a great part of the day we stretched ourselves on the dry hides at the top of the cargo, watching the scenery, and occasionally trying the range of a revolver at some of the huge birds which were fishing on the banks of the river. Once we passed two or three boats full of nutria-hunters, creeping along close to the marshy land, but we could not get near enough to ask them what success they had met with.

On the morning of the third day we passed the Ybiquy, and reached the main stream of the river Paranà, which we ascended for a few leagues, instead of descending, as I had expected. The object, however, was to reach the Palmas channel, and so avoid the necessity of crossing the wide open water from Martin Garcia to Buenos Ayres, which would have been dangerous with our light but bulky cargo. After a short time we turned westward through a deep-water channel, at least 300 yards wide, which was known to have been begun about twenty years previously by a man digging a ditch as a short cut for his canoe. This is a wonderful instance of the rapidity with which the face of the country can be altered by the agency of these mighty rivers. On the other hand, near the mouth of the Pavon, we passed a considerable island covered with trees, the whole of which had been formed within the same period by the deposits of the stream.

Hitherto the weather had been perfectly fine, though exceedingly hot, but bad symptoms appeared in the south-east, and a squall so frightened the captain and his men that they ran the vessel on shore, and made her fast to the trees with a couple of hawsers. It would be difficult to imagine anything less picturesque than this part of the country. The land on both sides for many leagues is so low that the greater part of it is frequently submerged by floods, and is covered with a jungle of huge rushes and scattered willow-trees. With the help of a plank we went on shore, if shore it can be called, where the mud is so soft that without the grass and rushes it would be scarcely possible to walk upon it. The change was considered beneficial to the two surviving sheep, which were dragged on land, tied to a tree, and left to eat anything they could find. The only creatures that I saw in a very short exploration of this dreary spot were gigantic snails, whose shells were about three inches in diameter.

Such was the place where we were to spend the night, with the prospect of being devoured by musquitos. A large piece of muslin had been brought from Gualeguay, and we employed ourselves with fitting up temporary curtains for our defence against these enemies: we were able by this means to keep out the great mass of them, and the attacks of stragglers, though by no means pleasant, were not altogether intolerable. A tremendous storm of thunder, lightning, and rain burst upon us in the evening, and as our cabin was not large enough for any amusement or occupation, we preferred turning into bed early. When the storm ceased we heard myriads of musquitos buzzing outside the curtains; but towards morning they were dispersed by a colder wind.

The next day was spent in beating to windward through a very tortuous part of the river, called Nueve Vueltas, or Nine Bends; the appearance of the country was still perfectly uninteresting, and our only excitement consisted in speculating about the number of tacks that would be required before we should get round a particular corner. When these difficulties were passed, we made good progress throughout a long moonlight night with a favourable wind, and ran many leagues down the Paranà, the scenery of which now began to improve very materially. We went to bed after a most delightful evening, with the prospect of reaching Buenos Ayres on the following day; but very early in the morning we were startled by the violent motion of the vessel, the roaring of the wind, and the execrations of the wrangling sailors. Jumping up on deck we found that a furious Pampero had commenced, and the

Italians, in a panic about the safety of their craft, had, after the usual amount of conflicting opinions, determined to let the ship run before it up the river again till they could find the shelter of a forest-covered part of the coast. Here we were, then, scudding back in the wrong direction! Happily this course did not last very long, and we were soon moored safely to a couple of large seibo-trees, under the lee of a large island, which was covered with forest sufficiently high and dense to protect us from the wind that roared among the branches.

Our situation was in some respects delightful. We lay close to the bank, and the masts of the schooner met the overhanging boughs and crimson blossoms of the seibos to which we were fastened. The variety of trees and shrubs was very great, and many flowers hung over the water's edge. Vast quantities of peaches grow on the banks and islands of this part of the Paranà, but unfortunately they were not yet ripe. In the season, people lay their vessels close to the banks, as we did, and load them with peaches and oranges, without taking any trouble or incurring any expense except that of going to gather them. All day long the wind blew furiously over our heads, but the sky was clear, and as we were in shelter, with a sheep and a half still left, we cared but little for the detention. The most remarkable result of the gale was the rapid rising of the river, which appeared to be here nearly two miles in width. I had observed the stump of a tree on the bank in the morning, and soon afterwards saw that it was covered. I then took another mark, which in its turn disappeared, and in the evening I found that the level of that immense river had been raised between three and four feet in less than twelve hours, by the force of the wind blowing up against the downward stream. This had nothing to do with the usual periodical rising of the Paranà, which is a very gradual movement, caused by the heavy rains of the wettest season near the equator, and extending over about four months, from December to April, during which it usually rises about twelve feet.

The captain did not venture to leave this safe hiding-place till nearly three o'clock in the morning, and when we came on deck the schooner was very near the entrance to the Boca del Capitan, leading to San Fernando. The wind being again contrary, no one could say how long we might be detained; and the captain agreed to let us take the boat, with four men, to row to San Fernando, while he and the cook and the ship remained tied to a tree at the entrance of the Boca. After our usual ten o'clock breakfast, we started under a blazing sun; I undertook to steer, and the crew pulled very fairly, relieving themselves now and then by setting sail when the wind suited the course of the river. This was really a pretty piece of river scenery, the banks being ornamented with beautiful flowers and overhung by delicately-green weeping willows, mixed with the splendid crimson of the seibos. After about three hours of uncommonly hot work, we reached the Porto Nuevo of San Fernando, and once more landed in the province of Buenos Ayres, about twenty miles from the city.

We found an old negro with a bullock-cart, who conveyed our goods up to the principal inn of the town, where we found that in another hour the daily *diligencia* would start for Buenos Ayres. We filled up this time with dinner in a comfortable room, which was doubly welcome after our close quarters for the last five days in the schooner. Then we started, passing through San Isidro and Belgrano, places which, though unknown a few years ago, are now being rapidly covered with houses and quintas; and, after about two hours of fast driving, we were safely deposited in Buenos Ayres, where I had long learnt to feel entirely at home.

Many people will probably think that it must be a very dull affair to navigate the Paranà in a wool-schooner; I can assure them, on the contrary, that though the country passed through in that way is far from picturesque, yet such a journey is in many respects highly interesting. It is at all times delightful to a lover of Nature to see her at work upon a grand scale. No one who has not made the experiment can have any idea of such a mighty river-system as that of the Rio de la Plata and its tributaries: the mass of water, the formation of new channels, the cumulation of new islands, and the rapid increase of their vegetation, must be seen to be properly understood and appreciated. The fast passage of a steamer, invaluable as it is for the developement of commercial relations, does not give such means for understanding these matters as are provided by the slower sailing-vessel; and those who may have tried almost every other variety of travelling, would admit that they had experienced an entirely new sensation in being moored to a forest of magnificent seibos in one of the islands of the Paranà.

Repose seemed strange after the constant movement and ever-varying excitements of the last three months; but I thoroughly enjoyed repose in its turn. We kept Christmas in Buenos Ayres right loyally, though the ideas of skating and holly-berries were marvellously at variance with the doings of a hot climate in its hottest season. The English church was beautifully decorated with wreaths and branches of olives and flowers, though the heat was so great in the middle of the day that walking was a severe exertion to many, whilst others scarcely liked to expose their carriage-horses to the blazing sun. Turkeys, however, flourish peculiarly in that part of the world, and the whole county of Norfolk could hardly have eclipsed that with which we celebrated the feast. I am certain that nothing could have surpassed the genuine enthusiasm with which we drank the health of 'Absent friends,' the favourite toast of the wanderer.

But my own wanderings in those regions were coming to an end. All my enquiries at Rosario and Paranà in November met with the discouraging reply that it was impossible for the present to communicate with the far west. The merchants on the River Plate could not send their treasures across the Pampas into Chili; the war had drained men and horses from the various rough post-stations between Rosario and Mendoza; the worst characters of the country had joined with run-away soldiers in defiance of the laws; Indians had taken advantage of troublous times for making further encroachments, and no man captured by them had a chance of his life. I could find no companion of any kind ready and willing to undertake the journey immediately to Mendoza and the Cordillera of the Andes; and the time which I had fixed for returning to England admitted of no further delay if I intended to make the long detour by Peru and Panama. The usual *diligencia* could not yet be depended upon, and everybody whom I knew at Buenos Ayres earnestly dissuaded me from making the attempt alone. I enquired about ships likely to go round Cape Horn to Valparaiso, and I found that, even if one were likely to start in the next few weeks, it would have a stormy voyage, with contrary winds, for a couple of months, which would be too long for my other arrangements. Sorely against inclination, I was obliged, for the present, to abandon my plan for seeing the Andes and the Pacific, and to confine myself to the pleasures of society at Buenos Ayres till the departure of a homeward packet. I had so completely enjoyed myself there, and had met with so much genuine friendship and hospitality, that, after a short further stay, I departed with the sincerest regret, not without an earnest hope that I might again be fortunate enough to visit the Rio de la Plata.

Before leaving, I called upon as many friends as I could, and had an interesting conversation at the club with Dr. Scrivenor, a scientific traveller among the higher ranges of the Cordillera. He accompanied Mr. Pentland in some of his explorations of the mountains of Peru and Bolivia, amongst which they ascended the Peak of Potosi, which they ascertained by two measurements with theodolite and barometer, to have a height of 15,900 feet above the sea, the barometer standing at 16 inches and the thermometer at 56° Fahr.

At last we started in the 'Mersey' once more, and had the most stormy of all the passages which I have made upon the coast of Brazil. The destruction of glass and crockery was very great, in spite of all precautions, and the ship rolled so heavily before the force of an easterly gale, that most of the swing lamps were broken against the ceilings of the saloon. For two days and nights no observation of any kind could be taken, but Captain Curlewis had a fine opportunity of showing his skill and seamanship. The patent log, which, when thrown overboard attached by a rope, works itself by an easily-revolving screw, with an indicator showing the number of revolutions, proved itself invaluable; and when the storm-clouds lifted, on the third morning, the first object seen was the island at the mouth of Rio harbour, exactly over the bowsprit, showing that, in spite of clouds and currents, the powers of calculation had triumphed, and we were exactly in the right course.

At Rio we found the heat excessive. I was transferred to the 'Tyne,' commanded by Captain Jellicoe, under whose agreeable charge we commenced our voyage to Europe. If Rio was hot, Bahia was still hotter; and the engineer declared that the temperature of the sea was 80° Fahr. We took in a fine stock of oranges, bananas, and mangoes, with sundry other fruits and vegetables. At Pernambuco we obtained a supply of enormous pine-apples, which, with bananas and moselle, provided the best of luncheons for the next three weeks. Lovely weather accompanied us to St. Vincent and England, though there was by far the most enormous swell that I have ever seen on the ocean, resulting from distant north-westerly winter gales. It was upon such an immense scale that it scarcely affected the motion of the ship: looking at it from the deck, we saw ourselves gradually lifted, as it were, to the summit of a hill, and then slowly sinking into a valley, without a single bubble of spray to disturb the purple serenity of the water.

Such was my last experience of the sea—a worthy conclusion to the pleasure of a journey among the sunny glories of South America.

CPSIA information can be obtained
at www.ICGtesting.com
Printed in the USA
LVHW110932160522
718424LV00014B/98

9 783375 005030